The Accidental Murder Club

an international murder mystery with Irish wakes, German weddings, and British humour

Stefanie Fletcher

Chapter 1

Stansted Airport's Executive Lounge (Margaret)

Margaret closed her eyes, inhaled deeply, and tried to quieten the nervous cross-chatter in her mind. Just because the last time she went abroad there were two murders, didn't mean it would happen again. And they'd managed to check-in and were now in Stansted Airport's Executive Lounge, and so despite all those weeks of mysterious prank calls, she must be wrong, no-one was trying to stop the wedding, and her friends were not in terrible danger, once again.

She let the breath out and loosened her impossibly tight grip on the passport and boarding pass.

A glass of orange juice was placed in front of her. She stopped nibbling on her cheek and looked up. Jim smiled down at her. "This'll help," he said, sliding into the booth next to her. He was in his beaten-up old brown leather jacket, two sizes too big, just like his head. Margaret imagined he wore that thing to bed, too. He raised his pint and took a first sip of Guinness, a little foam settling on his top lip. He turned towards her to make it easier to meet her eyes. "About 3c too warm."

She picked up her glass and sniffed it. "Vodka?" she asked,

incredulous. She put it down and pushed it away. Jim held up a tiny space between his finger and thumb. "Just to take the edge off. You're all edge today, Maggie. It's like sitting with a ruler."

"Margaret, and you know I don't drink."

His eyebrows jumped. "Yeah, but I still don't know why. Or why you're so tense."

She looked over at the others, either attacking that sad buffet or on their way to and from the bar.

"Why I don't want to diminish my judgement, lower my concentration, slow my reactions, decrease my problem-solving skills, impair my memory, and disturb my sleep? It should be self-evident."

"Have you forgotten about the two-drink buzz though? How the edges of life," he gripped the table then yanked his hands away, "melt away."

To her right, on the wall, was a framed picture of the Queen Mother, who'd only died about a month earlier, in late March. Very sad, the whole affair. She wasn't a royalist, per se, but a respecter of traditions long held. Of the status and its magnificent quo. "The buzz?" she repeated, slowly. She had felt it once, and all its ugly repercussions. "You sell the buzz well, you common drunkards, when you're fighting over nothing at 2am, or vomiting into shrubbery."

Jim flashed another of his make-mine-a-double grins. "Supposed to be a party, this. We're in the Executive Lounge." He whistled appreciatively. "Hell of a buffet out there, if I do say so myself, and I've seen a few in my time. The sausage rolls are a 9/10. Yeah, Con's spared no expense, surprisingly, being he's usually tighter than a duck's–"

"Vulgar," she said, cutting that sentence off before it could reach its anatomical destination. Connor was the groom, Lise his bride. Connor and Jim were off to Galway in Ireland, Connor's family home, while Margaret, Lise and Pat would

The Accidental Murder Club

visit Leipzig, Germany, where Lise had grown up before being forced into exile when one country became two, and a very large wall was built. "A bachelorette party, at our age?" She said. "Aren't we a bit too…"

"Don't say old," he said. "Age is just a number and I've never got on with numbers. And they call them Stag and Hen do's now. Try and keep up."

"You know precisely hold old I am," Margaret said, because they shared a birthday, month, date and year. A coincidence that Jim liked to read more into. They'd even celebrated with a big joint party last year. They were sixty-two, not that she felt it. He might have felt it, she'd never asked, but he never acted it.

"And they're twenty-one at most," Jim said, nodding towards Connor and Lise who were giggling over by the buffet. Their romance had certainly scandalised Cahoots Coliving, where they all lived. After all, Lise hadn't been widowed for much more than a year and the way she fell for Connor, the intensity of it, how they fawned and draped over each other, the kissing sounds from the back row during Cahoots movie nights? They were like teenagers. And then the fast engagement. They liked spectacle, and so, yes, she had to admit that a trip like this was in character for them.

Once they made it to Germany without anyone mysteriously dying, Margaret was sure she'd get into a more celebratory mood too.

"Are you afraid of flying?" he asked.

"That would be illogical," she said, and tried to remember the micromort score for flying. It was low. She always looked up the micromort score of an activity. Unless you knew how likely it was to kill you, how could you decide if you wanted to do it? She undid a button on her blazer as she watched two women flirting with a man half their age and a quarter their intellect. Her shoulders felt tight, like they were a size too small. The lounge was warm and full of little whizzy suitcases and large, breezy dispositions she couldn't find a way to share: travel's a con, because, wherever you go, you're still yourself when you get there. "Actually, Lise paid for the buffet," she said.

"Really?" Jim chuckled as he took another long sip from his Guinness then licked the foam moustache from his lip. "Figures. Nah, let's enjoy ourselves, aye? I've got a clean shirt on. New jeans. I'm going on holiday. You look cracking as always. No-one rocks the neckerchief like you, Mags."

"Margaret," she corrected, glancing down at her standard, trusty travelling outfit - navy-blue blazer with gold buttons. Underneath, a delicate blouse in a soft pastel shade, perfect to minimise perspiration up to 25c and exquisite, tailored black trousers that fit just as well as the day she bought them, more than ten years ago. Buy cheap and you pay at least twice; it's a false economy. She straightened her back. "Flattery won't get you anywhere, Mr Whitecastle."

Jim's eyes circled. "I say it how I see it, is all. Always have, always will."

"Yeah, but you have cataracts."

"Always the headmistress," he said. "Got to have the last word." Jim got out his comb from his inside pocket and neatened what little hair he had left. He was a surprisingly vain man, she felt, for his age. It was almost cute. Pat slipped in opposite them and opened her notepad. Pat was mute, but never stopped communicating in other ways. She loved a bit of drama. Not that there was going to be drama. Not with Margaret in charge.

"I'm retired," Margaret said.

He scoffed, turning his attention to Pat now too. The man loved an audience. "We never retire, we just stop getting paid. Yeah, you work in a pub as long as I have," his chest expanded, "and you learn to read people. Look at Connor over there, see how he's still wearing that big sheepskin coat even though it's boiling in here? You can be sure sausage rolls are slipping into those pockets."

They both watched and not twenty seconds later, Connor did, indeed, slip in a handful of mini sausage rolls. Jim cracked up, as did Pat, who had already caught the conversation's thread. Margaret hadn't known you could laugh silently, not until Pat had joined Cahoots, something Margaret had voted against, but lost.

"Probably the same with journalists, right, Pat?" Jim asked. "You get a sense for people. Have to. It's what makes you damn good at the job."

Overconfidence would be Jim's downfall, Margaret had always been sure of that. What was hers going to be? Had that downfall already happened? Pat looked up from her trusty notebook, always with her, raising both her eyebrows at Margaret's vodka-tainted orange juice, her large brown eyes widening, making her face, with its long, beaked nose even more owlish. She hadn't spoken a word since she'd arrived at Cahoots the previous year. Margaret still couldn't believe someone who'd made words her living, a prominent investigative journalist, would take a mysterious vow of silence. Or, that someone who'd once hobnobbed with prime ministers and been a regular on Newsnight would choose to retire somewhere as dull as Bury St Edmunds. Margaret liked dull; dull was predictable, you knew where you were with dull. Dull you could control. Pat didn't even have family nearby, unlike Jim. Not that Cahoots ever saw Jim's family.

"I read people," Margaret said. She also snooped on people, was a regular reviewer of the Cahoots Visitor's Book, which was how she knew Jim hadn't had a visitor in more than a year.

"My Trudy's wedding was in Dublin," said Jim, putting his almost-empty drink down. A drink that size would take her all night to finish, alcohol or not. "Massive affair, it was. Five hundred guests, maybe more. Irish, you see, her Danny."

There was almost a sneer when he said his son-in-law's name. "Not his fault, I suppose." Jim chuckled again, to himself; he was a happy drunk, which was lucky, considering how often he and Connor were inebriated. They treated life like it was a party and they were its guests of honour. Margaret treated life like it was an unruly child that just needed a bit of discipline.

"I'd like to hear your speech, someday," Margaret said. "I bet you put a lot of work into it, not to mention footballing idioms."

"Game of two halves," Jim said. "Football idioms."

She remembered a deputy headteacher, Mr Wallis, a die-hard Arsenal fan who'd be in a bad mood until Wednesday if his team lost on Saturday. Why would anyone outsource their happiness to an entity over which they had no control? It was absurd. She didn't understand fandom.

Jim stared down into his pint, his eyes glazing over. "Family's everything, isn't it?"

Pat drew an exclamation mark and held up her notebook. Of course she would agree with Jim. Everyone found Jim so very agreeable. It was part of why he had such a big head (that and the booze), and why he considered himself such a man of the people. It's easy to make people like you. Margaret had always known that. It's harder to make them respect you. Everyone at Cahoots respected her. It's why they'd voted her on to the management committee. As for Pat, well, Margaret vowed she'd solve her many riddles on this trip.

There was a flash to the left of Margaret's vision. A staff member was taking a photo of Lise and Connor. Memories surfaced, unbidden. Before she knew it, she'd grabbed the edge of the table. Emotions arise and pass away, she repeated to herself, one of many of her personal mantras.

"What is it?" Jim asked, noticing her unease.

"You know what it is."

The Accidental Murder Club

He rolled his eyes. "Not that again. You've been a stuck record these past weeks. You're paranoid, is all."

"Paranoid?" she snapped, then tried to slow her speech down. She didn't want to appear hysterical. "I'm not paranoid, I'm prudent." She let go of the table and pushed down a crease in her blazer. If you can't argue without emotion, you shouldn't argue. Not that they were arguing. She would merely present the facts and only the facts. "And after what just happened at check-in? And before that. All the weird phone calls? The heavy breathing? At all times of the day. And the night. Don't forget the night. The most dangerous time, the night. Statistics are clear on that. 9pm is peak crime time."

His shoulders bounced. He seemed to be enjoying her show. She wasn't sure how she felt about this. "How do you know this stuff?"

Her eyes narrowed. "How do you not?"

Pat clicked with both hands. Margaret smiled at her, happy she was in her camp, for once. Jim blew out a breath. "Pranks," he said, "in my humble opinion."

"Nothing humble about you."

Pat made a gun and fired it at Jim. Gotcha.

Jim leaned back. "We used to get a ton of prank calls in the pub, all sorts of weirdos, asthma

breathing or asking if Seamore Butts was there–"

"Do you have your fact file?" she asked both him and Pat. She'd been up until 1am finishing those. They both nodded. "Good. I have a feeling we're going to need them."

Pat turned towards the buffet, eyeing Lise and Connor. Lise was whispering sweetly into his ear while he chewed, open-mouthed, on an onion ring nearly as big as a hula hoop. Connor was in a sheepskin jacket, flat cap, and a thick red woollen sweater that was more tear than wear. Five feet and change, he still loomed long and large in the minds of everyone he interacted with. There was a good heart in there. A fiercely loyal one too, but in a challenging, often hostile, frequently drunk wrapper. Margaret liked him most of the time; which didn't mean she trusted him. But then, who did she trust? Jim?

Connor and Lise would be parted soon and that couldn't be easy for them. They'd not been out of each other's sights since the chaos of the Cahoots trip to Berlin, one year ago to the day; what a farce that had turned into. Margaret shuddered at the memory of the media circus that followed it. All those cameras pointed at her and Jim. How they tried to make heroes out of them, for doing what anyone would have done. She took a deep breath. This trip would be different, she promised herself, despite all the prank calls, the unhelpful tour guide who never responded to Margaret's letters or phone calls, the venues that kept cancelling their bookings and the vague, non-committal responses from Lise's sister, Tilda, and supposed best-friend-forever, Nele.

"It'll just be kids," Jim said again, finishing both his drink and his thought. "The calls. Probably."

Pat, a person who never shirked eye contact, looked away and down. It was subtle, but all the good things, all the important things, are. Pat knew something. And that 'probably,' the slight uncertainty in Jim's voice, always so sure of itself. Margaret shivered. Too much air-conditioning, probably. "There's something you need to tell me," she said, banging her fist on the table. "Both of you. Now."

"Is there?" Jim asked, wide-eyed. Pat bent the exclamation mark into a question mark and held the paper up.

Nice try, Margaret thought. "That's why it wasn't a question," she said, doubling down. Her friends were in danger and they needed her, even if they didn't realise it yet.

Margaret felt two hands on her shoulders and jumped in the air. "What do you need to tell Margaret?" When she turned around it was Lise, bright blue eyelashes fluttering like rare butterflies. Connor was just behind her, in mid-scowl, as usual.

The Accidental Murder Club

"Just highlighting the importance of family to Margaret here," Jim said, "What with her being an only child and all. How long since you saw your sister, Lise?"

He improvised well, Margaret had to admit, but then he had to, since he was such a bad planner, unlike her - always so meticulous. Lise fell heavily into the booth next to Pat. "Thirty years," she said quietly. "I wonder if she'll even recognise me? Or me her? And Leipzig? It must have changed so much. Is this a good idea?"

"No one could forget you, my love," Connor said, standing at the table's edge and reaching down to grip her hand. She smiled up at her husband-to-be. Margaret grimaced at his paint-flecked black jogging bottoms. He looked like he'd just finished renovating a particularly difficult shed while Lise, her bright blue hair, heavy makeup and gold jewellery, had the air of a discount fortune teller. She'd become unapologetically herself after her husband Dieter's death; a self no longer holding back.

"Galway won't have forgotten me, either," Connor said. "Although it'll certainly have tried." He slapped his thigh. "Good one, C. Now who's up for a last drink before boarding?"

A young, female staff member appeared behind him, clearing her throat loudly. "Mr McGinley?" Connor turned on his heels. "Not if it's the tax man asking, darling."

"Follow me, please," the young woman said. Connor turned back to the group, stuck out his tongue and flapped it. "Didn't we agree, no strippers?" he said, far too loudly for the young woman not to hear.

Connor followed to the bar where Margaret spotted the telephone receiver laying on its side. Another prank phone call, perhaps? But who would know they were here, now?

Too many people. Another shiver. She really needed to tighten her neckerchief. Margaret watched Connor on the phone. How his face, so breezy when the call started, hardened and then cracked. He walked back towards them trying to rebuild his normal, nonchalant self as he went.

"Everything okay, mate?" Jim asked.

"Peachy," Connor said. "Except my old man's just died, so I'll probably need another onion ring or two."

Margaret gulped. It was happening. It was happening again.

Chapter 2

Galway Airport (Jim)

"Drizzle," Jim grumbled as the airport doors slid apart and he and Connor stepped out of Galway Airport's modest arrivals building. The news had been bumpy but the flight as smooth as churned butter.

"No welcome quite like it," said Connor, tipping his head back and sticking out his tongue. He had a hard time keeping that tongue to himself. It had been in Jim's ear more than once at the tail end of an all-night bender.

"Tastes like home, it does."

"You remember the taste after twenty years?" Jim asked, looking around for any sign of their welcome party. Months ago, at Margaret's prodding, he'd reached out to Seamus, Connor's sort of brother, to arrange things over here. Seamus had been very vague about who Connor might want to celebrate his nuptials with, what with it being so long since he'd graced Galway with his... unique presence. He hadn't sounded exactly thrilled at the idea of having Connor back in his life, even if it would be for just a week.

Might be for much longer now.

Jim looked around but couldn't see anyone loitering with

purpose. "Shall we just hail a taxi?" he asked, disappointed - he wanted, no, *needed* this stag-do to go well. Partly to do right by his buddy, partly to impress Margaret, and to prove something to himself—that he could still do hospitality right. He certainly hadn't planned on the groom's father snuffing it while they were en route.

"It's Ireland," Connor said with a wink. "No-one's ever on time."

Jim had never been to Ireland before but with so many young paddies cavorting around London--where he'd spent most of his life and thought of as home--he often wondered how anyone could be left over here. And why, since they all swore what a paradise the Emerald Isle was, they all buggered off at the first opportunity. He dropped his sports holdall to the floor, unsure how long they'd have to wait, and zipped up his trusty leather jacket. Took ten years off him, that jacket. Connor didn't have any luggage, which Jim also found odd. If he really was coming home for the first time in thirty years, shouldn't he at least bring a gift or two for the family? A top-shelf whisky or middle-shelf champers, at the very least?

Connor wiped his eye. "You okay, chief?" Jim asked. If he was cut-up about his father, he hadn't shown it on the flight, well, other than only drinking two Bloody Marys instead of four. Jim couldn't remember Connor ever talking affectionately about his father, Willie, but still… Jim's dad had been an alcoholic, degenerate gambler and yet if anyone dared slander him, he'd punch them straight in the nose. Your dad is your dad, always.

Connor wiped his eye. *Emotion?*

"You okay, fella?" Jim asked again.

"I'll miss her," Connor said.

"I thought, maybe… your dad?"

Connor lowered that proud chin of his. "Yeah, him too."

"Shall we cancel the stag?"

The Accidental Murder Club

"Never."

Jim got out his trusty pocket comb and neatened his thick brown hair. "Fair 'nuff."

A middle-aged man with curly dark hair, a huge backpack on his back, exited the airport and looked around and up and down, map in hand. He scratched his head with a gloved hand--what kind of pansy wore gloves in May? Or at all. The man approached Jim and Connor. "Excuse me," he said, but Connor didn't even acknowledge him. He would have, had he been a woman. The tourist cleared his throat. "Err," he said and thrust the map he was holding at Connor, "do you think you could be so kind as to point me towards Ashford Castle? I was supposed to meet my group here, but I seem to have--" Connor stepped back and the map fell to the ground as a stretch limo glided to a stop opposite them. The passenger window lowered and music blared out - *Streams of Whisky* by The Pogues. Jim had always had a sweet spot for The Pogues; they had spunk. Jim liked to think he still had it, too.

"There they be," said Connor, skipping across the road towards the limo, his delusions of grandeur acting up again.

"Stop," Jim shouted. "That's not ours." Seamus would have said if there was a limo coming, not that he'd been able to get Seamus after the first time he called, everything running through someone called Bill. Jim gave an apologetic nod to the wimpy tourist with the backpack as he scooped up his bag and ran after his friend. He couldn't help the man, he'd never even heard of Ashford Castle.

He jumped down from the curb into the road as a portly man popped up through the limo's sunroof, pulling a cigarette from his mouth. "Is that Galway's least eligible bachelor I see before me?" he yelled at Connor.

Connor stopped, then opened his arms wide. "Gary Mine's-A-Triple Kelly, as I live and breathe. Get down here right now, big fella."

The passenger window lowered as Jim caught up with Connor. Inside, he could see a giant of a man in what looked like a cassock, dog collar visible. "That a priest?"

"Bloody hell, Tad lad," said Connor. "I didn't know we were doing fancy dress." He turned to Jim. "Why didn't ye tell me? I'd have packed me PVC nurse's outfit."

Tad and Gary, Connor's childhood friends. Jim had heard many a yarn about them. Tad indulged with his fists, Gary with the bottle. Jim actually quite liked what he'd heard about Gary––seemed like a salt of the earth type, just like him. Also worked the pubs. But they can't have heard, Jim decided––not about Willie, Connor's dad. Or they wouldn't have come in a limo, boozed up. *Tacky.*

Tad got out, and in the process, unfurled himself. Jim got a crook in his neck just looking up at him. Had his own weather up there, he did. Wet and windy too, by the look on his gaunt, almost skeletal face. A scar ran the length of his left cheek. He had scraggly, black, scarecrow hair. Thin, not naturally tousled like Jim's. You certainly wouldn't stick him on a door, that's for sure, or you'd always have an empty bar. The man was the stuff of nightmares.

"It's good to see you, Connor," the unfriendly giant said, leaning down and trapping Connor's hand in a shake that almost lifted him off the ground. Connor tried to extricate his hand and reach in for a hug, but it was like grappling with a lamppost, and anyway, Connor was little higher than his belly button.

"And it's not a dress, it's a cassock." Tad's voice was deep enough to shake the leaves from a tree.

"It's ridiculous is what it is," Connor said, tugging a great handful of it. "I'd heard the rumours, but I didn't believe a word."

Gary appeared at Jim's side. "You must be Jimmy," he said,

sticking out his meaty hand, his fingers swollen chipolatas. "'Tis a pleasure to meet you. Seamus said good things."

"Jim," said Jim, "and pleasure's all mine, fella." He recognised Gary's nose––he had one like it; swollen, with a bulbous end; a tippler's nose. Rhino something or other, it was called. Jim could never remember the name, but he'd seen many in his long career. Gary's was more pronounced than his own––purplish and bumpy.

"Take your bag?" Gary asked, reaching for the strap of the holdall hoisted over Jim's shoulder.

Jim resisted. "Light as feathers, it is."

"Still," Gary said, tussling with Jim over the strap. "Let me."

"It's fine," Jim said, stepping away. How old or weak did this guy think he was?

"Get in then," Gary said, slapping him on the back. "I've already opened the bubbly. We've what, twenty years to catch up on, C?"

"We all, like sheep, have gone astray," said Tad, his raspy voice and dead eyes adding menace to what Jim guessed was a bible verse. Jim wasn't really up on his scripture. The only churches he went to were the ones they turned into wine bars.

"Baa," Connor said.

"Baa," Gary mimicked, and the two fell into easy laughter as they walked arm in arm to the open limo. They were going to be quite the double act; a real Shearer and Sutton. Sensing there was going to be no good moment to bring it up, Jim blurted out, "You've heard the bad news, right? About Willie?"

Tad and Gary turned to Connor and their silence was the answer. "Me old man's pegged it," said Connor with a shrug. "But he wouldn't want the bubbly wasted."

Tad took a long, deep breath. "When?"

"'Twas this morning, far as I know."

Gary lowered his eyes and put his hands in the pockets of his scuffed anorak. "Poor Seamus."

Tad made the sign of the cross. "May his soul rest in peace. Something denied us living."

Jim shuddered. Connor clasped his hands together. "The show goes on, boys, always. Have your man take us through Galway proper, Taddy. Jim's never seen it and I haven't in too long."

They got in, spreading out, luxuriating in a space for twelve. Jim ran his hands across the crisp black leather of the seats, of which there were many. And a full bar too - whisky, gin, rum - all in decanters. He reached for what he was sure was cognac, removed the stopper, and inhaled.

"Crystal," said Connor, tapping a different decanter of rum and whistling appreciatively.

"Glass," Jim corrected. Connor scowled, didn't like being corrected. Jim handed the decanter to Gary, who sniffed. "You can tell by the smell, right, Gary?"

"Yep."

"They use glass because it's porous," Jim explained, happy to be on a subject he knew well. "A little air gets in that way, opens up the spirit. You don't only get the fruit notes of your cognac. Your apricots and your raisins. You also get your earthy ones too--cinnamon, nutmeg. Crystal doesn't... It's not," he hesitated, "it's subtle, but, well..." he faded out, not wanting to brag.

"Yeeeeeaaaah, bollocks," said Connor, lifting the glass decanter, "and anyway, it's not for sniffing, it's for gulping," he said, chugging down a generous sip.

"Not from the..." Gary recoiled. "*Ugh.*"

"Why's Tad in the front?" Jim asked, looking at the partition (also glass).

"Unbecoming," Gary said, with a roll of his eyes. "He's very pious these days. I barely see him about town anymore."

The screen lowered with a pleasant whirring sound. "Like

God himself, I hear everything, fellas. Watch your tongues lest they be cut off."

Lurch, Jim decided, that's who Tad reminded him of. Connor farted. "You hear that, me old mucker? Or shall I do it again, and louder?"

The driver, who had not been introduced, laughed. Tad dinged the dividing window back up. Gary poured Jim and Connor champagne in glass tumblers, not flutes. Wasn't this guy supposed to be a barman? "You get more per pour this way," Gary said, as if hearing Jim's thoughts. Gary held out the full glass. Jim hesitated. He didn't want to embarrass himself, fall asleep, or both.

"You're not a teetotaller, are you, Jimmy?" Gary probed. "If you are, you can get back on that plane."

"Nah," said Jim, taking it and swigging, trying to understand why he was so on edge - things were going well, weren't they, or as well as could be expected? Connor's friends were here, which meant Connor still had friends, which meant they'd have company for the activities of the following days. Still, something sat heavy in his chest. Maybe it was the death, timely though it was. Willie had to be late eighties or early nineties, even? He felt like he was looking at the world through Margaret's eyes, detective-ing, as she always was. They'd spent a lot of time together in the past months, and he had to admit that she'd rubbed off on him. Not as much as he wanted her to, but that was up to her; he had time.

He hoped he had time.

Connor stuck his head out the window like a dog and howled. Through it, Jim glimpsed some of the island's famous rolling green hills. Connor pulled his head back in, threw his feet up on an empty seat, and propped his head on some cushions. "What are you up to these days, G? Do you own this fine city yet?"

Gary looked away. "I'm keeping busy, yeah."

"Got your own pub? Got a string of them?" Connor winked at Jim. "When he's drunk, Gary's the best barman in all of Galway, Jim. Sober, he's a useless sack of–"

"Feck off," Gary said, punching Connor playfully on the leg, the drink in their tumblers splashing. "And I'm never sober." The two men howled with laughter. There are some stories in this friendship, Jim thought, sliding back in his seat and crossing his arms.

"I've booked us the VIP area at the dogs," said Gary. There was a click of what sounded like a speaker.

"Gambling's a sin," Tad cut in to say.

"That's the best bit about it," Connor quipped. "And stop listening, unless you want to join in?"

"Got more tips than a Vegas hooker's G-string," Gary said. "We'll clean up. Just make sure you bet differently to Tristan if he insists on coming."

"Who the devil is Tristan?" Connor asked. It was all a blur to Jim. He was struggling with all the names and everyone's thick accents. He felt like he was watching a film at double speed. One of them foreign ones with subtitles. Not that he watched those. Margaret did, sometimes.

"Works for your father." Gary cleared his throat. "Worked for your father. *Shit*, I still can't believe it."

"I've lost enough to your tips," said Connor, after the briefest of pauses, trying to shift the topic.

"Like it matters how much you lose," Gary said.

Jim sat up. "Why wouldn't it?"

"Do you need someone for the service?" Tad asked over the intercom. "I deliver a firm but fair sermon. And I *knew* your father. What kind of man he was."

Jim scratched his ear. Was that a compliment? It didn't sound like one, but maybe that was because of the deliverer. Tad's tonal range seemed only to have one level--ominous.

The Accidental Murder Club

"I'm sure Seamus will have it all under control," Connor said, holding his empty tumbler towards Gary.

Jim lowered his window and stared out at the town, or was it a city? He wasn't quite sure. It reminded him of Cambridge, where he'd lived for a few years in his twenties. He'd been dating… what was her name? *Brenda.* A redhead and a real wild thing, she was. A biter. Yeah, it was the Georgian architecture, the bridges and narrow, cobbled pedestrian streets. Loads of people sitting out too, drinking on what was one of the first warm days of the year. Well, warm for Ireland. The limo was getting a lot of looks and a few jeers.

"Is everything here a pub?" he asked.

"No," Tad said. "Some things are an off-license."

Connor howled with laughter and even slapped his knee. The randomness of Tad's contributions and how far-off the speakers made him sound, gave his interruptions a 'voice of God from up high' feeling. Maybe that's why he had chosen that seat. A group of young lads in sportswear gave the limo the finger, and Connor popped out the sunroof and lobbed a few choice words at them. And then the content of his glass. "This is the Corrib," Connor said when he popped back down. "Runs up to the waterfront. They've spruced it up, they have."

"Connor owns half of it," Tad said.

"What?" Jim asked.

"I do?" said Connor, laying back and lifting his feet up onto the seat next to Jim. "But I don't even own shoelaces."

Jim looked down at Connor's scuffed leather boots with their big chunky tongues; yep, matching, but lace-less. They seemed to be secured by only a layer of grime and bravado. "The McGinley stock has risen," Gary said, his cheeks reddening on Connor's behalf. What had Connor said his family did again? *A market stall? A clothing shop? Something to do with jumpers?*

19

"You own *Neachy* now?" Connor asked. Jim wasn't sure if that was a pub or a sneeze.

Gary's mouth narrowed. "I wanted to talk to you about that actually. There's an opp–"

"I have the people's ear now, Connor," Tad interrupted. "We could do some good."

"You used to take ears, as I recall. And a tongue once, if the legends are true?"

"Legends rarely are. I've found the Lord. Found my calling. Found my peace."

"You've lost me," Connor joked.

"Have you changed?" Tad asked.

"You joking?" Gary asked. "He's still wearing the same jumper he left in."

"Well, he's getting married," Jim said, sticking up for his friend.

"Aye," said Gary, poking Connor in the side. "Never thought I'd see that day."

"And he came home," said Tad. "To make amends."

Connor laughed. "Make amends? But we've only got a week." He raised his voice and glass. "To the McGinley mansion, driver."

"Mansion?" Jim spluttered.

Chapter 3
Leipzig Airport (Margaret)

Lise marched out of Leipzig Airport, head swivelling, soaking everything in, basking in the background chatter of her native language. The tour guide they'd hired hadn't been waiting inside for them, as instructed, nor was she answering her phone, again, so they'd come out in search of a taxi. Margaret felt like everyone was staring at them and the banality and stupidity of the feeling annoyed her. It was a fallacy - *The Spotlight Effect* - because if everyone feels like they're being watched, logically, there's no one free to do the watching. Still, it was a feeling she couldn't shake with just rationality alone - she was on edge.

"Poor Connie," Lise said. "I should be with him."

"Jim's there," Margaret said. "And he was adamant the show must go on. His words. Did you ever meet Willie?"

"No," Lise said, rummaging through her shoulder bag, probably hunting for one of her very intense mascaras, as she power-walked away from Margaret towards the taxi stand, not noticing she was about to fall off the pavement.

"Look out," Margaret shouted, as a huge, old Mercedes swerved to avoid her, beeping aggressively. A brief shouting match occurred that Pat, forearm draped over Margaret's shoulder, found hilarious. Margaret couldn't follow the angry volleys flying between Lise and the driver, but she felt Lise held her own, even though she'd been clearly in the wrong. Margaret had spent the past year trying to learn German. Lise had started an afternoon class at Cahoots, mostly for Connor, who turned out to be its most challenging, unruly, and frequently drunk student. Margaret had improved enormously and yet to her fastidious ear, the language was still, mostly, just a cacophony of harsh sounds. She was excited to spend a week in Leipzig to see if those sounds would bend and fuse and soften, no longer noise, but signal.

"You okay?" she asked after the Mercedes drove off, the driver shaking his head. Pat gave him the finger.

Lise lifted the strap of her bag higher and settled her sunglasses back onto her face. "Of course. Don't turn that into another story about how everyone's out to get us. Some people are just bad drivers."

Margaret bit her lip, thinking, yes, and some tourists really should pay more attention. Wait, did Lise count as a tourist?

A voice called out from behind them. "You ladies from Bury St Edmunds?"

Turning on their heels, they saw a young woman with a short, silvery-blonde perm–the curls gathered high on top, the sides shaved–striding towards them. She didn't look so much as glare at Margaret, who was not going to be intimidated by her leather jacket, ripped jeans, and huge, shiny, black Dr Martens boots. You wouldn't just tread on someone's toes in those, you'd break them.

"Daniella," the woman said. Margaret held out her hand. Daniella snubbed it, simply giving a sharp half-nod, the audacity of youth.

"So nice to meet you," Lise replied, hand to her chest. Pat clicked with both hands in agreement. Margaret had briefed the travel agency in advance about Pat's curious form of mutism–one that allowed writing and embraced the full rainbow of body language, yet forbade talking.

"We thought you'd stood us up," Margaret said, putting her hand into her blazer pocket. She wanted to establish who worked for whom, and that they were not intimidated by this woman's... confidence. It's the same with unruly children in a classroom. You pick the gobbiest and you rein them in, the rest then fall into line.

Daniella shrugged. "First of May, you know? City is..." She was chewing gum, leaving her mouth open as she did so. *"Lively."* She pointed. "Car's that way."

Carrying all their own bags, they walked towards a tiny, blood-red hatchback car. "It's like with *Tschüss* all over again," Lise chuckled.

Daniella's head jerked. "What?"

"Nothing," Lise said quickly, although Daniella wouldn't have understood the reference to *Tschüss Tours*, the company that had taken them all to Berlin last year, coincidentally, on exactly this date––May 1st, Day of the Worker in Germany. They had driven right into an anti-capitalism demonstration last year as well. The first in a disastrous series of events that culminated into two murders. Margaret shook Berlin from her mind as Daniella walked them to her car, a dented biscuit tin on wheels, its rear end hanging off a nearby pavement directly below a large no parking sign. Margaret was relieved it still had all its wheels. It was more rust than metal and appeared to be held together by a huge sticker running the length of its side––*Im Osten geht die Sonne auf*. That she could translate: *The sun rises in the east.*

The car's boot was so badly dented it no longer opened and so they had to load their luggage onto the backseat. Fortunately, only Lise had those two big suitcases, while Margaret and Pat had packed modestly, with just roll-on cases. Margaret ducked her head in through the open rear window and sniffed. There was a strong smell of marijuana, an odour Margaret knew well. She'd found it everywhere at her school, *Righteous Path*: stashed in a toilet cistern, in a hollowed-out tube of toothpaste, and once, well, let's just say, a student smuggled it on a school trip in an intimate orifice.

"Get in," Daniella said, or rather barked, seeing Margaret hesitate. And why shouldn't she hesitate? Neither the car nor its driver were particularly reassuring. She glanced over the roof at Pat, who was similarly apprehensive, pacing back and forth. She wiped sweat from her brow then kicked a bin. What was she so nervous about?

"You okay?" Margaret asked. Was she always like this with cars? Margaret had never seen Pat drive, come to think of it. The bus stopped just outside Cahoots, so you didn't really need one.

"Come on," Daniella said, opening the driver's door. "With the protests it could be tricky to get to the city centre. The longer we wait, the more things will be on fire."

Margaret ducked down and slid in, slowly. After handing the luggage in, Pat joined her. Margaret was thrilled to see there were working seatbelts. There was so much luggage piled between them they had to hold it with their arms to stop it tumbling down, and so she couldn't see Pat without leaning either all the way forward or back.

"Did you say city centre?" Margaret asked, as she'd checked their hotel's location several times on her map. It would have been beyond generous to call it central. She wouldn't have called it at all, actually, based on the miserable reviews, but Lise had insisted on it. Apparently, Dieter and her had spent a very special night there once, long ago. Which, according to those reviews, was around the last time they'd washed any of the bedding. Margaret had brought her own.

"Change of plans," Daniella said. "*Hotel Hofhandel* called me

The Accidental Murder Club

earlier. There was some sort of mix-up. Fully booked, if you can believe that? But it's fine, I sorted it, got you much better rooms at the Westin. And it's right by the train station, it'll be much easier to get around. Five stars, of course."

Lise's crestfallen face in the front passenger seat told Margaret this was very bad news. *Hofhandel* was two stars, although the photos hid them both well.

"I don't understand," Lise said, turning around to Margaret, "Didn't you book the rooms months ago?"

"Yes," Margaret said, "the honeymoon suite, even." And at more than €100 a night, a price neither the location, photos, or reviews could justify, Margaret thought, and just about managed not to say. Why would the hotel cancel their bookings last minute? And how could a place that flea-infested and far from anything be fully booked?

"Who did you say called?" Margaret asked, rummaging into her bag with her left hand, looking for the booking information in her folder.

Daniella was checking herself in the rear-view mirror, lips puckered. "I didn't, because they didn't. They also seemed to think the booking was for a Veronika Fleischer when I called last week to confirm it. Weird, right?"

Tilda had made the booking, from before they'd hired Paula. "Anyway," Paula said. "The Westin is so much nicer. It's where all the VIPs stay. You ladies will fit right in." There was an undertone of sarcasm. She turned the key, but where Margaret would have expected the engine to purr, it gave only a dull, repeated sigh. Her meticulous preparation should have made last-minute changes extremely unlikely. And now one, before they'd even reached the hotel?

"Didn't Tilda make the original booking?"

"I don't know," Daniella snapped. "You've dodged a bullet. Just let it go."

"Hmm," Margaret said, not enjoying that turn of phrase or

its implications. She reached for the door handle. "If this ride is going to take longer than expected, I just need to nip to the lavatory. Won't be a minute."

Pat tutted, which was a sound, at least. And one of her more common utterances. Before Daniella could complain, Margaret had the door open and was out, striding back towards the entrance. "Bring me back an Aperol Spritz," Lise shouted. "For the road. Or maybe two. One for the car park, one for the road."

We're not in a car park, Margaret thought, because apparently Daniella just parks wherever she wants. Does whatever she wants, or so it seems. Had she changed the booking to make their location more convenient for her?

Tucked under her arm was Margaret's trusty folder. She was going to get to the bottom of this and without Jim or anyone else pulling favours and cutting corners. They'd passed several pay phones and her travel package contained some small change of euros. She reached a phone and dialled.

"Hallo," said a grumpy male voice.

Shouldn't he answer with the hotel name? *"Hotel Hofhandel?"*

"Ja–Ja," the voice said, as if he wished it wasn't, but couldn't deny that it was.

"Margaret Barrett here from England."

Silence.

"We've booked three rooms."

Silence.

"Just calling from the airport as a courtesy."

"Huh?"

Did they not have courtesy in Germany? "We'll be there in thirty minutes or so." She would have liked to be more precise, but Daniella was an unknown variable. Better to be cautious.

"Klar. Ja. So?"

"For our rooms," she said, to double check.

Silence.

"That we booked."

"*Ja,*" he said, eventually and reluctantly, as if someone was pulling the word out of him with tweezers.

"That you still have available, yes? The honeymoon suite?"

"*Na klar,*" he said, irritated, and then hung up. *Of course.*

How rude, she thought, as she turned, satisfied but not reassured, tucked the folder back under her arm and marched back to the car, trying to work out what to do next. A direct confrontation with their so-called tour guide probably wasn't the best approach. She didn't know if Daniella was lying. Maybe someone really had phoned her, the same person trying to sabotage this trip, and Lise's wedding. The prank caller. No, she had to play it cool, for now, and so she put on a wide, fake smile as she reached the car. Inside, Lise was talking animatedly, and Pat and Daniella were in various states of pretending to listen. Pat's was more convincing than Daniella's, who drummed her fingers impatiently on the steering wheel. Margaret got back in, wedging herself into the tiny amount of free space allotted her, righting a suitcase that had tumbled into her footwell. "Everything's sorted. *Hotel Hofhandel* has the rooms for us after all."

"Really?" Lise asked, grinning, hands clenched together. "How wonderful. Thank you."

Daniella turned. "You called them?" Her voice was flat and un-emotional.

"Yes."

She started the engine. "But then why did they call me?"

"I don't know."

"That place is a dump," she said, crunching the stick into gear, turning the steering wheel and accelerating away after the most cursory of checks over her shoulder. "I don't know why you booked it."

"I have my reasons," Lise said, giggling. Daniella shrugged, jumped a gear, honked at a tourist, and cranked up the stereo, seemingly all at once. The car filled with loud, bass-heavy punk music. It's hard to overcome a bad first impression, and Daniella had sure made that. Lise's childhood friend, Nele, had recommended her. She'd prod Nele later to find out why.

"How did you end up becoming a tour guide in Leipzig?" Margaret shouted after they had reached the motorway.

"What?" Daniella said. Lise pointed to the stereo. Daniella turned the music down. "Huh?"

"How did you end up becoming a tour guide in Leipzig?"

"Because people who look like me can't be from around here?" Daniella snapped.

"Yes," Lise said, "I was also wondering where you learned such perfect English?"

Daniella honked at a slow-moving motorhome. Six times. "I grew up in the UK, but my dad was born in Germany."

"How wonderful," Margaret said.

"Oh, we're close to the *Auensee*," Lise announced, as they passed a sign. "Dieter and I had our first date at *Haus Auensee*. We often went there with Nele…" Her voice trailed off, lost to the memory. Margaret pulled out her map and tried to figure out where they were. *Auensee*, a lake, was pretty easy to find, and it looked like they were on the right, albeit scenic route towards *Hotel Hofhandel*, which she'd marked with an X.

Lise dabbed her eyes with a handkerchief, now dotted with blue eyeshadow. "He was such a great man. Always kind, always happy—even after everything that happened to him."

Margaret dove deeper into her map, looking for *Cospudner See*, where they'd spread Dieter's ashes in a few days' time. Good riddance to them, too. The walls of Cahoots were thick, but not enough to muffle Lise's first husbands loud, nightly tirades. Everyone at Cahoots was happy when he'd get one of his lorry delivery jobs and disappear for a few days. He always came back with odd souvenirs from random places and peace would be restored with Lise, briefly, before they'd flare up again. Maybe he had been different in the past, on that first date at *Auensee* and the many that must have followed it, and long before he went to prison, or maybe Lise was just kidding herself. Their history together was complicated. Lise had confessed it all one night, after a whole bottle of bubbly, Margaret on the tonic and just the tonic. The topic of why they'd both never had children had come up. Margaret had explained that her students were her children. And that she'd never met the right partner. Lise had revealed that she'd been pregnant, had found out just after the wall went up. She'd written to Dieter who was trapped on the other side, in socialist East Germany. He then masterminded the building of a tunnel with friends. On the night of their escape, he went last. Everyone else got out but he was chased, mauled, and caught by two dogs, and then set upon by many, many guards. Lise lost the child just after, in month five. She blamed the stress of his capture for that miscarriage. He was in prison eight years. By the time he was free, her career as a violinist had flourished, and he was too damaged by his ordeal to try for another pregnancy. Margaret could imagine Lise felt guilty that she'd been the impetus for his rushed, botched escape. It couldn't be easy to come back here now, visiting a city, family, and friends you left forty years earlier, armed with just two new Cahoots housemates–one as straight as a ruler and the other a mysterious mute–and an urn of your dead husband. It was a very unusual way to celebrate your upcoming nuptials. But then, Lise was very eccentric, with a capital e.

"Very passionate," Lise shouted as the latest of several songs with really, really angry singers demanding regime change faded out. "Dieter and I were very passionate in our youth, too."

"You and Connor are still very passionate now," Margaret said, with what she hoped was disguised disdain.

"Well, the man's a beast," Lise said, turning to Daniella.

"Can't keep his hands off me. Oh, you'd just love him, Daniella. He's a riot. Have you seen The Bodyguard? Of course you've seen The Bodyguard. Well, he's *my* Kevin Costner."

Margaret began to cough and found she couldn't stop.

"Men," Daniella said, proving one word can be a whole sentence, as she swerved into a small side street decorated with overflowing trash cans, rusted bicycles, and empty beer bottles. She parked in front of a grey, three-story building. "Here we are." The sign read 'H tel H fhandel'.

Lise gasped. "It's just as I remembered."

"O?" Margaret said, but no-one seemed to get the joke. Scooping up all their luggage, with Daniella's reluctant help, they shuffled into the lobby.

"It's the same carpet," Lise said, as if this was good news. "The burns I had on my knees." She licked her lips. "Totally worth it." She then seemed to float to the check-in desk on a cloud of erotic memories - quite a feat considering the stickiness of the carpet. Pat stopped wheeling her suitcase and gave the lobby a double thumbs down. Margaret nodded her agreement and trudged past the comically fake-looking potted plants and moth-eaten furniture towards the bored expression and greasy, swept-back hair of the receptionist – Herr Schulze (according to his smudged name badge). Would they have their rooms? What would the person who'd tried to stop them getting them do next?

Daniella lingered by the electric doors. "It looks like a crime scene," she said ominously.

Chapter 4

The McGinley Mansion (Jim)

"Christ on a bike," Jim mumbled as he climbed out of the limo, his jaw slackening, staring up at the enormous, three-story monolith; mansion really, yeah, that was the right word. It had taken five minutes just to get down the long, winding gravel driveway.

Connor's family home had tall, imposing pillars gracing its entrance and a massive wooden door that would sustain a mighty siege, wrought-iron balconies on the upper floors, and slate covering the roof that was weathered and moss-speckled. There were also lot of small poncey details that Jim lacked the vocabulary to describe, but knew Margaret would love. She wouldn't have liked the stone gargoyle staring threateningly down from the first-floor balcony, but he found it to be a real highlight. This place was like something the National Trust would charge entry to. He'd never pay, too tight, although in his younger days, he'd have jumped the back fence and had a poke around.

"It's smaller than I remember," Connor joked.

"That's what she said," Gary said. "BOOM."

The car parked to the right wasn't too shabby either--a

blue Range Rover Sport, custom plates: Tr1stan. Jim didn't care for that ostentatious detail, but the car was sleek. He'd had a Range Rover once, twenty years ago, although parking it in central London had proven an endless nightmare.

"Let me help you with your bag," said Gary, his hand grasping the strap of Jim's holdall.

"It's really fine," said Jim, stepping away, or rather trying to.

"Irish hospitality."

"I thought that was the booze?"

"I insist," said Gary, tugging harder. "You're a guest."

Jim swatted him away. Gary gave up, reluctantly, wiping sweat from his forehead with his sleeve. "And aren't you a guest too?" Jim asked.

Gary didn't answer.

"Hasn't changed," Tad said, stroking his endless chin slowly, eyeing the mansion's upper floors with suspicion. Jim had the feeling he viewed everything that way.

"When were you last here?" Jim asked.

Tad let out a deep moan that morphed, eventually, into the words, "A lifetime ago."

"Tell me about it," Connor said, moving nearer to the stairs.

"Have you forgotten?" Tad asked, to his back.

"And you, Gary?" Jim said, asking a different way. "You here often?"

"That your best pickup line, Jimmy?" Gary's cheeks had a red glow. Before Jim could come up with a snappy retort, a shape emerged from the mansion's open front door.

"The man of the hour," said a good-looking young man, skipping down the stairs, hand thrust out. He was maybe thirty or thirty-five and in a tight, navy, woollen jumper, gelled hair slicked back. His skin was glowing. Never trust a man with perfect skin, Jim knew, because it means he's using *product*. Which tells you he's got his priorities all wrong. He thought about the old geezer at the airport wearing leather gloves to read a map - real men should look, at all times, like they've just fought a bear and won. *Narrowly.*

The youngster clasped Connor's hand, then placed his other on top while flashing the widest of crocodile smiles. Polyester poser. His teeth were probably fake too. "An honour to finally meet–"

"We'll see about that," said Connor with a wink. "Who the devil are you then, young fluff?"

"Tristan," the man said, chastened, not letting go of Connor's hand. The reflection from his silver watch blinding Jim momentarily. "Vice President of the Trust, and, of course, a dear friend of your late father." He bowed, sort of. "My deepest condolences for your loss."

There was something in his voice that rang hollow, like he was reading from a teleprompter. A throat was cleared, elaborately, from up near the door. Connor turned to a butler who was making his way down the steps, his back comically straight, arms behind him, penguin-esque.

"Butler Bill," said Connor gleefully, throwing open his arms. "As I live and breathe."

"Butlers are real?" Jim asked. This one was clearly past his best, older than Connor, even. In his eighties, if Jim had to guess, but still––he was wearing an impossibly dark black suit, white shirt, gloves, and a neat bowtie. Impeccable was the word.

"Mr Connor, sir. What a delight it is to have you here once again." His voice was like a creaking door. "You look exactly the same. And by that, I mean, is it possible you're wearing the same jumper?"

Jim cracked up at the wonderful deadpan delivery. "I swear you're not a day older than when I left." Connor pinched the butler's cheek. "And just as cheeky."

"Service keeps one young." Butler Bill turned and coughed into his hand.

Jim prodded a finger into his ear. A priest *and* a butler? It had all gone very Agatha Christie. Jim had only just recovered from the excitement of Berlin, the last Cahoots holiday. There were some great memories mixed in there too, and it was the first time he and Margaret worked together, showing how compatible they were, at least in his eyes, which definitely didn't have cataracts.

"Where's Seamus?" Connor asked, turning towards the entrance, which was up the wide, five-step stone staircase. Jim craned his neck to look inside. Seamus was actually an orphaned cousin that Willie and Sophie, Connor's parents, had adopted when he was just a kid, and so by now was more like a brother – only one that didn't visit, call, or write.

"Emotion has overcome Seamus, rather," said Butler Bill. "His disposition is," the butler cleared his throat, "*unchanged*. We will join him shortly for the reading of the will."

"Feck me," said Connor. "The old man's only just pegged it."

"Still," said Bill. "McGinley employs many, and so there is great interest–"

Jim pulled his finger out. 'McGinley employs many?' What? Why? Although, you'd need a football team's worth just to dust this place.

"Uncertainty *is* costly," Tristan added.

"Just be a formality anyway," said Connor, moving up the steps, everyone trailing after him. For the thousandth time, Jim had to admire his friend's confidence, which was a kind of armour. A formality? That it would go to Seamus? Or to Connor? Who, while loyal and protective of the people of Cahoots, never mentioned anyone over here and hadn't thought to visit in decades?

They entered the foyer, a grand, double-height space that served as an entrance hall. It had marble floors and ceilings adorned with ornate mouldings. The focal point was a grand, curved staircase that led to the upper levels. He noticed framed photos of Connor's father and mother, Sophie, all along the walls. A blonde, and good with it, if you were into noses, which Jim certainly was. She had died young, when Connor was in his early teens. Had Willie, Connor's father, never remarried? Odd for someone this rich. There were photos of Connor too, as a younger man, the crook in his nose giving him away. Seamus was ten years younger than Connor, if Jim remembered right, but there were no photos of him anywhere.

By the time they found the library–through a drawing room, a sitting room with open blazing fire, a snooker room, and down a corridor as long as Italy––Jim felt thoroughly lost and dangerously peckish. The library turned out to be as equally grand and impossible to heat as all the other spaces - its walls lined with ceiling-height bookshelves with leather-bound books he was sure no bugger had ever read. On top of the hardwood floor lay a large rug showing a shepherd and his happy flock. In the centre, an enormous dark oak table surrounded by comfortable, high-backed chairs upholstered in velvet. Fine crystal glasses on the table. Real crystal, too. There were also a couple of comfortable armchairs and a large leather sofa next to the fireplace. At the table, sitting with his back to the enormous windows, despite the magnificent view, was a portly man with frizzy white hair and thick black glasses, blowing his nose into a tissue. There was a small mound of them in front of him.

Seamus, Jim guessed.

"Oh," the man said, jumping to get up, then banging his knee on the table. *"Balls.* Sorry, I was just... well." Next to the mound of tissues were long, shiny knitting needles and white yarn that looked like it was becoming a scarf. He was both wearing a fluffy white jumper and had one tied around his neck, an odd combination, especially with it being so unseasonably warm. He'd probably been too distraught to notice. Jim only had a plain black shirt under his leather jacket. The man was clearly in tatters - his eyes red and the skin at the edge of his nostrils cracked.

"*Sea*, my man, what's the craic?" said Connor, keeping his arms fixed to his sides.

"Hello, Connor," Seamus said, lowering his eyes. His voice was an octave higher than Jim would have expected. There was a stiff, formal, sad air to the reunion and Jim wasn't sure if that was by design: Connor's. "Hello, Father. *Gary.*"

"Jim," said Jim, introducing himself.

Seamus raised his puffy eyes and gave a muted half smile. "I might need a lie-down," he said, slapping the back of his palm to his forehead.

"Where's Bill disappeared to?" Connor looked around. "I've a mighty thirst on, and I could murder a sausage roll."

"You and me both," said Gary, rubbing his prodigious stomach.

"Robin just pulled up," Seamus said. "He's probably with him."

"Who's Robin?"

"The family lawyer. Here to read Dad's will."

"There's also some paperwork," said Tristan, gesturing to an open briefcase on the table. "And a few people you need to meet–" He opened and closed his hands.

"Not now," said Seamus.

"I meant Connor," Tristan corrected. "He's the heir, after all."

Seamus stiffened. "We don't know what's in the will. And obviously I know the estate better than–"

"This is probably a family thing," said Jim, edging back towards the door and away from the awkwardness.

"You'd think so, wouldn't you?" Connor said, glaring at Tristan.

"Maybe someone can show me to my room?" Jim asked, taking another step back. "Or draw me a map?" He let out a

The Accidental Murder Club

nervous chuckle. If Margaret had known about this place, she'd have put one in his pack. Did Lise know about this place?

"Gary knows his way around," said Tad.

"Me?" said Gary, flustered. "Didn't you work here that summer, too?"

"Under sufferance."

Connor beckoned them all to sit. "Stay, pals. This won't take but a minute. After all, there's only one son. And then we can go start the stag proper."

Seamus blew his nose into a tissue that had hidden until now up his sleeve.

"I've had several conversations with Willie," said Tristan, hands now open, playing peacemaker. "I know that his wish was for the trust to continue its strategic, innovative supervision of the entire McGinley estate. I don't know how up to date the will is, but I'm just here as a formality really, to make sure that happens. In case there's Ts to dot, Is to cross, reassurances to give, generous monthly stipends to approve, that sort of thing. I've actually prepared a short PowerPoint presentation." He took two steps and rustled in his briefcase. "Where did I put my laser pointer?"

"Mr McGinley," said Connor, through gritted teeth.

Tristan froze. "Sorry?" he said without looking back.

"His name was *Mr McGinley*, to you. As is mine."

"Right, of course," said Tristan, blushing.

"McGinley," Jim said, finally connecting dots - *that shepherd rug, the knitting needles, the double jumper.* "McGinley Knitwear? You're those McGinleys? *Crikey.*"

"Sharp as a box of knives," Connor said. "Nothing gets past him."

"Yes," Tristan said, beaming. "That's us."

Jim whistled. "Famous, right? I think I had one once, back in the seventies." He looked at the opulence of the room anew. "You're telling me jumpers bought all this?"

37

Connor blew a raspberry. "All property is theft. Wool is too, and we've taken plenty. It's time to give back, I say. Well, maybe not the wool. Not much use to the sheep now, is it?" He laughed. "The proceeds from it is what I'm saying. Turn the business into a commune is what I'm thinking. I've got a lot of artist friends back in Norfolk. Vagabonds and troubadours. Maybe even relocate Cahoots here? We could do a lot of good and have fun while we're at it. Give plenty to the workers too, of course. Power to the People, and all that jazz." He slapped Tristan on the back. "You with me, T?"

The colour drained from Tristan's face. Seamus's had no colour to begin with. He looked like he was in some kind of trance. "He was still so young," he said, quietly.

"He was ninety," Connor corrected.

Seamus dabbed his eyes with a balled-up tissue. "At heart, I mean."

"He died of a heart attack."

"We only had breakfast together this morning. He was still as sharp as a tack." Seamus wailed. "He had so much left to give."

"There are many good causes," Tad said.

"And business opportunities," Gary added meekly.

"What will we do without him?" Seamus whimpered.

Before anyone could answer, Butler Bill and the solicitor arrived. "Gentlemen, this is the honourable Robin Hughes, Esquire." Robin was a short, mole-like man, with rounded shoulders and thick, silver, bottle-top glasses. He shuffled in, his steps short, barely lifting his feet, and took the place at the head of the enormous table. He was holding a mustard-yellow A4 envelope. Everyone sat down, Tristan moving nearest the lawyer. Jim was facing Connor, who had his usual disaffected air.

"Terrible business," Robin said, with a smack of his lips. "Death, I find." He looked around expectantly, as if for applause

The Accidental Murder Club

at the clarity of this insight. "Wills too." Another awkward pause. Connor rubbed his temples. "I've read a hundred of the buggers," Robin continued. "Even saw a fist-fight once. And a stabbing. Cocktail stirrer, but in the eye." His eyes swirled. "No-one's ever satisfied is what I'm saying. That's the problem." He glanced at the folder. "Keep that in mind."

Connor drummed his fingers on the table.

"Anyway," Robin said, "I don't want to drag this out. But first, I do just want to offer my deepest condolences. Terrible business. Dear old Willie. And he was dear, wasn't he?"

Butler Bill cleared his throat. Robin turned. "Right, right."

"The envelope, man," Connor growled.

Robin turned the envelope in his hands and tried to stick his nails under the flap on the back, but his hands were shaking too much. "Terrible business," he mumbled again, after an awkward thirty seconds. "Envelopes."

Why was Robin nervous? Shouldn't there be more family at this? How big was the McGinley clan? Jim was swimming in questions and he'd never been much of a swimmer. His calves were too big.

Butler Bill moved across with an ornate gold letter opener and swiped deftly. Robin pulled a few pages of paper out of the now open envelope and squinted down at them. The room hushed. Jim took a moment to drink it all in; to just savour the drama. He was already thinking about how he was going to describe the scene to Margaret. Tristan sniffled and rubbed his nose with his index finger.

"A very wise man, Willie," Robin began.

"Yes, he was," said Seamus, gripping the edge of the table with both hands. "Always put his family first." The in-progress scarf had grown an impressive amount in just a few minutes, its end now falling off the table and into Seamus's lap.

"Good heavens," Robin said, having read the first few lines to himself.

"Just read it, man," Connor growled. "Before the rest of us croak."

"Yes," Robin said. "Right. Well, in my role as Executor, I stand before you today to read the last will and testament of Willie Darach Seamie McGinley." He cleared his throat. "To Bill, my faithful, loyal aide, and the man who has run my home and domestic life for decades, it is only fair to finally pay my debt to you, old friend, as much as could ever be possible. Accordingly, I bequeath you the sum of one million euros. May it provide you with the comfortable retirement you deserve."

The room turned to Bill, who was standing ramrod straight, one hand behind his back, the other supporting a tray. "Fiddlesticks," he said, his face expressionless until... it cracked and a wide grin leaked out. He lobbed the tray like a frisbee into the fireplace, lifted his left hand, and with the right, and a great deal of ceremony, yanked off its white glove. Then he pulled off the other one, threw them behind his head, unbuttoned the first three buttons of his white shirt, turned on his heels and strode out of the room.

They were all too shocked to laugh, until, from the hallway, there was a loud scream of joy. "Good on him," Connor said, smirking. Service might keep you young, but apparently you still didn't do it even a minute longer than you had to.

"Seamus, my dear boy," Robin continued, paper just centimetres from the thick lenses of his glasses. "No words can express how grateful I am for your contribution to the family business - your knowledge, your designs, your impeccable eye, your skill with those ever-present knitting needles. Like a golden retriever, you have been a faithful, loyal companion."

Jim winced at the comparison.

"How I missed you each year when you'd take your annual holiday to Mykonos. How pleasant it was to see you return, that skip in your step and twinkle in your eye. I hope you'll

The Accidental Murder Club

find similar joy in looking at this painting, commissioned for you in honour of your time here."

'Time here?' He made it sound like a long holiday, not almost all of Seamus's life. Robin went around the table and handed Seamus a small painting that had been between his legs, so small, in fact, that Jim hadn't even noticed him carrying it in. It was scarcely bigger than a hardback book.

Seamus got up to receive it. "Oooh," he said, his eyes filling with tears. "How... magnificent."

"Give us a gander?" said Connor. Seamus angled the picture towards him and Jim got a quick glimpse. There was a small white house with some kind of shrubbery around it. A couple of sheep too. Cracking view, very modest abode, and it looked more like Wales than Greece, although maybe the difference was mostly weather? Jim had never been to either.

"Compact," Connor said, pointing. "What's it say there, then?"

"Eleftería," Seamus said, reading from a small bronze inscription beneath the picture. Stupid name, Jim thought. Sounds like one of them tongue twisters.

"I... love it," Seamus said, after a slight pause. He looked back at his empty seat, seemingly unsure whether to return to it or to stay standing.

That was it? A crappy picture for a lifetime of service to the family business? And when even the sodding butler got a cool million? Connor moved his chair out and put his feet up on the table and both hands behind his head, a power stance. "Keep reading then, chief."

Seamus stayed standing, wiping his eyes with his tissue, holding the picture by the small hook on its back. Tristan poured himself a generous glassful of water without offering anyone else any.

"We Irish," Robin continued, having returned to his spot at the head of the table, "know that blood is always thicker than

41

water. I rest easy knowing that Connor, as my only heir, now finally settling down and abandoning his frivolous, flagrant, scandalous ways, will do right by you and the business, Seamus. The Trust has long served its purpose and can now be dissolved, should Connor decide he doesn't require its services."

Tristan sprayed a mouthful of water across the room. Seamus crumpled forwards, leaning on the table with his free hand for balance. Tristan leapt up from his chair, tipping it over as he did so, yanking a Blackberry from his briefcase and storming out of the room. Gary drew in a sharp breath. Tad mumbled something inaudible, his eyes up on the ceiling.

"Well," Jim said, which felt not like a full sentence, but an entire paragraph.

Robin placed the will down in front of him. "Terrible business," he said again, excusing himself. The latest in a line of sudden exits that had started with Butler Bill's unforeseen, instantaneous retirement. Connor sat motionless, lips pushed out, rubbing the back of his head, looking like a cat that hadn't asked for cream but wasn't going to push the saucer away, either.

"Well, well, well," he said.

Seamus put the picture under this arm and swallowed a sob. "Such a wonderful man," he said, as he walked to the head of the table to pick up the papers. "When was this will dated? January 2002. *Huh.*"

Four months ago, Jim thought, watching the sob grow in Seamus's chest. "I mean. Such kind words." He looked at Connor, or rather tried to look, but kept missing. Soon, the dam holding back his emotion collapsed, and he too, made a run for the hallway, chased by his disappointment.

Tristan strutted back in, plastic smile reset on his face. "Congratulations," he said, shaking Connor's hand. "Everyone at the Trust is excited to show you just how good a job we've done and will continue to do, day to day, what with you being retired and having a new wife to enjoy."

Connor let his hand be shaken. He still had his feet up on the table. Finally, his lips parted. "Trissy. You mind if I call you Trissy?"

"Nothing needs to change," said Tristan. "You'd still receive generous remuneration each month and yearly dividends, of course. Let knitwear be our forte and... hedonism yours?"

"Smart," said Connor, tapping the side of his head after yanking his hand out of Tristan's. He got up. "Well, Trissy," he said, flicking him in the chest. "Lots to think about, I have. And I don't know about you all," he looked at his three friends, "but I think best at the bottom of a bottle. Gary, you said you've had something planned, right?" Connor gave some jaunty elbow. "The dogs?"

"I guess we know who's paying?" said Jim, standing up, happy at the idea of leaving both this room and the situation, which had grown uncomfortably awkward.

"Connor never pays for his sins," said Tad.

"Or his rounds," Gary agreed.

Jim clasped the back of his neck and rubbed, increasingly certain that the situation, whatever it was, was coming with them. He'd hoped they might quickly resolve any resentment at Connor's long absence and then be able to move on to celebrating his engagement. But after that will, and the snide comments flying in all directions, there was no chance. Everywhere he looked, he saw daggers pointed at his friend, and it was his job to protect him.

Chapter 5
The Night Walk (Margaret)

"It's so wonderful to be home," Lise said, as the three women strolled, arm in arm, through Leipzig city centre. It was getting dark, the streetlights casting long shadows. Every sight warranted Lise, walking between Margaret and Pat, to pull enthusiastically either left or right on their interlocked arms. "Wow," she said, stopping to stare up at the strangely shaped prism of the *City-Hochhaus* skyscraper. "The view from the top is almost as scary as Daniella's driving," Lise said, poking Margaret in the ribs with her elbow. She yanked the three of them left. "Look, there's the *Nikolaikirche*. That's where the protests that brought down the wall began. Tilda volunteers there from time to time. It's all so wonderful here, no?"

Pat nodded and grinned. Margaret let out a "hmmm," while actually thinking that the historic city centre was a rather odd mix: beautiful, arched renaissance buildings shoved up against modern glass skyscrapers and austere offices. The juxtaposition was too jarring for her refined tastes. Not that they had much time to look at anything. Lise marched them on, soon passing a building with a big glass facade. *"Zeitgeschichtliches Forum,"* she read. Pat's eyebrows arched. "The GDR spy exhibition," Lise explained. "It's on the itinerary for tomorrow, right, Pat?"

Pat nodded. Margaret wondered again why Pat had insisted on adding this exhibition to their already full itinerary. It seemed an odd choice for a hen-do. But then so was scattering the ashes of your dead husband at a lake, and they were going to do that too. And to come to a place so rich in recent history, a city that played a crucial role in the final destruction of the German Democratic Republic (Germans called it the DDR, the *Deutsche Demokratische Republik*) but then not engage with that history? That would have been strange too. Ignorant, even.

The GDR, despite its name, wasn't democratic in the slightest. Margaret had checked a book out from the library about it, to refresh her knowledge. It was formed after the second world war, in the soviet-occupied Eastern part of Germany and became an increasingly brutal regime, characterised by central planning, state control of media, and an extensive security apparatus, including the infamous secret police – The Stasi.

Somehow, it lasted until 1989.

They walked closer to the museum entrance and as they did so, the features of a small, rather bony woman with puffy grey-blonde hair came into view. She was staring into the large window with her back to them, her face only visible through her reflection. She looked like she was mouthing something, then frowning.

"Nele," Lise screamed out and ran, stumbling before her on the cobbles. The woman whirled around towards them, effortlessly catching Lise as she did so. *"Ich kann es nicht glauben,"* Lise said, enveloping her in a tight hug. *I can't believe it.* The rest of Lise's words were unintelligible between sobs into Nele's shoulder, who frowned while patting Lise stiffly on the back, her green eyes darting around, never focussing for long on either Pat or Margaret.

"Shhhhh," Nele said, as Lise tried to pull herself together, laughing and crying, as if she couldn't believe Nele was really there.

"Sorry," Lise said eventually, after an awkward minute. She turned back to them and, fanning herself, said, "Girls, this is Nele, my dearest, oldest, sexiest friend." She pulled Nele's hand, which she still hadn't let go of, to her chest. "And Nele, this duo of quietly devastating femininity, is Pat and Margaret."

"I see that," Nele said, giving a narrow, uncertain smile. The contrast between Lise's overflowing emotion and Nele's restraint was striking, but that's probably what people thought when they saw Margaret and Lise together, too. And it was a public setting. Who knew who was watching and judging? Not everybody could be so casual with their emotions as Lise.

"Margaret doesn't speak much German yet," Lise said to Nele. Margaret wanted to correct her. She was improving rather quickly she felt, with the help of Lise's afternoon class and her own private studying. Lise was a rather scattered teacher and never took Margaret's advice on running a classroom--the importance of structure and preparation—but Margaret enjoyed attending her lessons nonetheless. If you can't be competent, you should at least be enthusiastic, and Lise was always that.

Nele studied Pat from head to feet. Pat had learned German at school. "You don't speak at all, right?" Nele asked. Pat's shoulders tensed and she gave a shy double thumbs up. Margaret didn't know a double thumbs up could also be shy, but Pat somehow made it so.

"I didn't expect you to speak English so well?" Margaret said to Nele.

Nele straightened. "Leipzig University is very international. I worked in the Dean's office for years." She seemed proud, despite her very thick German accent. "Unlike Tilda."

Lise's head cocked. "Tilda? She did some courses. I don't think she's bad at it."

"Really?" Nele asked. Margaret had spoken with Tilda, Lise's sister, on the phone and had no difficulty conversing.

"Yes, she hosts bird watchers from around the world."

"That makes sense," Nele said, head tipping back. "Leipzig is an international jewel."

"And every tourist visits Nikolaikirche," Lise added. "She leads tours there, I think."

Nele gave a subtle half eye roll. Margaret interpreted this as a dig at the church and not that they'd let Tilda lead tours of it.

"How's Christian and Julia?" Lise asked Nele.

"They're," Nele lowered her gaze, "far away."

"Your children?" Margaret asked.

"*Yes*. One's in Peru and the other New Zealand. Or Australia. Papua New Guinea? Who knows?" She cleared her throat. "They're fine enough."

"How wonderful," Lise said, with a double clap. "And Friedhelm?" Husband, Margaret guessed.

Nele cleared her throat again. "Still here. Where's Tilda?" she asked, looking around, trying to move the conversation on. "I thought she'd be with you?"

"We're supposed to meet her at the statue of Faust and the Devil." Lise pointed towards the entrance of a glossy shopping mall. *Auerbach's Keller*, Margaret read on the old-timey sign. "Leipzig's most famous restaurant," Lise said, pointing at two bronze figures. "And there's the statue."

No-one was waiting. Who'd be late to a reunion this long awaited? "Come on then," Nele said. The group walked the short distance to the statue as a thick-set woman in a frumpy green jumper and wax anorak came around the corner, hands in her pockets.

"Tilda," Lise yelled and broke from the group to run to her sister, engulfing her in another enormous hug. Lise's sobs and wailing were even louder this time.

Margaret adjusted her neckerchief, watching. Tilda did

resemble Lise, she decided. Just a wider, dowdier, less colourful version. Margaret had been nervous about meeting both Lise's sister and best friend, Nele. She didn't know what they'd been told about her, and despite promising herself she wouldn't take over the hen-do's planning, she'd stepped in rather frequently.

"I forgot your gift at the hotel," Lise said, patting her sister's arm. "Didn't I girls?" She looked at Pat and Margaret. "They've seen it. I'll get it to you tomorrow, I promise."

Instead of answering her sister, Tilda took a few steps forward to both shake off her sister and to shake Margaret's hand. Tilda had a firm grip and callused hands, like someone who did manual labour. "Nice to meet you," she said, her voice deeper than Lise's.

"Likewise," Margaret said. "We've heard so much about you."

"Really?" Tilda said, glancing at her sister, who blushed. "Well, only the bad stuff is true."

"You badass bitches ready?" a voice asked from behind them. It was Daniella, their so-called tour guide, who had emerged from an alleyway.

"It's more a question of whether they're ready for us?" Tilda said. Daniella and Pat laughed.

Margaret knew from the itinerary that the *they* in this sentence referred to the actors who were going to take them on a Ghosts and Ghouls tour of the city. Daniella's idea.

"I was ready half an hour ago," Nele needled.

"Our hosts will be here any second," Daniella said unconvincingly, ducking back towards the alley. Margaret followed her.

"You'll be glad to hear everything's in order with the rooms," she said. 'In order' was a stretch. Lise's room – the bridal suite - was more like the brothel suite because of its red velvet walls and furniture. The curtains had moth holes you could put your fist through and the towels were starched enough that they could stand up on their own. The whole place smelt as if it had a sixty-a-day smoking habit, but Margaret wasn't going to make a fuss. She'd stayed at worse on school trips. And Lise loved it.

"I have a few questions about tomorrow," Margaret said.

"Cool, cool," Daniella said, still hotfooting it down the narrow alley. "Later, yeah? I just need to... where are...?"

"Fine," Margaret said, annoyed, but knowing that leading groups, while not as difficult as Daniella made it seem, wasn't easy. She walked back to the others. "Probably best someone else is leading the Ghosts tour," she said in a quiet voice.

"She seems nice enough to me," Tilda said.

So, there was definitely a cultural divide concerning customer service. "I might be harsh," Margaret conceded.

"Or traumatised," Lise giggled.

"Because of what happened last year?" Nele asked. "Your big detective adventure in Berlin? It was in all the newspapers. How you caught a murderer."

"No deaths on this trip," Lise said.

"Not sure I can promise that," Daniella said, back from the alley with reinforcements. "Because that's exactly who's arrived." Three shapes darted out from behind her—a witch in a comically high black hat and fake nose, a devil with horns, and a hangman with a deep hood that hid his face and a rope with a hangman's noose—arms up, swirling and moaning as they circled the group pressing them closer together, the witch cackling loudly, head tipped back. The hangman got right up in Margaret's face, lifting his rope, teasing to put it over her disapproving head. Her teeth chattered. She must be cold.

"Stay back," she said as the devil danced in front of her, letting out a loud, unhinged, high-pitched laugh.

"Ladies," the witch said, with a sweep of her arm, "tonight is not for the faint of heart." The women bunched together, back to back. "Historic Leipzig is about to reveal its many ghouls and ghosts."

"Oooh, how fun," Lise said. "Huh, ladies?"

"Fun?" the devil mocked. "Hung murderers and witches burnt at the stake won't take too kindly to being disturbed." Margaret pushed him gently away with her forearm.

"Watch your backs," the devil said, then clapped once, loudly, like a gunshot. They circled the women faster. Margaret felt a rake down her back and turned sharply, but there was only Daniella there, arms crossed.

"You're very jumpy tonight," Nele said, looking very nonplussed by the show so far, hand on her elbow. "Good thing Nurse Tilda is with us, in case you have a heart attack." Her laugh had a cackling quality too. Tilda said nothing, just pushed her hands deeper into her anorak's pockets. If she was having an emotional reaction to any of this--seeing her sister, meeting the others, the bad theatrics of the theatre ensemble-- she was hiding it well.

"Follow," boomed the hangman, face lost in his hood. And so, they walked, following Daniella and the actors who proved stubbornly committed to their roles, either swirling around them or disappearing in alleys and side streets to jump out from behind bins or a parked car to scare them. They'd take turns talking, the other two playing the different roles of each story--that of an infamous midwife from a 1573 murder spree or mentally ill Johann Christian Woyzeck in a straightjacket, executed in 1824 in front of thousands. "They chopped his head off right here on the market square," the hangman said, while the witch flapped around them.

Margaret hated every minute, but tried not to show it. Firstly, because she thought it would egg them on and, secondly, because this wasn't about her. Lise was thrilled by it all, swirling with them, geeing up the others, clapping at the end of every story. She tried several times to interlock her arm

The Accidental Murder Club

with Tilda's, but somehow her sister always slipped away, quicker-footed than she looked.

"I do like a bit of bloodshed," Lise said during a lull in the tour by a van selling *Bratwurst*, the go-to German sausage. "Very intoxicating, isn't it?" she said. "I mean," she continued, "it's already very intoxicating just being with you two again." She grinned at Nele and Tilda. "I've all these memories here. With you both. With Dieter. When we were all young."

"A long time ago," Tilda said, as if she wasn't in any of them anyway.

"Yes," said Nele. "Gone and forgotten, just like the good old DDR."

"We're still young," Margaret said, but they ignored her.

"We have to keep them alive." Lise firmed. "What are we without them?" She patted her sister on the arm. "That's why I've decided, after thinking long and hard about it, and some gentle nudging from Pat." Her eyes met Pat's, who winked. "To get our files from the Stasi archives."

The light turned green, and the group walked on. "I thought that was a joke when I saw it on the itinerary," Tilda said, a half-step behind the others. Margaret had thought the same, but didn't want to get involved. It was Pat encouraging Lise to go to the Stasi archives, even though Pat had never even met Dieter. She'd only arrived at Cahoots after the lorry accident that had cost him his life. Jim had joked to Margaret, cruelly, that at least Lise could save on the cost of the crematorium, as Dieter had been burnt to ash along with his vehicle. The ash that was now sitting on Lise's bedside table in *Hotel Hofhandel*. It all felt strange to Margaret. This trip should be about the future, not the past.

"I don't understand it either," Nele said.

Okay, now Margaret felt she had to join in, she couldn't have Lise being ganged up on. "Don't you want to know what's written about you?" she said. "Who spied on you?"

"The past has passed," Tilda said.

"Sometimes the past comes back to haunt us," the devil said, appearing to Margaret's right. As if she didn't know that. She followed his finger, pointing towards an old cemetery. Inside it, great billows of fog––must be from a machine, Margaret decided––wafted down from the trees and cloaked the tombstones. On the far side, Margaret could just about see an old mausoleum. She swallowed. This really wasn't her idea of fun––that was reading (the classics), watching a nature documentary, hiking, rearranging and sorting a drawer, or, if feeling social, hosting an intimate dinner party.

Margaret trudged down a narrow centre aisle between collections of tombstones, paying close attention to her steps until, "Stop," the devil boomed, raising his hands, looking like a bat ready to take flight. Nele bumped into Pat, who was at the front of the line. "We've reached one of the most famous graves in the *Johannesfriedhof*."

Even in the almost-dark, Margaret could see Pat give the hangman a healthy serving of her trademark vicious side-eye. Having an inquisitive nature was the right character trait for an investigative journalist, but Pat seemed to have forgotten she'd retired. Or maybe Jim was right about us becoming our jobs. Pat had already rankled many *Cahootians*, especially Graham Littlejohn, almost a mute himself, whom she had accused of being the night-time flasher plaguing the community, and who was very much circumcised, unlike poor Graham, who'd had to expose himself just to clear his name. Sordid affair the whole thing. Margaret blushed just thinking about it. Graham had moved out shortly after, not that she blamed him.

After another gruesome story, their guides ushered them on and they followed, dutifully, all except Daniella, who sat down atop a tombstone––her face illuminated by the small, flickering flame of her lighter as she lit a cigarette. The rest walked, or rather stumbled, after the lantern, now held by the hangman, as more and more shapes emerged from the darkness, lit by the flickering light of the candles their guides held aloft. To Margaret's right was a statue of a bare-breasted woman, raising her hands to the sky. "Begging for forgiveness for her sins," the hangman said, as the witch, or perhaps the devil, scurried past on their left, using the cover of the many dilapidated tombstones, some of which had fallen over. "This graveyard is full of the victims of Leipzig's greatest, bloodiest ever battle. Listen carefully and you can hear the clatter of their sabres."

Behind them, next to them, in front of them--seemingly from all directions, Margaret could hear metal banging against metal. How were only three people doing all of this? Or were there more of them? Hidden speakers, maybe? That fog was obviously fake too; she had to admit they were putting in a lot of effort, she just wished it wasn't directed at terrifying them. Not that she was scared. That would be irrational. They had paid for this service and experience. The eerie dirge of an organ began to play. She shuddered. She really should have brought a thicker jacket. "Bach," said Lise.

"Toccata and Fugue in D Minor, to be exact," Nele said.

"This way," shouted the witch. Margaret did as she was told, still paying close attention to her steps down the narrow, twisting, overgrown path. With each fall of foot, she expected the vines to come to life and ensnare her. The witch stopped so suddenly Margaret bumped into her. She turned to the others. No-one was following them. "Where are they?" On tiptoes she could just about make out the figures of Nele and Tilda in a section of graves behind them, murmuring to each other, seemingly uninterested in the tour.

What had happened to Pat and Lise? What was that feeling in her stomach? Margaret darted back down the path. The wind was howling around her, broken only by the sounds of clattering sabres. The shadows grew and shrank as she ran, as if lunging for her. "Lise," she shouted into the darkness. "Come quickly. We have to stay together." She rushed past trees and gravestones as panic wrapped its tendrils around her. She heard Lise's voice in the distance. She got on her tiptoes, trying to see over a hedge blocking her view. Then she heard rushed footsteps. There must have been another path to her right somewhere. Was someone following her? The hangman? The devil? She ran around the hedge and saw Pat and Lise hunched over a gravestone, reading an inscription.

A gate creaked open to her right. She turned and saw a hooded figure by the railings raise a knife, metal glinting in the moonlight. "LOOK OUT," she screamed, but the dagger was already airborne and flying at her friends. She felt her eyes close, a reflex. Then the sound of metal on stone. She opened her eyes. Pat had her arms over Lise, seeming to have pulled her down to the ground.

"Help," Margaret called out, looking around frantically. "Daniella. Nele. We need help here." She wasn't sure whether to rush to her friends or chase the figure that had thrown the knife in case they had more weapons. Weaving between tombstones, sharp hedges and overgrown foliage, she darted for the railings, screaming "stop" and "help", just in time to see the figure running around the next corner and out of sight. They were dressed all in black, like their guides.

"Fire!" she screamed into the street, a new approach, one she knew got people's attention more than 'help', Bystander Apathy being so hard to overcome. "Feuer," she yelled next, but there was no-one around to respond. Out of breath, she moved back towards Lise and Pat, who were inspecting the knife. Daniella was behind them, having finished her cigarette break.

"That was spectacular," said Lise, holding out the knife for Margaret and Daniella to see. "They really put on a show, don't they?"

"That wasn't part of the show," Margaret said, incensed, waving back towards the fence. "That was *real*." She yanked the knife from Pat's hand and ran her index finger along the blade, which nicked her finger. Someone had thrown it, full force, in the dark, at two people who hadn't been expecting it. "They were trying to kill you."

"They probably want that back," Daniella said, ignoring what she had said. She nodded towards their guides standing a few metres away, still striking theatrical poses, staying doggedly in their roles.

"Was it one of your three?" Margaret yelled. "Tell us now."

"Yes," Nele said, arriving with Tilda, "that was really dangerous."

"Everyone stay calm," Daniella said, raising her hands. "It was all just part of the show. I only hire the best."

The hangman spun on his heels. "Make haste," he said. "We have more gruesome tales yet to tell."

Could it have been them? But who would think someone would want a sharp knife thrown at them in a dark graveyard? And even if it was, how easily could that have gone wrong? "No, no, no," said Margaret. "Not good enough. Come back at once."

"Leave it," Lise said, reaching out an arm. "They obviously weren't going to hit us. It was part of the show, right? Don't overreact."

"Overreact? You could have been killed."

"They're professionals," Tilda said. No matter what she was saying, or how good of a sport she was trying to be, Margaret could see that Lise was trembling in her fur coat. Pat let her incredulity be known by throwing some dagger-sharp glares at the actors, who seemed to sense that they'd lost their audience.

"Okay," Lise said, or rather, admitted. "Maybe that is enough thrills for one night."

"Should we finish the tour early?" the hangman asked Daniella. "We didn't even reach the grand finale."

"Like I care either way," Daniella said with a shrug. "Your call. Ladies?"

"See, this happens when you drag up the past," Nele said.

"I'm tired," Lise said. "Let's go back to the hotel and have a nightcap. Or three."

"We need to look for the dagger thrower," Margaret protested softly as they walked towards the exit. No-one else seemed to find what had happened as chilling as she had. The actors had finally decided to drop character and were now walking in a clump, whispering to each other.

"It was just part of the tour," Lise said meekly, as if she was trying to convince herself as much as the others.

"But–" Margaret started, before Lise interrupted her: "Don't make this into something it isn't. Don't ruin the night."

"I know what I saw. And how sharp that knife was."

"They took it a bit too far, that's all," Tilda said.

"It was a good show," Nele said. "They were very… professional."

"Yes, but professional what?" Margaret challenged. They reached the gate, Margaret letting the others pass so she could stop and sweep her eyes one last time over the shadows, looking for movement. As much as she wanted to go back to the hotel, she felt sure something monumental had just happened, and that there might be clues here.

"I'll get you a cab," Daniella said. "My car's being repaired."

Lise turned to the actors. "Thank you for a marvellous experience. You're very…" she paused, looking for the correct wording, "committed." She initiated a clap that everyone except Margaret joined. The actors bowed magnanimously, and the hangman held out his hood long enough that Lise took the hint. She removed some money from her purse. Several notes.

Too much, Margaret thought, whatever the denomination. There were certainly a few tips she'd like to give them.

Daniella returned from around the next corner where she'd been hailing a cab. "Got one," she said as it pulled alongside. Lise, Pat, and Margaret got in, Lise waving at the actors. "Tschüss," they called back. "Oh, sorry Daniella." The last thing Margaret saw as the taxi pulled away was Daniella's pained face.

"Did you-" she started, but then stopped herself. They wouldn't want to hear any more of her wild theories. There was only one person who might be able to help her with her suspicions. What time was it in Galway?

Chapter 6

The McGinley Mansion #2 (Jim)

After a promise to Gary that he'd be back at the library in thirty minutes, Jim made it to his room, although he still wasn't sure where in the labyrinthine mansion--full of narrow, twisting corridors, dusty oil paintings of sheep, and a knight in full knitwear armour--he was. His room was enormous, about the size of a football pitch, and in its centre was the biggest bed he'd ever seen; it could have slept five.

He opted for a quick shower, something to help rinse off his disbelief. Connor was rich now? Jim's Connor?! Why would Willie leave all he'd built to a man whose only talent was destruction? And what about Seamus--that poor, sad lump? How could he have been bequeathed just that piddly, amateur painting?

As he turned the dial to off and climbed out into the steamy bathroom, wrapping a fluffy white towel around his waist, he heard what he thought was footsteps out on the stone floor. Was he late already? Was someone coming by to pick him up?

He opened the bathroom door and poked his head out. The bedroom was empty, but the door was open. Had he left it like that? No, he'd closed it, hadn't it? Yes, he remembered how much lighter it had been than it looked, how he'd really thudded it shut. Tightening his towel, he walked over and stuck his head out into the corridor. No-one. He sniffed. What was that? Waft of aftershave? Citrusy.

Confused, he stretched his lower back and walked over to the bed. Wait... hadn't he left his copy of Kafka's *The Trial* on top of Margaret's information pack? Because it was underneath now. He scratched his stomach while trying to decide how much he could trust his memory.

Not much, he decided. It had taken a real beating from all the drinking. Not to mention his diet, which was unmentionable in polite company. He made a note to ask Margaret what the micromort score of eating a sausage roll was; he ate little else. Totally worth it though. It's better to live well than to live long.

He picked up his silver watch from the mahogany bedside table and put it back on his wrist. There were still a couple of minutes before they had to leave for the dog track. He laid down and tried to relax, but no matter how he arranged the pillows, he just couldn't shake off a gnawing sense of unease. It was as if the walls were watching him. His instincts never failed him––if he felt like something was up, he was right. Why had Gary been so insistent about carrying his small, light bag? There were no valuables in it. Well, a passport, but really how much use is that? There was information––Margaret's excessively detailed itinerary, and a bunch of contact numbers, but if even he didn't care what the girls were doing and when, why would anyone else?

The uneasy feeling remained, kept gnawing, like he was a bone and it was a slobbering dog. Why had Tristan announced he was coming to the racetrack? They weren't friends. He looked over at the door again. It was off, all of it. He had a good rummage up his nose and then got up, a plan having formed in his mind. He went to a nearby chest of drawers and tugged it open: just woollen jumpers. Nothing he could use. He moved over to the mahogany desk by the window and rooted around in there until he found a red marker pen and a small reel of tape. He finished getting dressed, opting for a tight white shirt this time, not wanting to be out-done by flashy Tristan, grabbed his wallet and left, closing the door behind him. Checking no-one was watching, he pulled the red pen from his pocket and carefully marked the underside of the door handle. Satisfied, he tore off a strip of tape and placed it across the gap at the very bottom of the door, between it and the frame.

He stepped back and admired his handiwork––not bad, not bad at all. He'd used something similar in 1989 (or was it 1990?) to work out which of his staff was stealing from the storeroom. It had turned out to be Clarice, his favourite. He didn't catch her red-handed in the usual sense, a case of Glenmorangie under her arm, but he caught her red-handed in a more literal way. She never admitted to the thefts, of course, but it was enough. He let her go, and they stopped. Messy business, all in all. He didn't enjoy thinking about it. His staff were his family. Actually, he'd spent more time with them than with his actual family, and he needed to believe he'd been good to them. There'd certainly been enough of them at his surprise retirement party, spilling out the *Red Lion* in Shoreditch into the road, stopping traffic almost. What a night that had been. The parts he could remember, anyway.

A limo ride, and two scotches later, Jim closed the car door behind him, gravel crunching beneath his feet as he hurried to catch the others, already approaching the entrance to Galway Greyhound Stadium. It was a large rectangular building, three stories high, with a long overhanging roof covering outdoor, terraced seating. Connor rubbed his hands together as they picked their way through the crowds and into the gallery, trying to get a good view of the track. Connor loved a crowd––loved working it, loved making it his audience. Tad, still in his cassock, inhaled deeply. "Sin," he said, as if it perfumed the air.

"What's it smell like to you?" Jim asked.

"Rot."

"Why come then?"

"Sin observed is sin halved."

"Fair enough, fella," Jim said, looking up at the screens. The first race was due to start in ten minutes. Through the enormous glass windows, he could see a few sleek greyhounds being led around, their coats shimmering, being shown off to the betting public, of which there were plenty, the background sounds of cash registers ringing and the soft, mechanical clacking of betting slips printing. Banter, too, lots of banter. Jim loved a bit of banter. A bit of the old verbal give-and-go.

A man in a smart red waistcoat approached the group. "Good afternoon, gentlemen. I'm David, your host for today. It's a pleasure to have you here once again," He looked from Gary to Tristan. "Follow me to the VIP area." He gestured towards a roped-off space with two tables and an enormous L-shaped couch, which looked down directly over the finish line; an exceptional view.

"What's the matter?" Tristan asked, seeing the pensive look on Jim's face.

"Must have eaten something funny," Jim lied. "You've been here before, fella?"

"No," Tristan said. "Not my scene."

Jim nodded and let Tristan walk ahead first, which was easy because he had long legs and young knees and when he turned sideways, there was nothing to the lad, you could barely even see him, slipped through the mass of bodies with no need for an "excuse me" or a "sorry, chap, can I just…"

Jim remembered a line Gary had said in the limo on their way from the airport, "Just make sure you bet the opposite of Tristan." He pulled Connor's arm back.

"What?"

"I need a favour, chief."

Connor reached for his pocket. "How much? Twenty cover you?"

"I don't need money."

Connor cracked a smile. "Seen a lass you like, aye? No problem, Jimmy lad. I know everyone in this town." He turned and swept his eyes across the crowd. "Which one would you…" His eyes narrowed. "The redhead at your 2pm. With the giant—" Connor started to point and Jim lunged to push his arm down.

"Don't," he said. "We've got enough eyes on us as it is."

Connor's tongue slid across his lips. "Well, we're VIPs, aren't we?"

"You might be." Jim sighed. "*Look*. When we get to our seats, lean over so no-one else hears, and then, casually like, or casually as you can, ask Tristan where the toilet is, okay?"

"What? The toilet's just—" Connor looked around, slowly noticing the same thing Jim had––that this place had very poor wayfinding; that's the technical term. Jim knew it from his days in the pubs. Signage, basically. How you help people move around a space. If you got it wrong, you had to point people to the toilet a hundred times a shift.

"What are you plotting?" Connor asked. "There should be no plotting on me stag, okay, fella? Well, unless I'm plotting, and it involves that red–"

"I'll explain later," Jim said, knowing that Connor would be too drunk to remember any of this in an hour. Jim didn't want Tristan to notice he was already suspicious of him. "But it's important. Ask him, okay?"

"Anything for you, chief," Connor said, tapping Jim on the heart with his fist. They threaded their way through the last of the crowd to their host, David, who was holding the red velvet rope open and closed it behind them, with a half bow. The VIP area had plush leather seats and its own private bar and betting booth, and they had it to themselves. "Champers," said Connor to their host. "Your best worst, like."

The others laughed. Well, all but Tristan. "We can afford the best."

"Who's *we?*" Connor asked. "You paying, young fluff?"

"The family."

"We family now?"

"Err... A business family, I meant?" His cheeks reddened. "Business is good."

Connor scratched slowly at his cheek. "So everyone keeps saying."

Tristan looked over his shoulder, towards the track. "Have you talked to Seamus yet about—"

"He's been quite busy weeping, so no, we haven't really had time to wag chins. And gambling's not his scene."

So that explained why Seamus wasn't with them. They settled into their seats. "First race is about to start," said David, returning and holding a silver tray with a bottle of champagne and four flutes. Jim angled his head to see the label - *Moët*. "Eh," he said, under his breath, but decided that, yeah, it did fit the description of best worst. A strong brand, you could certainly impress a date with it if she didn't know her bubbles, but it was too acidic; had a poor mouth feel. Jim looked up at the many TV screens, squinting to make out the names and odds.

"Seven times they will fall," said Tad as the dogs entered the starting enclosure for the first race.

"What's that, Taddy?" Jim asked. "They don't have to jump anything, do they? Why would they fall?"

Tad stoked his long, hairless chin, staring off into space. Not that there was much space. Tristan pulled out his phone and typed furiously. The surrounding crowd turned towards the track, the excitement thickening the air as the race began. Cheers and jeers filled the room, shouted words of encouragement, as if the more vocal they were, the harder the hounds would pound the turf out there. The dogs were just a blur as they shot past, like bullets from a gun, their long legs stretching with each enormous stride, really more of a gallop. Jim found himself swept up in the atmosphere and got up out of his seat and even pumped a fist as if he'd won when the third favourite came in by a whisker.

"Winner is 7. *All Change Please*," the announcer said as the cheers died down.

"Beautiful, it was," said Connor, hugging Gary, as if that was his dog, raised from a pup.

"I love it here," said Gary, downing the rest of his glass. "It's bloody electric."

The next race soon came and, ready to bet, they picked up the stack of slips on the table. Connor put a hundred on the second favourite. "Why the second favourite?" Jim asked.

"I was the favourite and look how I turned out."

"You were the only, weren't you?" said Jim.

"Seamus," Gary corrected.

"Ah, right, yeah," Jim said, thinking that Connor didn't consider Seamus worthy of the title 'favourite' and, having heard the contents of that will, he wasn't sure Willie did either.

"Plus," Connor said, holding his glass out for a refill, "with a name like that, it can't lose, can it?"

Jim squinted up at the screen: it was called *Can't Lose*.

"I like the sound of that too," said Gary. "Stick me down for fifty. No, wait, forty. No, sixty. Go large or go home, right?"

"You betting, Taddy?" Jim asked.

"Nooooo," said Tad. "I've long given that up. This place is corrupt to its core. Like everything in this forsaken town."

"They could really use you on the tourism board," Jim joked, but Tad didn't laugh. "Had a problem with it when you were younger, did you?" Jim probed. "I know I did. Nearly cost me my wife." He hoped by being confessional, Tad might too. There was a lot about Tad he didn't understand, such as, well, everything. "In the end, it was probably the late nights and the heavy drinking that did it, but the gambling didn't help." He should really call his daughter, Trudy, to see how she was doing. How his two grandkids were. How long had it been? She hadn't called him back the past few times. Understandable, what with her being so busy. Tad's narrow brown eyes bored into him, his pupils just pin pricks.

Jim waited and eventually, when he didn't break eye contact, refusing to let Tad off the conversational hook, the big man said. "I've had problems with many things, Jim lad. Some my creation, some that of others." He shot Connor a daggered look.

"Can you stick these on, David?" Gary asked.

"I'm afraid that's not allowed," David said, turning and sweeping a hand towards the betting window. "But you have your own booth."

"I'll put them on," said Tristan. "I'm the youngest here, after all. You old timers sit back and take it easy."

"Cheeky fella," said Connor, but settled back on the sofa, clearly going nowhere at all.

"Only... I'm not quite sure how to do it," Tristan said, suddenly, after standing up. "It must be simple, mustn't it?"

"Form. Money. Receipt," said their host.

"Right." Tristan nodded, straightening his white shirt, its creases much sharper than Jim's. "Good then."

Who to choose? Jim wondered. *6. Samuel's Inheritance,* at 12/1, and, *8. Last Call,* at 9/1. He checked his wallet and pulled out a crisp, new, ten euro note. They'd changed them at the airport as per Margaret's instructions. "Ten on *Last Call*, please," he said, marking the 8 on the form and handing it to Tristan.

"Folly," said Tad.

"What's that?" Jim asked.

"After six days Jesus took with him Peter, James and John

the brother of James, and led them up a high mountain by themselves," said Tad, staring down at the table.

"That... right?" Jim said. "Not a big nature guy, me. Always like to be near a bakery in case I get the munchies. Actually, you know what, T, switch it to *6. Samuel's Inheritance*. Got a feeling about it in my waters," he said, smiling at Tad, who didn't lift his eyes.

"Why are your waters still water?" Connor said, pushing up the bottom of Jim's champagne flute as he sipped from it. It banged against his teeth and a little of the bubbles spilled down his chin.

"Hey, watch it."

"Get more of it down ye. We're here to have fun and pious Tad and all-work-no-play Tristan are not going to provide it. I need a wingman."

"You need a restraining order if you don't already have one." Jim downed the rest of the glass, then wiped his forearm across his lips. David refilled it, waiting impatiently for the bubbles to dissipate so he could pour more. Jim leaned closer to Connor. "Did he know?"

"Who?" Connor asked, looking directly at Tristan, who was over at the booth, placing their bets.

"You know who."

"Aye, he knew."

A bell: last bets. Tristan returned. A firing pistol. *Bang*. The starting trap fell open, and the dogs emerged. "Come on, come on," Connor said, up and out of his seat; still light on his feet. "*Can't Lose*, you can't lose!"

Can't Lose did though, resoundingly, ambling in last. Might as well have had three legs. Maybe it even did. "Woohoo," said Jim, when *Samuel's Inheritance* sauntered home first by several lengths. "Get a round in on me, please, fella," he said to the host whose name he'd forgotten. Not that it mattered, that's why we'd invented *mate, fella, buddy* and *chap*. "But bring something real men drink, yeah. Glenmorangie?" He could almost taste its subtle vanilla and almond notes on his tongue.

"Not for me," Tad said.

"Of course, Father," said the host, giving a small bow as he backed away towards the bar. It's amazing what a bit of white felt and a fancy black smock can do to people, Jim thought. The next races followed the same format. Gary and Connor bet big and lost just as large, too. Tristan didn't bet, but seemed to get more agitated with each passing race anyway. Jim won every time he heard what he was listening for from Tad.

"How are you doing it?" Connor said, irritated by Jim's fourth win.

"Beginner's luck," Jim said. "Right, Taddy?"

"You've the luck of Irish, you have," said Gary.

Tad intensified his already formidable scowl. "Never understood that expression. The plantations. Potato Famine. Partition. The Troubles." He flared his nostrils at Jim. "Your lot had your hand in most of them, actually. And don't even get me started on the Ballymurphy massacre, Bloody Sunday, and The Birmingham Six. It should be the bad luck of the Irish, if you ask me."

"In which case, I'd say me and Gary are doing a fine job upholding our terrible reputation," said Connor.

"It's good fun here," said Tristan, trying to change the subject, Jim guessed. "I should have come earlier. I mean, I'm against gambling, of course. I only play games of skill, not luck. And the third of the Buddha's Five Precepts says to abstain from intoxicants and, well," he looked around, "it is intoxicating, isn't it? I mean, not for me, but I see how other people might become a little drunk on it."

"Hear, hear," said Connor, chugging the end of a whisky and tapping the glass in David's direction. David buttoned the top button on his red waistcoat, nodded, turned, and walked away.

A few drinks later, Jim finally lost the battle with his bladder, timing it just before a race was about to start. When he returned, he caught Tristan at the betting window. He sneaked up behind him just in time to see him paying for that round of bets, not with the cash they'd been giving him, but with a gold card, which he rushed back into his wallet when he saw Jim. How many credit cards had Jim run through a machine in his life? Tens of thousands? Must be.

"0211," said Jim.

"What?"

"Nothing, fella," he said, then mumbled, "for now."

Chapter 7

The Spy Museum (Margaret)

"At last," Daniella said, arms crossed, standing outside the *Zeitgeschichtliche Forum*, where they'd been last night before that ill-fated Ghosts and Ghouls tour. Margaret had been up half the night mulling over its dramatic ending.

"At last?" Margaret asked, irked at this latest impudence. Why hadn't she picked them up from the sauna, as agreed? Before she could give Daniella an earful, Lise stepped on her foot.

"We ran late at the sauna," she said. "You know how it is once Nele gets talking." She looked bashfully at her friend. "And then the tram didn't come."

"Don't blame me," Nele said. "You brought up the DDR."

"Yeah, but I forgot it's your specialist subject."

"Mine's bad boyfriends," said Daniella. "How was the sauna?"

"Less rejuvenating than whatever it was in the mini-bar last night, right, Pat?" Lise said about *Sachsen-Therme*, the sauna where they'd spent the morning. "It was like Underberg but radioactive. The kick, Daniella." She whistled appreciatively. "We went to space."

Pat mimed a rocket launching.

"I went to bed," Margaret said, not that she'd been able to sleep.

"Figures," Daniella said, dismissively.

After realising that the phone in her room didn't work, and Herr Schulze had waved away her protests about that with a nonchalant 'Morgen, Morgen', she'd tried to reach Jim from the phone in the very dark and teak and dusty bar. If you're going to have that much brass, you'd really better polish it, something they were also neglecting of the bar's glasses. She'd tried Jim a few times but got no answer. She didn't know if that was because they were out mourning or celebrating. Frustrated, she'd retired to bed, unable to tell him what had happened in the graveyard. He'd have believed it was not all just part of the show. Without him, she felt very alone with her fears and suspicions. It was hard to tell if that was why she'd slept so badly, or because of the mattress, which seemed to be made entirely out of bricks.

"Shame Tilda couldn't join us," Margaret said, watching Lise's reaction closely.

"Yes," Lise said. "Especially because I wanted to ask her for a favour and it's always better to do that in the nude. Lowers people's defences."

Pat laughed as silently as possible, but a little of it escaped from her nose with a hiss. Margaret hadn't been nude, despite the local (scandalous) spa custom. You can take the woman out of England, but not England out of the woman. And it had been a mixed spa, too. As for the favour? Margaret knew Lise wanted their mother's ring for the wedding. She'd mentioned it on the plane over. She seemed nervous to ask for it and with Tilda's standoffishness and Nele's incessant needling, it was clear to Margaret there was a lot more to these relationships than anyone was admitting.

"She was never one for letting loose, was she?" Nele said.

"Remember when you wanted her to come out with us after she finished her final exams but she had to get up early because *Mauersegler* were arriving from Africa?"

"Friends of yours?" Margaret asked.

"A bird," Nele said, with a roll of her eyes.

"Swifts," Lise clarified. "Everyone's different, I suppose. Is she here yet?"

"She's inside already," Daniella said, tossing her thumb over her shoulder.

"Whose idea was the spy exhibition?" Nele asked. "We already have the musical instrument museum exhibit at *Nikolaikirche* tomorrow. Isn't that enough culture for a hen-do?"

"It can't all be bubbly and gossip, can it?" Margaret asked. "We need to exercise our brilliant, still youthful minds."

"Speak for yourself," Tilda said, emerging from the doorway. "Mine's already an old lady in her rocking chair."

"I'd prefer to exercise my brilliant, youthful body," Lise said, running a hand down her body. "Right, Patty? Where do Leipzig's most eligible bachelors hang out, Daniella?"

"I've been wondering that myself," Daniella said.

"Divorcees are also fine," said Nele.

"And widowers," Tilda added with excellent comic timing. "You can't be too choosy, can you?"

Pat stuck out her tongue, but seemed, broadly, to agree.

"Day's still young," Daniella said. "I'll see what I can do."

Lise moved to hug her sister. "I hope you didn't have to wait too long?"

"Is an hour long?" Tilda asked.

Lise pulled her head back. "Oh, I'm so sorry. It wasn't our–"

"It's fine," Tilda said, breaking from the hug. "Not like I have other stuff going on, right?" She looked back at the enormous, glass-fronted museum. "Let's do this," she said, with what could only generously be called enthusiasm.

Daniella went in to arrange the tickets, something Margaret

figured she would have done already in that hour. "Are you interested in spies?" Margaret asked Tilda, as they both scanned the posters in the foyer.

"Did you know the Soviet Union trained birds for espionage? Not just for transporting messages, but actually listening to conversations and reporting back." She bobbed on the spot, the lights behind her eyes having switched on for the first time. She looked suddenly ten years younger. "Isn't that just incredible? Ravens can mimic humans very well."

"I didn't know that," Margaret said. "That is incredible."

Daniella appeared with their tickets. "Anyway," Tilda said, then slunk back towards the cloakroom.

"Talking to her is about as rewarding as talking to you," Lise joked behind Margaret who turned around in time to see Pat playfully punching Lise on the arm. While Lise faked being hurt--she never let a chance for drama pass by--Pat yanked her ticket from Daniella, striding first into the museum, notebook in hand.

Waiting on the other side of the ticket barrier was a tall man leaning heavily on a metal cane. He cleared his throat loudly. "Welcome to Hidden in the Daylight," he said, his eyes--behind their thick metal-framed glasses--staring at Pat. As he did so, Margaret saw that patches of his thick, coarse black hair at the back of his head were missing. Scars also covered one side of his neck. A fire, perhaps?

"I'm Thorsten and I'll be your guide for the next hour, and in English I hear? Jolly good, as I zink you Brits say?" He laughed at his own joke but got not a titter in return. "I talk you through two unresolved cases of the GDR's most notorious spies, Tick-Tick and The Ghost, two of the Ministry for State Security's most famous *Kundschafter des Friedens.* Operatives the Stasi usually placed in foreign countries, but sometime their operations took place right here, in Leipzig. Hidden in the shadows."

"Scouts of peace," Lise said, translating *'Kundschafter des Friedens.'* Margaret had known what *Frieden* meant, but not *Kundschafter*. "Perfect name, right?"

"*Ja*," Thorsten answered, "excellent double-speak. Orwell would be proud." He straightened and looked at all of them individually, as if telling each of them a secret. Margaret spotted scarring on the back of his hands too. The man had obviously suffered something horrific. He turned and opened a huge metal door to his left, revealing a staircase draped in darkness. "Travel back with me to the year 1956 and Operation Gold - the heart of *Europa's* espionage activities," he said, then slowly descended the stairs, limping heavily, the sound of his cane echoing out into the hallway.

"Less a history lesson and more of an amateur theatre performance," Nele said. "Like last night."

"Yeah," Tilda said. "I'm on a knife edge. That's the expression, right?"

The air surged from Margaret's lungs. It was too soon to joke about that. Every time Margaret closed her eyes, she still saw the glint of the blade and then the feeling of dread and horror as it somersaulted through the air towards the heads of her friends. They followed the man down, Pat first, Nele last.

"It's all so sensationalised," Nele said. Their guide stopped on the bottom step and turned around.

"Have you been here before?" he asked, but it was too dark to tell to whom he was talking.

"Me?" Nele answered. "No."

"I...," the man started, but then turned and walked down the corridor, tap, tap, tapping with his cane on the concrete floor.

Over the next hour, despite the labyrinthine structure of the museum, their guide–from whom Daniella could learn a lot–Thorsten skilfully weaved the webs formed by the different groups of operatives working for the Stasi. Margaret had heard of the Cambridge Five, of course, had even read *The Spy Who*

Came in From the Cold and so knew about its alleged real-life inspiration--'The Man without a Face'--Markus Wolf, its head of foreign intelligence, but she hadn't known he'd placed so many GDR agents in other countries. Thorsten--who more than made up for a lack of charisma with an abundance of knowledge--regaled them with different rules for creating codenames, dramatic stories of famous prisoner exchanges, poisoned toothpaste, and umbrellas guns. All the stories were told in slightly broken English, and with their tour guide leaning heavily on his cane.

"Hoover preferred one-word codenames," Thorsten said, "but the MI6 was--despite what you might have gathered from the movies--sometimes a bit more playful when it came to their naming strategies, especially regarding foreign suspects."

"Do you have an example?" Margaret asked. She knew from teaching that one good example was worth ten minutes of explanation. They were standing in yet another hallway, this one cramped and dimly lit. He pointed down to the metal door at the end. "The names might highlight a unique physical feature or refer to their character or ability. For example, 'Father Death' was the codename of someone who infiltrated a church group. He's in there."

"Church groups?" Tilda asked, clasping the tiny gold cross on the chain around her neck.

"Yes, I'll tell you more about those activities in our last two rooms, dedicated to the two most prolific, successful, brutal operatives never caught. The Ghost—"

"I ain't afraid of no ghosts," Lise sang in a low voice, elbowing Pat, who didn't react, her eyes and ears glued to their guide. "Tough crowd," she said, under her breath.

The guide sighed. "And Tick-Tick." He sounded like someone who'd just been told his condition was terminal. "It's hard to know where to start with Tick-Tick."

The Accidental Murder Club

"Did they call him that because he set bombs?" Margaret guessed.

Thorsten nodded. "Presumably, yes."

Nele smiled. "Not very imaginative, that one."

"Oh, Tick-Tick was very imaginative," he said, opening a door to his right. They followed him into a windowless room. Margaret's eyes slowly adjusted to the gloom. The air was heavy, laden with a faint, musty odour, as if every artefact was a hundred years old. Directly in front of her, dominating the centre of the room, were two glass display cases. Inside one, arranged with meticulous precision, were various components of homemade bombs. She recognised wires, switches, and the unmistakable bulk of a detonator. Each item was labelled with neat, typewritten cards, providing terse descriptions in German and English. The second display had a model of a bridge that had collapsed into a river. The walls held large, faded photographs of crime scenes. Each image was a frozen moment of chaos and devastation: a shattered storefront, a mangled car, a crater in the middle of a cobblestone street. Some showed firefighters and police officers, their faces grim and haunted as they worked amidst the wreckage. The black-and-white photos lent a ghostly quality to the destruction, as if the past were reaching out to the present. On the wall in front of them was a giant world map marked with crosses in multiple continents and at least a dozen countries, no obvious link between them.

"These were where he was active? It was a '*him*', I guess?" Margaret tried to backpedal. "I've been presumptuous. Sorry."

Thorsten lifted his cane and used it to gesture at several points on the maps. "Orange is where *he* was stationed, like here, Zanzibar and Cuba. Green are the locations of *his* crimes. All evidence suggests that it was a 'him', yes."

Margaret liked this phrasing––precise, measured, but careful. "We nearly caught him once in Spain," Thorsten continued.

75

"He acted like an undercover police officer and slipped away, somehow. He was a gifted technician and bomb maker and his skill was only matched by his," he paused, looking for a word, Margaret guessed, "*rücksichtslosigkeit.*"

"Ruthlessness," Lise said.

He nodded. "Yes. Thank you." His hand lingered close to the picture of a burnt-out Trabant, the iconic GDR car. "Only one of his targets ever survived."

Margaret scanned the room, taking in this CV of terror and destruction. One man did all this? As she turned, she saw Pat still standing in the doorway. Why? She'd been the first one in and often the last one out of the other rooms. Why was this one different?

"Although, he worked closely with ETA and the IRA, among others," Thorsten clarified, "he wasn't picky. Any terrorist organisation intent on destroying the West."

"I can't believe he's still out there," Nele said.

"Yeah, he must be really good at what he does," Daniella said, with what sounded more like pride than revulsion in her voice. *Unlike you*, Margaret thought.

"Yes, but we will catch him," Thorsten said. *We?* That was the second time he'd used that pronoun. He seemed barely capable of finding his own balance, never mind a master criminal on the run for decades.

"A monster," Lise said, under her breath. Pat clicked with both hands, still lingering in the doorway.

Thorsten cleared his throat. "Now," he said. "It's time to meet a Ghost. Or rather, *The* Ghost."

"We met enough of those in the cemetery last night," Margaret said, but followed him, fascinated. They returned to the narrow hallway and shuffled towards the last door in single file. Margaret felt someone's elbow poke into her ribs. "Hey," she said, turning around to see who it was just as the lights above them buzzed, then cut out, plunging the windowless corridor into darkness. She gasped. *Was this part of the tour? Or the work of whoever threw that knife last night?*

"It's The Ghost," Daniella mocked. "OOOOHHHHH-HHHHHHH."

"Sorry," Thorsten's muffled voice said from the front of the line just before the fire alarm kicked in, deafening everyone. Margaret covered her ears. "Just. The. Fire alarm," he shouted, unnecessarily, into the brief breaks in the siren. "A TEST. Keep. Walking. Straight. Emergency Exit. On. The. Right."

They moved slowly forward. "Are we all here?" she shouted. "Lise? Pat?"

No answer. The siren stopped, but the lights stayed off. Reaching with her arms, she touched both the walls. Then the sound of someone running behind her. She was about to turn around and see who it was when someone pulled her through the open door, plunging her back into the light. They were at the top of a metal staircase. Daniella let her shoulders go, roughly.

"Hey," Margaret said, straightening her blazer. Lise tumbled out after her.

"How exciting," she said. "Was that part of the show? The big finale?"

"It's a museum," Thorsten said soberly. "So, no. And sorry for the abrupt end."

"Right," she looked down. "Yes. I just thought–"

"I'm starting to think we're all cursed," Tilda said.

"You might be," said Nele, then laughed, as if it was a joke. Margaret wasn't sure if it was.

"Unfortunately, we'll have to end things here," Thorsten said, leaning with both hands on the top of his cane. "We seem to be having problems with the power." He seemed weirdly unflustered. Maybe this happened often? "Sorry, *Ja*. The stairs will return you to the foyer."

"Now we'll never know about The Ghost," Lise said. No, we

won't, Margaret thought, looking at their guide, who unclipped a walkie-talkie from his belt and talked into it, too fast and muffled for Margaret to understand. *But whose fault is that, and why?*

Chapter 8

The Wake (Jim)

Jim swallowed, gripping the arms of the chair, trying to push back down what was threatening to swell up and out. His stomach was annoyed, his head was angry, but his kidneys were downright furious. His wallet, however, was so full it scarcely fit in his jeans pocket. He certainly wasn't as rich as Connor, but he'd left the dog track a lot flusher than he'd arrived, and there weren't many who could say that.

He took two Alka-Seltzer from the silver tray to his left, dropped them into the glass of water, waited a minute, then knocked the whole thing back in one. It was probably very-late morning (or early afternoon?) but his sleep was erratic and fitful. Hands gripped to the arms of his chair, probably five-hundred years old, exactly the age Jim felt, he waited for the next wave of nausea to pass, and then asked: "What room is this, then?"

The room, like so many others, was full of heavy dark wood furniture, books and oil canvases of Willie and the wider McGinley family, but not poor Seamus.

"Buggered if I know," said Connor, sitting in dark sunglasses and a cowboy hat, looking both sorry for himself and the world. "Drawing room four?" He tipped the front of the hat up. "Does your head feel like mine?"

"No," Jim said. "Mine feels worse. Gary can sure knock 'em back, aye?"

Connor laughed. After the dog track, they'd returned to the mansion for a nightcap and a hand or two of poker in the games room. Gary's idea and probably a last-ditch attempt to separate Jim from his winnings. Or what was left of them after he had been stiffed with the three-digit drinks bill, which he couldn't really argue about paying, since he'd won so much following Tad's tips. How no-one else had cracked the code, he didn't know. But he wasn't going to share his secret, and he didn't think Tad would either. At the end of the day, a win is a win, and Jim had won big.

After a few hands of poker, Gary had excused himself to go to the toilet, then returned to deal. Jim spotted a certain red smudge on the bastard's right hand. He hadn't been gone for more than five minutes, either. How had he picked his way through the maze to Jim's room that fast? And why?

Gary, the rat.

Anyway, it was no surprise to him that a little later, when Jim stumbled to his room and bent down, he found the tape he'd placed on the door broken. Inside, everything was still there, best he could see. He'd have it out with Gary later, after he'd shifted a bit more of this hangover. He yanked the comb from his shirt pocket and methodically flattened his magnificently thick brown hair.

"Put that damn comb away, man," said Connor.

"You're just jealous."

"What could I be jealous of?"

"That I still need a comb?" They'd named a type of eagle after Connor.

"But do you, aye?"

Jim froze. He'd had a weird encounter at the barber's

recently. Had gone in without an appointment and the guy had been shirty with him; almost like Jim had been wasting the man's time.

"What?" Jim asked, confused.

"Would you still wear gloves if you had no hands?"

Jim stopped combing. Jim didn't wear gloves, of course he didn't, real men just suffered the cold, silently. "What do you mean?"

Connor looked away. He was obviously too hungover to talk any sense. It was silent for a while.

"Nervous about it?" Jim asked, being deliberately vague with the 'it'. Connor turned his head just a little, enough to make eye contact, were his pupils not hidden behind his sunglasses.

"Why would I be nervous, fella?"

"The will and then the wake today, I suppose? Seeing all those old faces?"

Connor's tongue poked briefly out from behind his teeth. "It's them who should be nervous."

Jim let the topic drop, didn't want to push too hard. "Why no Seamus?" he asked, finally, after scanning every photo above the mantelpiece.

Connor blew a raspberry. "Probably out shagging some poor ewe."

"No, I mean, on the walls. Where's–"

The door blew open and in strode Tristan, Blackberry clamped to his ear. The colour of the jumper had changed, from navy blue to black, but little else. Not a slicked back hair out of place. Same annoying Tigger bounce in his step. Looked as fresh as a field of daisies. He lowered the phone. "Afternoon, gentlemen," he said. "And a fine afternoon it is, too."

Jim groaned. Connor turned away in disgust. Tristan lifted a messenger bag onto a side table, the thick Velcro making a loud ripping sound as he wrenched it open. He removed the first of three black sports flasks. "I brought you some kale smoothies. I make them myself. Add in probiotics, of course. And flaxseed. And a nootropic supplement I was an early investor in. Breakfast of champions. It'll get you feeling as right as rain."

"Rain is wrong," said Jim. "Unless you're up 2-0. Nothing demotivates like a second-half drizzle."

Tristan handed a flask to Jim, who scowled down at it. He didn't trust any drink invented after he was born. Tristan jiggled it, which was when Jim noticed something else was different this morning: his watch. It was just as flashy as yesterday's, but gold now instead of silver. Jim waved the bottle away. Tristan thrust it towards Connor, who lowered his sunglasses, looking over the top.

"Nudetropics? Good for the old pecker, is it?"

"Nootropics," Tristan corrected. "Cognitive optimisation. Fascinating area, I've a presentation on the laptop if you're interested to know more?"

"Have ye?" Connor took the bottle, tipped his head back and took a generous sip, before coughing violently, spraying the contents back out over himself, the chair, and Tristan. "Feck. It tastes like roast ass, man."

"It grows on you," Tristan said, taking a seat at the long table, wiping the spit from his neck and jumper with his sleeve.

"So does cancer," said Connor.

"What time does it start?" Jim asked. They'd heard cars driving up while they'd been waiting for Butler Bill to serve them breakfast. The lawn was so full of them by now they were parking down one side of the long gravel path. Butler Bill had not come to give them breakfast. Jim suspected the man's days of giving anyone anything were long over. Fair play to him, too. What would Jim buy with a million pounds? A season ticket to Chelsea, for starters. Two, actually, so he'd have company. Maybe he'd even get Margaret to a game or two.

"Got any real food?" Jim asked hopefully. Tristan rummaged in his bag and threw over a protein bar.

"It'll do," Jim said, opening it and taking a huge bite. Jim was looking forward to the wake. Get a few drinks in someone and they'll lower their guard. It would be an excellent opportunity to probe Gary, Tristan, Seamus and Tad further. Maybe even Butler Bill, if he showed up in some capacity. The man must have a closet full of secrets.

"It's already started," Connor said, standing up gingerly. "Let's get changed."

"Do you want to take these with you?" Tristan asked, nodding down at the flasks. Connor opened his mouth.

"I think we're good, pal," Jim said before an insult flew out of it.

Twenty minutes later, adjusting his suit's left cuff, Jim entered the noisy ballroom––which must have had a hundred people in it already, all dressed either in sombre black or knitwear, a nod to the family empire, Jim supposed. A few of them were even in black knitwear. Dotted around the room were several tables holding large decanters of whiskey set before a dozen glasses stacked into a pyramid, rapidly being plundered. Despite the early hour, people were imbibing enthusiastically. Jim craned his head upwards. Above him was the showpiece––an enormous chandelier made of glass knitting needles like the ones Seamus had been knitting with when they'd first arrived. Jim couldn't decide if it was a stunning architectural triumph, a torture device, or both.

Looking around, Jim could tell––had a keen sense for it––that he was one and a half drinks behind. He needed to get started. Settle his stomach by getting back on the horse, as it were. Bad enough that he was the only person here who'd never met Willie. No need to look more out of place by being the only idiot sober. He undid the button on his borrowed waistcoat, part of the suit that had been hanging on the back of the en-suite's door when they'd arrived yesterday. He assumed Butler Bill put it there before he rushed off into retirement. Jim had spent the past five minutes in front of the room's full-length mirror, twisting back and forth, just admiring how well it fit. The suit's black fabric was as smooth as silk, might even have been silk, he wasn't sure. He was more of a polyester man. The seams of the single-breasted jacket were precise, sharp, the stitching immaculate, and there was a subtle sheen that caught the light. Jim was elephant calved and often had a problem buying trousers, but these hugged him like a new lover. He felt confident and sharp. He felt... youthful.

He weaved through bodies as a loud wail broke the background chatter and sounds of revelry. Over the tops of heads, he spotted Seamus, banging his fists on the green felt of the snooker table that was the room's other centrepiece and where, laid out--candles illuminating his head and feet and dressed in an immaculate, dazzling white McGinley sweater--was the body of Willie McGinley himself, much shorter than they'd painted him in the home's flattering artworks. Barely jockey height, really. So that's where Connor got it from, or rather, didn't. Willie's hands lay clasped over his stomach. Jim moved closer, excusing his way through the crowd. Yep, that was unmistakably Connor's father-- the same narrow, deep-set eyes, the same long thin, crooked nose, an edge of the pirate about him.

"Father," Seamus sobbed, holding the dead man's hand. "We miss you. We love you."

Jim's nose wrinkled. He didn't go in for big displays of emotion, not unless it was a cup final. Two people, probably members of the wider McGinley clan, tried to move Seamus along to make space for the next mourner, of which there was a line, but Seamus accidentally got his hand caught in the middle pocket of the snooker table. A woman helped him get it out. Jim couldn't help but laugh. He really was a bit of a wet blanket, old Seamus. Not that he was particularly old, just seemed to act it.

Jim scanned the room for Connor. He'd be near the biggest drink, Jim decided, and then he saw it, a large punch bowl over to the right, beneath a large painting of a black horse in profile, wearing the number seven. Around the bowl were platters of meats, cheeses, and fruits. Jim stopped scanning heads--Connor wasn't tall enough--and swapped to feet, deciding that Connor would wear something traditional, yet attention grabbing.

He spied a rapidly tapping foot adorned in a brogue with the straps that wrapped up around the ankle--and, yes there he was, the prodigal son. A man was leaning into him, shouting into his ear. There was a small line waiting to talk to him, too--he was rich now, and so, of course, he had many friends. Word of the will must have spread. I knew him before he was wealthy, Jim thought. Or before we knew he was wealthy. Had Connor already known he was rich? He'd certainly not acted it. Jim moved closer to the punch bowl, curious what it might contain. He loved the atmosphere of an Irish Wake and had tended many of them in the various watering holes he'd worked. You knew you were in for a hard night, sure--if it was held on a Saturday, you'd still be mopping vomit on Tuesday--but he loved them too; the mix of sorrow and jubilation, party and funeral, mourning and celebration. Anything went, just as long as it came with a shot, snifter, or pint. He bent over and inhaled. The rum hit him first, but then something else--some background vanilla and oak. He stirred with the ladle, bent deeply, his nose just centimetres away. *Allspice.* He nodded appreciatively. Good shout, that. Someone knew what they were doing. He spotted Tad over by the door and nodded at him. Tad didn't respond. Jim raised his glass, held it under his nose, swirled it, and chugged. His throat warmed and his chest caught fire and he knew--indisputably and joyously--that he was alive.

"What's with the shoes?" he said to the woman next to him--red frizzy hair and splattering of freckles, pointing at the extra pair of brogues near Willie's feet on the snooker table. Jim loved a redhead, Connor was right about that, but so few redheads had ever loved him back. Only his wife, until, one day, or so it had seemed, she told him she didn't anymore.

"For the walk through purgatory," the woman said. He liked the Irish accent on men, but on women... wow. He rubbed at the stubble on his chin. "Long is it?"

"For Willie, I imagine it will be, yeah."

"Friend?" he asked because why not? He was in a fantastic suit and he felt like what Butler Bill had--a million pounds. No, euros. She didn't hear, and so he shouted it. "FRIEND?"

She turned a little. "Family."

"You're too young to even be a niece."

"You charmer," the woman said, digging him with her elbow. He smelt--bergamot and rose, her perfume. Classy. Understated. He grinned. "Thanks for not saying old."

"Second cousin," she said. "You?"

"Friend of his son, Connor."

"Connor will need his friends," a man to Jim's left cut in to say. Jim turned, scraped his teeth across his lip, annoyed at the interruption. The man smiled, revealing a wonky front tooth. He had a proud nose and prominent cheekbones. Might have been handsome in his youth, Jim decided. Now he was about Jim's age, early or maybe middle sixties, and in a crisp suit but with a black toupee Jim found very uncompelling. Baldness is only a sin if you don't embrace it. Jim would embrace it when the time came, but the time wasn't coming; he pulled out the comb from his inside pocket and brushed a hand through his still thick, still shiny brown hair--the jewel in his crown.

"Your accent?" Jim asked, because the man clearly wasn't Irish. The man licked his lips.

"I get around."

The alcohol was making Jim chatty. He angled himself from this man back to his classy redhead. "My father always said the only difference between an Irish Wedding and an Irish Funeral is one less person," he joked.

It was the man that answered, even though he wasn't interested in the man. "He was Irish?"

Jim chuckled. "No. Just wanted to be. You're a fun bunch."

"They are. *We* are," the man corrected. "If you can stand the drizzle." Another lip lick.

"Did you know him well?" Jim asked, noting he was the only man in the room without a drink in his hands.

"No," the man said. "Second cousin."

"Tara," the woman said, reaching round and shaking the interlocutor's hand. "You must be on Willie's side then?"

"Callum, and, yes," said the man, stepping back. "Excuse me, must attend the little boys' room."

Jim watched him disappear into the throng - arms in arms, arms draped over shoulders, clusters of bodies in tight embraces - and then he saw him pop up on the other side of the room, the same door Jim had entered, turning right. It's left, Jim thought, right is the games room and the cinema room and some sort of office, more of a boardroom really. He felt proud he'd been here long enough to know where the nearest toilet was, although he'd just stopped there for a whizz on the way here, and so it was the last place he'd been. It was the one with the stained-glass window of a flock of fluffy sheep marauding over a hill; almost enough to put you off your business, too.

Gary sidled up next to him. If he'd borrowed his crap-brown suit, he'd borrowed it from a man half his size. If he'd coughed, the buttons would have popped off. It was lucky Gary hadn't helped himself to Jim's suit while he'd been in his room.

"Nice spread, right?" Gary said. "Do you know where Bill kept the Tupperware?"

Jim laughed, albeit a fake one, then turned in a circle. "So, this is kind of embarrassing," he said, "but I've left a gift in my room and I'm kind of lost. Do you know which way it is, by any chance?"

"Sure," Gary said, pointing to the door Jim had entered. The red mark on his hand was gone, but then even a scruffy bugger like Gary must wash his hands once in a while, mustn't he? Gary's face suddenly scrunched up. "Oh, actually, no I don't."

"That's a shame," said Jim. *Liar.* He sniffed and there it was - the same citrusy aftershave he'd smelt after his shower. Juniper, actually, he decided. Slightly sour, though that could have been because of Gary's rampant alcoholism. Gary took a glass of punch, clinked it to Jim's, then disappeared into the crowd too. Jim stood a while, drinking, watching, making small talk, wondering where his redhead had gone to. Then the four-piece band, set up near the fireplace, a feature of seemingly every room in the mansion, whirled into life with a loud, "1-2-3-4". The fiddler cut in, and the crowd whooped with delight. Jim was not much of a dancer, two left feet, two left hands, two left calves, but he felt his hips groove to the beat. He downed the rest of his glass, dropped a shoulder, and joined the fray. The band's leader, an older man with a bushy white beard and twinkling eyes, called out the tunes and both the room and time whirled until they hit a particular song, one he'd heard before, back when he worked in an Irish pub in Tottenham, where it would, occasionally, end a raucous evening.

Of all the money that e'er I had
I spent it in good company
And all the harm I've ever done
Alas it was to none but me

And all I've done for want of wit
To mem'ry now I can't recall
So fill to me the parting glass
Good night and joy be to you all

Connor's arms were in the air now as several people jumped on him as the party moved up through the gears. The crowd sang their lungs out, so loud you could barely hear the band as the second verse tugged at Jim's heartstrings, a lump forming in his throat.

So fill to me the parting glass
And drink a health whate'er befall
And gently rise and softly call
Good night and joy be to you all

Margaret would love this, he thought. Would she dance? No. But could she resist the emotion? The room was drenched in it, and you couldn't fail to be moved by it. Not that she really did emotion. On the surface, at least. You can push stuff down, sure, that will work for a while, but eventually it will all come roaring back to the surface; and never how or when you want. He wiped a sly tear from the corner of his eye as he spotted Seamus slipping back from the crowd to stand against the wall, staring at his shoes, shoulders bouncing, wailing, and crying. Should he go help him? But then to leave this...

Of all the comrades that e'er I had
They're sorry for my going away
And all the sweethearts that e'er I had
They'd wish me one more day to stay
But since it falls unto my lot
That I should rise and you should not
I gently rise and softly call
Good night and joy be to you all

It was wild now––hugging, being hugged, a great big puddle of people drunk on life and loss, as much as booze. Magic, he thought, and yet me, well, I didn't even know the guy. And in the middle of it, drinking it down like the finest of wine, was Connor––the born showman, the mad old attention whore. Did he know Willie, really?

Jim felt an arm link into his. He turned. It was the redhead, pulling him along in a kind of conga of jigging bodies, swirling first left then right, swapping partners, cheering, slapping heels. The song finally ended several verses later, to deafening applause.

Butler Bill cleared his throat at the microphone. It was the first time Jim had seen him since the will. He was dressed like everyone else, like a civilian––smart suit but no tailcoat, no white dress shirt, no gloves––not on duty anymore. "Ladies and gentlemen, dear friends of our beloved Willie McGinley. We thank you for your attention, your kindness, your merriment, and next… for your memories." He gestured towards an ornate, high-backed chair that must have been brought in while Jim was dancing. It was only two metres away from him and looked more like a throne. Its back faced the centre of the snooker table, directly below that chandelier. Jim didn't want to be so close to it, didn't want everyone looking at him when whatever was about to happen happened, but it would be awkward now to try and move away, would look like he had something to hide. Seamus was on the other side of the snooker table, tissue to his eyes, in his white woollen jumper, another around his neck. That had not been a clothing mix-up, as Jim guessed when he first arrived. The man just valued cosiness so highly that he always wore a spare jumper. A sweater-on-sweater combo that only accentuated his natural cuddliness. He was gripping tightly to a piece of paper like it was a life raft.

"Starting with immediate family," Butler Bill continued, "you're invited to sit on Willie's chair and regale us with your favourite memory. Without further ado, I hand you over to Sea—"

Connor lurched past, almost tripping over Jim's feet as he did so, swaying like a man in high seas. He dropped clumsily into the throne-seat. Seamus recoiled, hand to his throat, scrunching the paper in his hand.

"Thank you, Billy," Connor yelled.

Did he have a speech written? Hard to imagine; speech writing was just not in his locker. The last day had been full of these little power plays between them, almost all won by Connor. Who cares less usually wins. Seamus cared about Willie, knitting, and McGinley. What did Connor care about? Cahoots, Lise, and himself––in that order too, as far as Jim could see. Everything Seamus had helped build was now at the mercy of a charismatic lunatic.

That would make anyone livid. Overhead, the chandelier rocked a little. Or maybe it was just the sun coming out from behind a cloud, the light shimmering off the glass, firing shadows in hundreds of different directions? Connor settled in, putting his arms up on the armrests. He cleared his throat, enjoying the attention, as always. His nose twitched. He stood up on the chair, gripping the back of it with one arm. "Better," he said. "Now I can see more of your ugly mugs. And now... story time."

There was a pop like a firework. Jim looked back towards the window, a spikey ball of nerves moving up his throat. Connor was going to make a fool of himself. There was no way he'd prepared anything. He tried to swallow; it didn't work. He tipped his head back. No. It wasn't a trick of the light. The chandelier really *was* swaying. How and why and WAIT... instinctively, he lunged for Connor, diving over the side of the chair, arms out, smashing into him just above his hip, sending them both careening over the arm of the chair and onto the floor, an almighty smashing sound as the chandelier crashed down, just missing the two of them, but raining needles down onto the snooker table, floor, and poor old dead Willie.

The room went deathly quiet. Jim was on top of Connor, who'd landed hard on the stone floor and appeared dazed, wriggling beneath him. "What the fuck?" he mumbled.

"Ow," said Jim.

"You've cheated death, man," Gary cheered, yanking one of the needles that didn't smash out of the cushioning of the chair and waving it at them both. "That was incredible!"

Jim rolled off Connor and sat up, ignoring the pain in his side and knee. A hundred eyes bored down into him. Then the clapping and whooping began. Arms helped him up and slapped his back as he looked, confused, at the chair, or what was left of it. Knitting needles lay scattered all across the floor, and many had punctured deep into its upholstery. Now the throne really did look like a medieval torture device. Those spikes. The damage. Connor. The ramifications arrived all at once: she'd been right all along.

He needed to speak to Margaret, urgently.

Chapter 9

Hotel Hofhandel (Margaret)

Margaret made her way to *Hotel Hofhandel*'s bar. Dinner in town had been ruined by Lise finally asking Tilda if she could borrow their mother's ring as her wedding's 'something old'. A request that had gone down about as well as the main course, Königsberger Klopse--meatballs in a creamy sauce that Lise had made once for Cahoots and had been a huge hit--but in the restaurant Daniella had chosen, were an even bigger flop, tasting like the soles of an old shoe dipped in vinegar. Tilda had recovered from her obvious disbelief at Lise's request quickly, but the quiet, "yes, well, I suppose, sure," couldn't have convinced Lise, even though she so wanted to believe her sister held her in high affection, something Margaret hadn't seen compelling evidence of yet.

She passed the older non-gentleman in tweed with the unconvincing comb-over who'd tried to chat her up earlier-- her German allowed for that much–while they'd waited for the only working elevator. She pretended to be engrossed in the very gross burnt-orange carpet and then squeezed herself into the claustrophobic telephone booth, which did a poor job of muffling the loud, repetitive music from the bar. What was it called again? Lager music? *Trager?* Almost... *Schlager,* that was it––Lise had told her about it, Germany's answer to pop music, only worse.

She took a deep breath and dialled. Would Jim believe her? Or would he dismiss her theories too, like everyone else here? There was no reason to. She followed the evidence, and only ever the evidence. Someone had thrown a sharp knife in a dark graveyard directly at Pat and Lise. Someone––the same someone?––had messed with the fire alarm at the museum. There was a three-way, very sharp friendship triangle between Tilda, Nele and Lise and a blunt tour guide who oscillated between hostile and indifferent, and it was only the end of day two. Something was very much up.

Pulsing and clicking as the phone connected. Then an unknown, posh voice. "McGinley residence."

"Margaret Barrett. Would it be possible to speak with Jim Whitecastle, please?"

"One moment," the plummy voice said, and then she heard the receiver being placed down. Getting Jim to the phone took way longer than she had expected, as if he'd not been in the next room, but two houses over. As she waited, her attention drifted to the music from the bar. A German singer was crowing about how life started at sixty-six. It had almost ended then too, for Lise, with help from that knife. A rustling, then breathing.

"Margaret," Jim said, quickly. She closed her eyes. "I was just about to call you," he said. "You're not going to believe it."

There was a certain sing-song to his voice, a little higher, a little faster, a little sloppier than usual. He was inebriated. She should have expected that, but still, it annoyed her nonetheless. She needed him to have his wits about him. What little he still had. She sighed.

"Why the sigh?"

"Jim, something serious has happened–"

"Here too," he said.

Why did he always feel the need to one-up her? Well, this would shut him up. "Someone tried to kill Lise," she blurted.

He took a deep breath. "Bugger," he said. "Because someone just tried to off Connor, too."

"What?" she said. She must have heard him wrong. There was a sound like something toppling over. No, him collapsing into a chair? That was more probable. You sit down a lot more than you fall over. "Well, I was right," she said, petulantly, and then hated herself for it. "Back at the airport. I wasn't being paranoid, like you and Pat said. Someone is trying to stop this wedding. Violently, even."

"Yes," he said. "It's good to hear your voice, Mags."

"Margaret."

They both went silent, just the sounds of their breathing. She found that she was smiling, despite the topic. "You in a bar?" he asked, his voice growing quiet. "The music."

"I'm in a bar, notionally. Although it's more of a morgue."

He chuckled. "And the staff? How's it compare to a British boozer?"

"We need to focus, Jim."

"I'm focused. I'm all focus."

"You're drunk is what you are."

He sucked in a breath. "I'm skirting drunk, perhaps, but with my two flat feet still very much on the safe ground of sobriety. I'm higher on adrenaline, tell you the truth. I just saved well, you wouldn't believe... I mean... I don't want to make it all about me but, Jesus, what a save. It was like Shilton against Dalglish. You ever seen that dive?"

She smirked; he very much wanted to make it all about him. "The point, Jim. Find it."

"Right, well." He seemed uncertain how to begin. "You go first," he said, after a few beats. "Who did what to Lise?"

She began telling him about the hotel cancellation and the Ghosts and Ghouls walk. He didn't interrupt her once – a miracle.

"And you've no idea who threw it?" he asked, then burped into his hand. "Sorry. The wake was pretty wild. *Is* pretty wild."

"Do you need to get back?"

"No. Well, maybe. But no more booze."

She thought she heard him wretch. "Jim? Pull yourself together."

"Sorry," he said. "I'm undercover, and you know how it is, don't you? Gotta keep your eye on the ball but also blend in. Tricky business, undercover work." He gulped. "It's passed, I think. Well, I suppose, you know…"

"Jim. Focus."

"Why would anyone want to bump off our Lise?" he asked. "That someone might want to kill Con, that's… well, it's a wonder they haven't done it already, right?"

"Right."

"Oh," he said, "bugger, I forgot to tell you. Connor's minted now. A lot has happened over here with the will."

"He ate mint? How is that relevant?"

He laughed. "Nah, he's loaded."

"Drunk?"

"Fat pocketed. Swimming in dough. Rich?"

"Wealthy. Just say wealthy."

"Yeah, that too." He quickly filled her in on the McGinley family, the mansion, the butler, Gary and Tristan, and the shocking will that had made their friend a rich man with many enemies. "If I had known that there was so much money in sweaters, I'd have learned to knit. You knit, Maggie?"

"*Margaret.* I know the basics, but let's not get side-tracked. You still haven't told me about the attempted murder."

"Bugger, right." He let out a long breath then recounted, in great detail this time--and with a light sprinkle of hyperbole, she was sure--the chandelier attack, focusing far too long and hard on his own bravery and kitten-like reflexes. Eventually, finally, he did move on to his suspicions that someone had been in his room, and that Tristan had a gambling problem. Several problems, even, Jim had said, judging by how much Tristan kept touching his nose. It was hard to keep up with Jim's storytelling, since he made himself the hero of every scene, but she could just about follow, and he patiently answered every one of her questions. It was good to talk to him.

"I believe you," she said, when her desire for information had been finally sated. Somehow, she knew that was what he needed to hear. What she needed to hear, too. "Fitting murder weapon for a knitwear mogul too," she added.

"I thought the same thing."

"Making a statement with that, you think?"

"*Seamus*, Mags."

She hoped he was in a more private setting than she was, because he was practically shouting into the phone now. "You should have seen his face by the end of the will. It was like a cracked egg, leaking despair."

"*Margaret*, and yes, I can imagine. But the way you've described him, he sounds rather..." she stopped, not sure how to finish her sentence in a non-insulting manner.

"Meek?" Jim offered. "I know. But this amount of money would make anyone crazy. And McGinley's his life's work. He's the reason it's successful, or so everyone is saying. There's also a heavily tattooed priest. I've barely touched on Tad the Psycho Priest. He's a thing of nightmares. Never been into the priests, me. Too handsy."

"Oldest motive in the book," she said.

"Sex?"

"No." She blushed and was glad he couldn't see it. "*Money.*

But why kill Lise and Connor now, before the wedding? Who benefits from that?"

"Stops them inheriting," Jim suggested.

"Lise wouldn't inherit. Well, maybe after Connor died? But then it would make no sense to target her now. I can't believe we're talking so casually about murder."

They both fell silent.

"Tilda?" Jim said, breaking it. "Maybe she has some long held sisterly grudge? You said they're fighting and sniping at each other." She heard doubt in his voice. "Although she sounds a bit Seamus-ey, actually. A wallflower. And how is she toppling a chandelier from all the way over there? Nah," he said. "Doesn't make sense. Any of it."

She wished she could disagree. "She's a nurse," Margaret said. "Took care of their mother when she got sick. Seems like she's mostly lived through others. Resentment could build from that, but statistically speaking, and statistics speak and should be listened to, a person's first crime is almost never murder. Why are we talking about it being Tilda? There's no evidence it's Tilda. And beliefs without evidence are just evidence of irrationality."

"We're just supposing, I suppose," said Jim. He burped again. "S'cuse me. She would inherit, wouldn't she? If they both snuffed it and there was no will? Seamus is only a cousin, after all."

"Supposing is not in my nature. If it was her, she'd wait until after they got married. Anyway, how could whoever rigged the chandelier have known Connor would jump in front of Seamus?"

Jim laughed.

"Okay," she conceded. "It was predictable, but only if you know him. Seamus could have expected it. Planned for it. Not that we have any evidence of that, either. There were a hundred people in there, that's a lot of suspects."

"Yeah," said Jim, relaxing into a new sentence. "But most of them don't seem to actually know Connor. Haven't seen him since he was a nipper. And would you try to kill someone so publicly and theatrically like that over money? My intuition is that it's more personal. That it's about vengeance."

"Your intuition is irrelevant."

"Intuition has a role to play," Jim said defensively.

"A minor, uncredited role, maybe. Back of the shot."

"Nah," he said, really stretching the word.

"Go shake the Seamus tree, Jim," Margaret said. "See what falls out. He has the most motive, we're agreed on that. But put pressure on them all."

Jim clapped. "Jim and Maggie back in business. What did we call it in Berlin?"

"Margaret, and I didn't call it anything."

"The Accidental Murder Club," he said, after a beat. "Yeah, that was it."

She remembered how he'd tried to make this ridiculous name for their detective duo stick. He'd even gone as far as using it in some of the interviews he'd done on their return. She'd declined all press requests, naturally. She didn't want the attention. As for the name, well. "That name made no sense then or now. You can't have an accidental murder."

"Nah, the club is the accident, you see? We sort of fell into it, didn't we, this detective lark? Well, you're always snooping about--"

"Excuse me." Her voice lurched upwards. "I do no such thing. I just happen to have a healthy interest in things is all. In keeping people safe."

"Controlling things, you mean?"

Is this really how he saw her? "For the good of everyone, yes," she said, prissily.

"Right, yeah."

"And if we're actively investigating this case, which we obviously are, we're no longer doing it accidentally, are we?"

"Too late," he said. "The name's stuck, hasn't it? It's just too good to argue with. Okay, I'm calling to a close this year's first meeting of the Accidental Murder Club. Let's get back to work. First one to get a confession gets a… steak dinner and back rub?"

Margaret was too shocked to answer.

"Keep Lise close, and be careful," he said into the void.

"I'm always careful."

"Still." His tone firmed. "A good Maggie is hard to find, and I've got quite used to mine."

"Margaret. And *yours?*"

"Call me tomorrow and don't do anything I wouldn't do."

"That rules out sobriety and showering then?"

He laughed, and the sound soothed her. She made more jokes with him than with anyone else. He was generous with his laughter. And in other ways. Not that she'd ever tell him that.

"Good night," he said.

"Good night." She hung up and rested her head against the dirty glass of the phone booth. So, it was happening both here and in Galway. She had been right all along, as usual. Someone was trying to stop this wedding, and they were willing to kill to do it. And it wasn't going to end unless *she* ended it. That was a lot of responsibility. And she didn't want any of it. But none of that was going to matter. It was on her. It was all on her.

Chapter 10
Inishmore (Jim)

Jim swallowed and sat down on the bench of the fishing trawler, weathered and worn, its once vibrant blue paint faded and chipped, planks warped in places, the bow curving upward, ready to slice through the water. Along the gunwales dangled thin ropes and frayed fishing lines. The boat was called *Fish 'n' Chics*. "Not my name," Tad had said. "Merely a kind donation."

Tad fiddled with the controls and soon the diesel engine coughed, hacked and spluttered into life, but wasn't happy about it. The seating was humble but functional: two weathered wooden benches across the middle, almost the width of the vessel. Jim felt the misty air on his face and the chill seep into his bones as he sat watching Tad jabbing at the controls. He wasn't sure how kind of a donation it had been. He'd hold off on forming a conclusion until they made it to Inishmore Island in one piece.

He lifted the zipper on his borrowed yellow raincoat all the way up to his chin. After the call with Margaret, he'd gone back to the wake to keep an eye on everyone. Quite a night it turned out to be. He was the hero, after all, the man who'd saved

Connor and everyone wanted to celebrate with him, to clink a glass and down a shot. They didn't see it like he did––that the falling of the chandelier was an attempt on Connor's life. You're just paranoid, they kept telling him, an accusation he'd fired at Margaret back at Stansted Airport. He should probably apologise again about that because he didn't think she was paranoid anymore, no matter how many people cracked jokes about shoddy Irish construction work. He hadn't even got a good look at the wreckage. It had been cleaned up too quickly. All those needles and glass swept up to make space to continue dancing. Jim had protested, of course, but from inside the middle of a jigging, dancing, singing huddle that wouldn't let him go. He'd watched as ten of the biggest men shuffled the snooker table out and the next time he saw Willie, at the end of the night, his lower torso was needle-free. What poor bugger had got the job of yanking those out? Probably Seamus. The scent, though, had given it away. A distinct burning smell chased by wisps of sulphur or charcoal. Gunpowder, if Jim had to guess. That's what had toppled that chandelier. That was bad news, but what was really terrible was that in the dive to save Connor, he'd ripped a twenty-centimetre gash into the back-side of his fantastic new suit.

Hell of a story though, all of it, and he'd be regaling them for weeks when he got back behind the bar of his unofficial Cahoots pub, *The Next Chance Saloon*.

Sitting on his left, shoulders folded in, Seamus coughed weakly into a fist. He had squeezed himself into his life jacket, which sat very high, hiding his thick neck. No-one else was bothering to wear one. Seamus had disappeared straight after the chandelier collapsed, never even giving his speech. Jim still didn't know what he thought about what had happened. He'd try and find out today. He turned to make eye contact, but Seamus had his closed.

"We really have to do this today?" Jim asked no-one in

particular. His head was throbbing and his stomach was undulating more than the waves the boat sluiced through as they departed the harbour, the breeze intensifying. Connor and Tristan were standing, looking back towards Galway.

"You're only here a few more days," Tristan said, wiping his nose and jigging on the spot to keep warm.

"I'm only here at all because of Jim," Connor winked. "My all-action hero."

"You're staying now, though, right?" Seamus said, half question, half accusation, and with his eyes still firmly shut.

"We've still a lot to arrange," said Tristan, who Jim assumed was here for that very reason––to try to ingratiate himself with Connor, to convince him not to dissolve the Trust, and thus keep the young man's cash cow alive a little longer. Jim was sure he was milking that cow more than even Seamus knew, but he couldn't prove it yet. On paper, Seamus was the most likely suspect, as Margaret had pointed out at the Accidental Murder Club meeting the night before. He thought of her and there was a pang in his chest. It wasn't his chest that interested him though, it was his guts, and the feeling in them told him Seamus was a goddamn teddy bear. Jim always listened to his gut. They were good friends. Although less this morning, perhaps, after the liquid excesses of the previous evening. Still, he'd interrogate Seamus today like Margaret wanted and knew that, under the glare of his direct, no-nonsense questioning, the big wimp would tear like a woollen jumper on a fence post; they always did.

Gary, sitting opposite Jim, tried to light a cigarette, but the spray and wind were too hostile now this far from shore. He put the soggy stick back in the pack, then tucked it in his inside coat pocket. Gary lacked a clear motive, but he'd been in Jim's room and that meant he was up to something. So, he was high on Jim's hit list.

"Where exactly are we going again?" Jim asked, playing

dumb, as the boat pulled out to Galway Bay, bouncing on the roiling waves, the smell of diesel from the motor assailing Jim's large nostrils. A smell he liked. He was happy Tad was skippering; the sea's meanness was obviously no match for that man's fierce inner demons.

"Home," Tad yelled, from over the groaning and grunting and wheezing of the engine.

"Inishmore," said Tristan, sitting down next to Gary. "Home of McGinley Knitwear's production facilities. The company's true home, I suppose."

"How long's the journey?" Jim asked. "My stomach's in knots."

"I — err, well…" Tristan looked down at the floor.

"He's never been," Seamus said, then began crawling to the edge of the boat where he kneeled and vomited over the side. Tristan let loose a disapproving roll of his eyes.

"You've never been?" Gary asked during a break in the puking. "As head of the Trust?"

"I…" Tristan tripped over his tongue. "Tend to be more strategically involved. The Trust's business headquarters are in the Latin Quarter."

"I bet they are," said Connor. "As are all the good bars and restaurants too."

"A flashy postcode, that one," Gary agreed.

"Is it?" Jim asked, or rather, noted verbally.

"We'll take you there later," said Gary.

Seamus stood, wiped his mouth with his sleeve and ran back to the bench, dropping down next to Jim, sitting on his hands, and closing his eyes once more. Did he have a hangover too? "Excuse that unpleasantness, everyone," he said. "I don't have sea legs."

"What legs do you have?" Connor asked.

Seamus ignored the question.

"Your eyes not working?" Jim asked.

"It's rather the opposite, actually."

"Fair enough. How often do *you* get out to Inishmore?" Jim asked him.

"Oh, not that often really," Seamus said, fumbling in a pocket to find a tissue to blow his nose.

"Every two or three days, maybe? The staff look to me for… well…" He faded out.

"I'm there all the time," shouted Tad, from the helm. "Inishmore is my home. Is home for my boys, too. And the peace of it is like nothing on offer in that den of debauchery back there." He tossed a thumb over his shoulder, towards Galway. "That squalor."

"You don't miss…" Connor asked, now sat opposite Jim and Seamus, "everything?"

"There is nothing we miss, me and my boys." 'Boys' was more of a long drawn out *baaaays*.

"We don't miss them either," Gary said dryly. "Done us a favour taking those scallywags away."

"What do you mean?" Jim asked. There were so many mysteries swirling around he was getting dizzy trying to keep up. Were these altar boys, maybe? Part of Tad's congregation?

"Tad has a school for troubled youths," Gary continued. "Takes the worst of the worst from Galway and does… well… what exactly do you do with them, Tad? All I know is that we don't see them again. Or when we do, they're…"

"Redeemed," Tad boomed. He turned his head now, although it had such a weird, wide grimace on it, Jim wished he hadn't. "You might see them." His top lip curled upwards in what Jim had now determined was his version of a smile. "But ye won't recognise 'em."

Gary rubbed both his temples and looked as rough as Jim felt. "Remember that time you convinced us to steal your father's boat so we could go out to Inishmore and have a crack at the Murphy sisters?" he said to Connor. "What were we, like twelve?"

"We didn't know how to drive it and crashed into a fishing trawler," said Tad, who had heard, somehow. He told the story like he was reading it from a charge sheet.

Connor, deep in the memory, slapped his thigh and howled with laughter. "We had to swim to shore, we did. Lucky me father had a sense of humour, the old bastard. Forgave us. Bless his dead cotton socks."

"What?" Gary said. "Forgave you, he did. Tad and I had to slog it out at the mansion for an entire summer, and for nought too. I mucked out the bloody horses. What did they make you do, Taddy?"

"Rose garden."

The idea of Tad gardening was too much for Connor, now a giggly mess. Was this a happy story? Reading Connor's face, Jim would have said yes, but the other two? He couldn't tell and so, instead, turned around to look ahead, to see if they were making progress. The sea was choppy and grey, a thick mist hanging over the water. The small vessel bounced, the spray whipping up, helping clear his hangover as, slowly, an island emerged through the mist––all rugged cliffs and green hills. There was smoke from a few chimneys, but other than maybe a dozen buildings, the island appeared to be wild.

"Just look at her," said Tad reverently, steering the boat towards an empty jetty. There, he tied a tight knot as if ringing a chicken's neck. They disembarked. The smell of peat smoke and seaweed filled the air. Seamus only removed his life vest when they were a hundred metres from the shore, leaving it atop a rock as they entered a small village. They were soon following down narrow streets lined with small flint houses and shops. In the distance, visible over a hill, was the steeple of a church. Tad's, Jim assumed.

"How many people live on the island?" Jim asked.

"647," said Tad. "Give or take. Ten times that if you include sheep."

"How many work for McGinley?"

"Pretty much all the adults," said Seamus, eyes open, but on the ground, walking like it was his first day on earth and he had no reason to trust in gravity.

"And *all* the sheep," said Tad.

"We've a very good, longstanding relationship with the island," said Tristan. "McGinley has been here for nearly a hundred years. You won't hear a bad word said about us."

"Wouldn't matter if you did," said Gary. "There's no-one else listening or hiring."

There was the sound of bleating up ahead - loud and urgent. Seamus skipped away from the group. A sheep had got its head stuck in a wire fence lining the path at the edge of the village. Seamus rushed over to it and bent down, stroking the animal's head as it thrashed, kicked, and now tried desperately to get away from the one person trying to help it.

"Keep your hands where we can see them," Connor joked.

"And your trousers up," Gary added.

"You poor, poor thing," said Seamus, yanking at the metal of the fence, widening the gap until the sheep could slip its head out. It darted away down the hill. Seamus stood and watched it go as if he'd raised it himself.

"When I look around here," Tristan said, hands on his hips, staring at the large single-story stone building up ahead, the McGinley name visible over the door, "you know what I see?"

"Sheep shit?" Connor quipped.

"Reasons to drink?" Gary said.

"Blessed solitude?" Tad offered.

"Potential," said Tristan, voice full of wonder, his hands parting the air in front of his chest. "Look at the space. At the landscape." He gestured to everything and nothing. "It is nakedly, vividly, picture-postcard Ireland. We should have an airport just here." He pointed to an empty field on their right, scarcely large enough for a six-a-side football pitch. "Direct flights to Tokyo and Bora Bora. Rich city people are desperate for authentic, small-town experiences." He nodded. "We have to think bigger than jumpers, Connor. I have some plans. The board wasn't necessarily interested but you're... well... a man of—"

"We make more than jumpers," Seamus barked, looking at each of them in turn. "How do none of you see that?" He grabbed a fistful of the extra sweater tied around his neck. "*This...* is art you wear. Each stitch tells a story. Some of those stories are hundreds of years old. We don't need to expand these stories. We don't need to modernise them. We don't need to take them to Bora Bora, wherever the bleedin' heck that is. We just need to stay here, preserve and protect our flock, and keep telling our ancient tales. Each time a little richer, a little better, a little longer lasting. We've a dynasty to protect. I mean, *Connor* has a dynasty to protect." He pointed at Connor's chest. "Your father's dynasty, and your grandfather's before him. Nothing needs to change. Should change." His voice softened and his chin dropped back, the spell of his certainty having worn off. "I think... I mean... Don't you think? You understand what I'm saying, right?"

It was the most passion Jim had seen from the lad, even if he'd cracked a little at the end. He agreed with Seamus, more or less. Just because you can do something, doesn't mean you should. It's why he refused to get a mobile phone. And why none of his pubs had ever stocked any of those fancy fruit beers or stupidly sweet, gimmicky ciders that were supposed to be for adults but looked like they should have a straw coming out of them that led into a six-year-old's cavity-filled mouth.

"I hope the weather changes," said Connor, tucking deeper into his shoulders. "I'm tired of this bloody drizzle."

"Change is nothing to fear," Tad boomed.

"It's innovation that distinguishes leader from follower," Tristan said.

Connor groaned like a bear had stood on his foot.

"That's Steve Jobs, by the way," Tristan clarified.

"Can't all be leaders though, can we?" said Jim.

Gary nodded. "And some would-be leaders just never got their break."

No, that's why they resort to breaking and entering, Jim said to himself.

"I like a jumper as much as the next man, Seamus," Connor said, throwing his arm around his shoulders. It was the first time Jim had seen them touch. "And yours, I mean ours, I mean, *mine* now––they're terrific jumpers. That's why you always wear two, isn't it? But what else could we do with our money? Think about how much fun we could have. How much more fun the poor bastards working the looms of our sweatshop could–"

"Weaving room," Seamus corrected.

"Our facilities are state-of-the-art," said Tristan.

"Out here?" Connor scoffed. "They're still shitting in outhouses. My father was tighter than a duck's ass, and you know it."

Seamus threw Connor's arm off. "How dare you."

"Oh, come on, kid," said Connor. "It's the truth, and there ain't no reason to be scared of the truth."

"How would you know anyway?" said Seamus, chest puffed. "You hadn't seen him in decades."

"People don't change."

"No," said Seamus. "Unfortunately, that *is* true."

Seamus strode ahead and so was the first through the open iron gates of the factory. He removed an enormous bronze key that opened a thick wooden door that looked like it had stood there since they were burning witches.

The space inside was enormous, with high, vaulted ceilings,

exposed wooden beams, and stone walls packed to the rafters with people and machines, creating a mix of clacking, banging, talking and laughter.

And then all of that stopped. Each of the about two dozen employees in this part of the factory turned and stared. Jim got the impression they weren't used to visitors.

"Cracking day for it," Connor said, to no-one in particular.

"Keep up the good work, everyone," said Seamus. "Got some mainlanders who want to see how the magic happens. We'll be gone shortly."

"Blimey," Jim said, surprised at both the scale and productivity. It was shocking to discover such industriousness in a place that seemed so desolate and forsaken, depending on how you felt about sheep.

After an awkward few seconds, the staff turned slowly back to what they were doing and this small group of mainlanders began touring the room, clockwise, Seamus explaining a little about every station. Jim was transfixed more by the walls than his words. They were adorned with newspaper articles and pictures of McGinley through the years. Black and white at first and showing a hirsute, grubby man standing stiff-backed and proud in front of a herd of sheep. Then a small workshop with just one loom. Two looms. Six looms, and maybe twenty staff. Fifty staff. Colour began to saturate the photos. A younger Willie handing over a sweater to Bono. A much younger Seamus driving a forklift loaded with fleece and already rocking his double sweater. So, there was a photo of him on display somewhere. In the centre of the wall was a framed picture of Willie and Connor's mother on their wedding day, dated 02/11/1947.

A woman with pigtails and an apron made a beeline for Seamus. "Shay," she said, and then continued in a thick, syrupy dialect that was impenetrable to Jim's ear. Something about dye and wool thickness, maybe, if he had to guess? The correct

The Accidental Murder Club

time to soak? Seamus answered her with ease and she thanked him and returned to her station, relaying his instructions to several others.

"Gilly," said Seamus. "She's the supervisor out here. Been with us since she was fifteen." He picked a jumper from the pile, carefully, as if to grip it any tighter might leave a bruise. "You see the raised pattern here, fellas? Aran sweaters are created with what we call cable knitting. Terribly old, 'tis. Passed down through the generations." He pointed to the twists and braids in the yarn.

"It's ribbed," Connor said. "For your pleasure."

Tristan cracked up, slapping Connor on the arm. "Good one, C."

Seamus cleared his throat, carried on, pretending no-one had interrupted him. "To create these cables, we use a special technique, crossing the stitches over one another. You need to be very skilled, which the people here are. They're true masters."

"When did you learn it?" Jim asked, noting Seamus's modesty of his own skill.

His head dipped again. "Father taught me when I was a child."

"Did he teach you, Connor?" Jim asked.

"He tried," said Connor with a shrug. "Was a bit too…" He dragged his tongue across his teeth, "I'm not so…"

"Patient?" Gary offered.

"Detail oriented?" Tad grunted.

"Dexterous?" said Seamus.

"Gentle," said Connor. "And finicky. I'm more your big picture kind of guy. Broad strokes."

"Well, you did become a painter," Jim joked.

"Exactly."

"Is it so different?" Seamus pressed. "Art is art, no?"

Connor's eyebrows lifted. "Well, Sea, my lad. No-one went

111

so crazy knitting they cut off their own ear, did they?"

"You'd be surprised," said Seamus. "The artistry here is exceptional. The stories too. For example, this honeycomb represents the lives of the hardworking bees, the other industry we have, I mean," his eyes lowered, "*had* here. Look at this cable, that's the fisherman's ropes. A single sweater might be forty hours of painstaking labour."

"Exactly," said Connor. "For a sodding jumper. And do the staff see more than minimum wage?" He scanned heads, almost encouraging them to join in, to strike right here and now. "I bet they don't. Is there even a union?"

"There was talk of a—" Seamus began.

"That matter was resolved swiftly," said Tristan, touching his chest. "I handled it myself."

A man passed, heaving wool in giant sacks. "Nice shoes," he said to Tristan. Jim looked down at Tristan's footwear, which had a heel and a point and were shiny enough to use as a mirror.

A young man approached Tad, mumbling something. "Excuse me," Tad said, leading the youngster to a room at the back.

Confession, Jim wondered? Didn't seem like you could sin much out here.

A heavily bearded staff member came up to Seamus. "Can I borrow you a second, boss?" he said. "There's a problem with the loom."

"There's a problem with my stomach too," said Connor. "Took a real beating last night. Which way's the... *oh.*" He'd spotted a small brass sign over Jim's shoulder and sloped off, grabbing a folded-up newspaper on the way. Which meant there was only Jim and Gary left. An opportunity. Jim cracked his knuckles.

"Gary," Jim said. "Me old mucker. Can you do me a favour and tell me what the hell you've been doing in my room?"

Chapter 11
Nikolaikirche (Margaret)

The women stood in a row, staring up at Leipzig's famous *Nikolaikirche*. Lise took a deep breath, as if inhaling something divine, when all Margaret could smell was another sausage vendor. There seemed to be a law in Germany requiring one every twenty metres. "Magnificent, isn't it?"

"I always thought it was a bit ugly," Nele said, nose upturned.

"Ugly?" Margaret challenged, gazing up at the tip of the church's gothic tower. Her eyes swept down the façade––a mix of Roman and Gothic styles with large, arched windows framed with tracery. "What's ugly about it?"

"It's a bit lumpy, I suppose," Tilda conceded. "They've added different parts over the years."

The church sat in the middle of a cobblestone square. Tourists milled around them, babbling in a cocktail of languages that mixed with the music from a nearby accordion player forming a pleasant background soundtrack. Around the square, cafés and shops mingled with historic buildings and narrow cobbled passageways. There was something else in the air now, too - the aroma of freshly brewed coffee, which had to be better than the slop they'd served at breakfast back at *Hofhandel*.

It had taken her a day or two, but Margaret was being seduced by Leipzig. There was a lot of charm to the place. You could feel its... she groped for the precise word--charisma? No, not quite. Potential? Close, but not it either. Resilience-- yes, that was it. The sense that it had endured a lot and yet still remained hopeful, positive, and proud. She thought of a day trip she'd taken with Jim to London and how that city, famed as it is, just didn't do much for her. It felt too... finished, accomplished, and confident. Smug, almost. She much preferred an underdog like Leipzig, where the best was yet to come.

"It played an important role in the revolution, right?"

"That's overblown," said Nele.

"Not at all," said Tilda as she met Margaret's eyes. "And yes, it did. It was a safe space for the earliest little pockets of resistance. All the way back in 1982, they were holding Prayers for Peace here. By '89, just before the wall fell, the Monday demonstrations here were attracting thousands. It played a huge role."

"Good to know who to blame then," Nele said, dismissively.

"I had a hot night here once," Daniella said. "In the back of the pews with a grizzly biker. Not sure if it was a Monday."

Margaret gasped. "In a church?"

"Yeah, he had a kind of fetish, I think."

"Scandalous," Margaret muttered.

"Yeah," Daniella said nonchalantly. "That was a big part of it."

Margaret looked to Tilda, assuming she would share in her outrage, but found she seemed as nonplussed about this confession--if it was a confession--as she had been about everything else thus far. Nele thumped the palm tree statue on her left. "This is new, and it shows."

"We better go in," Margaret said, glancing at her watch, "we're twenty-two minutes behind schedule."

Inside, the church was vast, majestic, and totally empty. The transition from the bright, lively outside to the serene but dimly lit interior was jarring. Soft light filtered through the stained-glass windows, casting intricate patterns of red, blue, and gold onto the stone floor. Tall, slender columns rose like sturdy trees, their tops branching out into elegant, palm-like vaults that held up the high ceiling.

"How often are you here?" Margaret asked Tilda.

"I help out around the services," she said. "At the weekend, mostly."

"It's beautiful," Margaret said.

Nele shivered. "It's cold."

As if to prove the stupidity of that comment, Tilda removed her coat and laid it reverently over the back of a nearby pew. "No matter what's happening out there," she said, glancing back towards the door, "when I come in here, I relax."

"More than when you're birdwatching?"

"No," she said. "But close."

A section of the nave had been cleared and the space, normally filled with pews, now showcased a dazzling array of instruments, including a polished, red grand piano. "Why would they hold an exhibit on rare musical instruments here?" Margaret asked.

"There used to be a priest here in the 60s, a Father Flasche," Tilda said. Pat tittered at the name. "He was a music buff," Tilda continued. "Could play like ten instruments. He built up quite a collection from all his travels. He passed away recently and left them all to the church."

"Lucky church," Daniella said, with what Margaret assumed was sarcasm. She moved ahead of them, to the instruments, and took some index cards from her back pocket. "I came the other day," she said, "so I'd be prepared."

Prepared? Daniella? Margaret's knees almost buckled in surprise. Daniella swept a hand over the first instrument. "This is obviously an umbrella violin," she said. "It looks like an umbrella, hence the name."

Margaret watched Lise frown. Why was Daniella, the world's most reluctant, disinterested tour guide, so keen on doing her job here? Maybe she felt guilty about the debacle in the graveyard, the abrupt end of their tour of the spy museum, forgetting to pick them up at the spa, or all the many other mistakes she'd made? But here, of all places? Where they actually had three experts––Nele and Lise for the instruments, and Tilda for the building itself. Lise had been a career musician and Nele had studied classical music with her. They'd played in the same orchestra, even. "Second fiddle to Lise's first," Nele had said on the walk over before Lise pulled her into a hug and several excited 'remember when' conversations about violin lessons with unreasonable teachers, clandestine smoking breaks on the windowsills of bathrooms, and nerve-racking public performances.

"No, I have that wrong," Daniella said, scrutinising her notes again. Pat let out another chuckle. Margaret's eyes wandered to a large tapestry on the wall that depicted colourful scenes of musicians and dancers. Beneath it was an intricately carved sitar from India, a West African kora, and an ornate oud with its pear-shaped body. Music was not Margaret's forte. She'd taught the recorder occasionally at her private reform school, *Righteous Path*, but only when the usual music teacher was unavailable, and never with any great enthusiasm. Fortunately, the kids were usually so disinterested, you didn't need anything more complicated than *Twinkle Twinkle Little Star* to fill a forty-five-minute lesson.

"It's a walking stick violin," Nele corrected.

"It's mid-nineteenth century," Lise added. "Spruce."

"Yeah, like I said," Daniella replied, narrow mouthed, as if the mistake had been theirs, not hers. Her confidence (or was it arrogance?) really was something to behold. Margaret had spent the first half of her life relentlessly people-pleasing, a fate that often befell children whose parents had made their love conditional. She'd grown out of the habit, thankfully, with the help of several excellent self-help books, and her own private study. She no longer cared how people saw her, but at Daniella's age, it had been everything to her.

Tilda was studying a nearby oboe, hands in the pockets of her jeans, lips pushed out, eyes as blank as a freshly cleaned classroom blackboard. Not only was the architecture of Leipzig incongruous––half of it running off towards a glitzy new future while the other stood clinging to a proud past––two of the city's daughters, Lise, constantly broadcasting every emotion and Tilda, reserved to the point of indifference, were also an odd mix. Pat leaned on the side of a plinth and wrote something in her notebook. Margaret stepped closer to her to try and sneak a peek. "I didn't know you had such an interest in musical instruments?"

Pat covered her paper with her arm and shrugged.

"How can you not have?" Lise asked, having overheard. "This is such a fun, eclectic collection. Look at that," she said, tugging Margaret's arm, and pointing. "Do you know what it is?"

"Err... another violin?" Margaret said, sheepishly.

"Not just *any* violin. It's a *Hopf*." Lise stepped close to its display case. It was the only instrument behind glass. She bent forward and basked, like a cat in the sun. "Just look at the purfling and f-hole." She flapped at her neck. "Gets me hot under the collar, it does."

"Okay..." Margaret said. "Fine, I guess."

"They're famous," Nele said, from behind them. "The best in the world, indisputably. And made right here in Saxony, of course."

"We played them once," Lise said.

"You played it," Nele corrected. "I wanted to, but the conductor favoured you, but then I suppose he would since you were sleep–"

"Oh," Lise said, chuckling. "I remember it differently." She waved Nele closer. "Let's get a photo. The two violinists and the hot *Hopf*."

"I don't have a camera, sorry," Margaret said. "Pat?" Pat shook her head. "Daniella?" Daniella did the same––just more aggressively. No-one asked Tilda, but she said, "Not my area, either."

"I thought you had that special camera Mum got you?" Lise asked. "With the mega giant zoom lens?"

"I do," Tilda said. "But it's not for... *people*."

Lise's shoulders dropped so low Margaret thought she was going to topple forwards. It was just how she'd looked earlier, when Tilda had told her she'd forgotten to look for their mother's ring. "I don't see myself as a violinist anymore, anyway," Nele said. "Or that I ever was, really."

"You were," Lise said. "You were incredible."

"Not as good as *you*," she corrected, and Margaret bristled at the sharpness of the tone. Lise blushed.

"I was just lucky."

"Yes," Nele said. "Not everyone gets to follow their dreams. Some of us end up in an office."

"Office of the president."

"*University* president," Nele clarified. "Tilda, you understand what I am talking about, right?"

"Me?" Tilda said as if being asked to describe the end of a movie she hadn't seen. "What?"

"Yes, you," Nele pressed.

"I..." she mumbled, stepping back, straight into the piano. "Ow."

"You had a place to study medicine in Berlin, no?" Nele

asked. "You were supposed to move in with Lise and Dieter. But then..." her voice trailed off.

"Things happened," Tilda said.

Lise's eyes filled with tears. "I'm so sorry," she said, moving towards her sister and reaching for her hand. "I didn't plan to leave, Tilly. I need you to know that. You know that, right?" She looked at the others. "Did I tell you the story? It was the craziest thing. I was in West Berlin--at the cinema, of all places. When we went in, no wall. We came out and they'd blocked the road already, and I guess, I mean, maybe I could have found a way across, but I just, well, I don't know... I stayed. By the next day or maybe two the wall was up. I didn't even think. I mean, I couldn't have known, right? How could I have known?" She turned back to Tilda. "You believe me, right?" she pleaded, tears streaming down her face. Tilda stared at the floor as if she hoped it would swallow her up. Pat turned around, pretending to read the small sign accompanying a drum. Margaret shifted nervously on the spot, not sure if she should intervene or give the sisters space.

It was a long time before Tilda answered. "It's fine," she said. "Everything happens for a reason."

Margaret frowned. She would not have expected someone as no-nonsense as Tilda to subscribe to such lazy, magical thinking. Everything happens, then we invent the reason. She was probably just saying this to appease Lise, to end the awkwardness.

"I would have had to give it up anyway," Tilda continued. "When mother got sick, because you were, you know..."

"Stuck," Lise said, between sobs, her voice unusually high.

Tilda patted her hand awkwardly. "Travelling the world."

"I missed out on so many years with you," Lise said, leaning her head on her sister's shoulder. "I will make it up-"

"Nothing to make up for," Tilda said, stepping away and

around the piano, using it to put space between her and her sister.

"You're going to love Connor. You just wait and see."

Tilda's face soured. "Like I loved Dieter?"

"Probably some great birdwatching on his estate," Margaret said, trying to paddle them all to shallower waters. The sisters had a lot of work to do, but was this really the place? With all of them watching on?

"Estate?" Lise asked, confused.

"Yes," said Margaret. "I talked to Jim last night. Why didn't Connor ever tell us he was rich?"

Lise's eyebrows knotted. "Rich in stories, you mean? He doesn't even have matching socks."

"But very good sweaters, I hear?" Nele said, a rare smile on her face.

"What?" Lise asked. "We're still talking about Connor, right? A man who complains that charity shop clothing's too expensive. He doesn't have a pot to piddle in."

"He wouldn't piddle in it anyway, out of principle," Margaret said. "He'd rather go on his own shoes."

Lise and Pat laughed.

"You knew?" Margaret asked Nele.

"Knew what?"

"About McGinley Knitwear?"

"Err... doesn't everyone?"

"Know what?" Lise asked, her fists balling. "What the hell is going on? How am I the last one to know things about my own husband?"

"Fiancé," Tilda corrected.

"Connor is the heir of *McGinley Knitwear*," Margaret said. "I just assumed you knew. That it must have come up?"

Lise gasped. "I always thought there was something familiar about his surname. My God." Her breathing accelerated. She

The Accidental Murder Club

placed her hands on top of the piano, as if to stop herself from fainting.

"Don't smudge it," Tilda said.

Lise ignored her. "Maybe it was a test?" she asked, both mind and speech racing. "To see if I'd still love him, penniless?" A wicked smile formed on her lip-sticked lips. "Of course I would. No, maybe it's all a big prank? You know how he loves his pranks. Remember when he hid that dead cat under Jim's bed? He found it hilarious. Jim barred him from *Next Chance* for a month. No, I bet it's not his mansion or family. I bet he's set Jim up."

"I remember," Margaret said, although the humour of that incident was lost to her, and she didn't even want to think about the violation of Jim's privacy and the risk to his health from having that decaying corpse under his bed for two days. She'd suggested they give Connor a final warning but he'd done so many favours for the rest of the Cahoots board, her suggestion had fallen on deaf ears.

"I'd have negotiated my rate higher," Daniella said. "If I'd known."

"A box came sometime last year," Lise said, ignoring the strange comment, because the women could, and in fact, were paying their own way; they didn't need their men. Not that Margaret had or wanted a man. "I was with him when he picked it up from the mailroom. He thought it was going to be Cuban cigars. He said he once dated a Cuban spy and she could still get the good stuff, from Castro's personal stash. Anyway, he opened it in the gardens and inside were three white jumpers. Exquisite, they were. He was so disappointed he took them straight to the charity shop. I thought it was odd, but then he's an impulsive man, and he does so like a cigar."

"He's probably waited to tell you for a good reason," Margaret said diplomatically, because despite all the abundant evidence to the contrary, she just couldn't accept that people did things for anything less. That we're all just blown around on the winds of each other's whims.

"Or he's just a liar?" said Daniella, pouting. "I've dated a million of them. They claim to be a prince and then you discover later they're actually a pauper with an irrepressible foot fetish." She shrugged. "So yeah, I guess it is better this way around, all things considered."

It was the most Daniella had ever said, yet Margaret wished she hadn't bothered. The women looked around the room, swapping puzzled expressions until, "How did *you* know?" Lise asked Nele.

Nele pretended to be very interested in some sort of double trumpet. "Nele?" Lise pressed.

"Hmm?" Nele said, as if the question was too vague to actually answer. "Tilda told me, I think?"

"Me? I didn't know."

"Sure you did," Nele said. "It's normal that you might do a bit of research about your future brother-in-law, no?"

"Why would I do that?" Tilda's voice sharpened, her indifferent veneer finally cracking. "What's it matter to me who Lise marries? And apparently she didn't do any research." Tilda moved away from the group and the exhibit, towards the altar. Lise followed her, trying but failing to whisper.

"It's fine, Tilda. I'm not mad. I'd look into whoever you were marrying too, to make sure there were no skeletons. I only want the best for you. I always have."

Tilda brushed her away. "Why would *you* have a reason to be mad? I don't complain. Never ask for anything from you. I keep accepting your constant apologies, even though your guilt is not my problem. Why would I care who your new husband is?"

"Tilda," Lise said, reaching for her sister's hand again, "I'm sorry."

"STOP SAYING SORRY!" Tilda pulled her hand away and

ran for the back door, which she'd opened earlier to air the church. Lise was going to go after her, before Margaret could call out.

"Stop. Wait. Give her a moment." She knew from her school days that in the first few minutes after an altercation, you can't talk to people. You have to wait for the red mist to vanish and their adrenaline to lower. Only then can you try to reach them. It wasn't only irate parents, any student sent to her office had to sit on the chair outside for fifteen minutes to cool off.

"But I have to–"

"You can't solve this today, Lise."

"I just want everyone to be happy," she said and Margaret believed her, but it was a naïve wish, like praying for world peace.

"I'll go," Margaret said, her voice soft, as if it were a burden she was gracious enough to try to carry. "Make sure she's okay." She didn't wait for an answer, moving the other way around the grand piano, past Lise and towards the door before anyone could stop her, sure this might be her only chance to talk to Tilda alone.

Chapter 12
The McGinley Factory (Jim)

"Your room?" Gary said, eyes skittish, turning to see if anyone had overheard. Some of the staff might have, but why would they care? "I haven't been in your room. Why would I–"

"Sure you have," Jim said. He tipped his head towards the door. "Smoke?"

"Err... sure?" Gary said, confused at the abrupt change in question. Gary followed him to the door. Jim braced for the cold, tugging up the zipper on his jacket, and then threw open the door.

Outside, he made a show of patting his pockets. "Shoot, I seem to have left my fags back at the mansion. Can I bum one?"

Gary held out his pack, nervous on his feet, aiming for eye contact but missing. The lighter was inside and there were just two smokes left. Jim hadn't smoked in a decade, well, not before his fourth pint, but Gary didn't need to know that. He took one, lit it, and took a long draw, the nicotine shooting straight to his head like a dart to a bullseye. He suppressed a cough into a shiver. While the island was only forty-five minutes from the mainland, it felt like it had its own climate, one best described as disagreeable. He handed back the pack but kept the lighter to help with Gary's, who immediately blew a thick cloud of smoke between them.

"There a pub on the island?" Jim asked, because it was their common topic, and he wanted to let Gary stew a bit longer.

"It's Ireland, of course, there's a pub. No barman, mind. You serve yourself. A trust kind of thing."

"Worth a look?" Jim asked.

Gary took another drag. "You know that sheep we saw with its wee head stuck? That's a pretty excellent summary of this place. Seamus likes it, for some reason, but we should get out of here as soon as we can."

"How do you know he likes it?"

His eyes narrowed. "Well, he said he's here all the time."

Jim nodded, his suspicions growing. "Connor told you I'm a publican too, right?"

Gary grinned. "Could have guessed. You've an ease around people, fella. An ease with yourself, mind. An ease with a yarn."

Jim enjoyed the compliments. "Have to, right? Pubs are melting pots, and we're their ladles."

"Couldn't have said it better."

"I've moved on, sort of," Jim said, neglecting to mention *Next Chance*, his illicit speakeasy, tolerated but not officially approved by the Cahoots board, since he didn't have an alcohol permit and Health and Safety certification and all that stupid nonsense, nor did he have any intention of getting them. "Or, I'm trying too. What about you? You must be thinking of retirement?"

"Chance would be a fine thing." Gary scraped his bottom lip. "You have a family? Kids?"

Jim thought of his Trudy, and how she hadn't even invited him to her wedding. Every time he remembered, it was like being stabbed in the heart. "Yeah," he said, resisting the topic change, needing to keeping the focus on Gary and why he was still working the pubs all these decades after he started, yet didn't seem to have reached management level, never mind regional manager for a chain of them, like Jim had been by age forty. "We're close. You?"

Gary gave a resigned shrug. "I do what I can for them, you know? Me and my ex, we don't see eye to eye anymore. Maybe we never did. And just when I think I'm getting ahead; the past has a way of catching up. This is really your first time in Ireland? Hard not to take that personally, if it is."

You know it's my first time, Jim thought, we talked about it in the limo. It's a common tactic––if you don't want to answer a question––ask one. "Was it a surprise when you heard Connor was coming over?"

"Yeah," Gary said. "Wasn't sure I'd ever see him again. If someone stays away for twenty-odd years, you assume there's a good reason."

"What's the good reason? There's a lot of stuff being hinted at, as I see it."

Gary scratched his neck. "You know what my father used to say? Nothing builds bigger resentment than a small town."

Jim laughed. It was a good line. He filed it away to use later about Bury St Edmunds. He tapped ash onto the ground. "Is Galway a small town, then?"

"Ireland's a small town. That's why most get out. Why Connor got out. Why he never came back, neither. He should have just stayed away."

"When I called Bill to set up the stag, he said Connor didn't have any friends left in Galway. Yet, you and Tad are here. Enthusiastic welcomes too. Limos. VIP areas at the track."

Gary sighed. "The limo was Seamus's idea, actually."

"Really? Why?"

"Jesus, Jim, what's all this about? Why do you care?"

He raised his hands. "I know, I know. Nosey old Jim, rooting around in other people's business. Thing is though, G, I really want to see Connor and Lise safe. They're good eggs, underneath it all. Don't tell anyone this, but when I had a delay selling my pad in London and I couldn't afford the fees at Cahoots for a few months, Connor paid them. I didn't even ask him to. At the time, I figured he'd robbed a bank for it, but I guess he has a bit more stashed away than he acts. I paid him back, of course. Still…"

Gary's eyes widened. "Wow… That's… I didn't…"

Jim bounced his eyebrows. "Generous, yeah. And after what happened with the chandelier, you can understand why I'm—"

"That was an incredible dive," Gary said, doing a mock lunge forward, cigarette dangling precariously between his teeth. "Were you a goalkeeper?"

"Nah." Jim laughed. "Didn't have the knees for it. Central defender, but I mean, really, the way I played, it was basically rugby." They swapped a knowing smile. Jim knocked some ash onto the ground and pressed it in with his shoe. "Nice as this is, Gaz, are you ready to tell me why you've been coming into my room? Rooting around in my stuff?" He tensed his arms. "Or do I have to get angrier first?"

Gary took a half-step backwards. "I don't know what you're talking about."

"Show me your hand," Jim said, reaching for it.

Gary kept the cigarette in his mouth but moved his hands behind his back. "Why?"

"You don't have to, fella. I've already seen it. Marked the handle of my door with red ink. I know it was you, G, that's settled. What I don't know yet is why?"

Gary dropped the nub of his cigarette on the ground with his weaker left hand and trod on it. Jim heard Connor's sloppy, raspy laugh from the other side of the door. He was back from the toilet; Jim didn't have long left. "The truth," Jim said, flashing his teeth. "Before I tell the others."

"I was looking for Seamus," Gary said, lowering his head.

Jim stroked his chin. "You talk about Seamus a lot."

Gary looked away. "I just... well... I feel sorry for him is all. He's misunderstood, like me. He was so close to Connor's dad... but then the will. That stupid picture."

"Do you see him socially?" Jim asked.

"Seamus?" Gary blew out a breath. He'd recently eaten something with garlic. "Nah, he called me about the stag, said he wanted Connor's old friends involved."

"Yet, you decided you just had to talk to him, privately, in his room? Late at night but then, somehow, ended up in mine?"

"There are so many rooms in that sodding place, Jimmy. I just got lost is all. His room is next to yours."

"Is it?" Jim hadn't seen anyone coming and going from the many rooms near his.

Gary nodded. "Bill said it was, anyway. But I couldn't find it. Found yours by mistake. Went in. Realised it was the wrong one. Gave up. Came back. Didn't want to disturb the poker game for too long, did I? Had a flush draw. The last time I had a hand like that–"

"Thing is though, G," Jim interrupted. "Someone was in my room earlier in the day as well, too. And you were very insistent about helping me with my bag when I arrived?"

Gary raised his hands. "Mate, seriously? I was just being hospitable."

Jim let out a long, weary sigh. He wasn't sure he believed this story; actually he was sure he didn't, but he might still need Gary as an ally. And he'd given him plenty he could ask others about, and more than enough to catch him in a lie if he was lying, which Jim strongly suspected was the case.

"Fair enough," Jim said. "Innocent mistake."

"Yeah," Gary said, but didn't meet Jim's eyes while saying so. "We best get back inside. I think I can hear Connor."

Jim nodded. "One last thing, yeah? Humour me. You people are famous for your humour, right? If someone wanted to kill

The Accidental Murder Club

Connor, and let's be honest, who wouldn't, who would your money be on? Seamus?"

Gary howled with laughter. "Seamus? He idolises Connor."

Jim tried the idea on, but couldn't make it fit. "Why do you say he idolises him?"

"Come on, anyone can see that."

Jim hadn't seen it, but he didn't want to let Gary know that. Jim prided himself on seeing more than everyone else. He always thought he should have been a therapist. In a way, from the other side of the bar, he had been. Gary stepped to the side, looked like he was going to move past Jim and back indoors. Jim stepped into his path. "Who then?"

Gary hesitated, then took a deep breath. "It's a small town. People talk. There's a name I hear in circles where I shouldn't."

"Tad," Jim guessed.

"Tad?" Gary scowled. "Nah. I'm talking about Tristan. Likes a flutter, I hear. Going to the greyhound track was *his* idea."

"What's that got to do with Connor, though?"

He looked up at the stone building. "Seamus is the power behind McGinley, but he doesn't know it himself. He lacks confidence. If Connor's gone, Seamus will leave the Trust in place."

Connor's loud laugh rang out from inside, and the door rattled behind them. Jim nodded his thanks to Gary and then stepped aside. Tad emerged first. "We're off to me church, boys," he said, striding past them and down the boggy path. Seamus came out last, answering a final question from one of the McGinley staff. Overhead, there was a break in the dark clouds and a little sun poked its head through. Jim's mood had lightened too. That interrogation had been a real six pointer, and he'd won it. Sure, he'd hadn't got a full confession out of Gary, but he had new leads, a very firm hunch about Gary and Seamus, and it was pleasing to see Gary found Tristan about as credible as Jim did: never trust a man that uses product.

Leaning forwards, braced against the wind, they trudged down the hill, trying not to slip on the narrow, muddy path, their boots sinking into the damp earth with each step as, up ahead, a small church sat defiantly against the elements, weathered and worn. A shiver shot down Jim's spine. The red of the church's spire was faded and its clock had stopped. Its stone walls, once sturdy and proud, now bore the marks of time and neglect. Patches of moss and lichen stained the façade. The wooden door, weathered and splintered, hung slightly ajar. On its left was a small, overgrown cemetery––now a tangle of wild vegetation, half-submerged tombstones, and sharp, twisty ivy.

"There she is," Tad said, as if glimpsing land after a long time at sea.

"Hmm," said Gary.

"Feckin' hell," said Connor.

"Yes," said Seamus, ever the diplomat. "I suppose it is."

Jim had to lower his head to duck beneath the hand-painted sign that hung on two rusty hooks over the entrance. It looked like a piece of driftwood and on it, in white paint, was scrawled: *Soft Knocks - Boys Reform School*.

"Blimey," Jim said, when the inside was no warmer than out, and, squinting, he tried to take it all in. The basics of a church were there––the tall, arched ceilings and enormous stained-glass windows, trying to make you feel insignificant, ramming the fear of God into you, and the nave and pews, rows and rows of them pointing in one direction, to the altar, ready to receive higher wisdom––but at the very centre of the room, lit by brilliant, gothic light streaming in from the red, yellow and green tainted stained-glass windows, was a boxing ring. A ring almost certainly older than Jim. Its ropes were threadbare, their paint chipped off, and now a dirty, faded red that Jim hoped wasn't from the blood of injured boxers. The turnbuckle pads at the corner were no longer soft and plump, but worn and unforgiving. Gary laughed. Connor whistled.

"Potential," Tristan said reverently.

Tad walked towards the ring, and the others followed silently. Jim couldn't remember the last time something had shut Connor up. He was sure Margaret's reform school was nothing like this. There were a few youngsters dotted around doing what looked like homework in the pews, or exercising in a makeshift gym set up in a far corner, where there were weights and several punching bags. When they saw Tad, they stopped, turned, lowered their head and said, "Father."

"My altar," Tad said, as they got closer to the ring and grabbed the top rope. "And ain't she a beauty?"

"You do your sermons here?" Jim asked.

"Every single one."

"Why's it so cold?" Seamus asked, shivering.

"It's warm in their hearts."

"Where do they sleep?" Connor asked.

"Upstairs. All together. Like puppy dogs."

"We could give them jumpers?" said Seamus, rubbing his arms and turning to Connor and then Tristan. "Couldn't we? We could get them right now from the factory. How many jumpers do you need, Tad? It's no problem, really. Right, Connor? We'd be happy to do it."

"They need much more than jumpers," said Tristan.

"It would be a start, though. And we could give them more. I could talk to the board? I mean, I'm on the board." He looked accusingly at Connor. "While there's still a board."

"Money's tight right now," said Tristan, sucking on his bottom lip. "We're a seasonal business, and it's a long time until Christmas."

"You said business was good when we were at the track?" Jim asked.

"Relatively," said Tristan. "To before I became so actively and strategically involved."

"Do they all train?" Connor asked, shadow punching the air.

Tad gave the slowest, deepest nod Jim had ever seen. He didn't like the answer.

"But they're just kids, T," Jim said, tugging at his neck. "They shouldn't have to fight." He looked with pity at the smallest lad. "Some of them are tiny little things. We're not all made for the ring. I know we were," he flexed his biceps, "but that's just… it's not *in* everyone." His eyes tried to find Tad's, but settled instead on Seamus.

"Judge not, that ye be not judged," Tad said and turned to that smallest, youngest boy––a waif with blond hair, parted in the middle, chewing on the sleeves of his grey school jumper, as he wrote on a piece of paper with a pencil.

"Kelly," Tad barked. Addressing his pupils with their surnames only added to the frosty atmosphere, Jim felt. Kelly jumped up from the front row of pews. Jim guessed he was maybe eight or nine, the gold-rimmed glasses on his small button nose wonky and tilting left. He was a bully's dream, the lad.

"Matthew 7:1, Father," the boy said.

"Good." Tad stared at the men one by one. "They don't choose whether to fight. They were fighting before they arrived here. And they'll be fighting long after they leave. But because of this place, they'll know love, warmth, and how to win those duels."

"Warmth?" Connor joked.

"Kelly," Tad shouted. "Lace up." The boy moved silently and obediently towards the ring. Two boys who had just begun sparring climbed out, first holding the ropes apart for the boy to enter. He handed one of them his glasses.

"Seamus?" Tad said, nodding towards the ring.

Seamus pulled his head back in alarm. "What? No!"

"Well, he needs an opponent, does he not?"

"Seriously?" said Gary. "He needs a hug, is what he needs."

"So, hug him. Boxers hug too."

"He's just a child, for God's sake," said Seamus.

"NOT IN THIS HOUSE," Tad boomed at this latest act of blasphemy.

Seamus looked down at the cold stone floor. Gary stepped forward. "You draw a line at blasphemy, but it's fine for a weedy six-year-old to fight?"

"I told ye all, they're already fighting." Tad pointed to the ring. "Tristan, you man enough?"

"An eye for an eye will only make the whole world blind," said Tristan, which Jim took to mean no.

"Ghandi?" Connor asked.

"Stevie Wonder."

Tad laughed, so deeply and loudly it echoed off the walls. "This is not violence, boys. It's poetry." He sniffed. "Connor, then? I know personally that you're no stranger to the brawl."

Connor raised his hands. "He's just a wee nipper."

"He's one of my boys. And if you don't," Tad circled his arms, warming up, "*I* will."

"Fine. *Fine.*" Connor winked at Jim. "I'll go easy on the lad. Don't you be worrying," he shouted to Kelly, mock skipping. "I'm only half as deadly as I look."

"That's not what I heard," Gary muttered under his breath.

One of the older boys, perhaps fifteen, helped Connor into a scruffy pair of blue gloves. "The whiff of these, Taddy," Connor said, pretending to pass out. "When did you last wash 'em?"

"When we wash here, it's only in holy water or blood."

It was really hard to tell when Tad was being serious. Jim had a sick feeling in his stomach, or near his stomach, but it wasn't the hangover; it was something else. A boy rang a bell.

"Begin," yelled Tad and Connor strutted over from the ropes, fists up, legs dancing a near Irish-jig, as he had so many times at his father's wake. He circled his arms through the air, ducking and weaving in his usually exaggerated, clown-like way, turning more towards the men than Kelly. Throwing shapes and encouraging them to cheer, really hamming it up for the crowd. But then, Connor was always hamming it up for a crowd, even when he was alone. "Show me what you got, kid."

"Defences, Kelly, don't let him push you around. He likes pushing," Tad said to the little lad who was standing in the corner, fists raised to his chest, watching Connor with a look not of fear, as Jim would have expected, but something more like confusion. His tiny head overwhelmed by his boxing shield. As Tad commanded, he raised his little fists higher—the gloves were also several sizes too large—until they blocked the lower half of his face. If he had a chin, he was hiding it well.

Seamus went and sat down in a pew at the end of an aisle, making a point of turning away from the ring. Jim was tempted to do the same, but had a feeling how this might play out yet. "You sure about this, Tad?" he asked.

"Yeah," said Gary, "someone might get hurt, you know. It happens faster than you think, right?"

"Don't be such a kill-joy," Tristan added.

"Yes," Tad said, "there's only one killer here, right?"

There it was again, Jim thought - the hints, the little extra left tacked on the end of a sentence. Throwaway remarks that were anything but. These friends, or family, in the case of Seamus and Connor, were bad at guarding the skeletons in their collective closet. Jim needed to find a way to get the doors open and those rattling bones out here into the light of the present.

"Begin," Tad shouted, and Kelly snapped into life, his back suddenly ramrod-straight, his small feet in their black plimsolls making a fast, soft, muffled sound as he shot towards Connor. The speed of his movements hypnotised Jim. He was always in motion and he began to stalk Connor, moving forwards twice, right once, back once, left once, forwards twice, right, back, left, slowly pushing Connor back to the corner, without him even noticing it was happening.

"He's full of beans, aye lads?" Connor shouted, fists so low he was barely even protecting himself. "But he ain't going to see my right hook coming."

"They never do, do they?" Tad said.

Connor hooked the air theatrically and at this moment, Kelly launched forwards, a quick step and then he took flight, both feet off the grimy canvas mat flecked with sweat and bloodstains, as he socked Connor with a wild uppercut to the jaw. Connor took it but, shocked, stumbled backwards, his calves hitting the ropes, which had no give, and so only shunted him forwards again where he staggered straight into Kelly's waiting left fist, slamming straight into his stomach, winding him and sending him crashing forwards onto the deck, yelling in pain. "ARGGHGGHHH."

Kelly turned and bowed first towards Connor, then Tad. "Father," he said, then went to the edge of the ring where the older boy who'd rung the bell to begin the bout climbed in and helped remove his gloves. Connor lay on the ground like a spilt sack of spuds, holding his stomach and spluttering, trying to get some breath into his failing lungs.

"Shame we didn't place any bets," said Tristan. "I'd have gone big on little Kelly."

"Lasted quite a bit longer than I expected," said Gary.

"That's not what she said," Connor croaked. "But it's not over. I'm just getting warmed up."

"Impressive in this place," Jim said, blowing on his hands.

Tad turned to Jim and the others. "My boys are learning much more than how to fight. You see that, right? They're learning discipline, strategy, and self-respect." His voice grew louder. "*We* don't talk of their past, *we* don't talk of their sins, nor of those who should have cared for them, loved them. They're loved here. Of that, *we* talk often."

For the first time, Jim could imagine Tad at the pulpit, delivering a sermon, even if it really did just happen at the centre of this ring. It was the repetition of the "we" and the changes in speed and rhythm. It was even more hypnotic than little Kelly's footwork. "Here *we* find redemption."

"I don't know," said Connor, on his feet now, but clearly still winded and clutching his stomach, helped to walk by two of Tad's disciples who split the ropes so he could climb down. "It's easy to swap one fear for another. And I see how they're looking at you, pal."

If he was embarrassed at his loss, he was hiding it well. But then Jim had never seen Connor do embarrassed, he seemed to be immune to that particular emotion. "Let he who is without sin cast the first stone, Connor," said Tad, irritated.

Connor tried to straighten up. "What do you mean by that, chief?"

"Byrne," he said to the boy who had both rang the bell and helped remove Kelly's gloves.

"John 8:7, Father," the boy said.

"Good."

"I've no sin," said Connor. "I'm basically a saint, I am. Ask anyone?" He looked around, challenging someone to disagree.

"Can be your sin," said Tad. "Can be the sins of your family. The sins of power. The sins of money."

"They make jumpers," Connor said. "My family make woolly jumpers."

"They've made more than that," Tad snarled.

"Let's go," Tristan said. "We've a board meeting soon and much to discuss."

"Yeah, you toddle off now," Tad said. "The day's public boat sails in fifteen minutes. But know that not everyone here can just leave."

"And we've plans tonight," Gary said. "Neachy."

Jim had figured out this was the pub Gary worked in, one

with a completely unpronounceable name. "I'll make your plans," Tad said, although it sounded more like a threat. "I'm a man of my word. *Always.*"

Gary nodded. Jim slipped Connor's arm over his shoulder and helped him through the pews and back towards the entrance, happy to have him away from Tad and whatever resentment he was failing to keep to himself. As they left, they heard the sound of punches ringing out from the ring, the next bout already taking place, the deep bass of Tad's voice as he guided, or maybe goaded, two of his boys. Jim was deeply conflicted about all he'd seen. Sure, they'd not got a look at the living quarters, classrooms, or met the other staff, and so there might be a home hidden here somewhere, a place of warmth and love and community, like Tad claimed, but Jim found it hard to imagine.

Chapter 13
Outside the Nikolaikirche (Margaret)

Margaret stepped out into the square behind the church, holding her hand up to block the midday sun of another terrific early May day. She looked around for Tilda, who didn't have much of a head-start. Holding the handrail, she moved down the ramp and there, off to the right, she spotted her silhouette. She was watching a bird drinking from a small stone fountain.

As Margaret moved nearer, she flicked through her mental playbook, trying to think how to best approach the conversation. It was something she did before each semester review session with one of her teachers. Everyone needs different things before they will open up. How we act begins with how we feel. Feelings were not Margaret's speciality, but she found them easier to recognise in others than in herself, was more respectful of them too, perhaps, despite their fleeting, untrustworthy and often downright contradictory nature. How did Tilda feel at this moment? Angry? Well, yes, but that was more symptom than cause. Resentment? That seemed to be what Lise suspected but Tilda claimed otherwise. Misunderstood? Yes. And that was a feeling Margaret did know well. What do misunderstood people want? To feel that they're not alone. To feel they're not crazy.

She approached slowly, as if she were afraid Tilda might fly away and not the bird she was watching with rapt attention, arms behind her back.

"Everything okay? I just came to check—"

"Passer domesticus," Tilda said, without turning around.

"Sorry?"

"The common house sparrow."

Margaret stepped closer until they were side by side, looking down at a small, plump bird with brownish-grey feathers and a black bib on its neck, its head bobbing up and down as it took quick sips of water, tiny throat contracting with each gulp. "Were you always interested in birds?"

A few seconds of silence. "My parents had an allotment," Tilda said, still facing forwards. While she occasionally stumbled and had a heavy accent, her English really was very good for someone who'd never left her hometown. "I used to go there every day after school and then sometimes while I should have been at school. Birds were always easier, somehow."

Easier than people, Margaret knew she meant. Books had been her solace. Knowledge. Study. An unrelenting focus on the verifiable and immutable. "Yes," she said. "I understand that sentiment completely." Agreement was good for building rapport, although in this case it was also what she believed. "People have often told me I come across as cold and distant. That there is something a little bit off about me." She paused to let the words sink in and turned sideways towards Tilda, willing her to do the same. "I don't mean to be like that. And I don't know what that thing is, even. I study people, Tilda, like you do birds. No-one sees the effort I put in."

Silence. Margaret considered if she'd been too direct, too soon. She had told the truth, but truths are heavy, anchors we drag around our necks, and not everyone wants to be burdened with the weight of someone else's.

"The bib," Tilda said, pointing down, slowly, so as not to scare the bird. "House Sparrows have a social hierarchy within their flocks. The larger the bib, the more dominant and higher status the male."

"Interesting," Margaret said, glancing at it. "And so, this one is–"

Tilda turned to her, finally, meeting her eyes. "Do you see a flock?"

"No."

"But then we don't all need a flock, do we?" Tilda said.

"Your sister does," Margaret said. "Was that always the case?"

Tilda's lips pursed. "She's always been emotional," she said after a few seconds of contemplation. Mother called it her art temperament."

Artistic, Margaret corrected in her mind. "Was she always artistic?"

Tilda nodded. "Mother said she sang before she spoke. They were all very," she paused, "*stolz?*"

"Proud," Margaret said, thrilled she knew a word Tilda didn't.

"She got piano lessons and then violin. My mother was so happy when she was accepted to the orchestra in Berlin."

My mother, not ours, Margaret thought. Interesting choice.

"I can still see my mother's face when she finished her solo. It was the last trip she took. Her *diagnose* came after. Then the wall and…"

Diagnosis. Margaret was surprised how forthcoming Tilda was being. It wasn't only birds that animated her, her sister was a topic that also unleashed strong emotions. While the sisters looked similar, it was striking how Lise seemed to have gotten all the colour and the effervescence, while her sister wanted to blend into the background.

Margaret glanced back towards the church to check if anyone was coming. "Just between the two of us," Margaret continued, lowering her voice, trying to suggest the sharing of a great secret, "but in the last years with Dieter, Lise lost almost all her sparkle. I'm not sure you'd have recognised her. It's come back recently. Mostly since Connor, I think. And now it's like she's trying to catch up for lost time. There were moments during our Christmas production of the nutcracker where I thought I was going to have to strangle her." Margaret chuckled, Tilda didn't. Instead, she pushed her lips out a little more and gave just the smallest hint of a nod, more in acknowledgement than agreement, before returning her attention to the sparrow. Margaret saw no choice but to plough on. "I can't imagine growing up with a sister who everyone found so charming, so talented. Not that I had a sister. Anyway, a career travelling all over the world, and now the chance of a second life with a rich husband and a manor house in Ireland?"

The bird fluttered its wings and flew away. Tilda turned. Her eyes were huge, angry saucers. "You're doing it too," Tilda hissed. "You're a snob like her."

Margaret took a step away and raised her palm. "Tilda, no. That's not... I'm not..."

"You can't believe someone could be happy with a simple life, can you? Just because I never left Leipzig and can't play Bach's *Violin Concerto in a-moll*. Yeah, I don't have a rich husband who pretends to be poor, but is that really what you think is important?" Like an angry snake, Tilda seemed to have risen a foot. She was leaning forwards as she spoke, jabbing her finger into Margaret's chest.

"Sor–" Margaret began, before catching herself. Sorry Syndrome, so terribly British.

Tilda snarled at her sorry, lowered her hand, and slipped it back into her trouser pocket. "Do you know what I see when I look at Lise's life?" Margaret waited out the short pause. "All that she's missed. The last years of our mother's life, for one. Holding her hand when she finally died. She even missed her funeral. Dieter didn't want her to come. Said it might not be safe. And anyway, she was on tour, in *Südafrika.*" She rolled her eyes, seemingly finding it ridiculous someone would be sent that far just to play a violin. *South Africa.* "Unforgivable, isn't it?" She continued. "She picked her career and now what does she have to show for it? Nothing. That's why she's going on some kind of tour of the past, dragging us along with her, running around with the *Asche* of her first husband, reading Stasi-files just because she wishes she picked differently." Tilda snorted. "But she can't. It's too late."

"Is that why you don't want to give her your mother's ring?"

Her nostrils flared. "What? Why are you bringing up that?"

"You didn't bring it today and you seemed taken aback when Lise asked you about it. What are the odds you'd have misplaced something so valuable to you?" *Long.*

Tilda frowned. "No. I... She only told me about two days ago. I'm just supposed to drop everything to look for it?"

"Of course not," Margaret said, reaching to touch Tilda on the elbow. "I think she really does just want to be close to you, you know?"

Tilda moved her arm away. "You all think I'm jealous of her. About her career. And Dieter. *She* thinks I'm jealous of her. But that was never me."

Jealous of Dieter? Why? Other than the fact he was away a lot, Margaret had never seen any other redeeming qualities in the man. The only nice thing he did was bring Lise souvenirs from the places of his lorry trips; she had a whole shelf full of knick-knacks from the most random places.

"Who was it then?" Margaret asked. "Who was the jealous one?"

They both heard footsteps and turned. Lise, Pat, Nele, and Daniella were crossing the square towards them. Margaret was running out of time. "Who?" she pressed. "Nele? You mean Nele, right?"

Tilda lowered her head. "Yes."

Pat and Daniella were ambling, but Nele and Lise were in front and only ten metres away now, their arms looped into each other, Nele talking animatedly, smiling, sun on her face. Margaret couldn't see her eyes, but felt them on her.

Chapter 14

Tigh Neachtain (Jim)

Jim took a deep sip of his stout, the bitterness of the ale complementing the uneasy feeling at the bottom of his throat. They were in the corner of the main room of *Tigh Neachtain* pub in Galway, a real warren, all narrow passages and hidden nooks. This was Gary's pub, well, Gary worked here. He certainly moved around it like he owned it. Jim stared over at the bar, a handsome, dark wood affair with smudged brass footrests. Crowded, too, the bar staff behind it moving with practised ease, almost like a dance - lifting, wiping, pouring sometimes to command, but often in anticipation - what does that punter need? A little grub too to mop up the booze curdling in his stomach? Toss him a pack of crisps on the house. He felt a twinge of envy, missed the rush of keeping up with the demands of a busy boozer, the buzz of being in the thick of the action, a key stitch in the tapestry of people's lives, contributing to their wild Friday nights and mundane Monday middays. He had *Next Chance*, sure, but it was more of a hobby, a man cave masquerading as a pub.

He lifted his glass to the room, just a little and reflected on what he'd learnt so far that day: the fruits of his usual brilliant interrogations and keen detective's mind. Gary was going into his room and lying about it. Gary and Seamus were shagging. Okay, that one was still a hunch, but one he was growing more and more confident of. Gary suspected Tristan was involved in Connor's near-demise. Tristan had a clear motive to be, as he needed the Trust to stay in place, and, despite his cool, calm demeanour, the guy was a hot mess with at least one addiction, although because of the amount he touched his nose and disappeared into toilets, Jim was guessing there might be another vice he'd lost control of, too. And last, but very much not least, based on all the snide comments fired at Connor during that boxing debacle, there was something violent in the groom-to-be's past, something the others weren't letting him forget.

He took another sip and then licked his lips; it was a good day's work. He looked forward to gloating about it to Margaret on their next call. Evidence is nice and all, but in lieu of it, you have to work with your gut and your instincts. He put the pint glass down and let his eyes wander. The surrounding walls were cluttered with vintage posters and old black and white photos of Galway. He was surprised by how much he already recognised--they could change the dressing, sure, add a park here and a lick of paint there, but the heart of a place will stay the same--Galway had changed remarkably little while Connor had been away.

In the opposite corner was a small stage for live music. They were too early for that, which was good, because Jim wanted to talk. Just because he'd had a good day didn't mean it couldn't get better yet. Opposite him, Tristan tapped at his phone--that damn Blackberry, always in his supple, moisturised hands. On his lap was a newspaper from the rack. Jim leaned forwards a little to get a look at it, to see what topics the young lad was interested in. Where he fell on the political spectrum, if he was on it at all. Seemed only interested in himself. Squinting down, he saw only a lot of small texts and numbers in strip panels. To his left, Connor and Tad were deep in conversation, or rather, Connor was. Tad was sitting like a sad totem pole, head slightly angled, listening. He'd been the first one here though, had kept his word, just as he said he would. Although having seen his church, Jim wasn't surprised––*Neachy* was a lot less draughty. He, Gary and Connor had spent the afternoon at the mansion, a nap to sleep off the wake's hangover, then Connor had given Jim a whooping at snooker. It was shocking to learn in just how many ways that man had misspent his youth.

Gary's seat was empty. Jim spotted him over by the bar, on another lap. Slapping backs. Shaking hands. Seemed to know everyone's name, he did. Was interrupting a card game now. Not everyone talked to him with enthusiasm though, Jim noted. There was a little something at the edge of their eyes, sometimes, and while he wasn't sure what, exactly, if he had to guess, like if you put a gun to his head, he'd have said it was pity.

Tristan got up and put the folded newspaper on his seat before walking away. Couldn't be getting a round in because as soon as they were halfway through their drinks, the next ones arrived, unordered, from the staff. Gary had obviously told them this was a VIP table. Jim watched as Tristan headed towards the toilets. He sighed, deciding he'd been, on reflection, too soft on Gary, and that was not a mistake he'd make again. He took out his comb, made himself correct, took another generous gulp of his pint, and stood up.

Chapter 15

Moritzbastei #1 (Margaret)

"What's with all the dungeon restaurants here?" Margaret asked, as the waitress went to check if their reserved table was free. A casual glance down at her watch told her they were seven minutes behind schedule. They were in *Moritzbastei*, another subterranean bunker, just like *Auerbachs Keller*––the most famous restaurant in the city and where Goethe had often dined, and even wrote into his play Faust. Unfortunately, it was closed for refurbishment.

Nele pouted. "Never noticed that."

"The GDR had a lot of dark corners," said Lise, then giggled. "And I would know. I explored most of them."

"And not alone," Tilda said, without making eye contact.

"Yeah, well, you always had such high standards," her sister said, pouting.

Tilda sighed. "I was just busy."

"Men are such a distraction," Nele said.

Lise rolled her eyes. "It doesn't take that long. Right, Pat?"

Pat wrote in her notepad and handed it to Lise: "Vibrators are faster," she read, and then howled a scandalised laugh, as did everyone else, except Margaret.

"Girls," she hissed, chastened; there were people around and she'd said it so loudly they must have heard. The waitress returned and beckoned to a booth right next to the bar. Too central for Margaret's tastes, but she wasn't going to make a scene about it.

"The DDR had a lot of light too, you know," Nele grabbed Lise's shoulders from behind, pretending to start a conga line as they walked. "And fun. We knew how to have fun back then, didn't we?"

"Fun's my middle name," Tilda said, with her usual flat tone. Everyone laughed. A rare moment of group harmony.

"Your middle name's Ilse," Lise said, shouting back down the line. "But it should be *fun*, yes."

Moritzbastei had to be more fun than lunch. Daniella had taken them to a restaurant whose theme was 'world cuisine', despite its furniture being scuffed, bashed, threadbare local leftovers of the GDR. It was unclear if the chef possessed a passport, but it was very obvious that Margaret's Hungarian goulash, Pat's Indian chicken curry, and Tilda's spaghetti Bolognese all had the same sauce. They hadn't complained, well, only amongst themselves, since the atmosphere was still tense from the *Nikolaikirche*, with Tilda clearly avoiding Lise's gaze. Things improved slightly when Lise presented her with her long-mentioned, often-forgotten gift: a *Birds of the UK* book and a plane ticket to come visit, but even that hadn't lightened the mood all that much. Tilda hadn't even opened the book to look inside and her 'thanks' was so flat you'd have thought something had run it over.

"Right next to the bar," Lise said, when they had reached their table. "Excellent."

"What else did you expect?" a smirking Daniella asked.

Margaret coughed. Their waitress smiled as she gave the table of their curved booth a quick wipe. She had thick, wavy, very dyed copper hair and was wearing a *Moritzbastei* branded black tank-top, two sizes too small, presumably to show off her arms and chest, which were completely covered in tattoos. "The *Junggesellinnenabschied, Ja?* Ireland?"

Hen-do. "*England,*" Lise clarified. "But close enough."

She turned and gestured at her colleague behind the bar, who was inexpertly pummelling the limes of a mojito. She made two shapes with her hand, what Margaret thought were an I and a W. She'd got a lot better at charades since meeting Pat.

The bar woman nodded, dropping the finished mojito on the counter top roughly, so that some splashed over the rim. She looked like she had just woken up from yesterday's shift, and left its shirt on, as well.

"I requested a special cocktail for you all," Daniella said.

"A house speciality," the waitress added with a wink. "Irish Wedding."

The bar woman's hands were shaking as she took the first of six champagne flutes out from under the bar, lining them up on the counter, which she missed with the last, the glass falling and smashing on the floor.

"Wahey," Lise said, and several other patrons cheered and clapped. The barmaid attempted a sarcastic curtsy that became a shambolic stumble. Jim would have read her the riot act, Margaret thought. Very unprofessional. Her eyes drifted from her back to their waitress, locking on the tattoo that covered her entire upper right arm and seemed to depict a female, homoerotic sexual… she shook her head, tried to pull herself together, and her attention elsewhere. She'd never understood tattoos. How could you be sure you wouldn't permanently brandish yourself with something you'd later regret? It seemed an awfully large gamble to take out against your future self. And anyway, Margaret didn't gamble. Life was already risky enough.

"Just an orange juice, for me please," she finally remembered to shout. The barmaid nodded, putting one flute, the only one she'd not poured champagne into yet, back down behind the counter.

"You're not even going to try it?" Nele said.

"No," Margaret said, which never worked as a complete sentence in these circumstances, people always wanted to know why you didn't drink, when Margaret felt the onus should be on the drinker to justify why they were poisoning themselves for pleasure. She settled deeper into the booth, enjoying how cool the back leather was. She'd done well with Tilda today. Tonight's goal was to get to Nele alone and see if the things Tilda had hinted at--a love triangle between Nele, Dieter and Lise--were true. Could love--that temporary mental illness used to trick us into propagating our flawed species--really be enough, decades later, to make you throw a knife at someone who had once called you their best friend? And especially with Dieter already dead?

Margaret didn't understand how it could be, but understanding wasn't important - the facts were all that mattered. Nele's behaviour didn't have to be rational, Margaret reminded herself. And jealousy was the most common cause of the violent skirmishes that had happened at *Righteous Path*. One student, Maria Watkins, had even committed suicide after being cheated on by her girlfriend, admittedly with her best friend. A real debacle that had been, and it still weighed on Margaret. Certain signs she could have spotted, because of, well, painful experiences from her past. They'd had to have a special assembly about it. Margaret had been unwell that day and couldn't deliver it. No, Tilda's hint of a love triangle, however unfathomable, had to be explored thoroughly, but neutrally, to see if Tilda was just trying to throw Margaret's attention off of herself.

"Five Irish Weddings," the waitress said, a few minutes later, arriving at their table, holding a tray that she slid carefully down onto the table with practised ease. The bar woman would have dropped them all. "Champagne and Guinness."

Margaret did a headcount. "Where's Pat?" she asked, noticing there was going to be an orphaned cocktail. Margaret had been too distracted by the bar woman and her explicit tattoos to notice her slipping away during the attempted conga.

"And why's Daniella not joining us?" Lise asked. She'd sat down on a bar stool.

"I thought she was just arranging something."

"Daniella," Lise called out to their guide, who had her back to them. Daniella turned her head. Lise raised one of the glasses. Daniella came over, took it and went straight back to her stool before anyone could protest. Not that Margaret would have. Probably busy researching an even more horrible restaurant for tomorrow, Margaret thought, and then chastised herself for her meanness.

Were they really going to drink this strange cocktail, the colour of mud? Was this how a mix of Guinness and champagne was supposed to look? Margaret sniffed the nearest flute to her, then grimaced. She raised it carefully to the light and inspected the rim. She realised she'd forgotten to bring any of her testing strips with her on this trip. *Damn.*

"A toast?" Lise said. "Who wants to lead it?"

"We should wait for Pat," Margaret said. "And for my orange juice."

"Pat disappeared at lunch too," Tilda said, her voice hinting at possible intrigue.

"As if she wasn't already mysterious enough?" Nele quipped. "How do you befriend a mute, exactly?"

"Proximity," Margaret said. "It's 90% of friendship. They've researched it."

Earlier, Margaret had gone to Pat's room during the ninety-minute slot on the itinerary reserved for rest and relaxation, to borrow some *Pepto Bismol* to help dislodge that disaster of a lunch, only to discover that Pat had gone out. She'd asked the hotelier, not that he deserved such a grand title, but he'd claimed not to have seen her leave. She'd waited in the lobby and Pat had returned just a few minutes before they were due to head out to Moritzbastei. Margaret had asked her where she had been, as innocently as possible, of course, but Pat ducked the question. And she'd arrived back so late she didn't even have time to go to her room to get changed.

Jim and Lise might think Margaret was paranoid, but she preferred to think of herself as prudent. While the adage that there's safety in numbers is overused, there's also an important truth to it. In a group, you have a larger range of skills and resources, therefore you can react better to challenges. You're also less likely to be targeted for crime and you have more people to notice abnormalities, like the smell of that cocktail. Cocktails, probably.

"I'll just go," Margaret said, reaching down and picking up her handbag. Sliding out from the edge of the booth, she let her handbag swing off her shoulder and into all the *Irish Weddings*. *Strike.*

"Margaret," Lise said, jumping back as a river of liquid flooded towards them.

"Sorry," Margaret said, rushing deeper into the bar. But she wasn't sorry at all.

Chapter 16

Tigh Neachtain #2 (Jim)

Jim pulled on the bathroom door and was assaulted by the smell--a mix of chemical cleaner and urine. Dark too, the floor sticking to the underside of his shoes. The row of three sinks along the wall had brass faucets, smudged and rusting, while two of the three mirrors above them were cracked. There were four urinals to the right, running down the opposite wall. Tristan had taken the one closest to the door and was whistling as he did his business. As the door thudded closed behind him, Jim shuddered. This place needed a deep clean. If it was his boozer, he'd have gone at it hard with a toothbrush. If you want to know how well a pub's run, check the lavs. Good cleaners are hard to find and only very committed pub landlords either keep looking, or roll their sleeves up and do the job themselves. If so, that's the kind of pub you want to drink at.

Jim sidled up next to Tristan, unzipping himself at the next urinal, in violation of the code that said he should have taken the one furthest away. "Just me, fella."

Tristan flinched. Jim pulled himself out, clearing his nose as he did so. "Cracking boozer this, right?"

"Yeah, I suppose." There was the usual snoot in his voice. "Consulted for them a few times. Brand's worth a fortune."

"Impressive. Regular in here, are ya?"

"I wouldn't say that, no."

It took Jim a little time to hit mid-stream, but soon there was a thick cascade of urine hitting the metal trough with a satisfying sound like rain on a metal roof. "Aaaaah," he said. "Where are you a regular, then, T?"

"I'm not a regular anywhere. Well, maybe at the Yoga studio. And there's this Ayurvedic Ashram out Abbeyknockmoy way."

The Irish and their names. Had that place lost a bet? Talking of bets. "Whose idea was it to go to the dogs the other night?" Jim asked, staring straight ahead.

Tristan's stream began to slow. "Who do you think? Gary's, of course."

"Ah, yeah, right." Well, that's not what Gary had said. Tristan shook himself dry, zipped and moved to the sinks. Jim was only halfway through; he had a huge bladder, trained from long shifts behind the bar and long nights cuddled up with a bottle, or four. He squeezed his pelvic muscles, trying to slow things down. He didn't want Tristan to get away. He managed to stem the flow, just about, and made it in time to catch Tristan just as he was turning off the tap and reaching for a paper towel, about to leave. It was now or never.

"Cracking watch," Jim said, grabbing Tristan's wrist with his unwashed hand. It was the silver Timex from the first day.

"Thanks," Tristan said, trying to pull his arm away, eyes narrow and confused. Jim clamped tighter to his wrist. "Could have sworn you had a different one yesterday? A silver Rolex. Trust paying you well, is it?"

Tristan's pupils became skittish, unsure of where to look. He was trying to pull his arm free, but Jim's hold was vise-like––a wide, unhinged smile on his face. He wanted Tristan on edge.

"Business is incredible," Tristan said, trying to play cool, to act like this exchange was normal, that they were still both on-script. "Thanks to my, I mean, the board's acumen."

"Acumen," Jim said breezily, with a short whistle. "That right, is it? Because a little dickie bird told me it's actually Seamus that makes business good? That he's the real mastermind." Jim released Tristan's wrist suddenly, knowing he wouldn't leave now, not after Jim had bruised his ego like that. *Control the tempo, Jim. Put your foot on the ball.* Slowly, he turned the tap on and washed his hands.

"It's a symbiotic relationship," said Tristan, balling up the paper towel he'd been holding and throwing it towards the bin by the door. It sailed through the air and landed about fifty centimetres short, Jim saw in the mirror. He left it there too, the sod. Tristan turned to admire himself in the mirror, sweeping a hand back through his gelled hair. "You shouldn't listen to everything you hear."

"That right? Because I also heard you like dogs, and I'm not talking about the ones with wagging tails that you take walkies, neither."

Tristan stared Jim down, shoulders back, mouth narrowing. He was taller, half a head or so, but not intimidating in the slightest. A face that perfect has never been hit, and if you've never been hit, it's likely you don't know how to fight, or that you've too much to lose to do so.

"Gambling's a scourge," said Tristan. "But what's any of this to you? Why don't you just enjoy your holiday and then you and your bald patch…" He mimed a plane taking off. Bald patch? That was a strange thing to call Connor.

"Well…" said Jim, taking a paper towel from the dispenser, drying his hands, balling it up and, mimicking a basketball player at the free-throw line, lobbing it at the bin. It landed perfectly in its centre. "Swoosh," Jim said, grinning. He got out his comb and studied himself in the mirror, neatening the sides of his hair, just as Tristan had done, only with his hand, not a comb. He turned and flashed his teeth. "I think it might be why you're trying to murder my friend. So, yeah, I suppose that's what it is to me."

Chapter 17
Moritzbastei #2 (Margaret)

Margaret hunted through another of *Moritzbastei's* many dark passageways. At an intersection, she stood on her tiptoes. Was that…? Over to the right? The beaked nose? *Maybe.* She excused herself, shimmying between necking lovers who should have got a room, and ducking under a low arch. Yes, it was Pat, back to the stone wall, scribbling into her notebook while talking to someone, their face obscured at this angle by the heads of several other revellers. The pub had a grungy student feel to it that made Margaret feel old.

She tried to part the crush of bodies to reach Pat but just as she approached, weaving and bobbing, trying to get a look at who her friend was talking to, a heavily bearded biker, clearly high as a zeppelin, cut across and stepped on her foot. "Owww," she said. "Watch where you're–" but her voice was too loud, and Pat spun towards her, her large shoulder bag slipping off her shoulder and falling to the ground. There was a clacking sound from somewhere, probably one of the many exposed pipes. The biker growled at her, baring teeth, eyes bloodshot. Cover blown, she hopped the last two metres to Pat, who was furiously gathering up the contents of her bag, spilt on the stone floor.

"Who were you talking to?" she asked.

Pat cupped her ear. *What?*

"Who were you talking to?" she repeated, louder, annoyed and unable to hide it. She scanned around again, faces and the backs of heads, but there were too many people around them, and too many nooks to hide in. So, she returned her attention to Pat, who was closing her notepad. "You're disappearing a lot. It's not safe. More than that, it begs questions."

Pat turned to the wall behind her, a giant info board that was festooned with adverts for concerts and events, seemingly five notices deep, new ads jammed on top of tattered older ones. She pointed at it and mimed writing. Margaret crossed her arms, angled her head, a mime of her own, one that said: *pull-the-other-one*.

Pat pointed behind Margaret, in the vague direction of the others, and gestured drinking. Before she could stop her, Pat slipped past and away. Margaret grunted but followed. They got lost once, but did eventually find their way back to the large main room near the entrance. As they neared the group's booth, she saw that there was a new face working behind the bar. The clumsy barmaid was gone. In her place was a bald man in a leather vest. He was in deep conversation with the young tattooed waitress, both gesticulating animatedly. Hopefully, Margaret's spillage hadn't caused too many problems.

"You found her," Lise said, when Margaret and Pat slipped in to take their places in the booth. The spillage had been cleaned up, as had the shards of broken glass, but no replacement drinks had arrived. The table was bare.

"We need something to distract us from our thirst," Tilda said.

"Margaret had an accident," Nele explained to Pat. "And then ran away."

"Sorry," Margaret said. "It was that lunch. I had to dash for the toilets."

The music grew louder, an English language pop love song about someone walking 500 miles to be with their lover. Connor was about three times as far away, but Margaret was sure he'd crawl that far to get to Lise, and over broken glass too.

"I love this one," Lise said, climbing up onto her seat in the booth with the help of Nele and Tilda's shoulders. Soon she was dancing, arms out, shrieking along to the chorus, in full hen-do mode now. "Girls, get up here." She reached down and tugged on Nele's arm. Nele fought her off.

"Girls?" Margaret shouted. "We're a long way from that."

"It's the Pretenders," Lise shouted. "Pretend."

"A lot of it about," Margaret said, glancing at Pat, whose mouth had dropped open. She followed her gaze to a handsome red-headed young man in a short kilt that was shimmying towards them, thrusting his hips to the beat, index fingers pointed at Lise. *Oh, no.* Was this why no replacement drinks had come?

"Girls," Lise mouthed, poking out her tongue, keeping her eyes firmly on him. "Have you been naughty?"

"He's going to be," said Daniella, who was now standing at the edge of the booth, next to Margaret, blocking her escape. Lise wagged her finger as the young man approached.

"No, no, no. Get out of here. I'm old enough to be your mother."

"Grandmother," muttered Margaret, under her breath. Everyone in this part of the bar had turned to watch. In fact, people were even coming in from the outside patio now, a crowd that, if not carefully managed, could become a mob. Margaret tugged on the end of her neckerchief, sinking deeper into her seat. Should she do something? But what?

"I said NO STRIPPERS," Lise shouted down at them. She

had, but maybe someone in Leipzig hadn't got the message? Daniella clapped to the music, head bobbing, not her genre but going with it. She let out a loud wolf whistle.

"Don't encourage him," Lise said.

"Doesn't look like he needs much encouragement," said Tilda.

"Any of you ladies order a hot highlander?" he asked, bouncing his eyebrows and giving his best smoulder. His accent was notably German, not Irish.

"Definitely not," Margaret said. "You must have the wrong table."

"And you must be Lise." He held his hand up and across the table for Lise to reach down and take it.

"Sure, she is." Nele grinned. Blocked in by Tilda on one side and Pat on the other, Nele ducked under the table and out of the booth before Lise could admonish her. Could Margaret leave too? Her breathing was rapid, but shallow. The attention. The awkwardness. The violation of privacy, trust and bodily autonomy. She wanted to be anywhere else, but that would mean abandoning Lise.

"I'm a gift from your highland man, Connor," the man said, putting a foot between Margaret's legs to climb up on the table, where he knelt in front of Lise. Margaret decided on a compromise. She'd get out of the booth but stay close. She tried to slide out but hit Daniella, who refused to move, even after she poked her several times in the leg and arm. The stripper, if that's really what he was, took Lise's hands and put them onto his thighs.

"Oh, I say," Lise said as she groped. "So firm. Like butternut squashes, yes?"

He stood up and slowly undid the last few buttons of his shirt and then whipped it off, spinning it around his head as the song changed to a techno version of *Danny Boy*. Margaret looked around, and, yes, just as she had suspected, every set of eyes in the room was on them. Pat was having a good time, pumping her fists to the music as Lise, hips thrusting, neck forward like a chicken, screaming and whooping with delight, was running her hands up and down the stripper's muscular, oiled chest.

"Get up here, Margaret," Lise said, turning and trying to yank her up onto the table. "If I have to, you have to." The stripper whipped off his kilt and threw it at Daniella, revealing just a string thong with the flag of Scotland on it. Lise laughed hysterically as he began grinding against her, pulling her in with a red scarf. Stuck in the booth, all Margaret could do to get away from this debauchery was to slide further and further back, until her body was pressed tightly to the leather of the booth, arms crossed, head turned the other way, looking over towards the bar. If she had a shell, something many people had accused her of, she would have retracted into it.

A bright light flashed twice. It was Daniella taking pictures with a small camera, grinning to herself and giving the occasional thumbs up. A bolt of electricity shot down Margaret's spine. This was the only photo anyone had taken on the trip so far, and it was of Lise's hands on the exposed, commendably pert buttocks of an almost-naked stripper-stranger?! Did Lise want this? Was she in control of the current situation? The stripper kissed Lise on both cheeks and slid his hands down her body, dropping down onto his knees. Two more flashes. She needed to find something else to focus on. Behind the bar, barely visible between a sea of heads, she spotted the bald barman struggling to manoeuvre the shambolic barmaid from earlier out towards the exit. The poor woman was hanging off his shoulder, head lolling around, being almost dragged away. Why?

Daniella stepped away, perhaps wanting to get more into the shot for the next photo, and Margaret practically leapt from the booth. She squeezed her way to the bar and then followed it round. The heavily tattooed waitress had come to help the male barman and together they were now winching their colleague towards the door. She seemed to be so drunk that she was barely conscious, and so in an even more vulnerable state than Lise.

"Kein Guinness mehr," the barman said. *No more Guinness.* The waitress said something in response, but it was lost in the ruckus, whooping, and chants of *"Ausziehen, ausziehen."*

That one she knew. *Take it off.*

Wasn't the stripper naked enough for these people? She turned back to see how much more compromised he'd become. In front of the booth, two young women were dancing wildly, bumping their hips into each other and into Daniella, who almost dropped her camera. She bumped them back with more aggression. One of the younger women, with exceptionally blonde hair and an exceptionally tight, short, silver dress, tried to climb up on the table too, which was when she slipped--or was pushed? She stumbled, grabbing aimlessly for a secure hold and found… the stripper's crotch. Falling backwards, she pulled him back to the floor, and he yanked Lise down with him into a puddle of limbs, a ripped thong, and with it, very indecent exposure. Margaret looked away. The shame. The embarrassment. She could barely breathe. A memory. With too many bodies in front of her, she pushed her way out, stumbling for the exit.

Chapter 18

Tigh Neachtain #3 (Jim)

"Ridiculous," Tristan said, turning and striding out of the toilets.

Jim tutted loudly; he'd blown his fuse again. It was just the calm of the guy, that was what had pushed his buttons, made him want to ruffle him, find out what was under that brittle, *Brylcreem*-front, but it had been too much, too soon, and if he made it back to the others, Jim would have lost his chance. He hot-footed it out after him, the sounds of the bar growing louder as he walked down the narrow corridor, past a couple of young'uns swapping tongues, him squashing her against the wall, hand on her bottom beneath a faded black Pogues poster.

Youth. Jim mourned it. Tristan was only two steps ahead. "T," Jim said, with urgency. "Wait up." He needed a new strategy and, with the bar looming, needed it quickly. "Thing is… I need your advice," he blurted at the back of Tristan's head. Appeal to the man's ego; he obviously had a prodigious one.

Tristan stopped. Didn't turn, just stopped, arms by his side. Jim squeezed next to him, sideways, back to the wall and gave him a friendly wink, affecting a funny-us-meeting here kind of vibe.

"You need a murderer's advice?" Tristan turned just his head, not even trying to hide the mixture of scorn and irony in his voice. There was an uncomfortably small amount of space between them. Jim smelled the sour waft of those disgusting flaxseed, seaweed and sealion sperm, or whatever else was in those horrendous smoothies.

"Right," said Jim. "*Yeah.* Sorry about the old, you know…" He flicked his head left, towards the toilets. "That was the stout talking. Don't usually touch the stuff. Get on with it like I do with my ex-wife. *Someone*, I meant to say. Someone is trying to murder Connor. Not *you*, obviously. And this is your town. You're the big man around here. I'm just a stupid tourist. That's why I need your help."

"Yes," Tristan said, smoothing a crease from his shirt. "That's both true and not."

Jim scowled. "What's the *not?*"

"It's true you need my help. It's not true that someone's trying to murder Connor."

"How can you be so sure?"

"How can you?"

"Look, we want the same thing," Jim said through gritted teeth. "Really, when you think about it, which you obviously have, because you're a man who sees all the angles."

Tristan's eyes narrowed, but Jim could tell he'd beaten the defence and was charging in on the goal. He just had to hold his nerve. Tristan wiped his nose again. Another bump in the toilets before Jim had arrived, perhaps? Wouldn't be the first, that's for sure. It was snowier than Lapland most Friday nights in a British public house. Behind Tristan was a small, empty nook, enough space for two, or three maybe, if everyone knew each other well. Jim pointed at it. Tristan sighed, considered it for a moment, and then acquiesced. Jim followed him there.

"What do you want from me?" Tristan asked after they sat down.

The Accidental Murder Club

"I want the same thing as y–"

Tristan tutted. "You keep saying that, but the thing is, Jim." He placed his hands calmly on the tabletop, fingers splayed, affecting the haughty air of someone who found the conversation beneath him, but was too dignified to make a stink about. "I'm the youngest Vice President in McGinley Knitwear's hundred-year history. I drive a midnight-blue Range Rover Sport with custom plates. I date models, and only models. I haven't cooked a meal or washed a plate in over two years." He smiled beatifically. "I'm living my dream life, Jim. And you are..." The smile faltered. "Not." Satisfied that he'd put the matter to bed, he closed his eyes and tipped his head back. "Sorry about the tut. Tuts aren't very Buddhist."

"You're V.P., are you?" Jim asked.

Tristan's head tipped forwards suddenly, eyes re-opening. "That's what I said, isn't it?"

Jim coughed, clearing his throat. "Right. Well, here's the thing, though, T. Indulge me a minute, will you? Because I knew a man once, see? Wasn't much when I met him, one of those BIG I AM's, to tell you the truth, when he barely had a pot to tinkle in. But then he started a business, right, one of them tinternet things." Jim mimed typing. "Websites, and the like. Shopping through your computer. No idea why any bugger would want to do that. I mean, what's wrong with Tesco? They do a bloody good job, Tesco, won't hear a bad word said about them. Some of the finest sausage rolls in the business," Jim noticed Tristan's eyes glazing over. "What was I talking about?"

"I'm not sure."

"Sometimes my mind sort of wanders–"

"Computers. Someone in one of your pubs?"

Jim clicked and, while doing it, thought of Pat. "Cheers, T. I remember now, the fable of Leisure Suit Larry. So, anyway, a couple of years back, Larry sells his company, right? Gets very, very rich. For a while, anyway, because the last time I saw him, must have been what a year, maybe eighteen months ago, he's looking worse than before. Holes in his shoes. Bedraggled is the word, I think, is it not?" Jim bounced his eyebrows. Tristan had pretended he'd spotted something fascinating on the tabletop. Jim carried on regardless. He loved a good story. "Dark rings beneath his eyes and his Ferrari's long gone, isn't it? Back in those awful tracksuits he used to wear, which is how he got that name. He's driving a shit-brown, rust-covered Ford Escort." Jim tapped the table three times with a finger. Tristan looked up. "So, I ask around, as I do. I'm inquisitive, you might have noticed that about me?"

Tristan rolled his eyes.

"Sure, you have. Anyway, turns out he's lost all his money, ain't he? That he has a particular fetish." He over enunciated the next two words, opening his mouth wide. "F-I-N-A-N-C-I-A-L D-O-M-I-N-A-T-I-O-N. Know anything about that, T?"

Tristan bristled. "Can't say I do, no."

"Well-"

"Or want to."

"Rude," said Jim, miming having been punched. He collected himself. "I've started, so I'll finish. It's the funniest thing, it is. Basically, you find women, also on the tinternet mostly, and give them access to your bank account and they just take what they want, when they want. They tell you about it first, like, tease you, and all that. Send you photos." Jim laughed. "And that's it. That's what did him in." He rubbed his hands together. "Incredible, right? Sure you've not heard of it?"

Tristan wiped his nose with the back of his hand. "No."

"In my day we called it having a wife." Jim laughed. Tristan stayed stiff as a plank. "Point I'm trying to make is, some people, they don't feel alive unless they've got one foot dangling off the old cliff edge. Know what I mean? Connor's a bit like that, and I'm wondering who else around here might be, too?"

Tristan locked eyes with Jim's and gave him very slow shake of his head. "I'm not like that."

Jim blew a raspberry. "That's a relief then. That's just great, that is."

"We done?" Tristan asked, going to get up.

Jim beckoned him to sit. "I know a bit about cars too," Jim continued. "My mate, Sparky, regular at my last boozer, *Red Rum*, he used to buy and sell them, he did. Wizard with a motor, Sparky. Could hot wire anything in under a minute. Your car, what did you say it was?"

"Midnight-blue Range Rover Sport."

"Custom plates," Jim added, with a knowing nod. "That's a very expensive car, that is. That's what, an €85k ride?"

"€99k, what with the heated seats."

Jim whistled. "Heated seats? Holy moly. Crazy that the Trust is paying you enough to drive a car like that round a small, flat town like this."

If Tristan thought his hard stare was intimidating, he was underestimating the kind of men Jim had served over the years. He'd even had Reggie Kray as a regular in *The Chariot*, in Tottenham. They'd had a disagreement one night about what was and wasn't an acceptable use for a snooker cue. Things had got a bit heated. A day later, Jim heard he was being transferred and now, with the reputation the Kray brothers later developed, Jim often wondered if that might have saved his life. When most people saw conflict, they turned the other way. Jim, well, he lowered his head, lifted his shoulders, and ran straight at it.

"Maybe it's leased?" Tristan said, with another wipe of that leaky nose. "You ever think about that, Sherlock?"

Jim set his jaw. "Thing is, T, you're showing a lot of flash, and you're the only one showing it - 'cos that mansion's sure seen better days. A lot of peeling wallpaper and don't get me started on the hollowed cheeks of the staff in that sad-sack of a factory out there on Bleak-Ass Island. So, I know you're not spoiling them." He settled back a bit in his seat. He was enjoying himself. "And talking of sad sacks, Seamus is modesty personified, poor bastard. His only indulgence is that extra sodding jumper, and he knits them himself. Yet, I'm also hearing about all these record years? I think you've been dipping your hands in the cookie jar." He mimed just such an action.

"I never eat sugar," said Tristan. "Sugar is poison."

"It's an idiom."

Tristan banged his fist on the table. "Don't call me an idiot."

Jim waited, sitting perfectly still. Tristan seemed to catch himself after this little outburst. He took a deep breath, letting his anger dissipate. "Sorry," he said. "Fist banging is not very Zen. Look, we at the Trust do a great job, and we're rewarded for it, sure, but not more than we deserve."

"Who decides what you're rewarded?"

"We… well… the board."

"Not anymore, not according to the will. Only maybe you can't walk away, can't let the Trust be dissolved? Someone will notice the debts, won't they? The missing money. The dog track money. The coke money." Jim wiped his nose one way then the other, fast, and with a certain drama, making sure Tristan got the point. "So, you're feeling the pressure. You need Connor gone, one way or another. You need everything back to how it was."

"You have everything wrong," said Tristan, moving to get up. "And we're done here."

Jim gestured to stay sitting. "Am I, T? Am I? Because what I know, or rather what I saw, was that when we were back in the bar, when you reached up to the newspaper rack, the nearest paper to you was The Sun. You read The Sun? With the nice big titties on page three." Jim mimed two full breasts with his hands. "And the footie on the back, and yet, what did you choose? The sodding Racing Post. I've also noticed you're always on your infernal Blackberry. Crackberries they call them, right? Fits in your case. Always checking something, aren't we? And that David, was that the guy's name, down at the track? Knew you well, and you knew your way around well, too, for someone who'd never been there. And for a place with such cruddy wayfinding. I also know that it was your idea to go there. And that you were pocketing our cash and yet paying for our bets on a gold credit card. A company card, I'm going to bet. Seamus probably has one in his wallet. Account number ends with 0211, which, coincidentally or not, just happens to be Willie and Sophie's wedding anniversary. Romantic, from the old geezer. It's small things, sure, but you stack up a lot of small things and you get a big thing." It was his turn to tip his head back and bask in the blazing heat of his own intelligence. He was so magnificent, he wanted to applaud himself.

Tristan's nostrils flared and his hands balled into a fist, or at least they tried to, but he couldn't seem to close the right one.

"You're an idiot."

"Name calling Zen, is it? We're not enemies, T. You want things to stay how they are?" Jim raised his palms. "I want that too. I don't care about McGinley's finances, not really. I just want to take my friend out of here, alive and happy and excited for his wedding, back to his lovely dull life in Suffolk, with his cracking, crackpot of a wife--to paint, drink, and frolic away however many good years he's got before that liver of his is finally fully pickled, his wrists are arthritic, and he can hold neither brush nor bride."

"It's not me," Tristan said, wearily. "I don't want to hurt Connor."

"Really, son, because from where I'm sitting, you've a whole lot of motive."

Tristan's mad animal glare subsided. He steepled his hands and his voice lowered, suggesting conspiracy was coming, and Jim was invited. "Look, when the wedding announcement came out, and I'm not proud of this, but I thought it was best for the company, I hired a private detective. Asked him to look into Lise. A new love at Connor's age? Come on. And any idiot, well, other than Seamus, could see Willie's days were numbered. The lights went out long before the house was abandoned, if you get my drift?"

"You wanted to know if it was a real wedding or if she wanted his money?"

Tristan nodded. "We didn't know what was in Willie's will, or even if he had one. And if he didn't…"

"Connor."

Another nod. "But the detective didn't find any skeletons in her closet. Tricky to research too, with her being, you know, a Kraut and all, but he did find some in Connor's."

Jim sat up. "Did he now?"

Tristan hung his head forwards to peek around the edge of the booth, checking if they were being overheard. "Tad," he said, when satisfied they were not. "He not only looks like a skeleton, he's one of Connor's. Very strange he should be hanging around all week because, really, they shouldn't be friends. And I'm surprised they even let him in here."

"In Neachy? Why? And why would Tad want to kill Connor?"

Tristan took a deep breath. "You didn't hear this from me, because obviously I don't gossip. But maybe it's more about who Connor killed?"

Chapter 19

Moritzbastei #3 (Margaret)

Hand on the brick wall, sucking in great lungfuls of evening air, Margaret knew that no matter what she was feeling (emotions arise and pass away, emotions arise and pass away), she couldn't stay outside long––her friends were in danger. She watched as the almost comatose employee was lowered into the back of a taxi. Was she drunk, sick, or something more sinister? The sloppy movements and smashed glass when they'd ordered their drinks made Margaret favour drunk, but then the smell of that Irish Wedding? The taxi pulled away and the barman and waitress had a short, hushed conversation before walking back inside. Margaret took one last long inhale and skipped back down the stairs behind them into *Moritzbastei*. Using them like an ambulance, she rode their strip stream all the way through the dense crowd until they made it to the bar.

The stripper was holding an ice-pack to the bump on his head with one hand, the other shielding his crown jewels. A different female staff member was there with a first aid kit and applying a bandage to the woman who'd climbed up onto the table just as Margaret was leaving.

"That's why you shouldn't dance on tables," Nele said, a wry smile of delight on her face, perhaps enjoying the drama. Pat was next to her, writing something down in her notepad, balanced on her thigh.

"I did get hurt," said the stripper.

"Do you have another cool pack for his crotch?" Tilda asked.

Lise turned towards the bar, now staffed again. "Shouldn't we at least get a free drink to calm our nerves?" she shouted over to the barman, who was opening the first of several bottles of beer he'd lined up. "Or because of the show we just put on for your punters?"

"I'd love to buy you a drink," said the biker that had stood on Margaret's foot earlier, when she'd been snooping on Pat. He was leaning against the bar, his meaty forearm very close to Margaret's hip. "You lot are my type," he eyed Margaret up and down. "Rowdy."

"Not interested," Margaret said, turning her friend around by the shoulders. "Now let's get out of here before the stripper wants a tip."

"I don't mind his tip," Lise joked.

"Lise," Margaret barked, almost shoving her away from the stripper, bar, and booth, back towards the exit. She'd spotted a free table in a secluded corner.

"And we can afford our own drinks, thank you," Tilda said, looping her arm through her sister's--pro-active physical contact. Had the stripper broken down more than one boundary?

"Where were you anyway?" Lise asked her.

"I made a run for it," Tilda said and Lise whispered something in her ear, which blossomed into a conversation Margaret couldn't hear, and in German, but she was happy to see it happen--the tension in the group had been becoming unbearable, and the sisters were the primary cause of it.

The Accidental Murder Club

Margaret pointed at the empty table, not because she wanted to sit there but with the sisters out of the way and Pat prone to disappearing, she might get a little time alone with Nele. The woman was still a puzzle to her, one that she didn't really like the picture of, and so didn't relish spending time trying to solve, but solve she must.

"I'll get the others," she said, turning back to look for Pat, who was watching the crowd, nodding her head to the music. She glanced at Margaret and made a T with her hand. *Toilet.* Nele was scowling at the biker, the staff, and, well, just about everyone, as usual. While she had no idea how long Tilda would keep Lise entertained, or when Pat would emerge from wherever the hell she was actually going now, this was a chance too good to pass up. After another deep breath, she took the few steps to Nele, whose arms were crossed over her chest. "Now that was really something, right?" Margaret asked, trying to sound casual.

"I'm not sure who I feel most sorry for. Him, or Lise," Nele agreed, meeting her eyes only briefly before returning them, narrow and condemning, to the stripper and two gate crashers.

Margaret laughed. "His entrance seemed to surprise you less than the rest of us."

Nele lifted a shoulder. "Takes a lot to shock me."

"I could shock you," said the biker, listening in.

Margaret spun around. "Since we've already rejected your advances, loudly and enthusiastically, to invest further time in us would be irrational. This is a private conversation. Leave it."

The man grumbled, but picked up his beer and moved away. "Not bad," Nele said. "Not bad at all."

"Did Lise have a stripper at her last hen-do?" Margaret asked, ducking the compliment, as there was no time––she had to get them off the present and into the past, somehow, however ungracefully.

"How would I know? I wasn't there, for obvious reasons,"

Nele said, her foot tapping. Her tone was petulant, as if being forced to explain something to a simple-minded child.

"Because it was hard to see the two of them get married?" she asked, crossing her arms to mimic Nele's stance, and to brace herself for the reaction to this question, as this was not the obvious reason that Nele wouldn't have attended. That was geography. Lise and Dieter married in England after he came out of prison, but before Germany's reunification.

Nele's jaw clenched and her eyebrows sank. "Why would it have been hard?"

"Because you were a three, I suppose? That's what Lise always said, but then they were obviously more. And then you were two and a leftover."

Nele pursed her lips. "I would have come to the wedding, if I could have. And we're still a three, thank you very much."

"Right." Margaret nodded. "Sorry." She wasn't sorry. Nor were they a three, because two of the three had moved away decades ago and one of them was now very much dead.

Nele sighed, and in it, Margaret got the sense that she was being forgiven. "Life was fine here in the DDR." Margaret had noticed that Nele never used the English name, sticking rigidly to DDR. "We had everything we needed. Everything that mattered."

"But the regime was so cruel to its citizens."

"Just those that broke the rules," Nele said through all of her teeth. "Every country in the world protects its borders. Even your lot, over there on your tiny island."

"We can leave our tiny island, though."

"You could leave the DDR, even to go to the West. There were legal ways. Dieter just jumped the gun."

Margaret glanced up and saw what might have been Pat's grey hair through a tangle of bodies. Was she coming back already? Margaret had to hurry. "Lise was pregnant."

"Even more likely that they'd have given him permission then, if he'd just waited. He was always so impulsive."

"Maybe," Margaret said, while actually thinking, that's a very unreasonable and uncharitable take on things. "I can see why he never wanted to come back after the wall fell though. That all those years in prison would have been traumatising."

Nele rolled her eyes. "So many things are 'traumatic' these days," she said, air-quoting the word with obvious derision. "And the DDR hasn't existed for a long time. He could have helped build the next thing. Not that we had much say in the terms of the reunification."

Margaret was so busy with Nele and watching for Pat that she didn't notice Lise and Tilda sidling up next to them. "What you two jabbering about?" Lise asked. "And why didn't you come join us?"

"Politics," Nele said, with relish.

"Sorry," Margaret said. "We were just waiting for Pat, so she'd know where the group went."

Lise groaned. "Ladies, there will be no politics tonight. Especially not with Nele. She won every debate at university."

"I thought you studied music?" Margaret asked.

"We all had to do courses in Marxist and Leninist theory," Nele said nonchalantly. Lise fanned herself. There was a strong smell of sweat. It reminded Margaret of the changing rooms after P.E., another class she did all she could to avoid teaching.

"I hated those courses," Lise said, then clasped her hands together. "Okay, ladies." She looked around. "Let's get that nice Scotsman back over here for a do-over. Did we hire him for the dance, or for a full hour?" She held eye contact with each of them, as if deciding who among them would have hired him. It could have been Connor, of course. It was his style, but Margaret took nothing about this trip or their relationship for granted.

"Where's Daniella?" Nele asked, "Perhaps she knows?"

"Doubt it," Tilda said. "How did we end up with her, anyway? I could have shown you around."

Margaret realised that she'd forgotten about Daniella, and that at no point in the past thirty minutes had she felt any concern for her, nor acted to protect her, as she had for both Nele and Tilda, neither of whom she felt close to. It was pretty damning and now even Tilda had soured on her, having stuck up for her just two nights ago, before the Ghosts and Ghouls walk. "What she lacks in experience, she doesn't exactly make up for in enthusiasm," Margaret said.

Tilda smiled. "That's what I like about you Brits, even your insults sound like compliments." She moved across to the bar. Margaret hoped she was getting the bill.

"She was good value for the money," Lise said, scanning heads. "Much cheaper than the others Nele suggested."

"We'd used her at the University as a translator sometimes," Nele said. *Cheaper*, Margaret thought, that was how they'd ended up with *Tschüss Tours*--and look what had happened there. Sometimes it's not buy cheap, pay twice, it's buy cheap, pay with your life.

"Let's dance," Lise said.

"Let's not," Margaret countered. "I'll just go help Tilda."

She went to the bar where several small shot glasses were being loaded onto a tray. "Yours is just orange juice," Tilda said.

"And the rest?" Margaret asked, not able to recognise what the mud-brown coloured liquid might be.

"*Jägermeister.*"

"What's that?"

"You don't know *Jägermeister*? It's like a thermal spa for the mouth. Really popular here."

"I've not heard of it, no." Margaret picked up a glass and sniffed. Then two more. Then her orange juice. All fine. She took another sniff of the *Jägermeister*. While she had no frame

The Accidental Murder Club

of reference, she found what she sniffed––a strange mix of cola, cinnamon and wet leaves––to be quite pleasant.

"It's a half bitter with more than fifty secret ingredients," Tilda said. A fact Margaret decided she'd memorise and use casually later to impress Jim.

"Let me pay," Margaret said. "I knocked over the other drinks."

"I've already done it," Tilda said. "And don't worry about it."

The barman leaned over the bar and handed over the receipt on a pad to be signed, which Tilda did with a large flourish of bad penmanship. Her handwriting was more expressive than Margaret would have guessed. The barman checked the signature and returned Tilda's credit card with a brisk nod. Margaret picked up the tray, and they returned to the group. Pat and Daniella were now also there. Tilda handed out the drinks. *"Zum Wohl,"* Lise said, leading the toast.

Margaret knew that phrase had come up in German class, but couldn't remember the meaning. *"Zum Wohl,"* she repeated with the others, knocking back her orange juice with the disappointing realisation that it was going to be a long night yet.

Chapter 20

Tigh Neachtain #4 (Jim)

Jim spent the rest of the evening trying to find an excuse to be alone with Tad, who didn't drink or smoke and, well, did nothing much of anything really, except glower, tight narrow frown on his tight narrow face, looking like he'd just seen the Grim Reaper out of the corner of his tight narrow eyes while all around them, the rowdy mob of revellers were getting looser, sillier, louder, and ever more bashful. A lock-in had been called, which got an even bigger cheer than the band's second encore. Connor was just about as happy as Jim had ever seen him—swaying as he walked, spraying smiles and loud, shouted jokes at anyone who'd listen, and plenty more who weren't. Jim drank it in, while pretending to drink. When no-one was looking, he was actually surreptitiously pouring his Guinness into one of several glasses on the table behind them. He needed his wits about him. On that table were a group of lads in their early twenties, a Gaelic football team or so it seemed, by the sheer girth of them. They were always on the move, flirting with anything in a skirt, and didn't seem to notice that they never ran out of booze.

Gary stayed close to Connor's side, very much the Robin to

his Batman. Tristan was glued to his seat, and while projecting calm, had to be fuming inside about that interrogation as he sipped from his second alcohol-free beer, eyes on his phone until... those eyes flashed wider in alarm and his Blackberry slipped from his hand like wet soap, plonking down onto the table.

"You alright there, fella?" Jim asked. "Seen a ghost?"

Tristan picked the phone up carefully, squinting at it like someone trying to read a map upside down, and then handed it to Jim. "Do you know who this is? Mo-ritz-bastian. Sounds German?"

Jim leaned over the table, took the phone and blinked down at the picture on its piddly little display. He smacked his lips and pulled the screen closer. There was a shape there, of that he could be sure. It kind of looked human. No, wait, two humans? He turned it one way, then the other. Then. Hang on. It couldn't be, could it? The blue hair. Ah, and there was Margaret, trademark serious half-smile on her face and neckerchief around her neck, nothing else visible, as above her, a shirtless hunk had his hands on Lise's hips and was planting a kiss on her cheek. The sign behind them, hanging from the ceiling, said *Moritzbastei*.

Jim turned to see how far away Connor was. He was yelling something in the ear of the fiddle player. Jim had known the lasses were going to this bar, it was on Margaret's itinerary, but a stripper?! Fair play to them. Why should the boys have all the fun? Who would have booked him, though? He scratched his stubble, considering it. It certainly wasn't Margaret's style, too prudish. They called her Sister Margaret behind her back. Patty the mute? Hmmm, maybe. Pat was a wildcard. It was certainly Lise's style; he considered if she might have arranged it for herself, but then why send the picture here, and to Tristan, of all people? Who even knew Tristan existed? Jim wished he didn't exist. No, it made no sense unless someone was trying to...

Tristan was shifting nervously in his seat. "Who sent this?" Jim asked.

"I don't know."

"Don't mess me around."

"Really, I don't know." He clamped a hand on his watch and twisted it. "I just got it. It's not from any of my contacts."

"It's Lise," Jim said.

Connor came back to the table and put his arm round Jim's shoulder. "Really rocking in here now," he shouted. "You didn't tell me Delores works behind the bar, Gary." Gary was in conversation with one of the football team and didn't hear.

"An old paramour, Jimmy," Connor continued. "The longest legs in all of Galway, old Delores. Can suck a–" His eyes wandered down to Tristan's phone. The idiot was still holding it out at arm's length, as if it would explode if he moved it even an inch.

"What you two looking at there, then? Skin flick?" Connor asked, snatching the phone from Tristan's hand. "Give us a gander, then?"

"I'm sorry," Tristan said, raising his hands. "It was just sent to me."

Connor stared at the small picture, and his face grew suddenly stern. Gary appeared next to him. "What's going on?" he asked.

Connor tilted the phone so Gary could see.

"I'm sure there's an innocent—" Tristan said, sliding back in his chair.

"Innocent, you say?" Connor's voice firmed and his breathing became louder and faster.

"Yes, just some harmless fun."

"A fella kissing MY woman is harmless to you?"

"You know, just a playful bit of–" Tristan was like a man in a sinking boat furiously bailing water.

"ADULTERY," Tad barked, the first thing he'd said in about twenty minutes.

Tristan, in his chair, was now flush to the wall. "Well… I mean… no–"

"And for some reason, you're the first person to know?" Connor said.

"Yes. That's not–" Tristan didn't have time to abort this attempted sentence because Connor's furious expression broke into laughter.

"There better bloody well not be an innocent explanation," he said, slapping the table. "Good on her. Hope she slipped him some tongue." He looked around the bar and then feigned an exaggerated, droopy mouthed sad face. "Now where's my stripper, boys?" He handed the phone to Tad. "Have a good look, Taddy. That's my Lise. A beauty, right?"

"Why would they send it to me?" Tristan asked, still more confused than relieved.

"You're the only one with a fancy phone?" Connor offered.

Gary pulled his phone out from his trouser pocket. "Nope, I got it too."

"Weird," said Jim, a prickle running down his spine.

"The subject was FOR CONNOR. All caps," Tristan said. "I don't know the number."

"Same here," said Gary. Tad, who had been looking at the picture, dropped the phone, letting it clatter onto the table.

"It's indecent," he said. "Unbecoming of a lady her age."

"21?" Connor joked.

Tad ignored him. "Of any lady, of any age."

Connor jutted out his jaw. "Watch your mouth, Taddy."

"*He* will be watching this sin," said Tad, eyes to the ceiling and then back down. "Sin of the flesh."

"Aye, it is," said Connor.

"No better sin, neither," Gary added.

"You're certainly one to talk of sin," said Tad.

Gary puffed out his chest. "What do you mean?"

"What kind of example does it set?" Tad asked, pointing at the phone. "To Men? Women? Children?"

"That women are entitled to bodily pleasure, just like we fellas?" said Connor. "What's wrong with that?"

"We are entitled to nothing," said Tad, looking up, slower this time. "Everything we have been given is a gift. A gift from Him."

"What happened to you, Tad?" Connor asked, shaking his head. "When are you going to drop this bollocks righteous act?"

"Our acts are all we have."

Connor pointed a finger. "Yours is getting boring. I remember us sharing a few lasses, sometimes even on the same night. Remember that redhead?" Jim's ears pricked up. "Siobhan, we met out of the back of—"

"Enough," Tad said, slamming his fist onto the table. The pint glasses jumped. "This place, you people. The sin. It's enough." He got up in such a rush his chair fell back as he stormed towards the exit, knocking a couple of that football team out of his path as if they were mere skittles.

Jim gave him a head-start and then got up too.

"Just going to drain the snake," he said, and then apologised to the young lads as he passed. He didn't need to pee, could have gone until morning, even, but he did need one thing urgently--to get to the bottom of this plot, which had taken a new, weird turn with the introduction of this photo. Having failed to kill Connor, was whoever was doing this now settling for merely stopping the wedding? But then it must have been orchestrated by someone who didn't know Connor well? Didn't know he wouldn't care if Lise cavorted with a stripper?

Jim didn't want to get too close and spook Tad, so he

lingered by the service hatch, checking he wasn't just going to the toilets. When he passed them, Jim chased after him and towards the front door.

Outside, it was still balmy weather for May. He took in a mouthful of fresh air as he passed the huddle of people smoking by the entrance. On the right, someone had passed out, their head resting against the wall. He looked around for Tad, who was a hard man to lose, on account of the fact he was the world's tallest, meanest priest. He spotted him standing in the shadows at the entrance of an alleyway, near a tattoo studio whose mascot was, ironically, the grim reaper. Tad was staring into a street full of revellers, arms over each other's shoulders, songs being sung into a warm night made warmer with alcohol and brotherhood. A smell was tickling Jim's nostrils... cooking oil. About six doors down was a chippie. Jim thought, fondly, of battered sausages.

Two men came down the street, saw Tad, then crossed to the other side. Guilty consciences, Jim wondered, or fear? Talking of fear, he felt that too. Jim could handle a Tristan, knew his sort well enough––high testosterone and narcissism, but brittle as brie. But a Tad? Tad was an enigma. And his reaction to the photo had been so extreme, Jim wondered if he had something to do with it. It was like those politicians who are strongly anti-gay and then get caught rustling the bushes of a beauty spot, playing how's-your-father with handsome, stubbly strangers. Jim didn't know why Tad would want the wedding scuppered, but Tristan had made some pretty big hints, and, anyway, that's what an interrogation is for. Jim took a deep breath and tried to slow the race car lapping tracks in his mind. He was a skilled amateur sleuth, a real man of the people, he reminded himself, and Tad was just a man. A scarred, sharp tongued, viper of a man––but just flesh and bone, like Jim. Less flesh, sure. Approaching him, Jim felt like he was about to take a last-minute semi-final penalty against Schmeichel, another man who loomed larger than life. The streetlight cast Tad in silhouette. Jim noticed he'd balled his fists. He shook them out and then slipped his hands into the pockets of his leather jacket.

"Not now, Tourist," Tad boomed.

"Fine night, aye?" said Jim, smiling and gesturing to the street full of revellers in various states of inebriation, bouncing like pinballs between Galway's various well-stocked, well-aged, well-attended bars. He'd like to bring Margaret here one day, show her a good night, get her on the Vodka Oranges, at long last. That was her drink, he was sure of it. He had a knack for telling people's drinks. Tad's chest inflated, then deflated, as he stared down into Jim's eyes and then deeper, into his soul. "I said–"

"What's got into you?" Jim asked.

"Sin tried to," said Tad.

"It's just a stripper, Taddy. And I've heard a rumour you weren't always so whiter than white, weren't a, well, you know…"

"Servant of our Lord and Saviour, Jesus Christ?"

"Yeah." Jim shrugged. "Pretty much."

"The tongue has the power of life and death, and those who love it will eat its fruit."

Jim frowned. "Err? Margaret always tells me I should eat more fruit and veg. That I can't live on sausage rolls alone, but I mean, I've lived this long, haven't I?"

"Who is Margaret?"

"Never mind. I guess what I'm saying is that I'm not so up on my scripture. The only altar I worship at is Chelsea Football Club." He might have pretended to be a Tottenham fan to win the good graces of that lad in the airport, but his loyalties were to West London, his dad's team. His daughter's too. Granddaughters alike, he hoped. He should really take them down to the Bridge. "I was hoping we could have a conversation man to man?"

Tad let out a peculiar, high pitch grunt. "I've been washed clean by the blood of the lamb, Jim. My past is behind me, and I live in the present, serving only the Lord and my boys."

Jim smiled, slowly. "Fine, fella. It's Connor's past I'm interested in, anyway. I think someone is trying to kill him, see, or at least trying to stop the wedding from happening. Maybe both. Maybe more than one person. It's a bit of a muddle." He swirled a finger by his ear, emphasising the craziness of it all. "First it was the chandelier at the wake. Now this thing we're not mentioning with the stripper. I hear other things are happening too, over there in Leipzig. Attempts on Lise's life. I haven't told Connor about them because I don't want to worry him, but I'm telling you because I know you can keep a secret." He took a deep inhale, almost as if he was smoking, which he'd like to have been; that ciggie with Gary had helped take the edge off that conversation. "I'm worried, Tad, is all."

Tad blinked slowly, not like he needed to, but because he'd heard that's what humans do. "This is not the confessional booth."

Jim worked a knot out of his neck, trying to act calmer than he felt. "You know, we're not so different, you and I, T. I was a barman all my life. The pub is the atheist's church, no? More secrets spilled there than in your confessional booth, even. You can keep your past, that's your business. I just need your help with the present. With who might have a reason to want Connor dead?"

That grunt again, longer this time. "How long do you have?"

"About three more days is all. The jokes you were making while he boxed. About him being a killer? What was that about?"

Tad's eyes held Jim's with a paralysing intensity. "You move easily through the world, Jim," he said, after ten awkward seconds of silence. Jim waited for this to become either a question or an accusation, but it became neither. Tad's sentences were just statements of fact that he entered into the public record. Jim stayed silent, trying to wait him out. Half a minute passed before he accepted that wasn't going to happen.

"Connor moves easily too," Jim said. "Gary doesn't. Seamus doesn't. You don't."

Finally, the big man seemed to crack, his eyes sweeping from Jim's and around to the pub's sign, then he seemed to dig deeper into himself, somehow finding an even sterner expression that pulled his bottom lip out and up. He looked like he was taking part in a gurning competition. "I used to…" he said, more of a moan, and then there it was, another impossibly slow blink. "But some things, once seen, cannot be unseen. Acts once acted cannot be undone."

It sounded like he was about to start in on another sermon. "What did you do?" Jim asked, assuming he must be hinting at something specific.

Tad sighed and the whole street seemed to shudder. "I helped a friend. Helped my family."

Silence again.

"But no-one helped you?" Jim guessed. "I know there was an incident." He looked over at the pub. "Here, even. I've all the pieces, mate. Just don't know how to arrange them. Help me."

Tad lowered his eyes, took a deep breath, raised his head, and blew air out. Jim wondered if he'd ever been a smoker too, if that's why he was standing out here, if he'd dropped the drug, but kept the tics. He reached up and ran his finger slowly along the scar on his cheek. "This was our first ever local. We started coming here when we were twelve, nay, thirteen. Babbies, really."

It felt strange to hear Tad use a word like *babbies*, a soft, sweet word, a diminutive. Nothing about Tad was that. You could use his little toe as a hockey stick. "But everyone knew

Connor and his family. They turned a blind eye to our age. We had energy then. Big mouths. No fear. Ireland was a different place too. A divided place. Connor, he had the biggest mouth of..." Tad faded out.

Jim kicked a pebble with his foot. Thirty seconds passed during which Tad stared over Jim's shoulder at the brick wall between the tattoo studio and a tanning salon. "Is there more coming?" Jim asked. "Because I kind of feel like there should be. That Connor did something here. Hurt someone?"

"They sold my ease," Tad said, swinging his attention down like an axe onto Jim. "The ease that you have. They sold it for fifty thousand pounds. Ironic, really, when I think about how many worse things I did after prison. And for much less money. But that night, in this pub, that was my original sin."

Jim stumbled back a step. "What was the sin?"

"A man lost his life."

"Connor killed him? In a fight? That's what the boxing stuff was about?" Jim guessed, his mind rushing with the implications.

Another rub of his scar. "They say *I* killed him."

Silence. "Who says?"

"The Public Record." Tad made the sign of the cross. "The Lord took him is what happened. A bar fight. Nothing special. But sometimes it's enough, if His desire is strong. A head hits a brass bar at the wrong angle." He whacked the back of his head with his palm, hard enough that he should have given himself whiplash. "A miracle, almost, but miracles are real. 'Tis a neutral word, miracle."

Jim put his head in his hands and rubbed. So, he finally had his answer, but he didn't like it. He thought about a story an old friend, Gobby George, had told. George was trying to be a musician, but pulled the odd weekend shift at a boozer down in Crouch End. It had a regular--a nice local lad, soft, or so Gobby George had said. George didn't know his name and maybe only a few in the pub did, as he kept to himself, didn't cause no trouble. Only drank halves. Anyway, one Friday night Gobby George is working and Half Pint's there too, on a bar stool, minding his own business when some loudmouth messes with him. No reason at all for it, just cruising around looking for a fight. Half Pint tried to shrug loudmouth off but couldn't. Loudmouth threw a punch, Half Pint ducked it, and then pushed the guy. *Once.* Hard in the chest. Loudmouth fell backwards, hit his head on the edge of the bar. Died a day later. Half Pint went to prison, not because anyone thought he deserved it, but because the law required it. Manslaughter, or so they called it. Tragic case, everyone agreed.

So, it had happened at *Neachy* too, with Connor as its Half Pint. They needed to pin it on someone, and Connor's family had the money to make it go away. Jim removed his hands. Tad's eyes were still boring into him.

"I'm sorry," Jim said.

"As am I."

"Connor's family paid you."

"We were dirt poor, always had been. They sold my future for fifty thousand pounds. I was an amateur boxing champion, and I had a mean temper, Jim, if you can believe it." He took another deep breath, not that Jim was convinced he needed oxygen. "The shoe fit and they made me wear it."

Hell of a motive, this, Jim knew, a grudge left to simmer for fifty years. But what could he do with it? If it was true, Tad was dangerous, and wasn't just going to confess. He had to tread carefully. "And now you're resentful. I get it. I would be too. I'd be more than that. I'd be livid."

"No," Tad said. "I've made my peace and found my calling. I do good in the world now. I teach my boys to avoid the fights, or to end them quickly."

"Why are you telling me this?"

Tad stroked his long chin. "You wanted my story. This is my

story. But it's not *me*. You saw the good work I do today out on Inishmore."

Jim had seen something, alright, but he would have described it differently. That place could use help, hugs and heating.

"And you have Connor's ear," Tad said, accusingly.

"If it's money you want, why not get it from McGinley? Or from Seamus? He practically ripped the jumpers off his body earlier to give them to you."

Tad lifted his head. *Really?* the look seemed to say. "I don't *want* his money. Don't want anything from his rotten family. But I *need* what's *owed*. My boys *need* things––tutelage, warm beds, three square meals. A new boxing ring. For some of them, unlike the McGinleys, it's not too late. I can give them what I didn't get. A future. A chance. It's a noble cause. A righteous cause."

Righteous Path, Margaret's school. He'd not expected to find any similarities between Tad and Margaret, but here was one. Was that why Margaret had been a headmistress for decades? Was there something in her past she was trying to make amends for? She rarely talked about her family or her youth. She was a closed book of indeterminate genre. Jim clicked his back. Focus, lad. She's not the case. This is the case. Someone trying to murder and/or frame Lise and Connor.

"They used to help. The Trust shut it down. Connor *is* McGinley now. And you have his ear," he said again. "No history. No baggage."

Jim sighed. "No-one has his ear. Well, maybe one person, but she's not here." Jim remembered the photo. "Did you hire the stripper?"

"Think, man," Tad hissed, tapping his head.

"Okay, okay," said Jim, flustered. "I'll take that as a no." Talking about the photo would end the conversation. He had to swerve. "How long did you go to prison for?"

"You never leave prison," Tad replied immediately.

Fifty thousand to go to prison for a murder, well, no, a manslaughter you didn't commit? As just a teenager? That was heavy. Jim could see how that would brand a man, especially a man who looked like Tad. How it might give you a reputation you can't shed. How you might have to lean into it even, become what people say you are, just so they leave you alone. It certainly gave Tad a motive for murder, but if he really did want money, he wouldn't get it by killing Connor. He'd need Connor alive, unlike Tad and Seamus. Which left only one other person.

"Gary," Jim said. "Does he have a reason to want Connor dead?"

Tad looked down at his hands. "Everyone has a reason."

"Was Gary in the fight?"

"Not a brawler," he said, dismissively.

"What is he then?"

Tad's head jerked up. "An almost."

"An almost-murderer?"

"I'm not the only one who didn't get what he deserved from Connor and the McGinley family."

Jim tried to picture Gary's face–the veiny, bulbous nose and lightly pockmarked cheeks–was it a killer's face? He nibbled on his lip and looked over at the pub's door, which opened to vomit out a woman in an impossibly short yellow skirt. How was she walking in heels that high? He'd never been in to heels, a lot of men were, he knew, but he didn't see the appeal. Focus, Jim. Gary. He'd been thinking about Gary. Was he a killer? His instincts–and he put a lot of stock in his instincts–said no. He swivelled back to Tad, only to find that he'd vanished. He looked down, half expecting to find a cloud of smoke.

"Motherlicker," he said. "We were just getting somewhere."

Chapter 21
Moritzbastei #4 (Margaret)

The tables around them were packed with revellers, but there was still a surprising amount of decorum. Margaret found it interesting to see how table service reduced the mixing amongst the inebriated crowds, well, as long as you didn't have a Scottish-Irish stripper to unite the room, and people didn't have to wait so long for their waiter or waitress to arrive that they gave up and made their own way to the bar. Also, Germans didn't seem to follow the flawed English round system, which only sped up drinking, she now realised, tying everyone to the recklessness of the fastest drinker. Okay, so maybe some things were better on the continent. Not the music, which had switched to wordless, repetitive beats––just a lot of thump, thump, thumping really. Music was not really Margaret's thing. She didn't mind classical or, at a push, a bit of Abba, but all-in-all, she preferred the written word to its sung cousin. Period novels, now those she loved. Anything at least a hundred years old. She believed strongly in the merits of the Lindy Effect and only sought out contributions to popular culture that had proven themselves over decades. She doubted anyone would be venerating this music in a hundred years. It just sounded like robots malfunctioning.

Tilda and Lise were enjoying themselves on the other side of the table though, somehow. Their conversation had slipped into German a while back and remained there, discussing a family holiday, at least the last time Margaret had tried to follow along. Nele was drinking but not getting any merrier. Pat had become lost in something about an hour ago and was furiously writing in her notepad. Margaret would try to move them outside soon, which would be like shepherding a rowdy mob of mountain goats, at least looking at their sloppy gestures and wild, unfocused eyes. She'd meant to not let them drink at all here, not after that suspicious first round, but it had proved impossible. Every time she turned around, they had a different drink in their hands, minor celebrities since The Incident. They wouldn't believe her if she told them her suspicions someone had drugged their *Irish Weddings*. She had too many of those and too often, and why not? It's better to mistake a rock for a bear than a bear for a rock.

"When *did* you last drink?" Nele asked her.

"Hard to say," Margaret said, although it wasn't - it was a date tattooed just as loudly on her mind as their waitress had inked her body.

"There's no point arguing with her about it," Lise said, trying to put her arm around Nele but missing and slumping forwards, catching herself just before she head-butted the table.

"Exactly," Margaret agreed. She had her reasons, and anyway, there was no point in arguing with drunk people. There wasn't much point doing anything with drunk people, that was why she avoided them so fastidiously. Jim was a bit of an exception. He was a happy, funny drunk, but still, after fifteen minutes of him, she'd usually had enough and would make her excuses.

"If Jim can't get her to drink, then no-one can," Lise added, much to Pat's delight, and some double-handed clicking. Margaret clenched her teeth and gave her mute friend a scorned look. What was it costing Pat not to talk? Did it frustrate her? It would have driven Margaret insane.

"Jim?" Tilda asked, face flushed. This would have been a good moment to talk to her again, to see if she was willing to give up more of her secrets.

"Jim's her partner-in-crime – don't deny it," Lise teased with a swirling finger. "They have a murder club. *Accidental.*"

"You murder people?" said Tilda. "You should be more secretive about that."

"How do you murder people accidentally?" Nele asked.

Margaret smiled. "Thank you. It's a stupid name, right?" she said, neglecting to mention they were at it again, the club, trying to work out who wanted to stop this wedding, and were willing to kill both Lise and Connor to do so.

"Shall we try for another of those *Irish Weddings?*" Lise asked. "I didn't even get to try mine before Margaret knocked it over."

"I asked earlier, and they said no," Tilda said.

"We have to get up early anyway," Margaret said. "To spread Dieter's ashes."

"Not that early," Nele said. "Another round is fine." She waved to the young waitress in the black tank top. "Could we have another round of *Irish Weddings?*"

The young woman bit her lip. "That one's out," she said. "Sorry. Anything else I can get you?"

"But I never even got to try it?" Lise said, with pleading in her voice.

The waitress's mouth narrowed. "Nothing with champagne or Guinness in it. *Tut mir leid.*"

I'm sorry. "You've run out?" Lise shouted, trying to be louder than the chatter from a table of young men, probably students.

The waitress's eyes wandered up and right. She paused for too long, then said, "Yes. We're sold out."

"Oh, that's funny," Margaret said. "I could have sworn I saw at least a half dozen bottles of it in the fridge when the barmaid, you know, the one with the shaky hands, poured our first one." She looked over towards the bar. Behind it was the man in the vest, the one that had helped carry the barmaid out.

"Listen," the waitress said, leaning lower to the group. "We had a bit of an incident earlier. Someone drank something they shouldn't have, and they started to feel very sick." She looked visibly uncomfortable telling them this. "But it's not a big thing."

"From an Irish Wedding? But you made them specially for us, no?" Lise said.

"Yes," she said.

"But you wouldn't need to order if you were working behind the bar, right?" Margaret said. *The puffy eyes, the shaky hands, the bloated face*––all signs of someone getting high on their own supply. Tainted supply, if Margaret was right. The waitress looked towards the bar, then back and gave a small nod. She brought her index finger up to her lips. "We sent her home in a taxi with a bucket to puke in. She probably just had too much, but my boss has stopped selling Guinness and champagne, just as a precaution. Everything else is good, of course."

"Hmm," Margaret said. "That inspires confidence in this establishment." Seizing the moment, she got up. "Girls, we're calling it a night." She gestured towards the doors.

"I suppose we should be fresh for Dieter," Lise said, with awkward phrasing.

"Fine," Nele said, with a tone that suggested it wasn't really.

"Sorry again," the waitress said as the others got up and retrieved their coats from the nearby stand. The waitress moved over to the next table, notepad out, ready to take their order. Margaret helped Lise into her coat.

"That was lucky then, wasn't it?" Lise said. "That you knocked them all over?"

"Yes," Margaret said. "If you believe in luck.

Chapter 22

The Mansion's Trophy Room (Jim)

After a long night at *Neachy,* an unusually sober Jim sat in the trophy room of the mansion. It was nearly midnight but there was no way he could sleep; he was too wired. He needed to tell Margaret all he'd learned. He shivered as his eyes traced over a rack of antique looking rifles, trying to ignore the feelings of guilt as he met the very dead gazes of the dozen stuffed animals hanging from the walls; the cold, black, dead eyes of an expired deer, rabbits, mink, and even a full-size bear in an attack pose. He opened his mouth, chucked two aspirin in, and swallowed (was the headache alcohol or stress?) with the help of a big glug of water. He picked up the rotary phone, determined to reach Margaret in Leipzig. They were an hour ahead, but this was too important to wait, and if they'd been at *Moritzbastei* having a wild night out, they might not even be back yet.

BING BING Please hang up the handset and try again.

"Dang blasted argh," he said, slamming the phone down. He never called internationally. He was forgetting something. *What though?* He looked down at the paper she'd written her hotel's number on. The plus: it had to be the plus. But there was no plus on this stupid phone. He shoved his fat finger into the small circle again and dragged it right, then waited as it slowly returned to the left so he could dial the next number. What did she say about the plus?

Please hang up the handset and try again.

With all the heavy wooden furniture and menagerie of murder, the room felt stifling. He stood up and paced, muttering to himself, then sat down, took a moment, closed his eyes, and concentrated. *Two zeroes.* That was it, that was what she'd said, that replaced the plus. *Hallelujah.* He dialled slowly, methodically, his tongue poking out of the corner of his mouth. "Come on, Margaret, pick up," he muttered, listening as it rang, his heart racing with anticipation until…

"Abend," a man's voice said, slowly and ponderously, as if awaking from a long hibernation.

"It's Jim for Margaret."

Long pause. "You want to go to the market?"

"Jim," he shouted into the phone. "In Ireland. I need to speak to Margaret."

"There is a weekly market. But it's the middle of the night."

"*Margaret.*"

"This is hotel. You need room, *Ja?*"

"Yes." He looked down at his information pack. "Room five, please. Margaret Barrett."

"Room five?"

"Uh-huh."

"You wish to *sprechen* with Frau Barrett."

"If *sprechen* is chat, then yep, you got it, fella."

"Who fell?"

"Just put her on already, wise guy."

"The phone is not working in room five."

"Go get her then. I'll wait."

"It's too late."

"It's important."

"Call again in the morning."

"It's an emergency, man. Just do it."

He heard a loud sigh and the handset being dropped onto something hard. Jim blew out a long, annoyed breath. Why did anyone ever leave England? He knew that every time he did, bad things happened. First Berlin, now Galway, and whatever shower of excrement was raining down on Margaret over there in Leipzig.

"Jim, that you?" A familiar voice.

"Margaret, thank God you're there," he said, trying to steady his voice. "Sorry I'm," he looked down at his watch, "it's so late, I couldn't find the plus and then that fella on reception was half asleep."

"I expect he was fully asleep, actually."

Jim laughed; it was great to hear her voice. "It's great to hear…" He stopped himself. "Well, I'm at the mansion in Galway. In the bloody trophy room, of all places. I didn't even know they had a trophy room. No actual trophies, just taxidermy death. I was actually looking for the second lounge, got lost, but anyway, there's a phone and it's quiet." He couldn't shake the feeling of being watched by the stuffed animals. "Enjoy the stripper, did ya?"

"Excuse me?"

"The stripper, Mags. Did he, err," his throat tightened, "dance with you, as well?"

"*Margaret*, and he certainly tried, but—"

"Succeed, did he?" Jim aimed for nonchalant, but feared he missed.

"Let's concentrate, shall we, Jim? How do you know about the stripper? Was it you who arranged it?"

"Me? *No.* Cracking looking fella, wasn't he?"

"Depends what you're into, I suppose."

"What are you into, if you don't mind my—–"

"Jim," Margaret said. "If you didn't set it up, how do you know about it so soon?"

Jim filled her in on the details of the evening, and the photo Gary and Tristan had received. After he finished, she stayed silent. Knowing her, she was probably whipping up a quick spreadsheet to model the odds and motives and opportunity costs, to see who was most likely to have arranged it. "Are you absolutely certain it wasn't Connor who booked him?" she asked, after what felt like an age.

"I've asked him a dozen times. Nothing doing."

"But can we trust anything the man says? He's a born... well... I don't know what he is exactly. Showman? Provocateur?"

"Shit stirrer?" Jim offered.

"Vulgar," Margaret said. "But not inaccurate. I wish I'd had him as a young man in my school. I'd have put him on the straight and narrow."

"He's older than you. And I think he prefers winding and wide." Jim waited for laughter that didn't come. A great cross, but no one there to head it in. Margaret was a tough crowd... of one. That was probably why he liked her so much; she really made him work for it. Not that there was an 'it', despite all that hard labour.

He told her about his interrogation of Gary.

"He's lying," she said. "I believe, but quite strongly. It's the specifics," she said. "When people lie, they don't omit. They're afraid they will seem vague or effusive, so they invent very elaborate, very detailed scenarios. The fact that he remembers having to rush back *and* the specific hand he had? Highly improbable. And does Seamus seem like the type of person who'd want a visitor in his room after midnight? The other times you've mentioned him, he was always leaving to go to bed early with a migraine. It stretches credulity."

"Yeah," Jim said, annoyed that she'd so succinctly condensed into words what he knew, instinctively, just by reading the man's face as he'd said it.

"If he was in your room, he could have taken a photograph of the itineraries and contact numbers. If he's willing to lie about that, he'd also lie about arranging the stripper."

"He contacted Daniella, you think? Makes sense and based on what you've told me, she's shadier than a north-facing veranda in November in Newcastle."

Still no laugh. "Almost certainly," Margaret said. "She was the one with a camera too, taking pictures. A camera she didn't have earlier when Lise wanted a photo in the Museum." She paused and exhaled. "The whole sordid affair is troubling and scandalous."

"The wedding?"

"No, the stripper."

Scandalous? It was just a stripper. Jim had had hundreds in his pubs over the years, walking in in fur coats and little else to liven up the birthday party at table seven, or the wielders' work's do in the function room. Harmless.

"Gary knows Connor well, doesn't he?" Margaret continued. "So, the stripper would be a strange approach. Connor's just not the jealous type. Maybe he left the method to Daniella?"

"Oh, I forgot to say, Jesus, how did that slip my mind? Connor is also a murder–" Jim stopped himself. Connor wasn't a murderer. You can't chuck words around like that. He'd thrown a punch or a shove, maybe. Nothing Jim hadn't done fifty times. "There's one other thing you need to know," he said, nibbling on his bottom lip. "Are you sitting down?"

"No, but I have pre-emptively braced myself."

He wasn't sure if this was a joke, and so just barrelled forwards into the story of Half Pint and Loudmouth, then on to Tad's confession, how he was paid off by Connor's family, how he took the rap for the person Connor had inadvertently killed. She listened in a silence only punctuated with three gosh-es, two loud gasps, and one, "well I never."

"The poor man," she said at last, when Jim finally finished his tale of woe, and fell, stuffing knocked out of him, against the back of the chair.

"Which one?" he asked.

"All of them, I suppose. Tad, Connor, Half Pint, as you call him. It's easy to make mistakes, as a young person, to pay a much higher price than you deserve."

"Are you talking about you or your students?"

"Do you think Lise knows all this?"

Ducking the question. "No chance. She didn't even know he's loaded. Nah, this is on Tad's record, not Connor's, so why sully his good name? And anyway, it was just a tragic drunken accident. A one-in-a-million. Wrong head, wrong angle, wrong brass bar."

"Don't be flippant, Jim. That head belonged to someone's child."

"Still. He's not a murderer, not even a manslaughterer, not in my book, anyway. And it's a good book, my book."

"Facts are facts. The law is the law. Criminal records are criminal records."

"Yeah, but in this case, the facts and the law and the records don't match. Connor's family paid to change them."

Another long pause. "Why would Tad tell you all this?" she asked.

"Because I squeezed him like a ripe and juicy lemon, Mags. He couldn't not tell me. It was glorious."

"Margaret," she corrected. "And how did you squeeze him, exactly, like I don't already know, since you only have one approach. Aggressive."

"How dare you," he said, but laughed as he did so. "I'm like a Swiss army knife, me, a different gizmo and gadget for every situation. I'm a social peacock."

"Chameleon?"

"That too."

"No," she said. "You're a hammer, so all you see are nails. Hang on, someone's coming." Margaret's voice grew louder. "Hi Pat." *Pause.* "None of your business." *Pause.* "Okay, fine, it's Jim. Why do you look like you've seen a ghost?"

Jim strained to hear what Margaret said next in the game of charades. With Pat, it was always a game of charades. "Someone rammed you? That makes no sense. Oh, they rammed the door. What door? The car door? You're shaking the room key. Oh, the room? Your room? Someone broke into your room? What? Why? Hang on Jim," Margaret said into the phone, her voice suddenly clearer. "That makes no sense. Pat, there's nothing valuable in there, right?" *Pause.* "I have to go, Jim."

The line went dead.

Chapter 23

Pat's Hotel Room (Margaret)

Margaret followed Pat into the elevator, which was still working, somehow, even though the safety sticker suggested it hadn't been serviced since 1987, before the Berlin wall had even fallen. Ordinarily, she'd have insisted they take the stairs, but they were also a death trap of loose floorboards and missing handrails. Few people knew that stairs are actually, statistically speaking, much more dangerous than elevators. Pat closed the security gate and while she did so, Margaret tried to read her facial expression––the large eyes, the trembling bottom lip. Had someone really broken into her room? Was that why she looked so scared?

The lift came to a swift stop with a disconcerting thud. Margaret pulled back the squeaking metal security gate this time, and they stepped out and turned right, then right again, their feet fast on the threadbare carpet, past the brown corpse of a dead plant by Pat's door, which was ajar. She pointed at the frame and mimed kicking. Margaret kneeled and checked the wood. It had split at around hip height, suggesting, yes, that someone had rammed or kicked it open.

"While we were out?" she asked.

Pat shrugged. Margaret remembered Pat's absence during the scheduled rest and relaxation time. It could have been then.

"Did you tell the manager? Is anything missing? Is he calling the police?" Too many questions at once. Slow down, Margaret. Pat nodded again. Then shook her head. Stopped. Shook it again. *Yes,* she had told the manager, *no,* nothing was missing, *no* the police hadn't been called.

She followed Pat inside. Pat's money and passport were still beside the bed, but it looked like a herd of elephants had trampled the rest of the room. Clothes were scattered all over the floor, as were pillows and blankets. The cover of the complimentary Gideon's bible had been torn off. There were scraps of pens and paper everywhere and a roll of duct tape near the bathroom door.

"Why would someone break into your room, Pat?"

Pat shrugged, feigning an innocence her face didn't show.

"Let's write," Margaret said, miming. "This is too important for charades." Pat took a piece of paper from the bed and a pen from her handbag. 'Robbery?' she wrote. Margaret spotted a fifty euro note on the other sideboard. "But then not steal your money?"

'Interrupted?' Pat wrote.

It didn't look like they'd been interrupted. It looked like a wild party that reached its natural conclusion. And why would Pat have left her money and passport out like that?

"It makes no sense," Margaret said, thinking aloud, tapping her chin. "Unless they were looking for something specific." *Something Pat had hidden.* Pat was always up to something, on this trip in particular, with the furious note-taking and the frequent absences and the meeting she was clearly having earlier in *Moritzbastei*. But then why bring Margaret up here, why even tell her about the break-in, if she wasn't ready to include her in the conspiracy?

"*Unglaublich,*" said a voice from the hallway. *Unbelievable.* It was Herr Schulze, the hotel owner, hair unkempt, shirt misbuttoned. They moved nearer to the door. Herr Schulze was kneeling and inspecting the wood. As usual, he looked like he had both just woken up, and woken up in a hedge. "What did you do, *Ja?*"

"Us?" said Margaret, incredulously. Was she here because Pat needed her voice to deal with Herr Schulze? "Why would we … why would Pat break into her own room for which she has a perfectly working key?"

He stood up and put a finger in his ear. "People do all sorts of crazy things. You sit hotel, you see. One man, he makes the *kacka* on his own bed then calls down and complains there is *kacka* on his bed." Herr Schulze sighed. "Now I write break into own room on list of crazy."

While it was a relief to hear him say more than one word, it was a disappointment that they were all so stupid. "Ridiculous," Margaret said, stamping her foot. "Someone has broken in here, obviously. You need to call the police."

"The *Polizei?* No." He shook his head, with perhaps the most enthusiasm she'd seen him display so far. "*Nein.* Did they take something?"

Margaret looked at Pat. Would she admit now that they had to get the police involved? Pat considered it, lips pushed together, then lowered her gaze to the floor. "But they ransacked the room," Margaret said, throwing her hands up in the air. "Come on Pat. Stop playing games."

"Is messy, *ja,*" he said, looking between them and into the room. "But how people keep room is not my business."

"CCTV?" she asked. "We need to know who was on this floor. Cameras?"

He pulled the finger out. "*Spiel.*"

Spiel… spiel… she wandered her memories. *Game,* that was it. Ah, dummy cameras. Margaret rubbed her temples. She had a migraine coming. They were getting nowhere.

"Our cleaners are very thorough," he said with a straight face, somehow. "I call them. They come tomorrow morning."

"Thorough?" Margaret said, taking her finger, bending down, and wiping underneath the bed, then holding her blackened finger aloft. "She can't sleep here tonight, and not only because of the mess. It's not safe. The person might come back."

"Is perfectly safe," Herr Schultze said testily, closing the door to demonstrate it was still possible to do so. "You can use the chain lock, see?"

Margaret and Pat moved closer. There was a five-centimetre gap between the door and frame. Enough that you could see out into the corridor. Pat wagged her finger. Not that it was necessary. There was no chance Margaret was going to leave her here tonight, alone. She'd never have forgiven herself. "She needs a new room."

Herr Schultz reopened the door. "We're fully booked."

"I find that hard to believe," Margaret said.

He turned. "*Warum?*"

"Because it's a fleapit," she said. Not only was the whole place falling apart, it smelt worse than a teenage boy's armpit, had more dust than the Serengeti, and they rarely saw any other guests. The reception was usually empty, besides Herr Schultz snoozing behind the desk. If you were going to pick a hotel to break in to, this was a good one. She wasn't sure if Herr Schultz understood the word fleapit, but he seemed to get the sentiment and stormed off muttering to himself.

"Sorry," Margaret said to Pat. "I reacted emotionally. Now Herr Schultz won't help us. Not that he was helping us. But maybe he would have?"

Pat flashed her teeth.

"Should we call the police?"

Pat gave a thumbs down. Margaret sighed, her suspicions

confirmed. The burglary was personal. "And you're sure nothing's gone?"

She watched Pat's eyes roam over the room, stopping at one spot for just slightly too long. A fraction of a second only, but sometimes, that's all you need. Pat shook her head.

"Is there anything in here someone might have wanted to steal?" Margaret pressed. "Something you might have hidden, perhaps? Something to do with whoever you met earlier in *Moritzbastei*?" She was losing control of her voice. She tried to slow down. Pat wasn't her enemy. *Probably.*

Pat crossed her arms. The problem, Margaret surmised, was that Pat didn't respect her. Pat hadn't been at Cahoots very long. Didn't know enough about Margaret's career as a headmistress, as a national Teacher of the Year winner. That was twenty years ago, but still. Maybe Pat thought it was easy to run an internationally recognised reform school, compared to being a hotshot investigative journalist, but she was very wrong. Digging her nails into her palm, it was to her teacher's tone that she turned. "I'm sick of your games, Patricia Williams. I think you're in over your head, and that you need my help. That's why you brought me up here."

Pat's nose twitched. She took a deep breath. Margaret could feel her resolve breaking. "So," Margaret pressed, foot tapping. "Here's what's going to happen, okay? I'm going to, very quickly, and with commendable ease, find whatever they were looking for. And when I do, you're going to let me in on what's really going on, okay? From then on, you're going to work with me, and we'll get you out of the pickle you're in. That Lise is in. That we're all in." She clapped her hands twice, then let her voice brighten. "Okay?"

Pat considered it, her head angling, then stretched out her left arm and made a beckoning motion with her hand. *Game on.*

Margaret let out a wry smile. Pat responded to forthrightness and games: good to know. Margaret moved to the corner of the room, just to the left of the door, and took a moment to appraise the space again, as if for the first time, letting her eyes wash over everything. She knew every nook and cranny where you could hide something in a dorm room. She'd found it all--cigarette, knife, love letter, condom, baggie of cannabis or coke, tab of acid, even next week's English literature exam on Macbeth stuffed inside the stomach of a plush Paddington Bear. And a hotel room was nothing but a dorm for adults.

She rubbed her hands together. If she had something she didn't want someone to find, but that she might need to access, where would she put it? Certainly not in the safe, she knew that for starters. Safes are the first place a thief would look. Their default codes are rarely changed, and are well known in the right, or rather, wrong, circles. Nor would she put it anywhere near the desk, because the mind associates documents with desks, and her hunch was that it was a document. Everything was falling apart in the hotel's bathroom, so that left no safe, dry space to use. Carpets are easily lifted, so that was out. She walked forwards and moved down one side of the bed, stopped, turned around, traversed the other, testing the floorboards beneath her feet. *No*, she decided when they all squeaked underfoot--whatever Pat had been hiding, she'd probably taped it to the underside of a piece of furniture. No-one likes bending. And the lower it was, the harder for the eyes to spot. She walked slowly around the room again, stopping at the shoddy desk, watching Pat's reaction from the corner of her eyes, the slight curl on the upper lip that said *you're wrong*. She already knew she was wrong. Pat had already given her a hint as to where it was. Suddenly, she grabbed the lamp from the nightstand, got down on her knees and, cursing the state of the carpet, shined its beam under the bed to the centre. A lump. Yellow. She shimmied in after it, mentally accepting the dry-cleaning costs to come.

"Aha," she said, from under the bed. There, in the middle,

sideways, next to the supporting pillar in the centre of the bed, was a folder duct taped to the frame. A pretty good, but not great hiding spot. It took some effort to find it, and if you weren't slim, you'd need to lift the whole bed up to do so. Bending. Carpet burns. You'd need to be committed. Margaret was committed. She ripped out the folder held by the tape, slid back out, and waved it in front of Pat's face.

Pat clapped, slowly. *Okay*, she wrote. *You're in.*

Margaret brushed the dust off her knees. She didn't want to be in this room any longer. It was like it was shouting at her. "You're going to tell me everything, but not here. This room is compromised. We're sleeping in my room tonight. Get your things."

While Pat packed some clothes into a cloth bag, Margaret thought more about the hiding place. It was okay, sure, but if someone had wanted those documents badly enough that they'd kick a door down for them, would they not also have the commitment to shimmy under a bed in search of them? She thought about how, often, when she stayed in hotels she'd leave a little bit of money in an obvious spot, then stash more somewhere much more difficult to find. The logic being a thief would find the small notes and think that was it. She looked around at the room again. Lots of effort had gone into making it seem like they'd thoroughly searched the place. But something about it was off. What if it was a decoy? She went to the bathroom. The toothpaste cap was open, a pet peeve of hers. It dried out so quickly. She was always on her students about it, the girls were never the issue, but the boys... Would Pat really have left the cap off? She was a very organised, methodical person. She squeezed the tube. A runnier than expected white liquid came out, chased by toothpaste. She didn't recognise the smell, but then this wasn't her brand. She took the tube and threw it in the bin. "I've thrown out your toothpaste," she said. "It had dried out. You can use mine."

A few minutes later, they reached Margaret's room. Her hand shook nervously as she put the key in, eager to get inside. She let Pat enter first, then shut and locked the door, securing the chain lock as well. Pat was sitting on the armchair, the folder clutched tightly to her chest.

"You're going to tell me everything," Margaret said. "First, do you know who's trying to kill Lise?"

Thumb down.

"Do you think someone *is* trying to kill Lise?"

A shrug.

"Well, what are you working on then? A story?"

'Yes,' Pat wrote, then crossed it out and changed it to 'probably'.

"About Lise?" Margaret asked.

'No.' Slowly, she handed Margaret the folder she'd taped under her bed. Margaret rushed to pull the half-dozen pages out. *Careful*, Pat wrote. These documents obviously meant a lot to her. Margaret sat down on the edge of the bed and began to read. She was torn between studying each page slowly or quickly scanning them to see how they might all fit together. She decided on the latter, perhaps worried Pat would change her mind and take them away. As she held them, her hands were trembling. The first two pages were poison pen letters addressed to Lise. Mouth opened in disbelief, she turned them around to show Pat, as if she'd not already seen them.

Pat blinked, heavily. The third page was a ransom note, like something from a movie––the letters wildly different colours and fonts, cut out from magazines. Her mouth fell open and she looked up at Pat, who was wiping a tear from her eye and seemed to be having a very different emotional reaction to this document. The next pages were several news clippings about bomb attacks in different countries, Spain, Mozambique, and England, glued next to each other. Two mentioned Tick-Tick, the undercover operative they'd learned about in the Museum.

The Accidental Murder Club

The last page was a map of living communities, including Cahoots, which had been circled.

"Tick-Tick?" Margaret said. "You think he's still active?"

'Maybe', Pat wrote.

"He's the one after Lise?"

Pat tapped the word again.

"Hmmm," Margaret said, disappointed that even if they were going to be allies now, they weren't working on the same thing. Tick-Tick was a monster, sure, but if there was no link to Lise, then Margaret had more pressing problems––keeping Lise alive. Pat mimed sleep, pressing her hands to her face.

'More tomorrow', she wrote. 'I drank too many shots.'

Margaret groaned. She was tired too, of course she was, but her mind was whirring; there was intrigue everywhere. She'd not be able to sleep for hours, if at all. She wanted to go get Lise, bring her to her room too, just so she'd know they were all safe. She'd stay up all night watching them, if she had to. But Lise would just become hysterical, telling her she was crazy, paranoid, ruining a hen-do that seemed to be self-ruining. If Pat slept, Margaret would be free to study the documents for as long as she wanted. Pat cleaned her teeth, climbed into bed and patted the space next to her and its empty pillow. It was a small double bed, really more of a large single.

"No," Margaret said. "I'll take the chair."

Pat turned the page she was writing on. 'Don't be silly.'

"It's about respect," Margaret said. "And decency."

Pat rolled her eyes and laid down. That was fine. Margaret pretended she was getting ready too, removed her mascara, cleaned her teeth for the recommended two minutes and an extra one, as always, and then flossed. Soon, Pat was snoring lightly. How do people fall asleep so quickly? Especially after all that had just happened? Margaret had struggled with insomnia at various points in her life, although things had improved since she'd retired. She curled up on the room's single-seater sofa and studied the documents slowly, starting first with the ransom letter, which read:

'Shut up, or I'll shut you and your family up.'

Hands trembling again, she took some deep breaths. Was this sent *to* Pat? Pat had it, so that seemed the most likely, and her reaction to it? But who would have sent it, and why? Tick-Tick or someone else Pat had investigated? It wasn't addressed to anyone but... she made the obvious connection to Pat's vow of silence. Surely you wouldn't take a threat that literally? And would a renowned spy do this just because she was looking into him for a 'maybe' story? Pieces of the puzzle were missing, she could tell. There was much more that she needed to know. She moved to the map of East Anglia with a number of living communities circled, then crossed out. Only two were left uncrossed, one of which was Cahoots. How did that connect? Did it connect? Was it why Pat had ended up at Cahoots in the first place, pretending she was just another resident while actually secretly researching them all? Margaret felt a sharp stabbing pain in her lower back and shifted in her chair. Community was so fragile, and hers was in danger.

Next up, she read and reread the poison pen letters. They were typed, not handwritten. Where were the envelopes? She checked the folder again, tipping it upside down. Two envelopes fell out. They both had a UK stamp and postmark and had been sent to Lise at Cahoots. All had the same postmark––'South Devon'. Dated at various points in the past few months. The letters were short and sharp.

'Lise,

Your life is at risk. No-one is what they seem. Stay close to home or secrets will spill like blood.

Anon'

Margaret tapped the end of the pen against her cheek. Were they this short to not leave clues? Why did they not reference the wedding directly? Why did Pat have them? Did Lise even know they existed? Another gasp as a penny dropped. "The basta..." she started to say, before catching herself. She'd remembered how Jim had scheduled all the planning meetings for the stag/hen trips with her for right after breakfast, at the time when she usually helped out in the mailroom, not because they needed the help, but because if you wanted to know what was happening at Cahoots, you followed its mail. The timing had felt suspicious––Jim wasn't a morning person. She wondered if the first poison pen letter had arrived, he'd not wanted her to find out about it, or intercept any others, and so he'd been keeping her out of the way. She pulsed with anger. She'd been so on edge about the trips too, so sure someone was trying to stop the wedding, and they were.

She'd been right, as usual. And her friends had denied her pertinent information she could have used to keep them all safe. It made her furious. Jim was going to get it in the neck. She ran a hand through her hair and tried to slow her breathing. There'd be time for that later. She needed to focus. She moved to the second poison pen letter:

'Lise,

The wise see danger ahead and avoid it. Call it off or carry the consequences.

Anon'

'The wise see danger ahead and avoid it'––was that a line from something? There was a glimmer of recognition back in the hinterlands of her mind. Had she heard it in a school assembly, maybe? They always rotated who chaired the assemblies. She liked the religious teachers' assemblies least, for they always veered into sermons. Pointless as children don't do what you say, they do what you do. You lead by example, not threats––so many teachers got that wrong. Margaret had no time for religion, superstition, or the sacred; everything must be questioned, held up to the light and examined. She pictured one teacher in her mind, Herbert Spriggs, glasses swinging on a chain around his neck. How he loved to look down his nose at the students. Literally. Always wore a grey jumper, patches at the elbow. A sneering, snivelling little man, and a poor educator, too. She had looked forward to firing him. Had been building a file of student complaints. Then he kicked a sixth former, or so the gossip mill said. Margaret was so close to convincing the student to file a report. That would have been it. The end. But Herbert heard about it, somehow, and marched straight into her office and quit. *The wise see danger and avoid it.* Yes, that was what he had said in her office, still smug and contrite. If he had said it, it was probably scripture. She turned the page over, held it up to the light of the bedside lamp, examining every centimetre. Nothing. She did the envelopes next and just when she was about to give up, spotted something in the bottom right corner of one, a single word written wonkily:

'Butter'

Part of a shopping list, perhaps? The T looped. Her head jerked back. She dropped the envelope. She'd seen that T before. She thought back through the night at *Moritzbastei* and then smiled victoriously, having figured it out. There was another clue too: 'carry the consequence'. You don't *carry* a consequence in English, perhaps because of the alliteration. You *suffer* a consequence.

"Pat," she said, quietly. "Are you still awake?"

No answer. Well, maybe her snoring was the answer. "No matter," she said. "You have your secrets and I have mine. And tomorrow, there's someone I need to confront."

And with the documents held tight to her chest, Margaret did sleep; slept well, even, curled up in the armchair, door double-locked, another chair pushed against it, after first having gone to check on Lise, hearing her muffled snoring under the door, which hadn't been tampered with.

The next morning, after another disappointing breakfast (she'd asked for her bread toasted not incinerated), they took two different trams and then walked through a wood to arrive, exhausted, at *Cospudener See*––Lise and Dieter's lake, and where she planned to spread his ashes. Up ahead, several small sailboats crossed the topaz-blue water of the lake. On the far side, there was a small and artificial looking beach, too perfect, Margaret thought. The excited voices of children carried on the breeze. It was almost serene enough to allow her to relax.

Almost.

"Lovely morning for a conspiracy, isn't it?" she said, walking along next to Pat, who had been gone when she woke up. Pat brought a finger to her lips. They were in the middle of the group and so it wasn't private enough to talk about anything that mattered. Margaret needed to know if that threatening letter had been sent to Pat. If so, it would explain so much.

They walked on towards the lake, Tilda falling behind them, as if her feet were cement blocks. Eventually, they made it, and Lise, at the head of the group, turned around at the water's edge to address them all. The other women, including Daniella, bunched in front of her. Nele slipped a full backpack off her shoulder as Lise dipped her head and cleared her throat, trying to master her emotions. She said, voice shaking, "Dieter and I used to skinny-dip here."

Dieter skinny-dipped? It was hard to square the grumpy old man with the youthful nudist of Lise's stories. Maybe before prison and losing the baby? His ashes were in the silver urn, gripped tightly in her hands. She unscrewed the lid. "We didn't call it skinny-dipping, of course. It was FKK." The memory seemed to warm her. "We used to come here in the evening, bottle of wine and some cheese, sitting at the water's edge, reading, talking, swimming and, well, you know." She winked.

"Stop," Tilda said, stepping forward. "*Please.* This is all a lie."
Lise's forehead creased. "A lie?"
"This lake was only built two years ago, in 2000."
"What?" she said, looking around at the others. Daniella

lowered her gaze. "It's true?" Lise asked her. So, thought Margaret, that's why it all looked so new and unsullied.

Nele let out a spiky laugh. "I didn't want to say anything. Seemed cruel," she said, glaring at Tilda.

Was it cruel? Margaret wasn't sure. The truth often hurt, sure, but the pain was short and sharp, then passed. "You're romanticising the past again," Tilda said. "Dieter didn't even like lakes."

"What can you tell us about it?" Margaret asked Daniella. Maybe a terrible, half-remembered anecdote would calm everyone down? Or, more likely, give them all a new target for their annoyance.

"Fake as the palm trees in the *Nikolaikirche*," Daniella said, nonchalantly. "They flooded an old mine to create it."

"Maybe there was a small lake here before?" Lise mumbled as tears pooled at the edges of her eyes and her shoulders began to bob. She screwed the lid back on the urn.

Tilda raised her hands and let them drop heavily. "No."

Pat moved to Lise and put her arm around her shoulders.

"Or nearby?" Margaret offered, reaching for the map in her bag.

"Yes," said Lise, brightening. "I'm sure."

"No," Nele said. "I think, maybe you confused it with *Auensee?*"

Tilda sighed. "None of this makes sense. You're on a hen-do for your new man, who has lied to you, with the ashes of your old one, in a city neither of you have been in for decades."

"I just thought that Dieter would like to come home," Lise said, gnawing on her bottom lip. Her voice broke at *home*. Pat hugged her tighter.

"This isn't his home." Tilda spat the words out. "He hasn't been here in decades. They put him in prison. Why bring him back now?"

Had something happened overnight? The sisters had

seemed to end the previous evening on better terms. Alcohol often did that, briefly. And Lise had asked Tilda about her mother's ring on the tram here. Tilda had made an excuse again, something about getting back home late, but it hadn't sounded like an argument, from what little Margaret had been able to hear and understand. Could it be that which had caused this flare-up?

Lise cleared her throat. She'd never looked smaller or frailer. "You know that it was hard for him. He just wanted to be with pregnant me. For that, he was sent to prison for years. Yes, he helped others escape, but that was just who he was. He was brilliant at technical things. They broke him in that prison, so of course he didn't want to come back."

"Yes," Tilda said. "So why bring him here now?"

Dieter had never talked about his time in prison and abruptly ended any conversation that went near to the topic. Margaret knew that he had been some sort of sound technician for orchestras before he was imprisoned. But that experience wrecked his nerves. In the UK, he'd become a long-distance lorry driver. A job he seemed to think was beneath him, while also enjoying the travel and solitude it offered.

"His home was England," Tilda continued, still out for blood. "As is yours."

Pat gave Lise a fresh tissue, which she used to dab at the tears streaming down her face.

"You can't just come back here after all these years and think everyone and everything is just waiting for you, the same."

"Tilda," Margaret said. "Please."

Lise shrank another five centimetres. "I didn't expect that you'd wait around for me. I think I just expected, no..." her back straightened, "*hoped* for a warmer welcome from the only family member I have left. But warmth was never your style."

"I guess not," Tilda said, turning and striding towards the

car park. Lise's resolve broke and Pat had to help her, sobbing and hysterical, to a nearby bench. Margaret followed after Tilda.

"Not sure we'll need all the bubbly I've *schlepped*," Nele said, gesturing to her bulging backpack, as Margaret passed.

"Tilda," Margaret said, speeding up. "Wait."

"Don't," Tilda barked over her shoulder. "Leave me alone."

Margaret got close enough that she could reach for her arm. "What was that all about?" she asked softly. Tilda pretended not to hear and kept walking. Margaret ran alongside her. A change of tone, maybe? Something fiercer and firmer. "That was wrong, Tilda. Cruel."

Tilda stopped, turned, and looked not at Margaret but back towards her sister. "She deserved it."

"Why?" Margaret coughed. "I mean… Well. Even if she did, you didn't have to give it. You could have been the bigger person."

Tilda touched the cross around her neck. "I'm not good with lies."

"She just misremembered," Margaret said, wondering if she meant about the lake or something else.

"She's *misremembered* a lot of things," Tilda said, hissing the word misremembered.

"Well, you've certainly said your piece now. Lise can process it and respond. She does mean well, however clumsily." Margaret did up a button on her blazer. "Look, I'm planning something. A little surprise for everyone. I can't say more, but can you write your address down for me?" Margaret pulled something from her pocket. "A car will pick you up in the morning. At 8am."

Tilda looked down at the notepad and the metal Parker pen tucked inside. "What if Lise doesn't want me there?"

"She will. You'll have made up by dinner. You always do."

Tilda's nose twitched. "Okay," she said hesitantly, taking the pen and paper. She lowered herself so she could lean on her knee, and wrote. There it was, the looping T on the word *Straße*, the German word for street.

"Thanks," Margaret said, taking it and tucking the notepad into her pocket. *Gotcha.* They could still hear Lise's sobs. "The wedding is a really special event for all of us at Cahoots," Margaret said. "The first within the family. There will be plenty more, I'm sure, but this is number one."

"Lise must enjoy that," Tilda said, a sneer in her voice. "The attention."

"Not everyone's happy about it." Margaret lowered her voice, letting the words hang in the air.

Eventually, the intrigue broke Tilda, and she grabbed at them. "What do you mean?"

She looked her square in the face. "Someone's trying to stop the wedding, Tilda. Making prank calls, cancelling our hotel reservation and flight. Or trying to. They also wrote letters. Threatening letters."

Tilda inhaled. "No," she said. "Really?"

As acting displays went, it was mediocre. "I wonder what goes through someone's mind when they do something like that?" Margaret pressed. "They must be evil, don't you think? To try and ruin someone else's happiness?"

"What do you know about evil?" Tilda said, lowering her shoulders and clutching her cross again. She made for the car park but Margaret jumped into her way.

"Did you ever study any graphology? The science is beyond shaky, but still." Tilda's face stayed blank. Margaret carried on. "It's the study of handwriting. Yours would be interesting, I think." She got the notepad back out. "You have a very distinctive T. The way the stem loops into almost a bulb. I first noticed it in *Moritzbastei*."

Tilda looked nervously around Margaret's shoulder to Lise, Pat and, a little further away, Daniella, all clustered around the benches near the edge of the lake. Margaret was confident they were out of earshot. "Why did you write those poison pen letters, Tilda? And why are you trying to stop this wedding?"

"I..." Tilda's voice was quiet and weak. She turned one way, then the other. "I didn't."

"Your T suggests otherwise."

"There was no T on the letters. They were typed."

Margaret's breath caught in her throat. "How did you know that?"

"You just said it."

She replayed the conversation quickly in her mind. "No, I didn't."

Tilda bristled. "I mean, poison pen letters are always typed, no? That's the point. To not reveal your handwriting."

"Yes," Margaret said. She still had the notepad in her hand. "But this letter writer was sloppy. On one of the envelopes, in the corner, they started a list. 'Butter'." She lifted the notepad to eye level and shook it. "I know it was you, Tilda. But not why, yet. And it's the why that I care about."

Tilda looked back at her sister, but said nothing. Margaret had her on the edge of a confession. She just had to push a little harder. "Consequences," she said. "In English, we suffer them, in German you carry them. Another small mistake, but it's enough, all together. I'm going to tell Lise and then you'll have consequences of your own to suffer."

"I-" Tilda stuttered. "Please. Don't." She began to cry. Margaret considered touching her, offering some kind of reassurance, but she didn't want to transgress any physical boundaries. "Do you hate her so much for leaving you behind? For making you nurse your mother alone?" she asked.

"I don't hate her. It's just..." Tilda's head jerked left and right, as if looking for some safe place to run, her hand still pulling on the cross around her neck. Suddenly, she turned, lowered her head, and set off back towards the lake. "I'll tell her myself."

Margaret watched, weight on the front of her feet, ready to give chase. Was Tilda capable of violence? Jealousy was a strong motive, but the letters and cancellations seemed almost childish. Nothing like throwing a knife in the dark or poisoning a drink, neither of which she had evidence Tilda had been responsible for. And she'd collected that round of shots from the bar, so she'd had another opportunity to slip something in their drinks, and yet she hadn't taken it. And anyway, to do something out here, with so many witnesses?

No, Margaret decided, as Tilda reached Pat and Lise. Seeing the state of her, Pat stood up and excused herself. The two sisters sat and began to talk. Would she really tell Lise the truth? Without knowing why she'd sent the letters, it was impossible to say. It was the not knowing that gnawed at Margaret, an almost physical pain. She often had it when information was withheld from her, and it had been there last night too, when she'd learned Jim had conspired to keep the poison pen letters a secret. She hoped Tilda would confess. It would be better if it came directly, not via Margaret. But if Tilda didn't tell her, she would have to. She couldn't risk more scenes like this one, or they might all have consequences too heavy to carry.

Soon, Lise and Tilda were hugging, or rather, Tilda was being hugged, sitting, stiff as a plank, as usual. Was it a reconciliation? Had she come clean? Margaret had her doubts. Not much time had passed. She walked back to Daniella who was sitting on a large boulder perhaps twenty metres from the sisters, the young woman's beautiful, symmetrical, high-cheekboned face angled up into the sun, eyes tightly closed, usual dour pout to her lips, like a lizard warming itself. Margaret sat down on the boulder next to her (were these also fake?) and sighed. "That was intense, right?"

Daniella lifted her chin a few degrees higher. Her eyes stayed closed.

"Did you drink the Irish Wedding last night?" she asked. Daniella had taken hers and left before Margaret knocked them all over.

Daniella's eyes opened briefly. "Yeah. Wasn't great."

Her eyes closed again.

"Been feeling okay, though?"

Open. "Sure. Would take ten of those to knock me down." Eyes closed. This was a minimum viable conversation. They sat in silence. Somehow, she needed to get Daniella to open up. She didn't know definitively who had sent those pictures to the boys or why, but it seemed like it had to have been Daniella. "Of all the places to fight. But then I guess weddings are a stressful time for everyone involved, right?

Daniella's silence was deafening. People usually care what you think of them and so it's disorientating to be in the presence of someone who doesn't. It made Margaret feel very... exposed. "So many things can go wrong before a wedding, can't they? Gary, one of Connor's best men–"

"Who?" Daniella asked petulantly, swatting Margaret's sentence like it was a fly.

"Connor. The groom-to-be."

Daniella shrugged. "Fine. Sure." She closed her eyes again.

"You must know Gary because you sent him the pictures of Lise with the stripper."

Daniella's head turned abruptly. Her eyes stayed open this time. "What pictures?"

"The pictures you took last night with the camera you said you didn't have."

Her focus flitted left, then right. "Oh, the pictures." If she was surprised, she was being very careful to hide it. It was almost like she'd started the topic, not Margaret.

"Yes, Daniella. The pictures that you took of us and then

sent to everyone in the groom's party. The only question I have is, why would you do that to Lise?"

Daniella sighed. Nothing followed it.

"Do you want me to show you the e-mails?" Margaret pressed. She pretended to rummage in her bag, not that she had anything to show, she didn't have a phone or any printouts, but Daniella didn't know that.

"I didn't send them to *everyone* in the groom's party," Daniella said eventually. "Don't be so dramatic. And it was just a joke. He said so, anyway. *Gary.* He called me and asked me to set up the stripper and send him the pics. I thought it would be fun. But you women don't really do fun, do you?"

Margaret looked away. What a callous, disgusting, disrespectful act. She tried to gather her thoughts, to control her tone, when she really wanted to scream HOW DARE YOU in Daniella's belligerent face. "And you just did it, did you? For a stranger? Sending pictures around without Lise's consent? In a compromising situation. That's... disgraceful, Daniella. You should be ashamed of yourself."

"What?" Daniella's cold, brown eyes bored into hers. "It was just a laugh."

"For you, yes. But what about for Lise?" She gestured with her arm. "And for Connor? That photo will exist forever now."

"So? She was having a great time. She's a great sport, unlike everyone else around here."

Margaret felt sick just thinking about it. It was Maidstone all over again. Something she'd never talked to anyone about. Would never. She stood up. "You're fired, Daniella."

Chapter 24

The Hunting Lodge (Jim)

As he walked down the narrow, overgrown path, Jim replayed last night's trophy room phone call with Margaret in his mind. How could it be happening both here and there? It seemed like too much to coordinate. And now, before he could use his prodigious smarts to solve it all, Connor had dragged him out into the woods. He'd protested, of course, but Connor was not a man you could reason with, which was what made it so strange that Tad felt Jim had his ear. Jim wasn't sure Connor had Connor's ear. He seemed to be driven only by impulse, opportunity, and incredulity; he was the jester, life was his court, and he felt it owed him its laughter.

Laughter. Connor's. Stepping over a fallen branch, Jim pulled back the branches of two enormous fir trees encroaching on the narrow path. He slipped through and the small hunting lodge came into view. Wide, single-story, made of dark, rough-hewn logs that helped it blend into the forest. Two large windows masked by heavy green curtains. The shingled roof steep and foreboding. A thin plume of smoke rose from the chimney. If you were looking for a remote place to murder someone, this felt pretty much perfect.

"Come on, Jimmy," Connor shouted from up on the veranda. "Before Tristan confuses you for a yeti and slugs you between the eyes."

"Yetis are less hairy," said Gary.

With Connor was Tad, Tristan, and Seamus, their laughter mixing with the wind whipping through the trees and the loud chatter of birds. Jim ground his fist into his palm. He was a city boy at heart and so out of his element in such wild, untamed, unpaved, and unpubbed environments. He trudged up the steps. The men were standing by a couple of wicker rocking chairs, Gary and Connor sipping the morning's first whiskies. Tristan chugged from another of his awful homemade sports bottle elixirs. Seamus was the only one sitting, knitting as usual, rocking back and forth, but with his chair turned from the others, facing the house. He looked like a character in a Stephen King novel who'd warn cryptically of bad news that had come to him in a dream. The sound of metal clanking and the sight of the rifles deepened Jim's unease.

"It's been too long," said Gary, slinging a rifle over his shoulder.

"Too right, fella. I've got my sights set on a big old buck," said Connor. "At least as big as Taddy here." He hit Tad on the small of his back. Tad didn't move.

"I think that one is mine, Gary." Connor held out his hand towards Gary's rifle.

"They're all the same," Gary said.

"First, no. Second, if they are all the same, what would it matter?"

"What's it matter to you then?"

"They're my guns."

"Fine," Gary said, handing him his. Connor swapped for the one between his legs.

"What Connor wants, Connor gets," Tad said.

Connor laughed. "Right. Listen to *Father* here," he said, the word dripping with sarcasm.

"Are you going hunting, Seamus?" Jim asked. Seamus hadn't wanted to come at all. Jim had had to talk him into it over breakfast. He'd argued he needed someone to keep him company, since he wasn't going to hunt, either. Seamus was reluctant, but Jim pushed and he fell. Seamus turned from his knitting. "I'm sorry to be a spoilsport but I don't understand the appeal. It just seems so... mean?"

"It's not about no killing, Shay," said Connor, taking another sip. "It's about the thrill of the hunt. Tracking your prey." He drummed his chest. "Man against beast."

"Beast against beast," said Tad.

"The adrenaline," Tristan added, slicking back his hair. "It's like nothing else. Well, like almost nothing else." He started cleaning his rifle, an oily rag in his hands, a look of intense focus on his face. Jim watched him fumble with the safety, unsure if it was on or off. Not as experienced a hunter as he's pretending to be, he decided. Jim knew his way around a rifle, having been part of the Territorial Army in his youth. His father had pushed him into it because, as a fifteen-year-old, he was showing only interest in football and women. That was a long time ago, of course, but muscle memory sits deep. He fancied he'd beat Tristan in a duel, but then he didn't have Tristan's shaky hands.

"Obviously, the Buddha was against killing animals, and so I am, too," Tristan said. "But it's part of our culture, isn't it? I'll donate anything I kill... I mean... help into the next cycle of life. Yeah, I'll give it to the local homeless shelter."

Connor opened his mouth, then closed it, perhaps unable to decide which part of this ridiculous sentence to mock first.

"I'm happy to stay here anyway," said Seamus. "Man the fort. Make the tea. I also packed some scones. And I've got me needles. You boys go have a grand old time."

"As you wish," said Connor. "We have a gun for you, Jimmy." He handed him a rifle. "I'll show you the basics."

Jim reached out his hand, but then pulled it back. "Nah, I'll keep Seamus here company."

"No," said Gary. "Come, it'll be a right laugh."

"Yeah," said Tristan. "Communion with nature at its most primal."

Jim clutched his stomach. "It's me stomach, see," he lied. "Been playing up all morning. Must be the Guinness."

"Nonsense," said Gary. "We'll not hear of it." He was leaning heavily on his rifle and panting as if he'd just finished a 10k. Jim wasn't sure how good of a hunter he could be if he got out of breath from just standing still.

"Can you show me where the toilet is?" Jim said to Seamus, squeezing his stomach tighter. He wasn't going to miss this opportunity to get Seamus alone. Seamus moved to get up.

"Just shit in the woods, Jimmy," said Connor, gesturing for Seamus to stay seated.

"I hear the pope does it all the time," said Tad. The group laughed, which Tad appeared to neither enjoy nor resent.

"And it's tradition," said Gary, tapping his pocket. "I'm bringing some shit rags and quite looking forward to the fresh air on me–"

"Gary," Seamus said, without looking up.

"Burning witches was tradition," said Jim. "So was locking up gay people." Tristan and Tad turned to Seamus, who looked up, briefly, then lowered his eyes and carried on with the next stitch with a speed and grace that captivated Jim. "But you're probably right," Jim added, deciding on a new tactic. "I'll hit the bog and then come along in a bit, yeah? Once I'm sure my stomach has settled. Leave me at least a squirrel." He grabbed the rifle from Connor and weighed it in his hands. At first glance, they all looked the same, so why had Connor wanted the one in particular? And more importantly, would anyone else have known he'd want that one?

"Fair enough," said Connor.

"Quick shot of cognac before you go, though?" Jim suggested, stepping next to Gary and subtly blocking everyone from leaving. "I found a bottle in the drawer in my desk. I reckon it's from Bill's secret stash and let me just say that the man had taste." He shook the small silver flask he pulled from his back pocket.

"Look at you, raiding my home like it's your own." Connor gestured for the flask, putting his rifle down against the table. Jim went to hand it to him, dropping it deliberately. "Ah, shite." Connor bent to pick it up and Jim, positioning his body to block the view of the others, quickly switched their two rifles.

After a quick round and many complimentary words about what actually was exceptional cognac–no burn at all, just a slow, growing warmth and exquisite depth of flavour with an aftertaste that hinted at ripe pears–Connor, Tad, Gary, and Tristan left. Jim turned a chair so he could see both Seamus and the view, keeping Connor's rifle on his lap. "Shall I show you to the lavatory?" Seamus asked.

"Thanks, pal, but things have calmed."

"Good to hear it," he said, returning to his knitting.

"You don't like the view?" Jim asked, removing his pocket comb and taming his magnificent mane. Barely even receding, it was, a real gift at his age.

"It doesn't like me," Seamus said.

Was that a joke? "Well, it's a lovely day for it," Jim said once the others were out of earshot.

"For knitting?" Seamus asked, looking up at him, but not stopping the rapid clacking of his needles. He didn't need to see what he was doing. "Every day's a lovely day for knitting."

"That right?" Jim alternated between scanning out in the distance and enjoying the view of a master puppeteer working his string marionette. He squinted at the needles. Yes, they were the same ones used in the chandelier. "They special needles?" he asked. "They look awfully sharp."

"And strong," said Seamus, running his hand up one. "Designed them myself. Tungsten carbide. Most knitters, your beginners, bless them, they use plastic, wood, or maybe even bamboo, if they're showing off. But they wear down frightfully quickly, they do." He rolled his eyes. "And my word, are they imprecise, Jimmy."

"That right?"

Seamus gave a nervous nod. "Tristan's pushing me to patent these and found our own company to sell them." While he was talking, Jim methodically examined the weapon in his hand. He could have sworn it was slightly heavier than the one he'd been given. Balancing it on both hands, it seemed to tip ever so slightly towards its front.

"You know how to use that?" Seamus asked.

"Sure," Jim reassured. "Why not sell the needles through McGinley?"

"That's what I said. No, what I thought." A pause. "I will say something, probably." He didn't seem certain.

"And why do you need Tristan? They're your invention, no?" There was something scratched into the butt of the rifle. Jim lifted it and noticed small letters: C McG.

"I guess," Seamus said. "It's probably just a lot of hullabaloo, anyway. And I doubt they'll be popular."

"You could see what Connor says about selling them, I suppose. Now that he's in charge. How does it feel to have your brother off the sub's bench and back on the team?" This choice of word, brother, was deliberate, and Seamus flinched, just as Jim expected.

"Wonderful," said Seamus, but a little too enthusiastically. "A family business needs a family after all." He flashed Jim a wide grin, which he held for a few seconds too long. Jim started to disassemble the weapon. He tried to look down the barrel, which was when he realised he couldn't: something was stuck in there. He kept that to himself.

"Did you always keep in touch with Connor?"

"Yes," said Seamus. "I sent him cards. Birthday, Christmas and that. I'd talk to him sometimes too, when father called him."

"Ah, yeah," said Jim, as if they were just two men shooting the breeze, discussing an iffy penalty decision in the match last night. "He send any cards back, did he?"

"Yes," Seamus said, but too quickly. Jim remembered a card Connor had painted for Jim's sixty-first birthday. On the front was a weary-looking chicken in a party hat, drinking from a full glass of Guinness. Inside it said: From one old cock to another, congrats on lasting another year. The chicken's eyes followed you; it had a haunted glare. The man had talent, that was obvious, but talent only gets you so far, and in a bare-knuckle boxing match, dedication beats it every time.

"Can I borrow one of those?" he asked, pointing at Seamus's spare needles. Seamus handed him one. It was incredibly light and strong. "The will must have been a shock, though?" Jim asked, poking the needle into the barrel. "For him too. You two talk about it yet?"

Seamus's nose twitched.

"He's going to need you, Shay."

"I don't know about that. And why a shock? He's the heir, after all. The eldest son. It was expected." Expected––interesting choice of words. Whatever was lodged inside the barrel was stuck tight. He jammed the needle in harder. "Did they not formally adopt you then?" Jim asked, wondering how far he could push this line of questioning.

Seamus's spine stiffened. "What do you mean, formally? They raised me after my biological parents died."

"Yes but–"

The Accidental Murder Club

"Took me into their home. Treated me like a son."

Didn't call you son though, did they? And there're no pictures of you anywhere in that big old windy house either, are there? "Is your room next to mine, Shay?" Jim asked, still poking, in more ways than one.

"No," said Seamus. "Why?"

"No reason." And after decades of work, you inherited what, Seamus? Diddly squat. "It's just, well, I imagine that you imagined," Jim stopped. "Sorry fella, a lot of imagination in that sentence." He slowed down, tried to think about his wording, didn't want to just lunge in as he had with Gary and Tristan. "What I'm hearing, and correct me if I'm wrong, is that it's not much of a family business. That really you're the brains of the whole operation…"

Let it dangle, Jim, let him pick it up. Jim put the rifle down, didn't want Seamus getting distracted.

"Me?" Seamus said, blushing. "Do I seem like the brains of anything much? I mean, I do the designs, and well, yes, I suppose I know the staff quite well. I go out often to Inishmore, even though I get dreadfully seasick, but that's… well, that keeps me busy. Out of trouble. Gary comes sometimes too. He likes the peace out there."

Jim smiled, yet further proof they were an item, and another lie he'd caught Gary in, the snake.

Seamus stared into the window of the lodge, what little you could see between a gap in the curtains. "The Trust handles the business side of things," Seamus continued. "They keep the lights on and everyone employed."

Jim nodded. "That's what Tristan said, too."

"Tristan," said Seamus, smiling softly. "I bet he did."

"But you trust the tr-, oh, I've done it again." He sighed. "Do you get on well with the Trust? With Tristan?" He probed his front teeth with his tongue. "His style is very… different to yours. He's… flashy."

"Well, he's young, isn't he?"

"Very young to be the Vice President, yeah."

Seamus chuckled. "Did he say he was V.P.?" There was a knowing look in his eye. "He's Assistant to the Vice President. His father is V.P. but he's... in ill health. The Trust has been looking for a replacement for ages now, actually. I was wondering about that, but I didn't want to pry and I mean, Tristan seems to be managing things fine enough, I suppose, for a young fella. I mostly just keep myself to myself."

"Sure," said Jim, picking the rifle back up. He poked inside from the front this time.

"I got a strange picture last night, actually," said Seamus. "A young man in... well..." Jim lowered the weapon. Seamus's cheeks reddened. "A state of mmmm... and then the boys were joking about getting a picture of a whatdoyoucallit over breakfast, and I suppose I've connected the dots and I just... why would they send it to me?"

To sow maximum distress for Connor, thought Jim, or so they had hoped, but Connor wasn't a man who was easily embarrassed. Seamus squinted down at his phone. "Let me see if I can... I don't... the Trust gave me this blasted thing for e-mail." He pushed some buttons, seemingly at random. "It's got all the bells and whistles, but I'm not very good at..." Seamus trailed off, then handed the phone over. "Scandalous, isn't it?"

It was the same picture. "I suppose," Jim agreed, just about. Gary and Connor's booming laughs echoed off the trees. They were going to scare all the prey away. "Did they treat Gary like a son, too?" Jim asked. "Being as Connor and Gary are besties."

"Are they?"

"I mean, they act like brothers."

Seamus laughed. "You're a very prying man, Jim. I hope you don't mind my saying so?"

"Occupational hazard," said Jim, and finally felt something inside the rifle dislodge.

"Aren't you retired?"

"Don't believe in it. You've got to keep busy, haven't you?"

"I'm not a gossip," said Seamus.

"Me neither, Shay. Not my style. Someone tells me something, in confidence, and they can be confident, oh, I've done it again, haven't I? Well, it will stay a secret, is what I mean. Is it difficult being the only teetotaller in all of Galway?"

"Teetotaller?" said Seamus. "What gave you that idea? In Mykonos, I've got quite tipsy, even. I once drank from a bucket, if you can believe such a thing?" He licked his lips. "I'm actually rather partial to a Bailey's Irish Cream."

"Really?" Jim shook his head, but he didn't find it hard to believe. Seamus's sweet nature matched a sickly drink like that. Not a real drink, that one, just a gimmick in a glass. "Too sweet for me." Something fell out of the rifle. He bent down and picked it up.

"Did you know it was invented in Galway?" Seamus asked.

"Was it now?" It was a piece of greasy wool, filled with stones. Jim's heart rate accelerated. Someone had stuffed something inside Connor's gun so it would backfire. Seamus didn't seem to notice it, was lost in his knitting and his story.

"By a barman here. A good one, I've been told."

Jim looked out into the woods and could just about make out the bulky figure of Gary. "Wait, Gary invented Bailey's Irish Cream?"

Seamus nodded. "He came to Connor for money to help him launch it."

"Huh," said Jim, settling back in his chair. "And let me guess, Connor did what Connor always does? Made fun of it first, and then, well, nothing second?"

BANG BANG

Gunshots. Jim lifted some binoculars off the side table and brought them up to his eyes. The shooter was Connor, laying down on his front. Jim couldn't see what he was aiming at. His gun seemed to work fine, though. He wondered who'd be surprised about that? Apparently not Seamus, judging by the steady rhythm of his needles. He lowered the binoculars.

"Not that you heard that from me," Seamus said, getting up. "Just nipping to the little boy's room."

Jim rocked back and forth a few times, enjoying the success of another deftly handled interrogation, and his brilliance at swapping the guns, but his joy didn't last long, was chased away by the anxiety that he had been right about the rifles. That, and how he'd uncovered yet another motive for Connor's murder, another long-simmering resentment - the most potent kind. Gary, sodding Gary. He watched a bird swoop through the trees. Realising he couldn't see the hunters anymore, he stood up and moved nearer to the edge of the veranda, lifting the binoculars to his eyes and scanning for them while trying to stay calm. Should he go after them? Eventually, through the lenses, he spotted Connor kneeling, and alone, aiming his rifle towards some bushes.

BANG BANG BANG

Three more shots rang out, puncturing the silence. Jim panned left and his binoculared eyes settled on the nozzle of a gun poking out from behind a tree. A rifle, best he could see, but this one had a silver tip, not black like the others - and it was pointing directly at Connor. "CONNOR," Jim screamed, but he was too far away.

"Seamus," he said, shouting back into the lodge. "Come quick." Jim rushed down and stairs and along the path screaming, "CONNOR LOOK OUT HE'S GOT A GUN." He was a hundred metres away and aimed his gun at the sky--POP-- The recoil from it jolted him backward, but at least he'd cleared the jam successfully.

"GUN! LOOK OUT!"

POP POP.

He glanced back, but there was still no sign of Seamus. He

ran deeper into the woods, crashing between two giant fir trees and out into a clearing and right into the backside of... "Get down," he said, lunging for Connor, a repeat of the wake, knocking him off his feet.

"Argh!" Connor yelled as they hit the ground, Jim on top of him, the guns somewhere in the middle of them, clanging together.

"Did you not hear me shouting, man?" Jim said.

"What the hell is wrong with you?" Connor said, wriggling free.

"Or the gunshots?" Jim asked, looking madly around. There was no sign of the gunman.

"Christ alive," Connor said, trying to get back to his feet. "If you wanna hug me, just ask, man. Stop all this hero nonsense."

Jim got slowly up and brushed himself down, his rifle laying on the ground by a tree stump. "Someone shot at you," he said, wafting his hand in the vague direction of where he thought the man had been. It was hard to tell. It all looked the same.

Gary appeared from behind a tree.

"Are you sure it wasn't the yeti?" he said, his voice thick with sarcasm.

Connor shook out his legs and massaged the back of his neck, scowling from the pain in his limbs. "And you saw him from all the way back at the lodge, did ye?"

"With me binoculars, yeah."

"Your eyes are playing tricks on you," said Tad. "Too much of the devil's liquor."

"Shay must have seen them too," said Jim, as Seamus stumbled down the trail. "I mean, he was on the toilet, but then when he came out. Seamus?"

Seamus ambled up to the group. "What's the commotion, lads?"

"Someone shot at Connor."

"On purpose? Are you sure? I didn't see anything."

"I know what I saw," said Jim, picking up his gun. "Why didn't you all stay together?"

"Connor kept farting," said Gary. "And Tad's got no stealth to him."

"Stealth is for people with something to hide."

"Did any of you fire your guns yet?" Jim asked.

"Nope," said Gary. Tad shook his head, once, just about.

"I did," said Connor.

"I'd have liked the chance to," Tristan said. "I'd just seen a rabbit when you ran up hollering. No offence Jim, but you do strike us as somewhat paranoid."

"Us? You've been talking about me behind my back, have you?"

Connor ruffled Jim's hair. "Look, it's good to have you in me corner, Jimmy, don't get me wrong. But you're awful jumpy these days."

Jim decided not to tell them about the sabotaged gun: they wouldn't believe him. They'd ask if he thought Connor was the kind of person who checked or cleaned his gun before use, to which he'd have to say, well, no. Connor was a slob. Bathed once a week, at best. Maybe the shooter had been forced to act because Jim had ruined his backfiring gun plot? Which he'd only have known when Connor first successfully fired his gun. Was Seamus already in the toilet at that point? "He ran away," Jim said. "As I shot. I saw the bushes rustle."

Gary cocked his head. "What did he look like, then?"

"He was dressed like..." he looked around at them all in their matching camouflage jackets. "I don't know. The gun had a silver tip."

They inspected their guns. "You saw the tip from all the way back there?" Tad asked.

Jim's nostrils flared. "WITH THE BINOCULARS, YEAH. Are any of you listening to me?" His anger was getting the best of him. He looked down at his hands, which were balled into tight fists. "I'm sick of you all looking at me like I'm some sort of whacko. I just wanted to come here and have a nice time with Connor, experience some of your supposedly famous Irish hospitality, but I can't ignore my own eyes, or ears, or the facts."

"I'm sure you pull a mean pint, Jim," said Gary, "but from all the way back at the veranda you couldn't hit a herd of elephants with one of these rifles. Your crappy shooting wouldn't have scared anyone away."

"I don't think I hit him. I hope I didn't hit him."

"You didn't hit him," said Tristan.

"Well, he's gone, hasn't he?"

"Yeah," said Gary, sarcastically. He made the word very roomy.

"Or…" Tristan added, as if there was a more likely possibility.

"Mmm," said Connor, gesturing back towards the veranda. "Anyway. Come on, that's enough excitement for one day. Let's kill a couple of Seamus's scones."

Everyone but Jim started to walk. "I know what I saw," he mumbled, taking off through the trees in the opposite direction, over to where he thought the shooter had been. Maybe he'd find footprints or a cigarette butt or something that would prove he was right. He staggered around for a few minutes, turning himself in circles before he had to admit he was lost. He heard the others laughing back at the lodge. Making fun of him, probably. Well, he knew what he'd seen, what he'd learned, and what it all meant. He needed to make a call.

Chapter 25

Cospudner See (Margaret)

Margaret looked out at the calm, shimmering water of the lake, wishing her insides were placid, rather than the churning, bubbling hot pool of anxiety that she could neither ignore, nor rationalise away. It would pass, but not soon enough, perhaps not until she got back to the safety of Cahoots.

Daniella had revealed she'd been Gary's accomplice, and so she couldn't be trusted, firing her had been the only option. But why had Gary come up with such a stupid plan? Did he not know Connor at all? A man who had dared, no, practically demanded that Lise kiss Geoff, Cahoots's (dashing) yoga instructor, when he was drunk one night at *Next Chance*. The tongue had seemed to surprise Geoff, but little else had. He'd been at Cahoots a while, knew it was a raucous place.

Margaret had to get the group together and away from the lake, to somewhere they'd be easier to supervise. Margaret squinted, blocking the sun. Where was Pat? Had she wandered off with Nele? The sisters were still talking things through. Margaret strained to hear. Every fifth word was "*Entschuldigung.*" *Sorry*. The word Margaret had always thought sounded like a sneeze.

Daniella had refused to be fired, saying it was Lise's decision, not Margaret's. Since then, she'd passed the time glaring at Margaret with such intensity it was like she was willing her to spontaneously combust. Margaret was trying to work out what her next step should be, when the theme song from James Bond rang out from inside Daniella's army jacket.

"How did you get this number? She's… well… dead to me… no, not actually dead… I mean… calm down… no… okay, fine, whatever, just stop talking already." She ambled towards Margaret, holding out the phone. "For you."

Margaret accepted it, tentatively, then took two long strides away for privacy, then lowered her voice. "Hello?"

"Maggie." Jim said, breathless. She was about to correct him when… "They tried to shoot him, I stopped them. They got away. But they tried to shoot him. Tampered with his gun."

Why did Connor have a gun? She tried to remember what activity had been scheduled for this morning. It had taken Margaret quite a lot of prodding to get any information out of Jim about what the boys would be doing, and where. Eventually, he had come back with something, just a single page, with a dearth of hard facts. For most of the time slots, he'd simply written the word, 'BOOZING'. Margaret, on the other hand, had provided a very comprehensive itinerary to Jim, which, because of its carefully thought out taxonomy and efficient use of colour coding, had only run to eighteen pages.

"Probably wanted to make it look like an accident," Jim rambled on. "It's real, this whole thing is real, and it's serious, and it's here and it's over there in Germany and they're not going to stop and you need to be careful. No, come home. Call it off. Tell Lise. We'll all go back to Cahoots. No, to the police. …"

"Deep breaths, Jim. Calm down." She looked around to see who could hear. "No-one believes us," she whispered. "The people in danger don't believe us. We stick to the plan."

"The Accidental Murder Club," he said, voice cheering at the notion, just a little. "The finest in the business."

She checked if Daniella was listening. "Err... well, fine, yes. We solved Berlin. Well, we also let two people die, so not a great performance but, still, we'll solve this. We just need to stay calm and rational and use our intellects. Now, is anyone hurt?"

"No, I scared them off."

"How?"

"I shot at the bastard, that's how."

"Did you see who it was?"

"Nah, could have been anyone. Connor was alone. It could even have been Seamus, technically, because the lodge has a back door. I just checked that. He'd have to be faster than he looks, though. I'm on Seamus's phone as it happens."

"Gary was the one who hired the stripper," she said. "Daniella confirmed it."

"Gary, that sh–" She heard Jim thump something.

"Keep your cool."

There was a tap on her shoulder. It was Daniella, gesturing to give the phone back. "I have to go," she said. "Be vigilant."

"I'm always vigilant."

She handed the phone back and then walked towards Tilda and Lise, who were coming towards her, holding hands. When they smiled, they really did look like sisters––it was the slightly upturned top lip and the pattern of crow's feet around those deep-set eyes. Tilda looked up into the trees and whistled a clear, high-pitched bird call with a trill at the end. It was remarkably well done and didn't sound like it was made by a human. Lise giggled and, wiping a single tear from her eyes, returned the call, just as perfectly. The sisters embraced––a real one this time, with warmth from both sides.

"We used to make that call to each other when we were young," Lise said, after the hug ended. "In the schoolyard or down at the market. It was a kind of code we had. We could find each other anywhere."

"Black-capped Chickadee," Tilda said, and nodded. She pointed up into the sky. "I just saw one. That's what reminded me of it. They're quite rare. This is a good day."

Was it a good day? It didn't feel like one. Perhaps Tilda really had told Lise, and Lise had already forgiven her? Margaret hoped so. Ah, damn, she'd forgotten to tell Jim that it was Tilda who sent the poison pen letters. She hadn't given Jim a telling off about them, either. Did the letters matter? It didn't seem related to what was happening in Ireland. Unless Tilda had an accomplice?

"Who's ready to race?" Nele said. Margaret spun around. Where had Nele come from? She'd been very subdued this morning.

"Yeah," Daniella said. "We're late."

"Forty-one minutes," Margaret said. "But you can go get lost." She pointed Daniella towards the woods. "I've fired her, by the way," she told the others. "The boys have photos from last night. You with the male performance artist." She couldn't bring herself to say the word stripper.

Daniella guffawed.

"It was her who hired him. Gary asked her to do it. She sent them pictures, if you can believe that? We can't trust her."

"Oh," Lise said, lowering her head. "I see."

"Who's Gary?" Nele asked.

"One of Connor's childhood friends," Lise said.

"I'm sorry," said Daniella. "He told me you'd find it funny. Stripper at a hen-do. It just didn't seem like a big deal, you know?"

"I did," Lise said, laughing. "Find it funny. And kind of hot. The voyeurism. All those people watching me. And Connor won't care. He's probably doing the same, or worse, over there, the kinky old fox. Actually, I hope he's doing worse."

"It was the highlight of the evening." Tilda beamed. Pat clicked in agreement. Margaret's arms went limp at her sides. And so, she was alone, again.

"Don't let her get away with it," she said. "It was a violation of your privacy. Of all our privacies. It was," she searched for exactly the right word, "malicious."

"Watch it," Daniella said, stepping closer to Margaret, pointing a finger into her face. Pat moved between them.

"Ladies, please," Lise said, stepping in as well. "I'm still holding a man's urn." She lifted it slightly. "I talked things through with Tilda, and I've decided to take him back to Bury St Edmunds. To spread the ashes there. At Cahoots. That's where I'll put him and our past to rest. Mistakes have been made," she said, placatingly, turning to Tilda. "By all of us."

Why 'all of us?' Margaret hadn't made any mistakes, other than trusting the people around her to not be inept and duplicitous, or worse, crazy knife-throwing killers.

"Things were said in the heat of the moment," Lise said. "Emotions ran high, right, Margaret?"

"I let mine get away from me," Tilda said, eyes downcast. "Sorry everyone."

"I was not... I am not emotional," Margaret protested with a stomp of her foot. "I'm seeing things for what they are."

"Let's finish out the day," Lise said to Daniella. "Sleep on it, and then see how everyone feels in the morning. Okay?"

"No," said Margaret. "How we *feel* is irrelevant. This is not a decision for feelings. What do you *think* about the fact she so gravely violated your trust?"

"Isn't that the same?" Lise asked.

"Look," Nele said, palms up in a placating gesture. "Daniella has the keys. We're all excited to drive a Trabi, the finest cars ever made. We're far out of the city. Lise's right, let's just finish the day."

"Fine by me," Tilda said. "Pat?"

Pat considered it for a few seconds and then gave a weak thumbs up. Once more, Margaret had been hung out to dry, as she had been so often on this trip. Even Pat wasn't her ally, and after everything that had happened the night before.

Daniella bounced her eyebrows. "Let's roll," she said, pointing over to the Trabis. "We're late enough, and that's not my fault this time, before anyone starts." She shot Margaret a look. "The itinerary said nothing about you crazy bitches needing three hours a day to bicker."

Everyone laughed, except Margaret, who didn't care what the others thought of Daniella; she didn't trust her, and would act accordingly. "I still think it was good to come here," Lise said as they all walked along in a row. "Not just to see Nele and Tilda, but to close this chapter of my life once and for all."

"Great," Nele said. "Because if it's closed, we can spend the afternoon doing something nice, instead of waiting for you to go read musty old documents in the archives."

Lise kicked a pebble. "I don't know," she said, looking down the line. Pat shook her head too. Was she doing that because she wanted Lise to go, or because she didn't? Margaret had tried several times to get Pat alone this morning, but it was like she was avoiding her. "No," Lise firmed. "I'm going to keep my appointment. It was so hard to get it. I mean, assuming nothing else goes disastrously wrong before then."

Daniella chucked Lise a set of car keys, and laughed.

Chapter 26

The Trabi Tour (Margaret)

Margaret trudged after them towards the car park, behind the docks filled with small sailing boats, and where two tiny cars were waiting, brightly coloured and glistening in the sun. She had read about Trabis, or Trabants, to use their full name, the iconic East German car, made by automaker VEB Sachsenring from the nineteen fifties all the way until the early nineties. They had a notoriously unreliable two-stroke engine and were made from Duroplast, a cheap material derived from recycled cotton waste and phenol resins. They were famous for their appalling performance, high emissions, and laughably long wait times for ownership that had sometimes run into decades, not years. They should probably never have existed, let alone still be being driven on public roads.

"Your chariots await," Daniella said.

"Oh, good," Margaret hissed. "You're waiting here then?"

"No, she's coming," Lise said firmly. "Because she actually knows how to drive one."

"I'm sure I'd learn quickly," Margaret said, more defensively than she'd intended and overlooking the fact she'd not driven anything in twenty years, after a small accident in which she'd reversed into a cocker spaniel. It wasn't her fault, nor was it the dog's--its owner had been beyond inebriated and negligent, but still, the whole incident had crystallised to her that there's just too much responsibility in operating a motor vehicle, for too little gain. It was not about her own safety, although that was a factor, but not a primary one. She had always felt responsibility strongly, physically, even, like a really, really stifling embrace. It was an aspect of her personality she didn't fully understand and found it confusing that no-one else seemed to share it. Her mother had developed breast cancer when Margaret was in her twenties and she'd even abandoned her teacher training to move home and nurse her. The right thing to do. Not that her mother had seemed grateful. Maybe that's why she'd been easier on Tilda than she could have been? Not that any of this mattered now, as they approached the cars and it only annoyed Margaret that it was taking up so much space in her brain when she needed to concentrate.

"I can drive them," said Tilda. "I actually had one until a few years ago. You just couldn't get the parts anymore."

They reached the two Trabis: ridiculous, tiny, two-door things. Their low roof was barely at the height of Margaret's shoulder. The interior was as sparse as a monk's cell, with hard, uncomfortable looking seats. They looked so flimsy that she could have dented them with just a hard stare. They were like something that would accept tokens at a funfair, but at least those cars had proper bumpers.

"Looks like they're made of Lego," she said. "Did you try them for spare parts?"

"Well, I was born for driving them," Nele said, sticking out her tongue, then ducking down to look inside through the driver's window of the nearest one--emblazoned with a Union Jack. Daniella tapped the roof of the other, which had the emblem of the GDR--the same black, red, and gold of the modern German flag but with a hammer, compass, and wreath. A logo she'd seen plenty at the spy museum.

They were obviously not safe for anyone, let alone a group whose members were having knives thrown at them, their drinks tainted, and hotel rooms broken into. Margaret crunched the heel of her shoe into the ground. What should she do? Try to convince them not to get in? Wasn't it a bit late for that? And this had been the activity everyone was most looking forward to. It had come up often in the previous days, so she didn't see how she could convince them to do that long walk back to the tram instead.

"I've crashed a few of them," said Lise, hand to her chest. "But that was the old me."

"Yes," Tilda said. "But the old you was less reckless."

Nele clapped her hands twice. "Enough trash talk. How about a race of nations? East vs. West, Republic vs. Empire, Good vs. Evil?" She lifted her hands in a gesture of defence. "Just kidding. Well, not on the racing part." Two more claps. "How fun. I can't wait."

"Are they safe?" Margaret asked, banging on the bonnet of the Union Jack one. The sound was disconcertingly hollow. "Not to race. There's not going to be a race. There's no advantage in racing. We're just going to drive slow, okay? In convoy."

"Don't be such a worry-wart," Lise said, bouncing up and down on the balls of her feet. She was so cavalier, so oversized and enthusiastic in her movements and gestures, so unguarded with her face, Margaret was terrified to see how she might drive.

"I'm just being pragmatic," Margaret said, pushing on the bottom of her spine. She gave the Morning Movers exercise class at Cahoots, and after just a few days without it, she already felt as stiff as a board.

"Come on," said Nele. "It's going to be fun."

"I think we should just sit in them," Margaret said. "Take

some photos. You have your camera, Daniella, or would one of us need to take our clothes off for it to appear?"

Daniella tried not to laugh, but failed. "Fair play."

Margaret turned to Pat. "You agree with me, right? That this is a bad idea? We don't want any more ashes to spread."

Pat inhaled deeply, then lifted her hands and let them drop. Margaret read this as 'when in Rome'.

"We're doing it," Lise said, opening the driver's side door of the GDR Trabi. "With or without you."

Margaret winced. Pat could take care of herself, but Margaret felt responsible for Lise. She'd never forgive herself if she ducked out, and then something happened to her. Jim and Connor would never forgive her, either. If they were going to have to drive these Matchbox cars, could she not at least use the activity to her advantage? Try to flush the villain out? If they had tampered with the car, and it would have been easy enough to do so at some point in the past hour, or earlier, then it would be interesting to know who wouldn't get into the same Trabi as Lise.

"Daniella, Tilda," Nele said, gesturing towards the GDR Trabi. She knocked on its hood and there was that same empty sound again, like MDF furniture. Tilda and Daniella were her chief suspects, so she needed to know if they'd get into a car with Lise.

"Why would Daniella be in the GDR team?" she asked, "Lise's claim to it is larger, no?"

"I can swap," Lise said, skipping across from the GDR to the GB Trabi. "I don't care which car I'm in as long as I get to drive it really, really fast and win."

"No," Margaret said. "We're just going to drive there slowly. Very slowly. I propose first gear only." The others laughed. "That wasn't a joke. Okay, second gear. Can we compromise on that?" She looked around, hopefully.

"I'll be using all the gears," said Nele. "You'll be choking on my exhaust."

"You'll be using none of them," Lise said. "Because I'm driving the GDR car. You can be my navigator."

"I'm not getting in a car driven by Lise," Tilda said, walking over to team GB. "No offence, sister, but I remember how long it took you to get your licence. And weren't you dating the driving instructor at the time?"

"That's why," Lise said. "We lost a lot of practice time, if you know what I mean?" She winked. "He always said I was good with the stick."

"Scandalous," Nele said, with a bounce of her eyebrows.

Daniella howled with laughter. "You crazy mofos."

"What's a mofo?" Tilda asked.

"Fine," Lise said, ducking the question. "You go with Pat and Margaret. I'll drive Nele and Daniella."

Okay, so Tilda didn't want to be in a car with Lise. That was clear. But what about Daniella? "Who's going to drive the GB car, though?" Daniella asked, right on schedule. "Have any of you tourists driven in right-hand side traffic before?"

Margaret tried to calculate the micromort score of driving on the opposite side of the road. Driving a car was usually around a one, high for a daily activity, but she had to factor in that it was a new vehicle to drive for everyone except Nele, Daniella and Tilda, and also the flimsiest car she'd ever seen. She gave it a score of twenty-five. Crazily high. Using heroin was thirty. And while this was a decision they were making, to endanger themselves like this, what about all the people around them? Pedestrians walking down the road, cyclists on their way to pick up their children, children playing in a park? The possible repercussions and negative externalities didn't bear thinking about.

"I won't drive," Margaret said. "The risks make it unconscionable."

The Accidental Murder Club

"What's that mean?" Tilda asked. "I thought you people speak English?"

"Show off way of saying no," Daniella said. "But fine. We can't all be brave. Pat, you want to drive?"

Pat made an X across her chest. Daniella walked across to Team GB. "I can drive." They were now four.

"So can I," said Tilda.

Nele wasn't making any effort to leave Lise's car, Margaret noted, unlike Daniella and Tilda. Pat then wandered a few steps away and dropped her head into her hands, as if she had a headache. "You okay?" Margaret asked. She took her hands away, momentarily, and Margaret saw that her eyes were bloodshot. She mimed a steering wheel and then made a thumbs down.

Did Pat drive? There were several shared cars available to residents of Cahoots, but she'd never seen Pat check one out.

"Are you okay to be a passenger, though?" Margaret asked. Maybe if enough people dropped out, they could still cancel the activity. Pat pulled a variety of tight-lipped, pained expressions, then gave a subtle nod.

"It's boring if I drive," Tilda said. "I know how to do it. There's no novelty."

"I haven't driven one in years," Daniella said. "I'll drive for Team GB. You can swap with me, Mags?"

"Margaret."

"If we delay much longer, none of us will be able to drive," Nele said. "And you've had too much bubbly at breakfast, Lise. I'll drive. Margaret, you can help navigate. Everyone, get in."

"Yeah, it's double price if we have them for over ninety minutes," Daniella said.

"Fine," Lise agreed, going to the passenger side of the GDR Trabi. "Pat, get over here."

Pat, head down, walked slowly across. Lise held the door open, and Pat climbed through the front door into the back-

249

seat. There were two seats in the front and space for two in the back, three, maybe, if everyone knew each other very well. Lise took position in the front passenger seat. "But-" Margaret started, only to be shouted down by Nele and Lise. Nele hit the gas, and the Trabi lurched forward.

"Get in," Daniella said. "Before I run you over."

Resigned, Margaret walked the few steps to the GB Trabi and opened the passenger door. Tilda was already settled in the back, filling all the space. "Winning the race is irrelevant," Margaret cautioned Daniella, as she lowered herself into the passenger seat and put her seatbelt on, relieved there was one.

"Maybe to you," Daniella said.

"It'll be forgotten in an hour, so there is no advantage in driving quickly. Let Nele win and drive slow enough that we get there safely, and can actually see something." She turned around. "Right, Tilda?"

"I've seen it all before," Tilda said. "So, no, I vote we make it fun."

Margaret groaned. There's almost nothing as exhausting as being ignored. In front of them, a young man with shockingly red hair and a red waistcoat waved them out of the parking lot into a wide street with three lanes. A hundred metres later, they rolled up side by side at a traffic light.

"Yours seems to be stuck in first gear," Nele shouted through her open window.

"Just warming it up," Daniella yelled back at her. "Finish line is the *Völkerschlachtdenkmal*, okay?"

Völkerschlachtdenkmal–Margaret repeated the word back in her head a few times, putting in the gaps *Völker* (people) *Schlacht* (slaughter?) *Denkmal* (statue, no, memorial?)–an ominous finishing point.

"Fine," said Nele. With the cars idling at the traffic lights, Daniella put her foot down heavily on the gas pedal, the piddly engine in neutral, revving and grunting like an asthmatic kitten as they waited for the green light. The light swung to yellow and after a quick thumb on the horn to shoo away a last pedestrian, their Trabi lurched away faster than the one next to them, both coughing great clouds of dark exhaust smoke Margaret could see in the wing mirror.

Daniella gripped the steering wheel tightly with one hand, accelerating up through the gears as she pulled in front of the GDR Trabi just as the road narrowed to a single lane. She howled with laughter and seemed to be enjoying herself, for perhaps the first time on the entire trip. Margaret's hands gripped the seat beneath her. "Slow down," she implored. "It's single lane now. They can't overtake."

"Losers," Daniella shouted back through the open windows. "Hmm, the brakes feel kind of spongy."

In front of them, an enormous concrete monument punctured the horizon. Built on top of a small hill, it was like the lair of a movie villain. Even from this distance, it was large enough to block out part of the sun. She'd read about it at the hotel, one of the few leaflets they actually had––albeit a very depressing one. The monument was dedicated to nearly 100,000 lives lost in an enormous battle right here in Leipzig in 1813, that Napoleon had lost.

The GDR Trabi was chewing at their back bumper. The road widened to two lanes and the two cars were soon side-by-side. "Red light," Margaret said, pointing.

"We'll make it," Daniella protested.

"We won't."

"Stop," Tilda said, the first noise she had made since the race began. It seemed to shift something in Daniella and there was a loud screech of brakes as their Trabi slowed, then came to a sharp stop just over the white stop line while the GDR Trabi raced through and away.

"Damn it," Daniella said, thumping the steering wheel, any harder and it would have fallen off.

"You did the right thing," Margaret said.

"Now we'll lose."

"Breaking the rules is losing," she said. "That was dangerous of Nele."

"Yeah," Tilda agreed, as they watched the GDR Trabi surge ahead and then take the sharp right turn into a small side street before what looked like a cemetery.

"I could have made it," Daniella protested, dropping to first, preparing for the light to change, "but I can't risk any more points on my licence. I've a lead foot."

"We don't care about the race, do we, Tilda?" Margaret said, looking at Tilda in the rear-view mirror. She had only cared about not being in the same car as her sister.

"I only care about there being no more arguments," she said, which Margaret found strange, as she'd started the day's biggest one with that largely unprovoked attack on Lise.

Slowly, after what felt like fifteen minutes, the light went green and they proceeded forwards, Daniella flying up through the gears again, already in third by the time they whipped around the corner, which was when they saw, perhaps a hundred metres in the distance, that the GDR-Trabi had smashed into a high brick wall at the far edge of the cemetery and was on fire.

"NO!" Margaret shouted as Daniella swerved towards it.

"Lise," Tilda screamed. "Help them."

By the time the Trabi had skidded to a final stop, Daniella had already removed her seatbelt, opened the door, and was getting out, ready to run towards the wreck. Margaret fought with her belt's release button and followed too, letting her eyes sweep across the scene––the thick, dark smoke and the enormous orange flames. Nele was lying face-down on the ground, at the front left of the Trabi. Had she been catapulted out? No, the windscreen was still intact. Where were Lise and Pat? She tried to see through the dense smoke and into the car. The front right of the vehicle seemed to have taken the brunt of the impact, and the whole bumper was mangled and crushed. Daniella pulled on the passenger side door, but it wouldn't open. Margaret rushed to the driver's side door, which didn't look as heavily damaged. Daniella tossed her phone to Tilda. "Feuerwehr."

Inside, Margaret could just about make out the two shapes, both screaming. The heat from the fire was already scorching. She covered her mouth and tried to hold her breath. They were conscious––Pat laying on the backseat, kicking at the rear right window. Lise was in the front, scrabbling around. "Help," she shouted at Daniella, between deep coughs. How could there be this much smoke so quickly? Margaret pulled on the driver's door some more. The handle was so hot it was burning her hand. She took off her blazer, wrapped it around her hand, and tried the handle again. And then again. And then again. And then screamed and shouted and pulled and tugged and...

"It's stuck," she shouted over the roof to Daniella.

"Here too," Daniella said. "I'll smash the window. Turn away," she shouted, presumably to Lise, who was on that side, in the front passenger seat. Daniella elbowed the glass, but it didn't break. Tilda was on the phone and had come around to Margaret's side, kneeling over Nele, checking her vitals. She seemed eerily calm. Was that due to years of tending to patients in various crises? Why wasn't she rushing to help her sister?

Daniella slammed her elbow into the glass again. The air was thick with smoke and the acrid smell of burning rubber. Pat screamed louder. As did Lise. More coughing. "Aaaaaarggh," Daniella said after another failed attempt with her elbow. At Righteous Path, there'd been a spate of break-ins from the teachers' car park. Ten in a year before they'd installed CCTV. Every single time they'd used a stone or brick, Margaret had noted. Car glass is thicker than people think, even on a Trabi. She turned and looked. A high wall. Bricks. Had the car damaged any? Yes. She ran towards it, passed Tilda, who was now dragging Nele further away from the car, presumably because she was worried about it exploding. Margaret picked up half a brick, ran back and smashed the driver's side window. She plunged herself into the car, grabbing Lise's outstretched arms, pulling her out, and then part carrying, part dragging her away from the car. Another window smashed. The back window. Daniella was getting Pat out, having smashed the rear window with her boots. Tilda rushed to help Margaret with Lise.

"Lise. I'm here," she said as Lise sobbed and coughed. Tilda took her from Margaret, squeezing her. "Are you okay? Be okay."

Margaret turned and saw Daniella cradling Pat in her arms like a baby, running from the car. Pat's trouser leg was on fire, but Daniella was trying desperately to get her away from the vehicle, now completely engulfed in flames. Eventually, Daniella dropped her, took off her army jacket and beat out the fire. "It's okay," she said. "You're safe. You're safe. It's over."

And then Margaret heard it. The explosion. The fireball. Sirens.

Chapter 27
Galway Gold Distillery (Jim)

Jim was at the back of the small tour group, walking down a wide corridor. "Now then, you ugly lot," Gary said, very much enjoying the group's attention. He threw a large metal door open, revealing an enormous room.

"Wow," Jim said, his head tipping back at just the sheer scale of it. The room was vast, with high arched ceilings, hefty wooden beams, shafts of sunlight streaming in through narrow windows illuminating the fine particles of dust that danced lazily in the air around the dozens of tightly stacked rows of barrels.

They walked inside, Jim bowing a little as he entered; a reflex. The floor was made of old, sturdy stone, worn smooth by years of footsteps. It was cool inside, the temperature obviously carefully controlled to support the aging process. It felt more like a monastery to him than a place of commerce, or like descending into the belly of a great ship. He could have sworn he felt the floor undulating under him, or the creak of wooden staves as the barrels expanded and contracted with subtle changes of temperature and the passage of time.

He sniffed and there it was - the unmistakable scent of

aging spirits meeting sturdy oak - the finest smell on earth. A sweet, honeyed scent with undertones of dried fruits—raisins, figs, and dates. As they moved towards the middle of the room, it shifted slightly, you got more alcohol. The barrels older, he guessed.

"I've died and gone to heaven," said Connor, turning around, his hands above his head. Jim chuckled at the irony in that statement, bearing in mind just how close he'd come to that very fate back in the woods.

"Now, if I were prone to seeing ghosts," said Seamus, looking up at the high, vaulted ceilings, "this would be the place."

"I don't see ghosts," said Jim, defensively, moving to the nearest stack of barrels and stroking his hand down their side. Each bore the mark of the famous 200-year-old whiskey brand they were there to taste––Galway Gold. The year each casket had been sealed was stamped on the side. This particular barrel had been there since 1927. Extraordinary.

"I see money," said Tristan, wide-eyed, looking around like someone who'd just been teleported inside a bank vault. "And lots of it."

"I actually see very little," said Seamus. "I should really go for an eye appointment. Can someone guide me, please? I'm not saying I'm afraid of the dark, but then I'm not saying I'm not, either."

"Here," Jim said, taking him by the elbow, following the group. The central corridor was just wide enough for a forklift to squeeze through, in between rows upon rows of barrels, stacked five high. The floor bore the marks of hard work, faded trails created by countless barrels being rolled into position. The lighting was dim, a little too dim, actually, and if one of those casks fell on you, you'd... not to mention all the dark, quiet corners where someone could... in fact, a hundred eyes could have been on them right now, and they

The Accidental Murder Club

wouldn't even have known. He tried to shake the thought away but failed. There had been a person in those woods, and that person would have killed Connor if Jim hadn't scared him off.

Gary had a grudge, he now knew. Tristan had his addictions and had hired a private detective. Tad's life had been ruined by a combination of Connor and Connor's family. Connor was going to ruin Seamus's present. No matter where you turned, you smacked into a cold, hard motive.

Gary led them all the way down the aisle to a clearing near the back wall, under the large windows. There were doors on their left and right. In the middle, directly under the largest window, was an upturned barrel from 1939, set up as a table. Gary uncorked a bottle.

Connor whooped. "I love it here."

Gary grinned. "Hasn't changed much since I worked here."

Connor's head tipped back. "Forgot you used to work here. Jesus, that takes me back. I almost got a job here too, character building, or so my pops thought. They gave you all the crappy stuff to do, as I remember it. Cleaning the bogs and the like? Worked you like a dog."

"Well, I had to work," said Gary. "Unlike some of us."

"You still work here," Seamus corrected.

Gary's eyes lowered. "The odd shift," he said, clearly embarrassed. "But not for long. There's an interesting opportunity, actually, Connor. I just need to find the right partner, maybe we—"

"No work talk," said Connor with a wave of his hand.

Gary's shoulders slumped. He began to pour into the first of several tasting glasses. In better circumstances, Jim would have been ecstatic to spend the afternoon here, but found his mood ever darkening: stormy in his mind. Not stormy enough for him to overlook the fact that Gary had just poured himself the first glass, and that was just rude; you pour yourself last, always. Gary turned to Seamus next, who covered the closest glass to himself.

"Still a wee bit early for me," he said.

"It's 2pm, and you look tense," Gary said, pouring Connor's instead.

"Lots to do later."

"Knitting?" Connor scoffed.

"Migraine?" Gary added.

"To Connor and Lise," said Jim, lifting his glass to interrupt, even though it was still empty, "and holy matrimony. Just adding that for Tad. Where did Tad go again?"

Gary filled Jim's glass.

"Church," Connor scoffed. "Gotta preach to the masses. Not that the masses are in churches anymore. Hopefully, someone will come and listen to the poor bastard."

"Tad's congregation is very faithful, I hear," said Tristan, as Gary filled his glass. "Gets at least two dozen, which is good for Inishmore."

Didn't seem like there was much else to do on Inishmore, Jim thought.

"To me and the lady-wife," Connor said, finishing Jim's toast and necking his drink before Tristan, Gary and Jim had even sipped theirs. Seamus's eyes explored the floor as Jim brought the small glass to his lips, closed his eyes, and focused as the liquid hit his tongue, savouring the complex flavours as they danced around his mouth. The buzz, the buzz was coming. He wouldn't let it be more than a buzz, of course, he needed to be on the ball.

"This has to be a higher ROI business than jumpers," said Tristan.

"Knitwear," Seamus corrected.

"We should diversify. I've actually got a PowerPoint I'd love to show you, Connor." Tristan looked around. "There are a lot of quiet corners here we could, I mean, my laptop is in my bag, so?"

"Me too," said Gary. "Well, I've no presentation. But I can... we could just talk?"

"We are the best in the world at what we do," Seamus said, quietly. "Don't you think, Connor?"

"I think it's been too long since I've had Galway Gold," Connor said, licking his lips. "And too long since you poured more of it, G. Pull your finger out, man. This is a tasting, not a talking. Or do I need to call your boss in here and get you fired?" He laughed at his own joke. He was the only one. Jim bristled on Gary's behalf. There's nothing wrong with working in hospitality. With improving people's day. Being there with them when they marked the most important moments of their lives. And anyway, Connor, other than a bit of painting here and there, didn't seem to have ever done a hard day's work.

"I'll be my own boss soon," Gary said, but did as he was told and refilled the glasses, himself first again, though. "That's what I wanted to talk to you about too. It's urgent."

Connor waved him off again. Jim stood on his tiptoes and did a quick sweep of the room.

"What?" Seamus asked, seeing he was on edge.

"Nothing," said Jim, taking a deep breath. "Just soaking it all in, you know? The heft of it. The history."

"Oh," said Seamus. "Of course."

"Worth more than gold," said Tristan. "And there's no way to actually verify it is a hundred years old. I looked into that. People just trust distilleries not to lie."

"Why would they lie?" Jim asked.

"People lie about all kinds of things," Seamus said, staring at Gary. "Even obvious things."

"They probably have their reasons," said Gary.

"Fear," said Seamus.

"Or family."

"Fear," he repeated.

"Or pride."

"Yeah, a lack of it," Seamus sniped. "Hey, they make more than whisky here, don't they?"

"No," Gary mumbled.

"I wondered why you didn't mention it on the tour?" Seamus pressed. Jim didn't like where this was going. Seamus was acting mighty feisty--a tiff between the lovers? Jim wanted the group together and as harmonious as possible.

Gary's mouth slackened. "Mention what?"

"That there's a whole other wing to this place. That they're actually famous for two drinks."

"Is there?" Gary asked. "I'm pretty sure I'd know about that."

"Yeah," said Seamus. Jim was thrilled to see Seamus did have some teeth to him, even if they were milk teeth, but not now, not here. "Bailey's Irish Cream," Seamus said, puckering his lips.

"Now that's a hell of a drink. A dessert in a glass. Whoever invented that must have laughed all the way to the bank, I reckon. Don't you, Gary?"

Gary gripped so tightly to the small glass in his hand that it cracked and split, cutting his palm, blood splashing onto the top of the table. "Shit," he said, stepping back, trying to collect himself.

"Don't know how that happened." He turned and picked up a tea towel that was folded on another barrel behind them, against the wall. He stacked the pieces of glasses onto it carefully.

"I've an idea," said Seamus. "You know what Tad would say if he was here, about lies?"

"If anyone's a liar here, it's you," Gary growled.

"Easy," said Connor, lifting his hands. "We're all friends here. Old friends. We have each other's backs."

Seamus and Gary laughed, more of a sneer, actually. "That right, is it?" Gary muttered under his breath.

"Always," said Connor. "We're family."

"Did you know they make more money with Bailey's Irish Cream than Galway Gold?" Gary asked.

"Why does everyone keep talking about Bailey's Irish Cream?" Connor asked. "I don't care how much they make with it. That's a wuss's drink. A lady's drink."

"It was my drink," Gary said, tapping his chest with his uninjured hand. Jim choked on a sip of Galway Gold. Gary stared Connor down, puffing his already large chest further. "God, you don't even remember, do you? You don't even bloody remember." He picked a last shard of glass from his hand and wrapped the tea towel tighter, to stem the bleeding.

"Remember what?" Connor asked, turning. "Do you know what he's going on about, Shay?"

"There's too much focus on the past," said Tristan. "Let's embrace the freedom of starting anew."

Connor and Gary groaned. Tristan closed his eyes reverently. "Oprah Winfrey."

"It's hard to leave the past when you've nothing to bring into the future," Gary said, eyes still fixed on Connor. "I invented it. Neachy. Do you really not remember, or are you just playing dumb?"

Connor's eyes darted around. "Did you, eh? How long ago was that, then?"

Gary's face was twisting into something monstrous, his eye and nostrils doubling in size. He pointed at Connor's chest, which would have been more menacing were his hand not wrapped in a tea-towel. "You laughed at it, you cock. Like you laugh at everything. And then some other bastard was in there and he heard me tell you the recipe. He stole it, sold it to Galway Gold, and now he's richer than all of us combined."

The longer Gary spoke, the more Connor's head angled. "Really?" he said, either calm or faking it. "That so. You know about this, Shay?"

"I've heard the story," said Seamus. "You really don't remember?"

"No," Connor said, filling his own glass and downing it in one. His eyes were already growing glassy. Why was Gary doing this now, Jim wondered. Just because Seamus was giving him a hard time? Or because he knew Jim was on to him? "I…" Connor exhaled. "Maybe, like? 'Twas decades ago though, was it not?"

"Decades of hard work and shitty jobs, yeah," Gary shouted, jaw clenched, teeth grinding. In the low light, there was now something ghoulish about his face. Jim looked around for a weapon. The nearest was the bottle. He felt sure, if he had to, he could lunge and get it before Gary did anything. He shifted his weight onto his toes, ready to pounce.

"Let's all just take a breath," he said.

"And I worked," said Connor, taking a half step back. "I painted."

"You painted?" Gary repeated mockingly. "While I scrubbed toilets and Tad rotted in prison. Yeah, you had a hand in that too, didn't you?" He threw back his huge head and gave a villainous laugh. "Literally."

"Jesus, what's got into everyone today?" Connor chuckled, looking at Jim. "Is this because I farted earlier and scared that damn fox away? I apologised for that already, man. It's me Irritable Bowel, it is. I've not had Camembert in five years. That's no way to live, man."

"My life could have been as easy as yours," Gary yelled, spraying spittle everywhere.

Connor wafted his hand dismissively. "And if your mum hadn't had that second Long Island, you wouldn't exist. So what?"

"So what?" Gary said, raising his arm. Tristan, who was nearer, put his arm across Gary, holding his fist back. "And you," said Gary, turning and flashing his teeth at him.

The Accidental Murder Club

"Leave it," said Tristan. "Violence is never the answer."

Gary pushed Tristan who, while slim of build, was muscular and, well, young. He held his ground before shoving Gary back, who hit the table and rolled off onto the hard stone floor. He cried out in pain. "Screw you all," he said, staggering to his feet and out towards the door.

Connor grimaced. "Jesus, man. I'm starting to remember why I left this place. Pour another round, aye, Jimmy?"

Seamus moved to follow Gary. "I'll just check he's okay."

Jim stepped into his path. "Leave him to me," he said, then winked. "No history, you know? No skin in the game. One publican to another. We'll be back in a minute and we'll drink to this and all move on, okay? Pour Connor another drink."

"I really think, I–" Seamus protested.

You're the real problem, Shay, Jim decided. There's a lover's tiff, and now Gary's lashing out at Connor. And I don't know what he's going to do next, which is why I need to be near him. "You, Connor, and Tristan need to talk about the business," Jim said. "We don't have long left, Con. You can't avoid it for much longer."

"It's me stag, man," said Connor.

"It's not a normal stag. Willie saw to that." Jim turned and started walking, not waiting for anyone to object. He caught up with Gary in the next room over, which was, indeed, full of cases of Bailey's Irish Cream. At the back, three huge metal vats, which Jim assumed were full of the stuff. The room was easily half the size of a football pitch, and so like a giant monument to Gary's failure and Connor's betrayal. Gary didn't seem surprised to see Jim approach. He was holding up an open bottle, reverently staring at it, open-mouthed, like you might the photo of your first lover. Jim rubbed his head, then carefully flattened and straightened his exceptional hair with his comb. He wasn't sure how to handle this conversation because he didn't know if Gary had been the shooter, only that he'd been in his room and hired the stripper. They were very different things. As different as Galway Gold and Bailey's Irish Cream, even.

Gary took a long swig. "I knew I had something," he said, after wiping his lips with his sleeve. "From the first sip."

"It's a good drink," said Jim. "The ladies lap it up."

"The ladies," said Gary, tapping his head. "No-one thinks about the ladies, do they? But that's half the pub and a short drink…"

"Is drunk the quickest," said Jim, nodding. "Yeah, smart."

"I'd planned it all," said Gary, his face still flush with anger, and even more veiny than usual. "It was in Neachy. I had the ingredients out, prepared a story, had blindfolds and everything. I wanted to cut Connor in fifty-fifty, or McGinley, I suppose. If he'd said yes, his father would have given him the money, no problem. Would have been pocket change for them. And then we'd have been off to the races."

Interesting choice of words, Jim thought. Maybe Tristan wasn't the only one with a gambling problem? "But he laughed at you, the sod?"

Gary stared off into nowhere. "Said it was too sweet. That no man would drink it. No woman, either. I don't know if he even tasted it." He put the bottle down. His arms hanging slack at his side. "I think he saw who made it, and that was enough. He decided failures can only make failures."

"There's a Chinese proverb," Jim said, remembering something Margaret had said in Berlin, "half what we see is behind our—"

"There's an Irish proverb," Gary interrupted. "God invented whisky to keep the Irish from ruling the world." Jim laughed. "And to think," Gary continued, "I invented Bailey's Irish Cream and could have ruled Ireland."

"It can't be all Connor's fault, can it, G?" Jim rubbed an eye. "There were other people who could have invested, surely?"

"I believed him. That was the worst of it. Doubted myself. I've often had a problem with, well…" He put a hand over his mouth.

"And whoever overheard in Neachy didn't have that problem?" Jim asked.

"Jack Malone, one of the stable lads," Gary said. "Turned out his grandfather worked here. Only as a cleaner, like, but it was enough. Stole the recipe nary a week later. Gets fifty cents on the bottle, I've heard, which must make him one of the richest men in Galway."

"He's still in Galway?"

"St Lucia, actually, that was just a figure of speech."

"Is St. Lucia in Ireland?"

"No, that's," Gary started, his voice quietening, "somewhere with much better weather and lower taxes."

"Lower taxes than Ireland?"

The two men chuckled. Gary picked up the open bottle and resumed drinking from it, but just sips now, not gulps, which Jim took as progress. The two men stood in silence for a while, but it didn't feel heavy. "That's the only drink you ever invented?" Jim asked. "All these years?"

Another flash of anger. "How many drinks you invent, wise guy?"

"Fair enough," said Jim, raising his palms. He had once experimented with a flaming cocktail until an unfortunate incident that burnt the fringe of a bleach-bottle-blonde named Belinda, who'd agreed to be one of an early test audience. After that, he stuck exclusively to the classics. People, they were Jim's gift. He looked backwards at the door to check no-one was coming. He thought he heard footsteps. It was now or never. "Why did you think seeing Lise with a stripper would stop the wedding?"

Gary put the bottle down and scratched his chin. "What? Why do you think–"

"Should I tell Connor what I think?" Jim looked towards the door. "Or, actually, come to think of it, maybe I'll tell Seamus what you did to the man he idolises? I think that would hurt you more, wouldn't it?"

Gary turned. "No. Please."

Jim poked him in the chest. "Let's stop messing around. You were in my room. You took Daniella's number and got her to arrange the stripper. She sent the photos. I know everything, G. Just not why you thought that would work?"

Gary gave a long sigh, then took a half step back, his shoulders dropping, his whole body seeming to sag. He looked like something left out in the rain. "Connor…" he said, while looking at the tabletop. "Well… I guess, because I haven't changed much." He glanced up at Jim. "He used to be incredibly jealous. That fight, the one where Connor, or Tad, well, I'm guessing you know about that, because you seem to know about everything else?"

Jim nodded. "I know."

"That was over a girl. This guy, he only looked at Connor's lass in passing, but Con was wildly jealous back then. Controlling. Lost many a lady to it. The red mist."

Jim had never seen Connor jealous. "Were you in the fight?"

"I was hiding," Gary said, the words glass in his mouth. "Under a table." He kicked some cases, but meekly. "I'm not a fighter. Not an anything, apparently." He took the tea towel off his hand; the wound had already stopped bleeding. He looked almost disappointed about this. "He's going to do the same thing to Shay that he did to me and Tad. He'll get nothing."

"Ah. It's not about revenge, it's love?"

Gary looked around frantically. "How did you–"

Jim lifted his hand. "Who you love's your business, fella, unless you make it mine. But why would stopping the wedding help Seamus? It was Willie that screwed him over, that left him nothing. Well, just some stupid picture."

Gary took a long, laboured breath. "If Connor has a broken heart, he'll run. He won't come back here, what with everyone whispering about him. The Trust can pay him off and everything can stay as it is. Shay can stay as he is."

"It's never that easy," said Jim, feeling pity for Gary, seeing how stupid this plan had been. He reached over and put a hand on the man's shoulder. 'An Almost', that's what Tad called him, and he saw it, too. How Gary botched everything. How he couldn't even be honest about who he was, who he loved. Jim thought of his ex-wife, Sally, who he hadn't spoken to in a decade, and his daughter, Trudy, who had neither time nor patience for him. There was resentment on both their sides––for the kind of father he'd been. Trudy had never even visited him at Cahoots, yet she was only forty miles away in Norwich. His similarities with Gary were larger than he'd like to admit. Cahoots was what had changed things for Jim. He'd found community. Found a second chance. Founded *Next Chance*, his bar. He was useful there. He suddenly saw a parallel to Tad and Soft Knocks. Oh, and to Seamus too, with the staff at McGinley. Most of us just need a reason to get up in the morning, a way to leave the world better than we found it. It's the people that don't have that you need to worry about––that left Connor, Tristan and Gary.

"How did you know?" Gary asked and flicked his head towards the door. About Seamus, Jim interpreted the gesture to mean.

"Same way you would have, pal. You work in a pub, you see a lot of people having affairs, right? Comes with the territory. Alcohol, well, bloody intoxicating, isn't it? Things happen. No shame in it. We're only human. And by that, I mean, well, we're basically monkeys, aren't we?"

Apes,' Gary corrected.

"Same difference. Anyway, you want to know who's shagging in a room full of people and isn't allowed to be? Look which sets of eyes never meet. People over-correct, basically. That's you and Seamus. From the minute I arrived, until ten minutes ago, when you turned on each other. Plenty of eye contact then, but very little before."

Gary's shoulders slumped even lower, making him look particularly ape-like. "Clever," he said, wearily.

"And then your stories. How often you mention each other."

"Maybe," he said.

"When did you decide to kill Connor?" Jim asked, casually, because he had to, not because he believed it, but just to see, just to say he had.

"Jim... I... no." Gary burst into tears. Bugger. Jim moved closer and patted him on the back as he wiped his eyes with a non-bloody part of the tea towel.

"Is that really what you think of me?" Gary asked, between thick sobs, his voice clogged with emotion. "If I'd hide from a bar brawl, would I really kill my childhood best friend? And my lover's brother? Former lover." His crying intensified. "And be asking Connor for money to buy Neachy?"

Jim pulled his head back. "Neachy's for sale?"

Gary nodded.

"Nice boozer."

Gary sniffed. "Sure is."

This was not hard evidence of his innocence, sure, but Jim could read a man, and Gary's genre was failure, not murder. He pitied him. He'd never feared him. The thing with Daniella and the photos was petty. And it's a long way from petty to taking a life. Jim fancied that Gary would have had more chance stabbing himself with the chandelier while rigging it up to fall, than getting it to plonk down at just the right moment onto Connor's head. And would he really risk hitting Seamus?

"Come back to the others?" Jim said, softly.

Gary lifted his chin a little. "Give me a minute, will ya?"

"Sure," Jim said, giving his shoulder a last rub before

walking back out to the main room. There, he found Connor at the table, knocking back another Galway Gold, but straight from the bottle now. "Tristan?" Jim asked Connor.

"Conference call. Or so he said."

"And Seamus?"

"Powdering his nose." Connor took another swig. "You work out what the hell got into Gary?" Jim heard at least two more double whiskies in his now very merry voice.

"You really didn't remember about the Irish Cream?"

His gaze wandered. He took a long time to answer. "Ancient history and we're here for the future, Jimmy. For love. Talking of which," he flashed Jim a grin, his voice brightening, "I was wondering, actually, how's your speech coming along?"

"Speech?"

"Your best man's speech. You started it yet? I'd love a little preview." Connor stuck his tongue out. "To hear someone say something nice about me, for a change. It's been beat up on old Connor day today, it has." He shadow-boxed, still holding the bottle. A little whisky splashed out.

"I'm more worried about when they tried to shoot you," Jim said, his chest swelling with pride.

"And isn't Gary or Tad best man?"

Connor lifted a hand loosely, then let it drop. "Has to be you, doesn't it, aye? You're the only one not harbouring a grudge against me, like these sad sacks of shite. I remember now why I never came back here. Small towns, Jimmy."

Jim nodded. "Nothing builds bigger resentment than a small town."

"What's that?"

"Something Gary said."

Connor cocked an eyebrow. "He probably stole it from someone else."

"Maybe," Jim chuckled.

"And mashed up all the words."

"I'd be honoured," Jim said, reaching out and clasping Connor's shoulder.

"You have to promise not to keep it clean," Connor said, pulling him in and kissing him on the top of the head. A sloppy one. "You know they do hair transplants now, right, fella?"

Jim laughed. The wee Irishman was delusional. Connor needed a lot more than a transplant. Connor poured another Galway Gold and then they clinked glasses and slammed it back. The intoxication was evident in the lilt of Connor's voice, his Irish accent growing thicker and thicker.

"We have to make it to the wedding first," Jim said.

Connor's eyes flicked upwards. "Oh, not that again."

"You don't see a lot of people with strong motives to harm you?" Jim asked, motioning around the room as if everyone was still standing there, feuding. "Because from where I'm looking, there's almost as much resentment in this place as there are barrels."

Connor laughed. "And you haven't even met me enemies yet."

"I wouldn't be––" Jim started, but before he could finish, an enormous explosion erupted to their right. The blast was a deafening wall of sound that knocked both him and Connor off their feet as barrels cascaded from their stacks, smashing open and rolling in all directions.

"Connor!" Jim yelled, struggling to get up, seeing a dozen barrels rolling down the central aisle, gaining speed, hurtling right at them. "Move!" he shouted, but his ears were ringing so loudly that he could barely hear his own voice as the first barrels surged towards them, about to crush them against the wall. Instinctively, Jim raised his arm in front of his face, bracing for impact. In that split second, his life flashed before his eyes. His thoughts went first to his marriage, then to his daughter, and a holiday they'd taken to Skegness. Him teaching her to swim in the pool when she was just two or three, her tiny arms in inflatable Mickey Mouse armbands. He recalled how tightly she'd clung to him as he waded them both into the deep end, her giggle the greatest sound he had ever heard—and will ever hear.

As the memory played vividly in his mind, his consciousness jumped to Cahoots and the sticky web of friendships he'd made there, one in particular with a woman who was, well, kind of particular, but in a way he liked; in precisely the way he wasn't. How cruel it would be if this was the end, when there was so much just getting started...

The barrels were almost upon them, and Jim's heart pounded as he prepared for the worst and then... out of nowhere, from their left, a forklift accelerated, its prongs smashing into the first barrel, just centimetres from Jim's face. It screeched to a stop in front of them, protecting them from the next wave of barrels.

"Get in," its driver said. Jim stared up at him in disbelief.

Chapter 28

University Hospital Leipzig (Margaret)

The antiseptic smell of the ward burned Margaret's nostrils as she stared down at her friend, gripping to Lise's limp hand tighter. The rhythmic beeping of machines echoed through the sterile room, synchronised with the mechanical rise and fall of her friend's chest. Bandages swathed her head and one arm, concealing angry burns beneath. A breathing tube snaked from her mouth, the hiss of forced air a reminder of Lise's fragile state. Harsh fluorescent lights cast a sickly pallor over her skin, accentuating the bruises and cuts marring her face.

The small private room, secured by Tilda's connections, still felt claustrophobic despite its comparative luxury over an open ward. Here, at least, it would be easier to keep Lise safe. Outside the window, the dark grey Leipzig sky matched the sombre mood in the room. Pat was being worked on in one of the operating theatres on the floor below. She hadn't regained consciousness during the ambulance ride. "*Grad II, Vielleicht schon III*," Margaret had overheard the doctors say. *Second degree, maybe third*. She'd been able to see from Tilda's face that these were not the good kind of grades.

Margaret's mind kept racing, replaying the chaos of the accident––the screeching tires, shattering glass, and acrid smell of smoke. She could still hear the screams and see the flames making easy work of the Trabi's flimsy frame. Fortunately, they had all survived and their injuries were not life threatening. Nele wasn't burnt, just had a neck injury from the impact of the crash. She was on the ward below them and had been incredibly fortunate to make it out just before the first explosion jammed her door closed.

Margaret buried her face in her hands and rubbed. How had this happened? No, how had she let this happen? She should have taken the keys to both vehicles and fled into the woods. She'd given in far too easily. Had not wanted to make a scene and now her friends lay broken and battered, victims of her weakness. Poor old Dieter had been set on fire again too. His urn had been in the backseat of the GDR Trabi, and so had been completely incinerated. She wasn't looking forward to telling Lise that when she woke up.

At least Connor and Jim were on their way. The thought warmed her more than she'd like to admit. She'd called them from a payphone just after the accident, and the confident male voice on the other end of the line—she still couldn't believe it was Connor's butler, that butlers really existed—had reassured her the message would reach Connor immediately. She knew how he would react to that message. That he would drop everything to come here. The butler had sounded jolly, drunk, or jolly drunk. What was it with the Irish?

"I'll check on Nele," Daniella said in a low voice from near the door, "be nice for her to see a somewhat familiar face."

"Thank you." Margaret, turning her head, hoped Daniella knew she wasn't just referring to this small act of kindness. Their tour guide had been so efficient, so quick on her feet, so willing to put herself in danger to save Margaret's friends that she saw her in a new positive light. Which wasn't the same as forgiving her. That might come in time.

"I can stay with Lise if you want to check on Pat?" Tilda said, on the opposite side of the bed, holding Lise's other hand, worry lines etched into her forehead. The sisters' complicated history hung heavy in the air, unspoken but palpable. Sure you will, Margaret thought. That was probably why she'd insisted on this private room in the first place. A night in a hospital had a micromort score of 75 already––not accounting for a sister with medical knowledge and a decade-long grudge.

"I'll stay," Margaret said, neutrally. "At least until Pat's awake."

Tilda's shoulders dropped, but she said nothing and other than the occasional beep from a diagnostic machine, the room fell silent until, and into it, Margaret's mind whirred with the mysteries and clues and lies and possibilities.

"The poison pen letters," she asked, when she could hold them no more. Her voice sounded unnaturally loud in the quiet room. "You said you didn't know you'd accidentally written on one?"

"Why do we need to get into that now?" Tilda asked, looking down at Lise, worried she might be able to hear.

Head-teacher tone. "Because your sister is in danger. We're all in danger. If you didn't know, why did you want to get them back so badly?"

"I…" Tilda's eyebrows furrowed. "I didn't want them back?"

"Yes, that's why you broke into Pat's room yesterday, wasn't it?"

Tilda's blinking grew rapid. She checked again if Lise had woken miraculously up. "Someone broke into Lise's room, you mean? At Cahoots?"

"No, into Pat's. And here, at the hotel."

She let go of Lise's hand and clutched her cross, mouth

narrowing. Disbelief seemed to have become confusion, as far as Margaret could read her face, never the most expressive.

"Why would Pat have Lise's letters? I didn't even know the letters were here. And why would I want them back? The damage is done." She was babbling now with the stress of the topic, and the reminder that she really had authored those letters.

"Pat is working on something," Margaret said. "Something about Tick-Tick or The Ghost. That's why she's been sneaking off."

Tilda's eyes suddenly focused. "Thorsten," she said. "I thought it couldn't just be a coincidence."

The name rang a vague bell. Was it Nele's husband? No, wait… "Our guide from the spy museum," Margaret said, sitting up suddenly.

"He was there at *Moritzbastei*," Tilda continued. "After you left the table to look for Pat, he came through the bar from a different entrance with his cane."

Margaret's mouth fell open. She hadn't noticed him there, but then it had been full, and she hadn't been looking for him, specifically, not that he was an easy man to overlook. What were the odds of him accidentally being there at that time? She'd read that based on a Bernoulli trial calculation, the chance of meeting someone you knew in a city like London was 2.2% per year. Leipzig's population was fifteen times smaller, but they'd been here less than a week, and so knew almost no-one. And yet he had been there. And Pat had documents about Tick-Tick. Pat. She'd been so focused on who was after Lise and Connor. Pat had been in the graveyard, standing next to Lise when that knife was thrown. Margaret had picked up and sniffed the spare cocktail--spare because Pat wasn't there. Could it be that Lise was laying in that bed as tragic collateral damage in some ruthless quest to silence Pat? It didn't explain what was happening in Galway, though.

Margaret stood up and began to pace the room--four steps one way, four steps back. She hit her palm with her other fist. Assumptions: they really do make an ass of you. "I've been looking at this all wrong," she said. "I assumed all the events served the same goal: stopping the wedding, even if it was by killing either the bride or groom. But correlation is not causation." She shook her head. It was Jim's fault. He had been so sure it was all about the wedding. She breathed in through her nose. Yes, Jim deserved much of the blame, but she could still solve this. She just needed to look at everything that happened again, individually and neutrally. There might be several bad actors, with differing motives. She remembered something else she hadn't yet solved. "Veronika Fleischer. Why did you book the hotel under that name?"

"I…" Tilda gripped her cross tighter, as if trying to rip it off. A sob grew in her chest that she struggled to contain. Her eyes flooded. "I didn't want her to come here. I didn't want," she looked around the room, "all this madness. Veronika Fleischer was in the orchestra with Lise. Flute. She was a Stasi informant. Informed on her parents, even, who were planning to escape a little after the wall went up. They were put in prison. Shocking, no? I told Lise about it during a phone call, after Mum died. She couldn't believe it, how someone could do that to family. I'm surprised she didn't remember. Didn't connect the name."

Margaret sat back down and gazed up at the bland, white ceiling tiles as a wave of realisation washed over her. Another mystery was solved, but like everything in this case, it seemed only to lead straight into several more. She remembered a phrase from one letter--'I don't care about the wedding'-- what an interesting thing to say. Because if Tilda didn't care about the wedding, what did she care about? What else were they doing in Leipzig that mattered? What other sins were threatening to escape the past? There was a fizzing in her mind as synapses connected. It was all there. She'd just been too distracted to see it. "The archives," she blurted. "Of course. You wanted to stop her from going there because," it was the only thing that made sense, "you informed on her. You are her Veronika Fleischer. That's why you picked that name."

Tilda gasped, probably shocked to hear the words uttered out loud at last. She leaned forward, checking Lise was still asleep. Then she looked at Margaret and while it clearly pained her to do so, she nodded with downcast eyes. She had let go of her necklace and was rotating a ring on her finger; a simple gold band. Until now, the only jewellery she'd worn had been that cross.

"You had the ring all this time?" Margaret asked.

Tilda's head lowered further, chin into her neck, and it was as if she was talking to the ring, when she said, "I put it on after the crash. I had it the whole time. Wanted to give it to her. I just felt, I know it doesn't make any sense, but it was better that she was angry at me about the ring than about…" Tilda broke off.

It was not an uncommon strategy to deal with guilt, Margaret thought, baiting the other side into a conflict that one had control over. Not something she would do, of course, but then she was acutely self-aware. Still, of all the names she could have picked, she chose Veronica Fleischer. She had wanted to come clean. Wanted to rid herself of the guilt and so, subconsciously or not, she'd left clues. "The sins of the past," Margaret said slowly. "Wasn't that what Thorsten said? How they cast a long shadow?"

"Yes," Tilda whispered, the word birthed slowly and heavily. "When she was living in Berlin." Her voice broke. Margaret handed over a tissue from her bag. "She had so much contact with musicians and other artists in the West that they came to me. They pressured me." Tilda raised her hand to her chest. "They weren't people you, well… you did what they said. I did what they said. I shouldn't have, but I did. I told them about Dieter, too. I hate myself for it. But I did it."

Was that why Dieter had been caught in his tunnel? If so, that must have been an awful lot to live with. "Thank you," Margaret said. "For being honest."

"I wasn't honest, though," Tilda said. "Was I? That's the problem."

"You were young," she said. "You had no idea what they would have done to you, had you refused."

"You wouldn't have done it," Tilda said.

Margaret took a deep breath. "I've made mistakes."

"I wonder now if I was maybe just jealous?" Tilda said. "I didn't enjoy it, though. I even vomited once, after meeting my handler. But I could have said no. Or given them false information. I'll never know if I was the reason Dieter got sent to prison." Her voice was pleading for a do-over. To go back to that time and make different decisions. Margaret sensed she was unburdening herself. Tilda took a deep breath. "She told Nele on a phone call that she was planning to go to the archives. Nele told me. I couldn't let that happen. I thought if I stopped her from coming here. If I could move the wedding to Ireland. But I've just made everything worse, again."

Margaret's gaze wandered to the window, which looked out at a car park. "Why didn't you want to be in a Trabi with her?"

Tilda's eyes flitted left and right. "What?"

"You tried hard to get away from her."

"I just felt so guilty after my outburst. Also," a hint of a smile, "she really is a terrible driver. My father only let her drive the family Trabi once and she crashed into a bakery. How do you crash into a bakery? They don't move."

The confrontation at the lake. This confession. If she wanted Lise dead, why would she tell Margaret all this? It was just more ammunition. More motive. Margaret adjusted her neckerchief. Tilda's story held together, her actions making sense, more or less. Tilda lifted Lise's limp hand and kissed it. "I've hurt her enough already. It might not seem like it, but the things I did recently were to *not* hurt her more."

Margaret nodded. "The prank calls, the cancellations, the letters. They're their own case. And they're solved, right?" She gave Tilda a firm stare. "You've told me everything?"

Tilda rubbed at her neck. "Yes. And I'll tell her everything too," she said. "When she wakes up."

"You didn't tell her at the lake?"

"No," she said, quietly. "But I will now, I promise."

If she didn't, Margaret would. Lies are a cancer that consumes the host. She got up and paced some more, holding her arms behind her back to stop them flailing around. She went right back to the start. "The knife was thrown at Pat, too. But due to my own confirmation bias, I saw Lise as the intended victim. Next, the poisoned drinks. Daniella drank one and was fine, so it wasn't the whole round that was tainted. Pat's glass was near me. The break-in. Pat again, obviously. Unbelievable." She could have slapped herself. "I've been so stupid. And then the Trabi race. Three people got hurt. Pat, again."

The archives. Pat had been the one pushing to go there too. Just as she had the Spy Museum. She replayed that visit in her mind. How Pat had pretty much refused to enter the room about Tick-Tick, had just hovered in the doorway. Margaret had interpreted it as disinterest, but what if it was the opposite?

"I want to make things right," Tilda said, looking forlornly down at her sister. "I just hope she'll forgive me."

"She'll forgive you," Margaret said, even if she wasn't quite sure she believed it. It seemed possible. She'd forgiven Dieter often enough, and let's face it, she wasn't going to win any Sister of the Year awards herself. Maybe their two guilts would balance each other out? Margaret looked up at the clock. "The appointment at the Stasi archives. If it was so important to Pat that Lise went there, we can infer she knew something we don't about what's in Lise's file. I think that's our best chance of learning what this is all about. It has to be the person themselves. That's what Nele said, right? Or a family member, if the person has died?"

Tilda nodded.

"Being unconscious in a hospital is probably not close enough, although it's far closer than I'd like her to be."

"Maybe we can get another appointment once Lise is better?" Tilda suggested.

"It took nearly a month's notice to get this one," Margaret said. "There won't be time. Or Lise will have to come back after the wedding. Assuming there's going to be a wedding. Assuming there's still going to be a L–"

"I'll do it," Tilda said, jumping up and grabbing what was left of Lise's wallet from a nearby clear plastic bag of her possessions rescued from the wreckage. It was burnt down on one side, but had fared better than everything else in Lise's handbag. She removed Lise's ID from it. "Look," she said, putting it next to her face. Margaret removed a blue beret from her bag and settled it on Tilda's head. With Tilda's greying hair hidden under the hat, the resemblance wasn't bad. She was double the width of her sister, but you couldn't see that from the headshot, and anyway, women in middle age do tend to fill out, it was a problem Margaret knew well, and the reason she no longer ate dinner, well, unless on holiday or a disastrous hen-do.

"Are you sure?" Margaret asked, knowing she couldn't come, that she had no right to enter the archives, and that someone must wait here to protect Lise, and Pat, once she got out of the operating room.

Tilda nodded. "I'm sure."

"Be careful," she said, as Tilda hurried from the room.

Margaret took Lise's hand once more, returning to the vigil she'd been holding for her injured friend, the warmth of her skin a reassuring contrast to the cold efficiency of the room. "We'll figure the rest of this out," she whispered, her words barely audible above the hum of machines. "I'll figure it out."

Chapter 29

University Hospital Leipzig (Jim)

Jim hurtled into the hospital, his knees throbbing from the mad dash from the taxi. He was trying to keep up with Connor, rushing towards the elevator, but each step sent a jolt of pain through his aging joints. The fluorescent lights buzzed overhead, casting harsh shadows across the faces of worried visitors and harried staff. Tad and Seamus were just behind Connor, in the medal positions, with Gary a slow, stumbling fourth, and Jim last, his heart pounding and lungs burning, desperate for more oxygen than they could take in. Panting, he just made it into the elevator before the doors closed. Connor and Gary were bent over, holding the rail as the box on wires rushed them up to the fifth floor. Jim's stomach lurched with the swift ascent, his anxiety mounting.

"Come on," Connor muttered when the elevator stopped on the third floor, and for no one. He hammered the door close button a half dozen times until an alarm beeped. "Come on, ye bastard."

Bing. Fifth floor. Connor was the first out, striding down the hallway, the others in tow. Jim's eyes darted from door to door, counting up toward room 5.12, the number Margaret had given them over the phone several hours before.

5.9 ... 5.10 ... 5.11 ...

Through the window, Jim spotted a familiar thick head of chestnut-brown hair and a tight, modest scarf. His heart thudded even faster, and that was nothing to do with the exercise. Connor launched himself through the door. "LISE!" The rest rushed in behind him, filling the small, drab room. "My Lise. What have the bastards done to you?" Connor gushed, draping himself over his bride-to-be, knocking Margaret aside. She got quickly up and moved away. "My darling Lise," he said, peppering her cheeks with kisses. "Oh, how I miss ye, you daft wench."

Jim stood at the back of the room, feeling like an intruder on this intimate moment. His eyes roamed, taking in the various machines and tubes connected to Connor's fiancée. This was all so much more serious than he'd hoped.

"Hello Jim," Margaret said with a narrow smile as she moved over to the window. He stepped forwards and around Gary and tried to hug her as she passed. She accepted it, albeit stiffly. Her coolness towards him stung.

"Thank God you're okay," he said. "You are okay, aren't you?"

"Only my pride's hurt," she said, ending the hug.

He smiled, weakly. I missed you, he wanted to say, the words catching in his throat.

"I miss—how is Miss Pat?" There was a pang of guilt when he realised how little he had thought about Pat on the McGinley private plane from Galway; he'd not thought about her at all, actually.

"We don't know yet," Margaret said, teeth scraping her bottom lip. "The doctor hasn't been in. We also don't know how long Nele has to stay here." Margaret glanced down towards the floor. "Pat took it the worst. She's in surgery. When she's out, we need to protect her. There's–"

"Nele?" Jim asked. He hadn't thought about Nele either. So, she'd also been in the car?

"Nele's fine," said a voice from the doorway. He turned on his heels to find a young woman, dark-skinned for a German, wait... was she German? There was something familiar about her face, too––those prominent cheekbones and high hairline. And then the Hawaiian shirt––fitted, tucked in, nicely complementing her shapely blue jeans with a tear across both knees, now dusty and full of black streaks that looked like ash. Don't look at her jeans, Jim. Focus on the bandages on her hands. "Who are you then, love?"

"Unless you fall in love at first sight, I'm not your love," the woman said, folding her arms across her chest, a move that was supposed to be strong, but because she was worried about the burns on her hands, came across as nervy.

"Okay," Jim said, raising his palms; young people were so touchy nowadays. "Sorry."

"That'd be a first," Margaret said. "This is Daniella. She saved Lise's and Pat's lives."

Daniella cleared her throat and looked over his shoulder towards Margaret. "Well, I had some help."

"You saved her?" Connor said. Jim didn't turn to see if he was actually looking at Daniella, but his assumption was that he wouldn't be taking his eyes off Lise, not even for a second. "I'll thank you properly and generously later."

Jim had given Connor a full debrief on the plane of everything that had happened on the hen-do while they'd been in Galway. Of course, after the explosion at the distillery, Connor already believed that someone was willing to kill to stop his wedding, a wedding that would make Lise the heir to the McGinley fortune, should anything happen to him. On the plane, Jim had seen how the realisation cut into him; slashing at his pride and ego. For not only did it mean he'd failed to keep Lise safe, he was also the reason she was in danger. The reason she was now lying in that bed, unconscious. It was his love that had done this to her.

"Irony is, Jim," he'd said. "They're trying to stop me from getting the McGinley money when I don't even want the bloody thing."

Daniella spoke towards him, but also over his shoulder, to Margaret. "Nele woke up. She's still a bit groggy, but the CT scan came back normal. Her vitals too, so other than a bit of bruising, she's okay."

He stepped to the left so he could get out of the volleys of their words and see them both. "That's good to hear," Margaret said. "She was incredibly lucky to make it out before the fire." She corrected herself. "Fortunate, I mean."

"Know who else was just wheeled past me?" Daniella said.

"Who?" Margaret asked.

"The barmaid from *Moritzbastei*."

"Interesting."

"What's she got to do with it?" Jim asked, but Daniella's attention had wandered to the other half of the room.

"Here for the last rites?" she asked Tad, standing in the corner in his cassock.

"Oh, right," Jim said, realising he'd not introduced anyone. He pointed. "This is Tad and Seamus and Gary."

"Excuse the formality," said Tad, looking down at himself. "I came straight from a service."

Jim nodded, because he knew this was true. He'd already chased up Tad's alibi while they'd been waiting for the McGinley private jet to fuel up, Tad to arrive, and Gary to scavenge a six-pack. He'd called, with the help of Directory Enquiries, Tad's church out on Inishmore. It was Kelly, the young lad Connor had fought, who'd answered that call. Jim had had only two questions for him––had there been a sermon today? And what was it about?

"John 8:32 - Ye shall know the truth, and the truth shall make you free," Kelly had said. "Father," and Jim had wondered again if he was using that in the religious or familial sense, "told a fable about people in a cave seeing shadows on a wall. And about you seeing shadows in the woods."

It was that last detail that clinched it for Jim. Whoever had been behind the attack in the brewery, it wasn't Tad; he had an alibi over in Inishmore. Perhaps not proof iron-clad enough for Margaret, but enough for him to make his mind up. Or, rather, for his gut to do so, then send word up the chain to his mind.

Seamus moved closer to Connor, squeezing him on the shoulder. "I'm looking forward to finally getting to meet her, although I'd hoped it would be under better circumstances," he looked upwards, "and in softer lighting."

"Any chance of a drink around here?" Gary said to Daniella. "Just to keep spirits up?"

"Do I look like a barmaid?" She scowled.

"You look..." said Jim, scratching at his stubble. "Your accent. Where did you grow up, if you don't mind my asking, which you probably do?"

"All over," she said, but the er slipped into more of an ar, like a certain regional accent that Jim knew well, one that belonged to Norfolk, the county just next to Cahoots. Daniella... Daniella...? She was the rubbish tour guide, who'd really seemed to rankle Margaret. Jim dug deep down into his memories. He had the recollection of an elephant, and the neck too. "Hartmut," he said, rocking on his heels. "You're Hartmut's daughter. Bloody hell. Now there's a blast from the past. He told me you were in the same business."

"What?" she said, taking a half step back, straight into the corner of the doorjamb. Hartmut had been the owner of

Tschüss Tours. Jim had never been a fan of the man, on account of the fact that he was a charlatan and a playboy and slipperier than an eel at a water park. Also, he wore Hawaiian shirts so gaudy you needed sunglasses just to look at them.

"Hartmut had a child?" Margaret said, her face inscrutable. Either she didn't believe him or so much had happened today, she'd transcended surprise.

"How did you–" Daniella began to ask.

"I can't believe I–" said Margaret, rubbing the back of her neck. Okay, maybe this was news to her after all.

"Who's Hartmut?" Gary asked.

Jim grinned, enjoying that he'd worked out something faster than Miss Margaret Marple. Had they been alone, he'd definitely have gloated about it for several minutes, but there was a room full of people staring at him, and one who probably would have been, other than the fact she was very unconscious. "Get someone drunk and you'd be surprised what falls out," he said, moving his arm up to scratch his head languidly. "He told me that every first-born son in his family was called Daniel. Tradition, and the like. As was his older brother. Anyway, he was sure you'd be a boy, but then, surprise." He grabbed his crotch. "No meat and veg. So, he went with Daniella."

"I'm confused," said Gary.

"Yeah, but you're always confused," said Seamus.

Daniella's brow furrowed. "That... he never told me that."

"Well," Jim laughed, "knowing Hartmut it might not be true."

"Hey," she said, jaw jutting out.

"How is this helping Lise, or the rest of us get a drink?" Gary asked.

Seamus tutted. "You can go an afternoon without a tipple, Gary. You might even like it. Might clear your head on a few things."

"Yeah, why are we talking about Hartmut?" said Connor.

"Why do we talk at all?" said Tad.

"I got my car," Daniella said to Margaret, trying to shift the conversation. "I thought it might be useful later, if you want to go to the hotel, or something?"

"You can drive?" Margaret asked.

"Badly," she said. "But yeah."

"You drove badly before."

The two women shared a short laugh.

"None of this is what I want to talk about," Jim said dismissively. He pointed towards the corridor.

"Let's talk outside, Daniella." He wasn't sure how she fitted into this plot, or if she did at all, but her being Hartmut's daughter was just a hell of a crazy coincidence, and while they did happen––he once had two brothers separated at birth, no idea the other existed, order the same drink, at the same time, with the same lisp, from neighbouring barstools. Now that was a night to remember, and not only because they'd both skipped out on their bill–they didn't happen often.

Daniella considered it, held her breath, then let a small nod escape, almost against her will.

"Margaret," Jim said, beckoning her to follow with a flick of his head. She followed them out. As they stepped into the hallway, leaving the cramped hospital room behind, Jim took a deep breath, steeling himself. He shut the door behind them. To the right, in the corridor, were three chairs with their backs to the wall. Jim pulled one out and turned it around to face the other two. The two women sat side-by-side. He got out his comb and slowly fixed his look as he tried to work out how to start. As he brushed his excellent hair, with the thickness of a man twenty years his junior, a small smile formed on Daniella's face. He ignored it. She wouldn't be smiling by the end of this.

"Jim," Margaret said impatiently. "We've a lot to talk about."

He carefully returned the comb to his shirt pocket. "Thing is, Daniella," he said. "You're a coincidence, and coincidences make me more nervous than extra-time corner kicks. You'd not like me when I'm nervous, few do."

She laughed sarcastically. "That supposed to be a threat?" She gave Margaret a quick open mouthed is-this-guy-serious look.

"Jim," Margaret said again, but he pushed forward, didn't need all the information to execute another of his flawless interrogations. He was actually at his best when off script and ad-libbing. He cracked his knuckles. "You messed with the car, didn't you?" Daniella went still. "We know you conspired with Gary, hiring the stripper and sending the photos. You're over here, the one-year anniversary of Berlin, where poor old Hartmut met his…" he swallowed. "Yeah, it makes sense." It didn't really make sense, but he didn't have to let her know how confused he was. He prodded a finger. "Time to confess."

Daniella laughed, which wasn't the response Jim was expecting. "You're an idiot," she said, a lightning strike of anger flashing across her face. "I don't care about their stupid wedding or this dumb trip or *Tschüss*." She glanced at Margaret. "All they all do is argue anyway."

Margaret put her hand on Daniella's knee: "You don't really mean that, Daniella."

What part, Jim wondered? "Don't let her wriggle out of it, Mags. She has means, motive and whatever that third one is you're always banging on about. We're standing in front of an open goal, the ball at our feet. We just need to keep our nerve."

"What goal?" Daniella asked, confused.

"Margaret," Margaret corrected. "And sorry, Daniella. He's got a tic. Footballing idioms. You get used to it."

Jim's mind lurched. "Like that tic-tic fella?"

Margaret shook her head. "It's not tic with a c, it's tick with a ck. Like time."

"Ah, I always heard it the other way."

"It's the same word in German, anyway," Daniella said. "It's all just tick with a k."

Jim scratched his head, beginning some of his legendary lateral thinking. His mind was full of dots and he was bloody well going to find a way to join some of them up.

"I helped him," Daniella said, adopting a defensive posture, crossing her arms slowly. The bandages on her hands a reminder of supposedly heroic actions, at least that's how Margaret told it. "Gary, or whatever," she continued. "He offered me money, and I helped him. Got him the stripper. Sent him the photos. And only him, by the way. I didn't send them to anyone else. And I'm certainly not trying to kill anyone."

The harsh overhead lighting cast deep shadows under her eyes, making her look older and more tattered than she had in Lise's room. He noticed a slight tremor in her bandaged hands, a sign of nerves, or just lingering pain from her injuries? The antiseptic smell of the hospital seemed to intensify as they sat there, making his head swim slightly. He took a deep breath, trying to clear his thoughts, and then hit her with one of his hard stares, studying her face for any hint of deception.

"I believe her," Margaret said. "Sorry, Jim. There's been a lot here that you haven't seen and..." she paused, "if you'd been there, at the crash, you wouldn't be suspicious of Daniella." She smiled softly at her. "I do wish you'd told me about Hartmut. There have been too many secrets on this trip and it would have helped explain some things. Your behaviour. There were some clues, after the cemetery, how you reacted, but I was distracted. Why didn't you take *Tschüss* over?"

Daniella's eyes darted between him and Margaret, her posture stiffening. "The business was in bad shape. When I finally saw the books, he'd, well, drunk it all away. There was nothing to save. Now I'm stuck here, a lowly tour guide once again, doing the same job I started doing for him when I was first like, what, twelve? First working for free for him, and now for a pittance for you people. The people that didn't keep him alive despite your stupid club."

"You heard about that?" Jim remembered how'd he been careful to always use the name in the media interviews he'd done when they got back to England, just in case they got a book or movie out of it. None of that stuff had materialised, unfortunately, and after about a day, the news cycle had moved on. People were fickle like that.

"Why did you have to ruin his reputation?" she asked.

Jim lifted his hands. "To be fair, he'd done a lot of that himself. But I regret calling him a plonker quite so often though, and on the news."

"You remind me of him," Margaret said. Daniella tried to shrug the compliment off, but Jim saw her fail, a small smirk sneaking free from the edges of her mouth.

"The good parts of him," Margaret added.

"Good parts?" Jim muttered before he even noticed he was doing it.

"Jim," she barked.

"It's your no-nonsense nature," Margaret continued. "Not everyone…" she paused. "We women… Well. Some of us struggle to carve out an identity for ourselves, is what I'm saying. Not you. Yours is striking. You've no problem taking up space."

Daniella lifted her hands to her head but seemed to realise touching it would be painful, and so lowered them again. "I had nothing to do with this," she said. "With any of it." She craned her head back and up towards the room and Lise, trying to see in through the window. "After the ghouls tour, I went to find the actors and had it out with them. At first, each thought one of the others had tried something new, but it wasn't them, I knew. There was some nutter in the graveyard that night."

Margaret's hand shot up to her mouth. "Why didn't you say anything?"

"It's my job to keep you safe. And you were already blaming me for everything. Excuse me," Daniella said, standing up. Jim could see she was having a hard time staying composed and didn't want to be emotional in front of them. "I'll be back shortly. I just need to…" Her voice trailed off, and she moved towards the toilets.

Jim and Margaret were alone for the first time. "You trust her?" he asked.

"Yes."

"Right answer," Jim said. "Because my money's on Gary, isn't it? Yeah, I feel it in my bones, Mags. I'd gone off him but I thought it all through again on the flight. The shoe is very much fitting."

"Didn't you just think that it was Daniella? You went piling in on her, as usual, bull in a China shop. Attacking people like that never works."

He crossed his arms. "Never works for you, no. And yeah, right now, I'm fancying Gary. He could have done all three attempts. He was at the wake, he was in the woods hunting, and he was somewhere during the whisky tasting." He realised she didn't know yet about the explosion at the distillery, so he filled her quickly in. "Gary could have got ahead of me, somehow. Knew the layout too, since he works there. We know he organised the stripper. And he's an enormous chip on his shoulder about Bailey's Irish Cream."

"It's not about the wedding, Jim. It's not even about Lise."

He tipped back in his chair. "Jesus. So, you don't believe me anymore, either? About the chandelier? The shooting? The distillery?"

"It's about secrets from the past," Margaret said. "About the GDR. About what's in the Stasi files."

The Accidental Murder Club

"Maybe it's both? It's rarely ever either/or, Mags," he said. "In my experience. It's usually *and*."

"This more of your pub wisdom?" she asked.

"It's just what it is," he said. "And what the hell's a GDR?" he asked, feeling like an idiot, which he so often did in her presence.

"East Germany."

"The commies?" he asked, incredulous. Why was she trying to distract him? No, bamboozle him.

"I don't think they ever made it full of communism, but that's beside the point."

"Produced a hell of a football team too, the East Germans." He dropped his arms to his side. "1974 World Cup final against West Germany. Wretched game, but what an upset. What a move. Keeper to the big lad up front in just two passes. Magic."

"Can you focus, Jim?"

"He certainly had it. Sparwasser. What a chest." Jim inflated his chest, miming cushioning a football. It had been too long since he'd had a good kick about. He really needed to get the Cahoots team back in the over-fifties league now that the match-fixing scandal had died down. No one had ever proven Connor was guilty of anything other than indecency, and was that really a crime? Not in Jim's book.

"It was the regime under which Lise, Tilda, Nele, and Dieter lived," Margaret clarified. "Pat is researching something. It seems to have put everyone in danger. I think it's about Tick-Tick. That he threatened Pat. That maybe that's why she's taken a vow of silence." She blinked slowly. "It's a lot. I don't have it all. Don't even know how Galway and Ireland connect."

"Tic-Tac? You've lost the plot, Mags. It's about the wedding, obviously. Has to be. Why else would they both have been targeted? There's nothing else that links them."

He watched Margaret take a deep breath and feared she was about to use her patronising headteacher voice on him. The last few days had been so stressful. He really needed to be believed.

"Margaret," she corrected and then told him what she'd been able to put together so far––Tilda having been some kind of informant, and also the author of the poison pen letters, the letters Margaret was really mad he'd not told her about. By the time she'd finished, he'd gone cross-eyed and had a headache only a pint of something strong could shift; a Stella Artois, maybe. He massaged his temples.

"Mighty interesting coincidence that all this started the minute Willie died, though, no? A real million-to-one that."

"There's nothing special about a million-to-one events happening. It's just the law of large numbers. Think how many lotteries are won every day. Billions of humans, doing hundreds of billions of things each day."

"I know what I saw," he said defensively. "I nearly died today."

She reached for his hand, a small act that took him so by surprise that he nearly fell from his chair. "I'm sorry," she said. "That's horrible, and I'm very happy you made it out, and I absolutely believe you. I don't know how it connects and maybe it doesn't. Maybe it's a separate thing."

He slumped lower in his seat. Hearing her say she believed him took a great weight from his shoulders and the warmth of her hand… "Thanks," he said, as she let it go, much too soon.

"And it did start before," she said. "Pat arrived at Cahoots already mute. The poison pen letters arrived too, both long before Willie died."

"Yeah," he admitted, albeit reluctantly. She turned to the room and lowered her voice. "Did Seamus have an alibi for the distillery?"

"No," Jim said. "He's still on the hook too, don't you worry."

"And where is Tristan? Last time we spoke, you seemed sure it was him? You seem a bit muddled."

The Accidental Murder Club

He noted the tightness in her jaw and the worry lines etched around her eyes. Could see that the past few days had been as hard on her as they had on him. He wanted to pull her head into his chest, to assure her that they would figure this out together––The Accidental Murder Club––just as they had in Berlin. But he didn't, couldn't. She wouldn't want that. Didn't want him. "Your face is muddled," he said.

She rolled her eyes. "How old are you?"

"21. And it's not Tristan," Jim firmed. "He saved us at the whisky tasting in a recklessly driven forklift. Really came through, the kid. And he can't have been the one trying to shoot at Connor. He has trigger-finger. Which is actually the opposite of being able to pull a trigger." He cracked his knuckles. "You get it from doing too much coke. Weird name. Stay on point, Jim." He circled his arms, getting the blood flowing. "Anyway, he's not going to try and off Connor with a rifle from fifty metres away. He admitted he's stealing from the company to finance his drug and gambling shenanigans. Fessed up in the limo. Cried too, the pansy. Not really the right time for a confession, either, with Connor so distracted. He's a plonker, the boy. I'm pretty sure Connor will fire him. But he's not plotting murder. Well, maybe his own. I didn't bring him because we don't need him."

"And Tad?" Margaret asked.

"Solved that as well, I have. He was preaching at his church while we were at the whisky tasting about truthfulness and forgiveness and all that good stuff. Might even be a good egg after all, although I wouldn't bet big on it."

"Hmm," Margaret said, with that lightly disapproving tone that she so favoured. It hadn't even been a week, yet he'd missed it. "I need to go to the spy museum."

"To a museum? Now? You're off your rocker."

"There's clues there. Pat knew it too. And someone I need

to talk to." She went to stand up. Jim jumped up too, knees be damned. He held out an arm to block her.

"No, you're bloody well not."

"Who do you think you're talking to?"

"It's not safe."

"I'll be fine." Her face was just a few centimetres away from his. He smelt her perfume with its notes of bergamot. Catnip to him. A shiver ran down his spine.

"Yes, because you'll be here with me, helping me keep our friends alive."

"The best way to do that is to solve this," she said. "I don't know how what's been happening in Ireland fits, but I do know we haven't been able to stop any of the attempts from happening. Whoever's doing this is good. We need to understand the why of it to reveal the who."

"We need to stay together," he pressed.

"I'm going," Margaret said, knocking his arm aside. "If you think this is about Connor and Lise, fine. You can stay. I've made it this far without you. I can do the rest too."

"Why do you have to be so bloody obstinate?"

"Look who's talking?" she hissed. "If you think Tad's trustworthy, put him in front of Pat's room. She could use the protection." She adjusted her neckerchief, getting ready for battle.

"I want you protected too," he said. "Take Gary with you."

"Gary?" she asked. "Aren't you convinced he's the murderer?"

"So?" He shrugged, and, well, had to admit to himself, yeah, maybe he was a bit muddled – but so what? So was she. So was everyone, all the time. And what he did know was––if Gary was the villain, he should be kept far away from Lise, Connor, and Pat. "It's best we get him out of here then, no? And he's no issue with you. And it might give me another chance to talk to

Seamus alone. And if he does agree to go, that's another mark against his involvement, right?"

She frowned, clearly trying to come up with a counter-argument, which was going to be difficult with a plan this flawless, however ad hoc. From further down the corridor they heard footsteps: Daniella's *Dr. Martens* on the polished floor. "Take her too," he said, with a lift of his head. "She speaks the lingo and has a motor."

Margaret nodded. So, Daniella was an easier sell than Gary. Jim walked quickly back into the room before she could argue about taking him. A minute later, he returned, flanked by Gary and Tad. Daniella was next to Margaret, discussing something, perhaps a plan of attack.

"Jim said you need help?" Gary asked.

"Music to our wee Irish ears," said Tad, straightening his cassock.

Perfectly in sync, as if choreographed, Margaret and Daniella rolled their eyes.

Chapter 30
The Spy Museum #2 (Margaret)

Margaret's footsteps echoed hollowly through the empty halls of the *Zentrum für Zeitgeschichte*. The stark white walls and fluorescent lighting created an almost clinical atmosphere, not unlike the hospital she'd just left. She was alone, had overruled Jim on that, sending away his makeshift crew of Daniella and Gary to the Stasi Archives to try and find Tilda; she'd been gone too long. Margaret feared the worst.

Checking her watch, she felt a surge of urgency and broke into a run, her shoes clacking against the polished floor. Breathless, she skidded to a stop before the final metal door-- the entrance to the room they'd been barred from during the tour, on account of a suspiciously timed fire alarm. The room held the special exhibit on the operative known as The Ghost. As she put her hand on the door handle, a chill ran up her spine. She pinwheeled around, but there was no-one in the corridor behind her. Emotions arise and pass away, she reminded herself. Taking a deep, steadying breath, she pushed open the door and stepped inside.

The room was dimly lit, more like a fancy art gallery than a museum. It was divided into three sections, each having its own wall. In the middle was a collection of open and glass-covered plinths holding objects, all sitting on an enormous rug with the GDR emblem on it. While Tick-Tick had been a master of explosives, The Ghost had excelled in subterfuge, infiltrating many "subversive" groups. A pair of blood-splattered Dr. Martens boots made her stomach churn as the soft whir of the reel-to-reel machine playing secret recordings filled the air with ghostly whispers. The area nearest the door was dedicated to a religious choir that The Ghost had infiltrated for the Stasi. Pinned to the wall were tattered yellowed papers of an agenda, flyers for concerts, and a framed pamphlet with two doves—that the description, in both English and German—said agitated for a peaceful revolution. The text was faded, and the font made it hard for Margaret to read but she found it hard to imagine that an entire regime could feel threatened by a leaflet featuring two doves. She moved on, not knowing what she was looking for, just letting her eyes wander over the exhibits. She'd been so focused on Tick-Tick, yet this was the room they'd been blocked from entering.

She moved to the far wall, which was about The Ghost's infiltration of Leipzig's punk scene. Then her eyes were drawn to a large, plush Indian headdress full of bright blue and yellow feathers. She got closer, bending down, her nose just centimetres from the pictures, scanning every small detail. The colour photos showed people in bright, feathered costumes, part of something called FDK Indianisk Hiawatha––a Native American enthusiast community. Yet again, The Ghost had infiltrated them only to uncover hidden, organised, dangerous revolutionary elements and agitators in their midst. She turned and let out a gasp seeing a picture of a knife throwing contest. In an instant, she was transported back to the graveyard, the memory of her own screams echoing in her ears. Guilt and self-recrimination washed over her. She checked her watch again. There were only fifteen minutes until closing. Not enough time to review everything in detail. She went back to the choir area, which had the most photos with faces. They were grainy, and on the bottom left she found a series in black and white, from a concert in 1978. She saw the happiness on the singers' faces - heads thrown back, eyes beaming, mouths open. The concert was right here in Leipzig. None of them were aware a traitor was amongst them. Someone who was sharing their secrets and betraying their trust. She shivered, pulling her blazer tighter around herself as she checked every photograph closely, looking for something, but she wasn't sure what. The Ghost was not going to be sloppy enough to have been photographed singing with them, right? Squinting, she did recognise something: not a person but a place: the palm trees of *Nikolaikirche*. She shrieked because there was someone she recognised there, just about. Something about the bridge of his nose. And that high hairline. High, back even then, before all the scarring.

Thorsten.

There he was again, in a picture nearer the floor. Just him, face to the camera, like a mugshot, almost as if she were looking at a criminal rather than a victim. His name was underneath 'Thorsten Endt'. To the right, a small write-up about him, less than a page of A4, in the original German and with a shorter summary in English. Her eyes darted between the German text and the English, piecing together the tragic story. Thorsten had been a member of the choir at the time a car he had been driving had blown up. His passenger had died. A woman. He'd escaped with extensive injuries. After, he'd been sent immediately to prison because he'd secretly been plotting with the choir to distribute leaflets against the GDR's government, something The Ghost had uncovered.

Margaret tried to slow her rapid breathing and concentrate. Had they first tried to kill him and the woman, then settled on simply imprisoning him? But then a bomb didn't match The

Ghost's MO. It was more the style of… she moved to the right, to the next laminated article, about the tenth anniversary of the crash. The German words swam before her eyes. She clutched at the fragments she could understand. This one mentioned Tick-Tick by name and that Thorsten and the woman he'd been driving with were *Liebhaber*. Lovers. Both were now believed to be Tick-Tick's first *Opfer*. Victims.

Margaret's mind flashed back to the horrifying scene of the Trabi crash again, just hours ago. She saw Pat passed out in the backseat, the shattering glass, and the searing heat of the flames assaulting her senses. She shook her head violently, trying to dispel the horrifying images to focus on the task at hand. Could it be Tick-Tick and The Ghost hunting Pat? Were they the same person, maybe? Or accomplices? That could mean one was here and one in Galway. But then how could he/she/they have known where Pat would be? And the crash was such sloppy work; everyone had survived. It didn't seem to fit. She remembered with how much venom Thorsten had talked about Tick-Tick. How he'd nodded when Lise called him 'despicable'. She needed to speak to him. She rushed back out into the corridor, towards the lobby.

The guard in his booth didn't want to give it up, but her demeanour, her firmness and certainty won him over in the end. He told her a room number, pointed her down a corridor, around a corner, and to a small office next to the toilets. Reminded her they were closing in five minutes.

She found Thorsen's office and knocked on the door.

"*Wir haben geschlossen*," a male voice said, irritated. She knocked louder. "*GESCHLOSSEN.*"

"You're closing in four minutes," she shouted back.

The door opened. "Ah," he said, seeming to recognise her, and not surprised she was there.

"I need your help," she said. "I'm looking for Tick-Tick."

He laughed softly. "Join the club." He gestured her inside.

His office was windowless and scarcely larger than a cupboard. He retook his seat at the desk, which was more of a nest, surrounded on all sides by mountains of paperwork and folders. She hovered by the door, as there was nowhere to sit. Seeing this, he got up and moved a stack of documents off a small chair.

Tentatively, she sat. "I don't have long," she said. "Something has happened to Pat and my friends, Lise and Nele." Was Nele her friend? She was Lise's friend, and that would do for now. "They were also here on Monday. There was an accident." She stumbled over the word. "Or not an accident. A car blew up."

Thorsten inhaled through this nose. "Are they okay?"

She didn't have time to get into all that. "Were you in Moritzbastei to meet Pat?" she asked, her voice taut. He slid a little further back in his seat.

"Yes. Is she going to be okay?"

She placed her hands on her lap. "I think so. What were you and her working on? How did you know her? I need to know everything, and quickly."

"Can I see her?"

"She's in hospital. Please, what were you two working on?"

He looked away, pained, his jaw tightening. Was he trying to decide how much to reveal? Margaret's eyes locked on his every movement, searching for tells, for any hint of deception. "Several lives are at risk," she pressed. "You will tell me everything, now."

A few moments passed. His back straightened and he raised his eyes and seemed to have decided something. That he could trust her, she hoped. "The same thing I've been working on for a decade," he said. "Catching Tick-Tick and The Ghost."

"Tick-Tick killed your lover?"

Thorsten's voice dropped to a whisper. "They both killed her. The Ghost is as much to blame. They said I was an agitator. That I was conspiring against the Government. Someone in that choir might have been, but it wasn't me. The Ghost's intel was bad."

"But they put you in prison anyway?"

"The GDR wasn't big on innocent until proven guilty."

"Why was Pat interested in The Ghost?"

"She wasn't. Well, not unless it got her Tick-Tick, and you know why she wanted him."

Margaret blinked. Then blinked again. "If I knew that, I wouldn't have asked. Why was she so interested in him?"

"Because of…" He paused. "You really don't…" His eyes narrowed. "She never told you? Wow." His head tipped back. "She's really one of a kind." He sounded almost… impressed? "I can see why she was such a great journalist."

Margaret noticed she was digging her nails into her arm. She tried to stop, but it was like her fingers were throbbing. Needed to do something. Her body coursed with adrenaline. He turned around and rummaged in a stack of folders and returned with a thin, red folder. She waited for him to hand it over but, instead, he began to talk. "Pat didn't tell me either," he said, gripping it tightly. "She just approached me for help." He shook his head. "She was scarily knowledgeable about him. I looked into her. I guess you do this kind of work for a while and you stop trusting anymore."

Her mind screamed, "Give me the folder. Come on, come on," but she forced herself to maintain a composed exterior.

"I wanted to know why she was so dedicated," he continued. "So zealous. That the right word? There was something personal about it. I didn't know she was mute then."

Like you, Margaret thought. You recognised that zealousness because you have it too.

Finally, he handed the folder over. She had it open the second it was in her hand, her eyes darting across the pages, absorbing information at a frantic pace.

"Take your time," he said, perhaps in response to her haste, but he was wrong––that was precisely what they were out of. Luckily, there were just three sheets of paper inside. The first was a short newspaper article from East Anglia's regional newspaper, the Eastern Daily Press 'Young woman dies in tragic car accident'. The second was a longer clipping, dated one day later, January 10th 2001, with more details. The car had gone off the road. Its driver, a young woman, had hit a tree and died on impact. Suspected suicide. Margaret checked the date again––it was shortly before Pat moved to Cahoots. An obituary was next to it, naming the victim as Maya Chopra, daughter of Amir and Patricia Chopra and showing a picture of a pretty young woman with a narrow face and large dark eyes.

Chopra? That name didn't ring a bell, but Patricia sure did. The third document was a photograph of a young woman in a graduation cap and gown, flanked by her proud parents: a handsome, ruffed Indian man with a huge grin on his face and next to him with an even bigger smile… Pat.

All the air surged from her lungs. She felt like she was drowning.

"I'm sorry," he said.

She remembered an article she'd recently read in the New York Times that had said 26% of married women used their maiden name professionally. For an investigative journalist like Pat, it might have made sense to use her maiden name. Not that it had helped keep her family safe, not in the end.

"It doesn't mention a bomb."

"They only found that a day later. Well, they never officially said it was a bomb." Thorsten rubbed at the back of his neck. "She was getting close to unmasking him. He threatened her. Well, someone threatened her. She ignored that threat." It was clear from his tone that he was impressed by Pat. He blinked slowly. "Her daughter paid the cost. I can't prove it, but I don't think he's retired. Tick-Tick. The BBC car bomb, the attack at Belfast airport. All fit his MO."

Margaret gasped. "Yes," she said. "I think he's here in Leipzig."

Thorsten looked towards the door, as if he might be on the other side of it, about to knock. His jaw clenched. She tried to read his emotions. Fear, she decided. Margaret suddenly remembered Pat's nervousness before the Trabi race. And, back at the airport, before they got into Daniella's car. It was logical she'd be scared of them after what happened to her daughter.

She told him about the threatening letter, then described the details of the crash to Thorsten. As she talked, his body stiffened. Even though he was seated, he reached for his cane. "Doesn't sound like him," he said, of the crash, his mouth narrow and tight, still seated but now leaning on the cane. "I'm the only person who's ever survived a Tick-Tick bomb. He didn't use enough petrol that time, but he was an amateur then."

"Maybe he's just getting old?" Margaret offered. "Or maybe it just wasn't a very good plan?"

"It sounds more like," he said, tapping his chin with his hand. A small smile. "There was a famous case with a Trabant that went up in flames shortly after the *Wende*." The word they used for the wall coming down. For reunification. It meant change or turn and was a word used everywhere in the Museum. "A family, mother, father and two children were driving on an empty country road. Somehow, the car swerved and drove against a tree. The car immediately went up in flames. The father got out with only small burns, but the mother and the daughters all died."

"Okay," Margaret said. "What's the connection to Tick-Tick?"

"It turned out later that the father crashed the car on purpose. He'd put an open canister of gasoline in the boot.

That's why it burnt so quickly. Not that Trabants need much help with that."

She took a deep breath, remembering how quickly the Trabi had caught fire. "It's clever, right?" Thorsten added. "Because who would be stupid enough to blow themselves up too? It helps throw suspicion off the driver."

She leapt up, having had a sickening realisation. "You can take them, if you want," he said, about the documents she had just shoved back at him.

"They're safer here."

She ran back through the empty museum to the reception. She had to wake the security guard to let her out. Outside, Gary and Daniella were waiting at the bottom of the steps. No sign of Tilda. "Where is she?" she asked as she ran towards them, jumping every other step. They had to get back to the hospital; no-one there was safe.

"Easy," Daniella said, as Margaret missed a step and stumbled forwards. Daniella caught her with two hands. "Tilda was gone already."

"We shook the security guard down, though," said Gary, pride in his voice. "He said that the last visitor left an hour ago."

Margaret looked at Daniella's car, illegally parked at a nearby bus stop. "But then she would have been at the hospital as we were leaving, right? Or if she arrived since, Jim would have called you? Seamus has a phone. He called you with it earlier, when we were at the lake."

"There's more," Daniella said. "The guard said a boy on a skateboard came while Tilda was in the archives, and left a letter for her. Tilda read it and walked in the direction of the city centre."

"What?" Why wouldn't Tilda have checked in with them first? She didn't know they were at the archives, of course, but she knew Margaret and Daniella were at the hospital, and so would have been easy to reach.

"We asked him how she looked when she got the letter," Gary said. "Apparently, she clutched her chest." He repeated the gesture, which looked weird, because there was nothing for him to clutch and so he just grabbed at a handful of his jumper. Margaret copied him. It seemed like an unnatural gesture to her unless… jewellery. Tilda's cross. Margaret had seen her grab it often, a reflex, or tic, even. Her stress response. She'd clutched it at the spy museum when Thorsten had talked about the Stasi infiltrating church groups, at the courtyard just behind the *Nikolaikirche*, when she'd interrogated her and learned about a very old love triangle, and when Margaret had confronted her about the poison pen letters at the lake. Some of the pieces she'd been spinning suddenly snapped together. "I know where they are."

"They?" Gary asked.

"Yes." She broke from Daniella, and ran towards the car. "Tilda and the person planning on killing her."

Chapter 31

University Hospital Leipzig #2 (Jim)

Jim wiped sweat from his forehead and sat down next to Seamus, who was knitting as usual, and who looked up and gave him a weak smile. Jim tried but failed to return it. His stomach bubbled, and he burped into his fist. He'd buggered it up with Margaret, and he knew it. He'd been too abrasive. Too forceful and controlling. It had been so good to see her and now she was gone already, and in danger. They were all in danger.

Should he have gone with her? He sighed, lowered his head, and rubbed his face with his huge, meaty hands. Nah. Margaret was tough and nowhere near as impulsive as Connor. It was better he was here, keeping an eye on his old friend. Maybe it was about this RGD or DGR or whatever it was called, the commies, but he doubted it. That was the distant past and there was a lot of money here, in the present, and all of it was in McGinley Knitwear. He lowered his hands and lifted his head. Connor was pacing back and forth. "Sit down, man," Jim said. "I feel like I'm watching a lion at the zoo."

Connor stopped abruptly and turned. Jim saw how cut-up he was, how close to tears. "What happened to us, Jimmy?"

"Nothing happened, fella. We're here. We're safe."

Connor's hands balled into fists. "I used to be a lion. When I entered a bar, the men quaked and the lasses melted like butter on toast."

Jim laughed.

"When did we lose that?"

It seemed like a strange question to be asking now, even though Jim shared in its sentiment, mourned his youth just as anyone who's lost it mourns. He made the sign of the cross, wouldn't have dared if Tad was here, but Tad wasn't--he'd sent him to keep guard outside Pat's room. "The old enemy," Jim said, lowering his eyes. "Time."

"Yeah," Connor agreed.

"But we still have something," Jim said, quickening. "It's easy to think we don't. To give in to self-pity. But we do, C. Look at us. You and," he gestured at Lise. "Me and Mags."

"I don't know," Connor said, wiping away a tear with the back of his hand.

"I know," Jim firmed. "Trust me. I'm not saying the best is yet to come, I'm just saying great is yet to come."

"What do you know about it?" Connor growled, somehow triggered by Jim's certainty.

Jim took a long breath. He wished Seamus wasn't there, that he and Connor could discuss this alone, but it felt more important that they did discuss it, because who knew how this day would end, how much time they would all have together, and so he decided to push his inhibitions away and just barrel on. "I know that it's not there, and then suddenly it is. It's like a light going on. Getting brighter. Warmer. Sharper." He exhaled. "Everything becomes more alive and you can't look away from it, even though it's blinding. Can't believe it, either. That it's happened again, at our age. But it is. It's there. And there's no escaping it."

Seamus stopped knitting. Connor wiped away a tear and

looked from Jim to Lise. "Close enough," he said. "She's going to wake up, isn't she?"

"Aye," said Jim. "Lise's tough as they come."

"Yes," said Seamus. "And who'd leave a love like that?"

Connor resumed his walking, six steps in one direction, six back. On the other side of the bed, a diagnostic machine beeped. A vase of flowers sat on a small table beside the bed. Jim couldn't smell them, so they must be fake. He turned to the door, wondering if he should position himself outside, in the corridor, to have a clearer view of the comings and goings?

Wait, what was that? He saw something in the corner of his vision, over by the bed. His head snapped towards Lise... yes, there, movement: a finger gripping, then relaxing. "Connor," he said, as Lise's eyelids began to flutter.

"Lise." Connor rushed two steps to the bed. "My darling, I'm here. We're all here. Are you okay?"

Lise's head angled towards him. She blinked slowly and gulped, her lips dry. She looked up at Connor and, with a soft beckoning motion of her hand, gestured him closer. Must hurt to speak, Jim thought, as Connor lowered himself, putting his ear right next to her mouth, almost touching her lips.

"Thanks for the stripper," she said in her usual loud voice. Connor howled with brittle laughter and the crying he'd been pretending he wasn't doing intensified. The man did melt, basically, he became a blubbering mess. Seamus handed him a tissue.

"I've been so worried, my love."

"It's good to see you." Lise's eyes moved around the room, taking in her surroundings until they rested on Jim, who was now at the foot of the bed, beaming down at her.

"You just had to upstage us," Jim said. "Didn't you?"

Even though her lips were trembling, they formed a narrow, pursed-lipped smile. "Always."

"How ya feeling?" Connor asked, as her eyes closed again.

"Sore," she said. "But I'll live."

"And well, my bride," Connor boomed, lifting her hand and kissing it. "We'll live well. Far beyond our means and station. We'll make them gossip and scorn. And I, for one, cannot wait."

Seamus laughed. "Oh," he said, looking down at this knitting. "I've buggered it up." He was crying as well. "It's just..." His voice broke. He wiped his eyes with the sleeve of his bonus jumper. "Oh god, it's so romantic isn't it? Rushing here. The private plane." He unpicked his last stitch. "It's even better than Corrie."

"Who's this?" Lise asked. "Seamus?"

"Aye," said Connor, and if Jim had to guess, he'd have said he heard pride in Connor's voice. Were Seamus's tears genuine or crocodile? Jim couldn't tell. How many times had Seamus wept over the past days? Jim had lost count. If Seamus was involved, and, on paper, a lot pointed to him, he was certainly a brilliant actor. But then he was used to hiding important things about himself, wasn't he? Jim let out a burp that smelt of the paprika crisps he'd bought from the vending machine at the airport. No, he still needed to confront Seamus, to tip him upside down and shake him in the strong breeze of suspicion. Until someone was ruled out, they were ruled in. No-one got a free pass; the stakes were too high.

"Do you need something?" Jim asked, moving towards the door. "I'm heading back to the machines to get some choccy–"

"Coke," said Connor.

"The kind from a can?"

"That'll have to do."

"Orange juice," Lise said.

Jim took another step towards the door. "Keep me company, Shay?"

Seamus looked up from his knitting. "Just about to finish this sleeve."

"I could imagine they need a little privacy," Jim said, flicking his head. "Don't you think, big man?"

"Oh, right," Seamus said, hopping up. Just as Jim expected, the knitting came with him.

"Leave that," he said. He didn't want Seamus relaxed, not for what was about to come.

"But—"

"Leave it," Jim barked.

Seamus's mouth twisted into a frown, but he turned and put his knitting reverently down onto the chair, then followed Jim out. The equally harsh lights of the corridor welcomed them. Two nurses were walking away, laughing at some private joke or public tragedy. Jim let Seamus pass him, then closed the door. "Sit with me," he said, gesturing to the same chairs Margaret and Daniella had sat at too, backs to the wall, under the window to Lise's room.

Seamus looked around nervously. "What about the drinks?"

"Won't take a minute," Jim said, noticing Seamus's legs were trembling. "Now sit."

Seamus sat, coming down heavily, the chair creaking beneath his podgy frame. He fiddled with the extra jumper tied around his neck. Jim turned his chair from the wall a little, so they'd be better able to make eye contact. He sat, giving a little involuntary groan as he did so. "I've been spinning all this round and round," said Jim. "It's a puzzle, Shay. And I'm hoping you can help me with a few of its missing pieces?"

"I love a good puzzle. I just finished a thousand-pieces of Michelangelo's David. It was surprising how long it took me to finish the shaft of the—"

"Why are you trying to kill Connor?" Jim said matter-of-factly. All the colour drained from Seamus's face. Poor bugger's going to faint, Jim thought. He'd wanted to fluster him. That had been part of the plan. He leaned forward and touched Seamus's knee. He jumped a foot into the air, looking down at

Jim's hand like it was radioactive. Jim pulled it back and put it in his lap. "I mean, why wouldn't you want to kill him? Half the time I want to kill him."

"This again?" Seamus asked. "We did all this at the hunting lodge."

"Lots happened since then, as I see it."

"I was in the toilet. I didn't see anyone. And I was out of the room at the distillery."

"Yes," said Jim. "You were. Convenient that. Or not. No alibi."

Seamus loosened the knot of the jumper around his neck. "I'm sure there's an innocent explanation for all this. For everything. For Lise, even."

"There's an explanation," Jim said. "But it's not innocent, fella. No alibi," he repeated. "Three attempts," he counted them out on his fingers, "and you've no alibi for any of them."

Seamus lowered both his chins into his neck. "Come on Jim, look at me."

"They come in all shapes and sizes," said Jim. "And what I think doesn't matter." Follow the evidence, keep your feelings out of it. That's what Margaret had taught him. "Means, motive and opportunity," said Jim. Opportunity - that was the third one. "You've all of them. In fact, you're drowning in them." Jim punched his palm. "And it would make my blood boil," he said, "if I'd worked for decades. Saved the company's ass and then someone like Connor strutted in, ready to piss it all up the wall. Your work. Your talent. That would really hack me off, Shay."

"I know," said Seamus, blinking away another tear. "I know it would. But I'm not you. I'm not like that." He seemed tired. "We've done all this already."

Jim leaned forward and jabbed one of his massive sausage fingers into Seamus's face. "So, you decided to do something about it, didn't you?"

"Yeah. I guess I have decided to, in a funny way."

Jim was just getting started. "Bitter, full of rage, cut out of the will, embarrassed, a laughingstock, old Seamus the softy, everyone's favourite doormat. Still living in that small box room. What is that all about, actually? Even the bloody butler has a room twice the size and with four times the view. The worst room in the whole mansion, a mansion covered in giant oil canvases of the many generations of the great McGinley family, and yet there's not a single picture of you anywhere, is there? Not one. I know, because I checked. I've walked that place up and down. Drew a map, even. It's why I know you have the box room. It was the last one I found. I've been in them all. No shame in it. Everyone was coming into mine, so?"

Seamus lowered his eyes and started picking the skin around his nails. Jim noticed now how bitten and sore they were. "Jim, you've got the wrong–"

"Something inside you snapped, didn't it?" Jim pressed. "You knew Connor would jump in at the wake and take the best spot for himself. So, you sabotaged the chandelier and my god, the poetry of killing your brother with a knitting needle? Would have been so perfect. Could have been. If it weren't for me." Jim thumped his chest. "When that failed, at the lodge, you prepped Connor's gun. Stuffed it full of greasy wool––so you knew that it would backfire. First the needles, then the wool. Your MO."

Seamus lifted and shook his head, just once and slowly. "Jim, stop."

"But then you saw me with it, so you pretended you needed the toilet, went out the back door, and ran into the woods with the gun you claimed you didn't know how to fire. At the distillery, you suddenly find your bark, and you use it on Gary."

"Jim, please. Listen."

"Maybe it's not even about Connor. It's about Willie. How he treated you. How he let his family treat you."

"How he treated me? I was his son, Jim."

"You were his gimp."

Seamus gasped.

"Gimp," Jim said again.

"Stop," Seamus said, his voice cracking.

"No," Jim said. "The truth, Seamus. *Now*."

"Agoraphobia," Seamus blurted, his throat clogged with emotion, the word coming out in a gulp. "Okay?"

Jim's forehead furrowed. "What?"

"I've got agoraphobia. Didn't you notice when I had my eyes closed for the whole boat ride? Or my back to the view at the cabin?"

"Fear of heights? How's that relevant?"

"Open spaces," Seamus said. "Opposite of claustrophobia. That's why I have the box room. Why it has no window. Now just stop, will you?"

Jim thought back and, yeah, there were some signs, come to think of it. Like how Seamus always sat with his back to the window whenever Jim saw him in the mansion. Most people would have sat the opposite way around, enjoying the view. And yeah, he sat with his eyes closed for the whole boat ride.

Seamus stood up, just enough to pull something from his back pocket. He handed Jim a folded envelope and sat back down. Jim opened it up. It was fraying at the edges and had been folded and unfolded many times. He opened it and pulled out a piece of paper. Official looking. The deeds to a house, maybe? The writing was foreign. He did recognise one word though: 'Elefthería'. There was more: a one-way ticket to Mykonos, and a note written in a small scrawl that bent to the right. When Jim squinted, he could just about make it out:

'I'm freeing you of the McGinley burden. Be bold and live free, my son.'

Jim took a deep breath, put the note, ticket, and deed back

into the envelope, and handed it back to Seamus. "Quite a valuable painting," Jim said.

Seamus lowered his eyes. "It was hidden in the frame. Believe me now? I don't want Connor dead because I want Willie to get his dying wish."

"I see," Jim said. Maybe he was convinced, and maybe he wasn't. He remembered the argument at the distillery. That lover's tiff. He joined dots. "You wanted to take someone with you? That's why you're still here?"

Seamus looked away, shifting in his seat.

"You don't have to say it," Jim tapped his nose. "Gary."

Seamus straightened. "How?"

"He told me."

"What? He did?" Seamus smiled.

"Yeah," Jim said, and something told him to leave the part out about him having figured it out first. How he'd revealed to Gary he knew. Seamus needed a win. Needed three points.

"Wow," Seamus beamed. "I don't think he's ever told anyone."

Jim wasn't surprised about that. Galway was a small town and Gary had said he had a wife and kids, although they might already be estranged. He settled back into his seat and let all this new information settle over him. If he was taking Seamus off the suspect list, that list was getting awfully short. In fact, as far as Jim could see, it only had one name left on it. The man they were talking about: Gary.

"Gary knows about the deed?" Jim asked.

Seamus nodded.

"When did you show it to him?"

"After you came back from the dog track. He came up to my room. I thought this meant we could be open now, about... you know, but he didn't agree and we had an argument."

Jim nibbled his lip.

"It's not Gary," Seamus said, reading his thoughts. "I know

why you think it is. That this is about Bailey's Irish Cream and protecting me." His sentences were racing out. "Getting me the money and security Connor never gave him or Tad. But it's not. Because I don't want it, and he knows that. Oh, and he has an alibi."

Jim's eyes widened. "Does he now? For which attempt?"

"The distillery. He was with me. I was hiding, watching you two talk. We'd had another argument the previous evening. An existential one. That's why I was so angry at the distillery. When you left, I confronted him, told him I was leaving for Mykonos that weekend and it was his last chance to come. Then we heard all that racket from the other room."

Jim remembered, dimly, that they had arrived together. "What did he say?"

Seamus sighed. "He's scared, Jim. But I think he'll say yes."

Jim nodded, because love certainly scared the hell out of him. He exhaled. If Gary wasn't involved and let's face it, he'd never really suspected Gary, then he had no more suspects from Galway. Which just left Margaret's whacky theory. Seamus's phone trilled in his trouser pocket. "Might be Margaret," he said. He took it out and read the message aloud, *'Tilda not at archives. Have theory. GDR. Got tip about Nikolaikirche. On way. Protect Pat. M.'*

"Isn't *Kirche* cherry?" Jim asked. He'd flunked Lise's German class in week four, but a few words had stuck with him. A dialogue in a pub in one of the textbooks about kirsch liqueur. They had the same word for liqueur, just different spelling, with the little eyes over the ö. "And who is Nicola?"

"It's a church," said Seamus. "In the city centre. I'm a bit of a history buff. It's where the protests that ended the GDR started."

GDR. There it was. Those bastard commies. "Why would Tilda be there?" Jim wondered aloud, holding his hand out to read the message for himself. While he did so, an older doctor in a white jacket walked towards them, pushing an empty wheelchair, its wheels squeaking on the polished floor. The doctor had a slight limp and seemed to shuffle. Doesn't have great feet for a big man, Jim thought, looking up at him as he parked the wheelchair outside Lise's room, and opened the door.

He turned, looked at Jim, and licked his lips. He was wearing leather gloves.

Chapter 32
The Nikolaikirche (Margaret)

Margaret's knuckles whitened as she gripped the door handle, her body taut with anticipation and fear as the car screeched around the corner of a very pedestrianised zone, before skidding to an abrupt stop. It felt like they'd only left the Museum twenty seconds ago before Gary (driving to spare Daniella's hands) was parking the car, very illegally, outside a shop selling tourist knick-knacks–and directly opposite the *Nikolaikirche*.

Margaret climbed out of the small vehicle and stared up at the church. It was underlit, casting an intimidating shadow. She was surprised the square was so empty already, Leipzig must get a lot of day-trippers. Behind her, the owner of that tourist shop lowered the metal blinds with a series of loud clunks.

"What's with the palm trees?" Gary asked, at her shoulder.

"Christian symbol of peace," Daniella said.

"And justice," Margaret added. She had a complicated relationship with justice; needed to believe in it more than she actually did. "We need to hurry." She was rushing on towards the entrance as Gary dawdled, reading a *Stolperstein*, a brass plate attached to the floor outside the former home of someone who had been a victim of Nazi persecution. They were everywhere. Simple, powerful monuments of remembering.

"It's closed," Gary said, rattling the doors.

"Back door," Daniella said, and they moved quickly around to the rear of the church, the same square where she and Tilda had watched that small bird—the name of which she'd forgotten—drink from the fountain. The rear door was slightly ajar. Daniella swung it open. Dim light from inside bled out into the square. As she prepared to enter, Margaret felt her senses heighten even further. It was as if she had stepped outside herself, watching the scene unfold from above, a silent observer to her own actions. This out-of-body sensation brought with it a strange calm, a detachment that allowed her to focus with precision on the task at hand.

It was eerily quiet inside. In the very low lighting, the nave, with its Egyptian-style columns and palm-shaped tops, loomed large over the space. She stopped to listen, but heard no-one, her eyes sweeping the floor until... She saw something: a tiny gold cross on a modest chain. The cross that Tilda had clutched so many times. "I bet she dropped it for us to find."

Having gone to check the front of the church, Gary rushed back through the pews, slightly out of breath. "No sign," he said. "I don't think there's anyone here."

She showed him the cross. "She's here. And there's plenty of places to hide in a church."

"Where would you be?" Daniella asked Gary, perhaps believing his Irish ancestry gave him some kind of special knowledge about places of worship?

"The sacristy?" Gary offered. "At least that's where Connor, Tad, and I used to hide as kids."

Daniella led them around the altar to a small, narrow set of stairs leading down to a wooden door that looked like it had been there for eternity. Daniella raised her finger to her lips as they prepared to descend. As silently as possible, Margaret tiptoed down to the door. From the other side of it, they could hear a shuffling or dragging sound.

As gently as she could, she lowered the handle, but the door was locked. Gary tapped Margaret on the shoulder, motioning for her to move out of the way. She nodded and moved up two steps to make space for him. Without hesitation, he jumped off the first step and hurled himself shoulder-first at the door, which smashed free of its ancient hinges. He fell into the small, dark room, brightened only by candlelight. They rushed in behind him. It took Margaret a moment for her eyes to adjust and then she saw it, the full horror of it--how he had landed two metres from a body tied with rope, on its side, facing them: Tilda.

Her mouth was taped, her enormous eyes full with fear. Kneeling behind her body, tying a hangman's noose around her neck with thick rope, was Nele. "SURPRISE," she said, her eyes wide and unhinged. "Don't come any closer."

If she was flustered by their sudden arrival, she hid it well. Daniella helped Gary up.

"I guess I'm going to need more rope, right?" Nele said, and then let out a loud cackle. She dropped the noose in her hand and grabbed the large chef's knife next to her on the floor. She raised it towards them.

The sight of the blade made Margaret's blood run cold, every muscle in her body tensing.

"What are you doing?" she asked. "Tilda's not your enemy."

"Collateral damage," the madwoman hissed. "Just like you all."

"It's not too late," Margaret said, her voice sounding foreign to her own ears--steady and calm despite the maelstrom of emotions roiling within her.

"Yeaaaaah," Nele said, lowering the knife towards Tilda's throat. "It kinda is."

Chapter 33

University Hospital Leipzig #3 (Jim)

Jim's heart pounded as he followed the fake doctor into Lise's room. He didn't call out to Connor or Seamus, wanted to be completely sure first. Inside, he discovered the impostor looming over Connor's sleeping form, white coat straining against his frame, a glint from a syringe that was raised high above his head, poised to strike.

"Stop," Jim barked, lunging forward, his fingers closing around the man's wrist in a vice-like grip, pulling him backwards, the momentum spinning him around and away from Connor.

"Hey," the man shouted, grappling with him, the fake doctor's face contorting with rage, his features twisting into an ugly snarl, revealing a crooked front tooth. His eyes, cold and calculating, locked on to Jim's as he thrashed against the hold, his free arm swinging wildly. A fist connected with Jim's ribs, sending a jolt of pain through his side. They grappled fiercely, bodies tangled in a desperate struggle. The syringe wavered dangerously between them, until, with a sudden burst of strength, the impostor shoved his forearm against Jim's chest.

The impact sent Jim staggering back, his grip loosening just enough for the man to slip free. The fake doctor stumbled away, his breathing ragged, his too-small coat rumpled and askew.

"Let me do my job," he growled, his voice low and menacing as he moved around to the head of the bed, putting the frame between him, Jim, and Connor. He released the foot brake.

"He's not the patient," Jim said, between breaths. "But I think you know that, right? Seamus, block the door."

"What? Why? Who's this?" Seamus asked, standing in the doorway, phone in hand. He crossed his arms over his chest, but looked confused and sad, more like a man about to herd unruly cats than one ready to wrestle with an international fugitive.

The doctor slipped the syringe back in his pocket, cleared his throat and smoothed down his white jacket. He picked up Lise's chart. Jim moved to the right, around to the foot of the bed, and clamped both hands on the rails, just to make it clear that it was going nowhere. His mind raced, trying to anticipate the fake doctor's next move, knowing that this confrontation was far from over, but that there were also three of them and just one of him. Well, almost three. Jim edged left and stuck out his leg, nudging Connor with the tip of his boot while never taking his eyes off the imposter.

"Leave at once," the man said. "Or I'll call security."

"Call them," Jim said, pointing to the red button at the end of the cord over on the nightstand. "It's that one, me thinks." He kicked Connor again, harder, who moaned as he came to.

"You know, doc," Jim said. "I think I've seen you before?" The imposter doctor put the chart back and took hold of the metal frame of the bed.

"I see a hundred people a day." He licked his lips.

"Ah, doc," Connor said, rubbing his eyes and standing

slowly up, stretching his arms. "About bloody time. What's going on, chief? She going to be okay, because if not, you're going to have to ans—"

The doctor licked his lips again. "I'm afraid Lise appears to have some swelling on the brain. It's important that we take her to surgery right now."

Lise, thought Jim. That's overfamiliar. Germany was formal. He'd been called Herr Whitecastle twice at the airport. A doctor would say Frau Weber. Lise's eyelids fluttered. "What's going on?"

"Good question," Jim said. The pointy nose, the prominent cheekbones, that lip-licking tic. The wig was different to the wake, and he'd shaved his moustache, but if you knew what you were looking for.

"Doctor's here," said Connor. "At long last."

"Did you ever make it to Ashford Castle?" Jim asked.

Lise tipped her head backwards, looking at the doctor, upside down. "Doc…" her eyes narrowed. "Is that?" she murmured. "Am I awake?"

"You're very much awake," Jim said. "But that's not a doctor." He wasn't sure how to reveal what he knew without freaking Lise out. Better to let her come to the realisation on her own, and slowly.

"I just…" Lise mumbled. "I could have sworn I heard the voice of…"

"Did you enjoy the wake?" Jim asked. "Cracking vol-au-vents, I thought. And those little sausages on the sticks? I might have eaten at least a dozen."

"What's going on, Jim?" Connor asked, looking back and forth between the two men. "Do you know this fella?"

"Not as well as Lise," said Jim. "No."

Connor's expression was a mixture of confusion and slowly-dawning realisation. His hands clenched and unclenched at his sides.

"It can't be," Lise said, beginning to cry. She tried to scrabble upright and out of the bed, her movements slow but also frantic and uncoordinated, her hospital gown twisting around her.

"This is Dieter," Jim said. "In a very bad disguise."

The doctor laughed. "What do you see in these idiots, my love?"

There it was, proof. "Dieter," Lise said, her voice slowly morphing from confusion to anger. "It can't... How could... No!"

"And there's no need to be rude," Jim said, although he'd been called a lot worse than an idiot.

"It's really you," she said, sitting up, head turned back. She tugged the IV from her wrist, moaning at the pain, her body trembling with a mix of weakness and rage as she lowered her legs to the floor. Could she even stand? "How can it... how could you?"

"I'll explain everything," Dieter said, breaking eye contact with Jim. "But stay in the bed." He took a step backwards, nearer the wall, opened his coat, and removed an antique revolver. His disguise, now obvious to all, seemed almost comical in its inadequacy––the ill-fitting coat, the hastily applied makeup, the askew wig.

"You steal that from a cowboy?" Jim asked, pointing at his pathetic relic of a gun.

"He's the cowboy," Connor said through gritted teeth. His back was arched and his fists balled.

A lip was licked. "Another step, gentlemen, and I'll be forced to use this." He waved the tip of the gun up and down. "Not that it won't also give me pleasure," he said, and ended his bad community theatre villain performance with an exaggerated wink.

"Does it fire bullets or water?" Jim asked sarcastically, shocked at how far this man had fallen from the brilliant, international master of espionage that Margaret had made him out to be. Time had done a number on him too.

"Idiot," Dieter said, his nostrils flaring. Lise moved gingerly towards him, supporting herself on the bed. He took another half-step back, but watching her, his face also softened. It was clear he wanted to lower the gun and help her. Instead, he said, "I've missed you."

"He's a killer," Jim said. "Did you know that, Lise? He's Tick-Tick. I always heard it as Tic-Tic, which is fortunate, since he's one of those too. I guess most of us are. Mine's footballing idioms, or so I've been told. His is lip-licking. Same word in German." He was babbling. It was the excitement of it all.

"Huh?" Lise said. "What?"

"We'll get to all that later, my love."

"You're not even denying it?" she asked.

"Later," he said, dismissively, with a wave of the gun. "Once we get rid of these two fools. Go back to bed. I need to focus."

"Three," Seamus said. "I'm also here."

Dieter laughed. "Great. You'll come in handy if any of us need another jumper."

"I've been such an idiot," she said, rubbing her head. Watching from behind, Jim saw her reach out to touch him with her other hand, as if to check he was real. "How did... I mean... I saw the police report of the accident."

"It's not so hard to find a body if you know where to look," Dieter said, "or rather, burn a body thoroughly enough that no-one looks closely at it." He flicked the gun left and right between Connor and Jim. "By the wall, now, you two." He looked down at Lise. "It's me who's been the idiot, my love. For thinking I could live without you. Please, I have a plan. Return to bed."

Lise paused, assessing what to do. Connor was at the very front of his feet. "Don't touch her. Don't touch him. Get back in the bed, my love."

"My love?" Dieter threw back his head and howled with laughter sharp enough to cut glass.

"You've lost, Dieter," Jim said. "Put the gun down."

"I guess I underestimated you," he said to Jim. "Not that I really estimated you. Now move back against that wall or I'll shoot you both in the face. Sit down, Jumpers," he said to Seamus. "Lise, lay back down, please. We're going to get out of here and begin new lives. Better lives. I've so much to tell you, so much to explain."

"Yeah," said Connor, with a jut of his chin and the circling of his raised fists. "That's not going to happen while I'm breathing. So how about you put that peashooter down and we settle this like real men, fist to fist. Just me and you?"

Dieter chuckled. "Cocky little imp, isn't he?" he said to Lise. "What do you see in him? Were you that lonely without me?"

"She was lonely with you, shitbird," Connor said.

Another lick of a top lip that became a sly grin. "Can I shoot him, honey, please? I so want to shoot him. You can pick where. And these fat little piggies here too." He twirled the gun at Jim.

"Fat?" said Jim, whistling. "Wow. You hear that, C?"

"Yeah, well, he called me an imp." Connor looked around, searching for a weapon. "Doesn't seem to know he's outnumbered."

"I have a gun, idiots."

"Barely," said Jim. "And I'm not fat, I'll have you know. I'm just a little sausage rolled."

"Solid," Connor added, inflating his cheeks. "That's how I'd describe ya. Imposing. Thick of neck, maybe."

"I'm fat," said Seamus. "So what? Life's short and curly wurlys are long."

How much did Seamus know about Dieter? Jim couldn't be sure, but he wasn't acting surprised, and he imagined Tristan might have shared around the fruits of his illicit research.

Dieter blinked once, slowly. "I'm sorry, love," he said, as if burdened by the weight of all the world's stupidity. "But I just have to shoot them." He turned the gun on Connor, who rolled his eyes.

"Do as he says," Lise implored, waving Connor back. "He will shoot you. Stop making fun of him."

"Why would we need to do that?" Connor quipped. "His toupee's doing it for him."

Jim laughed, more loudly than the joke deserved; he wanted Dieter to feel mocked. To understand how out-numbered he was. "He'll have to shoot us, right, Con? No-one gets away with trying to kill our friends. Of messing with our women."

"Your women?" Dieter said, frowning at Lise.

"He'll have to kill me too," said Seamus, striding suddenly from the door to Connor's side. "That's my future sister-in-law there. You don't fiddle with a man's family." He took off his extra sweater and threw it onto the ground.

"Stay back," Connor protested, but Seamus pushed his arm away.

Dieter sighed. "*Idioten*. Lise, we're getting out of here. Go back to the bed. I don't want to risk shooting you."

Lise tried to move the hand with the gun away so that she could... Jim couldn't tell if she wanted to hug or hit him. Dieter didn't seem sure either, and pushed her back with his free left hand. Which meant that for a brief second, his attention was on Lise, not Connor, or Jim.

Connor's eyes swivelled to meet Jim's and a silent understanding passed between the men. He could sense - in the same way a football team that regularly plays together learns to anticipate the run each other will make - that Connor wanted him to push the bed into Dieter, squashing him against the wall. And if he got the angle right, he could probably hit Dieter but miss Lise. He leaned forward and shoved with all his might.

The Accidental Murder Club

The bed hurtled forwards at an angle, smacking straight into Dieter's midriff just as a loud gunshot reverberated through the space.

Seamus hit the floor.

"No," Jim shouted, sure the gun had been a bluff, a replica, a bad movie prop. He dropped to his knees and crawled left around the foot of the bed towards Seamus and Connor. Connor was next to Seamus, hands on his stomach, blood already pooling beneath him, shouting, "Seamus. Seamus, are you okay?"

"He... shot me?" Seamus said, his voice thick with disbelief. With everyone on the floor, Jim wasn't sure where the gun was and so how to keep himself safe. With no time to think, he was acting purely on instinct.

"Stop it, my love," Dieter yelled, but Jim couldn't see why. There was something laying on the floor: Seamus's phone. Jim kicked it towards himself. A fine bit of footwork under the circumstances. He then crawled back around the bed to check on Lise. He found her on top of Dieter, raining punches down onto his face.

"You bastard. You bastard. You bastard. Were you even in prison?" She ripped his toupee off. "It was all a lie, wasn't it?" She socked him on the nose. "You were never coming." Her fists were swinging wildly. "The baby. I hate you."

Where was the gun? Dieter rose up, throwing her off like she was a doll, climbing to his feet and sweeping her tiny frame up and over his shoulder. She yelled out suddenly, in some kind of pain, although he couldn't see why. Jim was hiding behind the end of the bed, not able to risk moving until he knew where the gun was. "Sorry," Dieter said. "That hurt me more than it did you, but it's necessary."

Maybe he'd lost the gun in the commotion? He couldn't just let him take Lise. Jim climbed back to his feet and into Dieter's path. Dieter thrust the gun towards him. "I think I've made my point."

Jim raised his arms. "Easy fella, easy." He gestured to the open door and the empty corridor beyond it. "Just walk on by." Why was no-one coming? Were gunshots a regular occurrence in a German hospital?

"Seamus, Seamus hold on!" Connor yelled, ripping a sheet from the bed and wrapping it around Seamus, torqueing the wound. "Doctors! Help!"

"You'll never know how much I'd have loved to kill you both," Dieter said. "I'd have really savoured it, but she'd never forgive me." Dieter's voice was unerringly calm. He pointed the end of the gun to a chair beneath the window. Jim turned around slowly, hands above his head, and walked to it. Seamus was making gurgling noises.

"Hang in there, brother," Connor said.

Jim was surprised Connor was staying so faithfully with Seamus and not trying to help him with Lise. Although, yeah, Dieter really had made his point––the gun was real, and he had no qualms about using it, and so they weren't going to win this one. Not in this room, anyway. Not without more people getting shot. Jim kept his hands on his head. Dieter moved around the bed and towards the door, carrying Lise, who was no longer resisting. Jim saw why when Dieter pulled the syringe out of her neck. Dieter passed, right next to Jim, stopping to turn and flash Connor one last unhinged grin. "We'll meet again," he said, leaving Jim just enough time to slip Seamus's phone into the front pocket of Lise's hospital gown. He hoped it was a deep one.

Dieter left, closing the door behind him. He heard him lower Lise into the wheelchair, its wheel squeaking as it moved in the direction of the elevators. Connor went and hammered the red button some more. "It's okay," said Seamus. "It's okay."

"Go get the bastard," Connor yelled, but Jim was already at the door, opening it slowly, and then creeping out, keeping low, wondering how he could raise the alarm without getting shot? Jim had only been on two foreign holidays in a decade and both had ended with someone trying to kill him. This was why people stayed domestic, just went to the seaside. He'd have given anything to be in Blackpool right now, a stick of rock in his hand, a cold bottle of Appleton Estate rum at his feet, wind tussling his excellent hair, Margaret one deckchair over, studying her cognitive fallacy flashcards, or reading a book about the Victorians. No, who was he trying to kid? This was exactly where he wanted to be--doing something that mattered, protecting the people he loved, not in the twilight of his life, but its glorious zenith, raising his middle finger to that old enemy, time.

"We need help in there," Jim yelled at two nurses running towards him as he made for the lift, which, while he couldn't see Dieter, he assumed he must have taken. "Someone's been shot." He kept moving. He was dragging his right leg a little but was nearly at the elevators when a shape sprang out... Jim hit the floor, then rolled towards the wall.

BANG

He felt the bullet whizz past his left shoulder. "Last warning." Dieter said before disappearing back into the elevator, the doors closing, as a different panicked nurse called security on a phone on the wall. Several patients in an open ward to his right screamed.

Jim got up, ignoring a sharp pain in his left knee. He ran for the stairs, knowing where Dieter was going. His legs burned with the effort, and his heart pounded furiously, each beat echoing in his ears. Sweat trickled down his forehead, stinging his eyes as he worked his way down three flights of stairs, his movements a frantic blur of exhaustion and adrenaline. Finally, he crashed through the doors of the ground floor, his eyes wide and wild as he looked frantically for the lifts, his chest heaving with laboured breaths.

Left? Right?

He spotted a sign: right. With a silent thanks to the Gods of Wayfinding he spurted around the corner and, yes, there was Dieter, maybe thirty metres away, pushing Lise—unconscious and slumped to her left—through the sliding entrance doors towards an ambulance, its back doors open.

"Stop him," Jim shouted, pointing and running, somehow finding a last, higher gear. "He's kidnapping her. Call the police."

Dieter looked behind, saw Jim, and picked up the pace too. Before Jim reached the entrance doors, Dieter had tipped Lise roughly into the back of the ambulance, jumped in after her, and slammed the door shut. Jim tried to open it, but it was locked. He pounded on it with his fist, but it was too late, and then there was the sound of the engine turning over. Dieter must have climbed through to the front. The sirens went on. Jim covered his ears as the ambulance lurched forwards out of its parking spot.

"Help," he screamed, looking around manically for someone or something until... yes... there... his eyes locked onto a pizza delivery boy, flipping open his blue scooter to remove his helmet. Who orders pizza to a hospital? Anyone who's eaten hospital food. The maternity ward, most likely, those poor bastards. He was there twenty-four hours when his Trudy was born, the longest, hungriest day (and night and then a bit more day) of his life. At one point he'd even ducked out for a Chinese. Sally never forgave him, even though he brought her favourite back--Chicken Chow Mein. He ran, reaching the young lad just as he was turning the key in the ignition. Jim lowered his shoulder. Distant, faded memories of school rugby matches playing in his mind as he charged the boy, hitting him

The Accidental Murder Club

hard in the chest. He screamed as he toppled heavily backwards, over his scooter, which wobbled. Jim grabbed the handlebars to keep it upright and climbed on. "Sorry kid," he said. "Emergency. Life or death."

"*Hilfe!*" The boy scrambled up as Jim was steadying himself on the seat. He'd had a moped as a teenager. Was the accelerator left or right? Frantically, he twisted both. Only the right turned, and with it, the engine revved and the moped lurched forwards and Jim wobbled precariously on it, as the boy, back on his feet, lunged for Jim who hit the gas. The wheels screeched beneath him as he swerved around two orderlies pushing an empty hospital bed, and a Good Samaritan security guard who had jumped off the curb to try and stop him, finally–where was that guy five minutes ago?

The delivery boy shouted a few last foreign obscenities, or what Jim was sure were obscenities, before he reached the road. He spotted the ambulance in the distance, turning right. The street busy with traffic. He gave chase, losing ground miserably until he worked out where the foot pedal was to change gears. Soon he was at the moped's top speed, maybe seventy-five kilometres an hour, the frame shaking beneath him, weaving through cars until he was tight to the back of the ambulance, its sirens on, riding its slipstream, almost touching distance until… he wasn't. Because, with the traffic parting left and right for it, Dieter had a good long stretch of tarmac and, floored it. The piddly scooter's engine was no match for the power in the ambulance. Dieter got on the highway and shot away from Jim who could only watch as it grew smaller and smaller until it was just a distant speck, the wailing sirens gradually fading into the background noise as soon, the ambulance disappeared entirely, swallowed by the horizon.

"Oh, you bugger," Jim said, still twisting the accelerator with all his strength. "And after I've been all heroic and everything." It was hopeless. Seamus was dead, Lise was gone, and Margaret was… He had failed them all. "Balls," he said, a bitter taste filling his mouth as he spotted a sign for the city centre. He swerved left at the last second, taking the motorway exit, the motion sharp and angry, and all while silently praying the *Nikolaikirche* would be easy to find.

Chapter 34

The Nikolaikirche #2 (Margaret)

Gripping the knife tightly, her eyes double their normal size, Nele cackled once again. This unnerving sound echoed loudly off the wooden walls and low ceiling. They had trapped a wild animal. Margaret took a small step closer, her heart pounding against her ribcage, her hand raised to her chest.

"Don't even think about it," Nele hissed, pointing the knife towards her, the blade shining in the flickering candlelight. Tilda was moaning and writhing on the floor, her face contorted in pain, but unable to get up.

"You're trapped," Margaret said, glancing left at Daniella and Gary. "We know who you are. We know what you've done. You're no longer a Ghost."

"Good on you." Nele sneered, a twisted smile on her lips. "You figured it out. If I had a free hand, I'd clap."

Margaret looked around for a weapon but there was nothing useful, just a lot of candles, crosses and several stacks of dusty bibles. She had no idea how to talk Nele down. Should she reason, placate, or antagonise? It didn't seem like Nele had a very good plan for any of… whatever this all was. Maybe after the knife in the graveyard had missed, she had to improvise in the later botched attempted poisoning and the Trabi explosion?

"It's three against one," Gary said, grinding his fist into his palm.

"Yeah," Daniella agreed. "Put the knife down."

Margaret knew she wouldn't do that, wouldn't just give up, because what did Nele have to lose at this point? "Second best," she said. "What you were to Lise in music and love, you were to Dieter, in spying."

"Dieter?" Gary asked, his confusion cutting through the tension.

"Lise's husband," Margaret clarified, her gaze never leaving Nele. "A bomb specialist for hire."

"How dare you?" Nele spat. "He's a revolutionary."

Present tense. Hearing it from Nele was like a physical blow that knocked her onto the heels of her feet. What would this do to Lise? Did Lise already know? "He seemed to enjoy our Western comforts," Margaret said. "I always assumed he was making up for lost time after prison, but he was never in prison, was he?" She thought back to the room in the museum. "He was in Zanzibar and then in Ireland, right? Creating horror machines for anyone who paid. ETA, IRA, the Mafia. That was what Pat found out." The souvenirs he brought home from his 'work trips' made sense now; they were his trophies.

"This was as much about killing Pat as stopping the wedding. At least, for Nele. For Dieter, on the other hand..." She let the words hang in the air, watching Nele closely. "It was about his true love."

Nele shivered, the knife wobbling in her grip. "Isn't Dieter dead?" Daniella asked. "Wasn't that whose ashes were in the Trabi?"

Margaret took another half step forward, her eyes still locked on Nele's. "I don't know whose ashes they were, but they weren't Dieter's. Dieter is Tick-Tick." He was still alive, which was why he cared what Pat researched, and who Lise married. Jim had been right back at the hospital when he'd said it didn't have to be either or, it could be both. In this case, it was about stopping the wedding *and* stopping Pat.

But Dieter had been sloppy in Ireland, and Nele equally so here, perhaps because of their age, perhaps because there was no state helping them, or perhaps because it was too personal this time, both of them driven only by rage and jealousy. She didn't know enough about each attempt in Ireland yet. She needed a full debrief from Jim, but her hunch was that Dieter probably wanted to watch Connor die, wasn't satisfied with just a bomb detonated from a distance. "Dieter killed Pat's daughter," Margaret said.

"Tiny bump in the road," Nele said, smirking. "Literally. He'd have been here too, taking care of Pat, but you know." She shrugged. The casual gesture at odds with the weapon in her hand. "Things came up."

"The wedding," Daniella guessed. "He got jealous."

"Yes," Margaret said. "If we've figured all this out, we won't be the only ones."

"Yeah," Gary said, voice hardening. "Give yourself up."

Margaret gestured down to Tilda who was moaning on the floor, her body curled in pain as she fought against her restraints. "What did she ever do to you, anyway? She's not involved, not really."

Nele shrugged. "No better than her treacherous sister, though, is she? And a lot of clues in those archives if the right person were looking for them. We really should leave the past where it belongs."

"She did it for her sister."

"The sister that abandoned her, yes," Nele retorted, her smile cruel.

"For freedom," Margaret said. "And for her unborn child."

"Freedom?" She cackled, her voice dripping with sarcasm.

The flickering candlelight cast grotesque shadows on her face, making her appear even more menacing. "The freedom to be unemployed? To have everything you knew become worthless?" Her eyes flashed with anger as she continued, "Capitalism is a lie. Just a system rigged for the wealthy. They get richer while the rest of us scrabble for crumbs. What kind of freedom forces people to choose between putting food on the table and paying for medicine? What kind of freedom leaves millions in debt just for getting an education?"

"Hurting Tilda won't bring the GDR back," Margaret said, her voice trembling but resolute.

"She knows too much now." Nele pointed the knife at each of them. "You all do."

"None of this matters," Daniella said, edging forwards. "Because you're trapped and outnumbered. Put the knife down before we hurt you."

"Never," Nele snarled, lifting her hand and turning the blade down as if preparing to plunge it quickly down into Tilda's neck, which made Gary launch himself, head-first, over Tilda and into Nele, like a kamikaze cannonball, the shock catching Nele off guard as he head-butted her hard in the chest and throat. She fell backward, him on top of her, their limbs tangling, knocking over a table, sending several lit candles crashing to the floor. Gary screamed in pain. Margaret lost sight of the knife. There was a flash of bright light and a whoosh as the rug underneath them caught fire. The flames spread quickly, licking up the walls and igniting the linen and centuries of candle wax coating the surfaces. Nele fought Gary off of her, as Margaret and Daniella grabbed Tilda–Margaret by her shoulders, Daniella by her legs– one pushing, one pulling her towards the door.

"Faster," Margaret yelled, as the flames licked at them, setting Tilda's feet alight. She gave a muffled scream. The smoke was already so thick it was growing hard to breathe.

"Get out, Gary," Margaret shouted over her shoulder as they approached the stairs.

"Leave me with her," Gary growled.

They hoisted Tilda up the stairs and away from the fire. Margaret left Daniella undoing Tilda's ropes and ran back down, fighting her way back through the smoke towards where she'd left Nele and Gary wrestling. There was no time to think, to appraise risk, and that was good. Gary was still on top of Nele, both of them motionless, perhaps from the smoke. "Gary," she shouted, pushing him awake. "Get up. You have to move." She managed to tip him onto his side, and that's when she saw it—the knife stuck in the centre of his chest, as deep as the hilt.

"No," she screamed.

Daniella arrived, coughing violently. "Get him up," she said between hacks. Margaret reached around and got under Gary's armpits, slowly hoisting him up with Daniella's help. He moaned several more times, low and guttural, a large patch of blood staining his sweater. He must have knocked Nele out, as she was lying lifeless on the floor. Together they winched him up the stairs, chased by clouds of smoke as thick as curtains. Margaret's lungs screamed at her to stay out, to stay away, to flee this burning church immediately.

"Thank you, thank you, thank you," Tilda was saying, when they got back up the stairs and she was removing the last ropes from her feet, which had been burned. They lowered Gary down on the floor and sucked in mouthfuls of unpolluted air. The speed the room had caught ablaze seemed faster than even the Trabi.

Daniella went to pull the knife out of Gary's chest. "No," Tilda said, jumping for it. "Leave it in." His eyelids fluttered, then closed. Margaret moved back down the stairs, wanting to free Nele, there would be no justice for anyone if she died like this, taking all her secrets with her. Lise deserved more than that, as did The Ghost's many other victims.

"Leave her," Daniella barked.

"We can't," Margaret insisted, skipping back down the stairs. She made it to the bottom step when a wooden beam holding up the door frame collapsed, straight into her path, knocking her back. The smoke was so thick she could no longer see inside. There was the sound of burning wood and glass smashing. "Help me," Margaret yelled up at the others. "We have to get her out."

"We don't," Tilda said, grabbing her by the shoulder and yanking her up the stairs. She was surprisingly strong.

"Come on," Daniella yelled from above them. "Help me with Gary." With another loud bang, a different part of the ceiling crashed down in front of Margaret and with it, she gave up resisting, turned, and followed Tilda up the stairs.

With Tilda and Daniella dragging Gary, and Margaret clearing the path and opening doors, they stumbled down the ambulatory and towards the back door they'd entered from. They fell out into the square, the clean air energising them. Tilda and Daniella were propping Gary against the wall when they heard the first sirens.

"Ambulance is coming," Daniella said, but Margaret knew it would arrive too late. She kneeled in front of him. He was coughing blood. His shirt and trousers were completely soaked with it. More sirens.

"Tell Seamus," he began, then spat blood onto the floor. He took a large, laboured breath. "I bloody loved him."

"He knew," Margaret said, because if you love someone like that, with dying-breath intensity, of course they would already know. No-one had ever loved Margaret this way, she knew, not even her parents, and in turn, she'd never loved anyone like it, either. Gary closed his eyes for the last time. Two paramedics rushed over and relieved Tilda, who was still trying to stop

The Accidental Murder Club

Gary's bleeding, while coughing violently from the smoke she'd inhaled, and ignoring the pain from her burnt feet and ankles. Margaret waved the next paramedics away from herself and towards Tilda, who was clearly struggling. The bells of the church rang out, clashing with the sirens of the fire engine, and ambulances, and a distinct 'Dum di-di-di dum dum dum dum' emanating from the phone in Daniella's hand.

Chapter 35
Outside the Nikolaikirche (Margaret)

Daniella looked puzzled, her phone pressed to her ear amidst the cacophony of sirens blaring through the city. "What?" she said, squinting one eye shut as if trying to focus better. She pulled the phone away, her brow furrowed, then pressed it back to her ear. "I don't understand," she said, and then handed the phone to Margaret.

Margaret glanced at the screen--it was an Irish number. "Jim?" There was no answer, just muffled noises. It sounded like someone was in a car. She pressed the phone closer to her ear, blocking out the ambient noise with a finger in her other ear.

"Where are we going, Dieter?" she heard a voice say, strained and tense.

"Ahnst du es nicht, meine Liebste?" a male voice responded. Margaret inhaled sharply. It had been a long time since she'd heard that voice, and almost never with such tenderness. It was quieter than Lise's, meaning she must be holding the phone, not him.

But why? And how? And where?

"English," Lise said. Yes, it was unmistakably Lise. Were

The Accidental Murder Club

they at the hospital? "My head hurts too much for German," Lise said, her voice sounding weak and distant.

"I remember when we switched to English," Dieter said. "It was our second week in England. At the seaside. We'd just had our first fish and chips. Terrible stuff. You made fun of my ths being zs. Said people would laugh at me."

"We wanted to fit in," Lise said, her voice carrying a hint of nostalgia.

"I had to fit in. You always just did. I'm so sorry about all this, *Schatzi.*" Darling.

"Who?" Tilda asked, gesturing for the phone. "Is it Lise?"

Margaret raised her finger to her lips.

"Where are we?" Lise asked again, her voice groggy. She heard a faint crunch, a mistimed gear change––they were definitely in a car. But where was Jim?

"You don't recognise it?" Dieter asked. "We're going to our special place."

"Our special place?" Lise's voice wavered, either groggy or stalling for time.

"Don't tell me you've forgotten?"

Margaret took deep breaths, trying to quell her rising fear.

"Can you take off these restraints?" Lise asked. "I'm happy to be with you. I just needed some time to... you know, the shock of it."

Margaret's heart sank. She lowered the phone. "Tilda, do you know where Dieter and Lise's special place is? Somewhere you could drive from the hospital? Probably something from their past?" Their real past, she thought, not Cospudener See, where they'd all been earlier.

"Why?" she asked. "Is Lise on the phone? Let me talk to her."

"It's urgent," Margaret said. "I need to know now and then I can explain. Think. Maybe something from when they were first dating?"

"Haus Auensee, I guess?" Tilda said, coughing into her fist,

343

snuggled in a blanket one of the paramedics had given her. The name struck a chord. Lise had mentioned it during the car ride from the airport and again at the lake. "It's been closed for a year or more," Tilda added, her voice weak and raspy. "Is that Lise? Is she okay?"

Margaret raised the phone back to her ear, not wanting to alarm Tilda and with no time to explain. "We're in an ambulance," Lise said. "I feel very protected, Dieter. Pull over and let me out of these."

Margaret covered the speaker, though she was sure Lise had muted it. "Daniella, we need to get to Haus Auensee, now!" Daniella was talking to a policewoman, likely giving a statement. Margaret's mind raced––Nele's dead body would raise questions. Abandoning her had been wrong, immoral even, but there had been no time. They could ask the police for help to rescue Lise, but would they believe them? That a madman had risen from the dead to kidnap their friend in an ambulance? It would all take so long to explain. A screech of tires snapped her to attention. A moped skidded to a stop near a police car, its handlebars grazing the wing mirror. The driver, helmetless and grinning, looked up at the burning church that two fire engines and their crews were dousing with water. "Hell of a barbecue. Any sausages left for me?"

Margaret rushed to him. "I know where they're going," she said. "Dieter and Lise."

"Hop on then," Jim said, gesturing to the space behind him.

Chapter 36

Haus Auensee (Jim)

"That's it," Margaret shouted into Jim's ear, pointing to the large building on their left.

"Hold on!" he said, swerving across the empty path and between two trees, the moped bouncing beneath them. The ride had been wild, some real Thelma and Louise stuff. Oh, no, wait, they were both lasses, weren't they? Well, anyway, Jim was proud of his very male heroism. He'd got them there in one piece, and had only forgotten to drive on the right twice. And, as an added bonus, Margaret had been forced to hug him tightly the entire way. Well, when she wasn't grappling with the phone and her map. He dodged between a tree and a pond as they approached Haus Auensee from the side, so not to be seen. Margaret threw her map into the air and gripped tight to his waist as he headed straight for the side of the enormous, stately building. Ducking under a low conifer branch, he brought them to an abrupt stop behind two thick bushes, perhaps twenty metres from the building.

"Quite stealthy for you," she said as she climbed off.

"Did you expect me to park in front of the main doors?"

"Yes."

He flashed her a toothy smile as he worked a twinge from his lower back. His heart was pounding in its prison in his chest, and for some reason, considering he'd only driven a moped, he was out of breath. He bent over, put his hands on his knees, and took a few deep lungfuls of air.

"It was both," she said.

He stood slowly up. "What was?"

"The past and stopping the wedding. You were right."

"Lucky guess," he said with a wink, knowing what she was talking about, impressed that she'd remembered that line from all the way back at the hospital. Inside, he did a cartwheel. Outside, he played it cool, simply looking up at the building, covered in ivy. At first glance, it reminded him of the McGinley mansion. "And I was making a lot of guesses."

His stomach was a mix of bubbling fear--at having to confront an armed madman--and icy thrill that he and Margaret were a team again, starting fires and evading gunshots and racing mopeds through foreign lands. He was not only in the story; he was already imagining how he'd tell it one day to the punters as he stood behind the bar at Next Chance, his favourite Chelsea F.C. tea towel over his shoulder. Assuming they lived that long. He hoped they would live that long. "The Accidental Murder Club's toughest case yet. No-one shot at me during the last one."

"And it's not over yet," she said.

"The bugger's armed," he said, thinking of poor Seamus, and what might have become of him. He ground the heel of his shoe into the dirt. That was no way to go. Vengeance, he wanted it.

"We're armed with our great brains and wits," Margaret said, voice low, peeking out from behind the tree, checking the coast was clear.

He'd given Margaret the broad strokes of what had happened at the hospital on the way over. While he hoped more than anything both of them would pull through, there was a certain poetry to dying together, after out-of-character acts of bravery, for which they could both be proud. "I feel like we're coming out for the second half at Old Trafford, 4-0 down, with two men sent off."

"I don't know what any of that means," Margaret said.

"It means the odds are against us."

"In anything worth doing, the odds are against you." She put the phone back to her ear. The call had continued for the entire journey. Jim looked through the bushes towards the building where sections of roof and guttering had fallen down, taking large chunks of white plaster and red dusty brick with it. A good place to… he shook his head. "What are they talking about now?"

"Dieter's grovelling, mostly, but I can't be sure. There's a lot of language mixing." She slid the phone back into her pocket. "I know where they are." She pointed him towards the front of the building.

They crept slowly along, staying low and close to the wall, ducking under the windows, until they reached the corner, and could peer around and left to the entrance. "Wow," Jim said, getting his first glimpse of it, all stately red brick with white accents. The façade's grandeur had long faded, and almost all its windows were smashed, but in its hey-day? A looker, for sure. Next to the five-step staircase that lead up to the entrance was an ambulance, its rear doors open.

"There's someone else here," she whispered, pointing to the small hatchback parked behind it.

"The plot thickens," Jim said, punching his palm. "And I do like a thick plot."

"You don't understand," she said, disapproving.

"What don't I understand?"

"Loss."

He scoffed. He'd lost plenty, his only daughter for one. And, yeah, sure, she'd just watched Gary die, but he'd just seen Seamus... well, he didn't know. He'd certainly been in dire straits when Jim had left him. Dieter had to be stopped.

He peered through the nearest window, cupping his eyes to better see inside. He could just about make out that the entrance opened into a large atrium. There was no sign of Dieter or Lise, but there would be plenty of places to hide in a building this large.

Dieter had a gun and they had the element of surprise. Often overvalued, the element of surprise. Yeah, you get to make the first move, but how many battles of brain and brawn can you win in just one move?

"There," Jim said, walking along the front, pointing to a broken window. Margaret pulled him back by his arm.

"We can't just charge in there. We have to be smart about this."

"Who said anything about charging in?"

She shushed him with a finger to her lips.

"I'm talking loudly?"

"You only have one setting––fog horn."

"Sorry," he said, trying to whisper. "And I'll have you know I don't just charge in anywhere. I'm subtle as a..." Jim's mind went blank. She cocked her head. Jim's mind stayed blank.

"See," she said. "You're so unsubtle you can't even think of anything from the entire genre of subtlety."

"Fine," he said. "But this loon has got a gun he's not afraid to use, so I'll lead. Cahoots would be lost without you. It'll be fine without me. I'll be as quiet as a mute mouse. You can direct me, and then when things look their bleakest, I'll swoop in and save the day. Deal?"

She adjusted her neckerchief. "I'll be saving the day, actually. I already know where they are. Lise dropped a million hints. They're in the main hall."

"They putting on a play?" he scowled. "Bunch of bloody crackpots, the lot of them. Connor too."

"Yes, but they're our crackpots."

Inside, they paused, listening to the sound of voices echoing. Margaret pointed, Jim nodded, and they crept out of this room and through the vestibule, Jim watching his every step, careful not to crunch any broken glass underfoot. He looked back at Margaret, admiring the look of stern defiance on her face. It was the face of someone afraid, but for whom fear was less important than what was right.

They passed a staircase and were slowly approaching the main auditorium's rear open double doors when Margaret pulled him back. She pointed at the doors and cupped her ear. Reluctantly, he let her lead. At the door, she bent down, peering slowly in. Jim couldn't bend that low, but hands gently on her shoulders, he looked over and around and into a grand concert hall. His mouth fell open. It was a huge, cavernous space with ornate stucco. Two levels. The ground floor was a jumble of chairs and tables. It looked like a rhino had stormed through it, scattering everything. At the very front—up on the stage, under an enormous lighting rig and between giant stacked speakers— were Lise still in her hospital gown, Dieter in his doctor's jacket helping a haggard-looking bottle-blonde woman, coughing into her fist.

"Nele," Margaret gasped. "She's still alive."

"That good or bad news?" Jim asked, squinting at Lise, trying to make out why she was sitting so strangely. Stiff and with her arms behind her back. Ah, she was taped to the chair. Dieter still had his doctor's jacket on and was guiding Nele— covered in soot and ash from the fire, blonde hair wild as if she'd been electrocuted—down into a chair. She must have just arrived too. Nele swigged from a bottle of water and coughed deeply, all chest. Dieter was talking, but they were too far away to hear, and it was probably in German, and so he'd not be able to understand. Margaret got the phone out and hung up the call.

He took a step back from the door and waited for her to follow. After a few seconds, she did so. "They're distracted, and not expecting us," she said. "That's something, I suppose. There's pretty good cover if we stay low. On the left, about three-quarters of the way to the stage, is a column surrounded by several stacks of tables on their sides. We can wait there and plan our attack."

He didn't really like the sound of an 'attack', but kept his feelings to himself. "Me first," he said, taking a deep breath and, bending down to his haunches, ignoring all the various pains as he slipped into the room and along the wall until his path was blocked, when he had to crawl between table legs and bags of rubbish and step over upturned chairs, alternating between watching the stage and the floor as he moved. He stopped several times when it looked like Dieter was turning their way, or Nele had spotted their movements. It was hard going, but somehow, they made it, settling behind a table flipped on its side, legs away from them. He tried to suppress his rapid breathing, in case he was panting loud enough that they'd hear him.

Margaret squeezed in next to him. Barely even out of breath. She couldn't be as calm as she looked, right? He wasn't calm. Her hand was on the floor, helping her balance. He put his over the top and squeezed and then they both risked peering over the side of the table. On the stage, Dieter was pacing back and forth, gesticulating wildly with his hands as if guiding down invisible planes.

"It's not too late," he said, in English. "Everything is fine. We have a plan. I have a plan. Complications? Yes, there are always complications."

"Dieter, dear," Lise said. "Cut me free. We're not in danger here."

"Soon, my love. We have to talk first. Agree on some things."

Nele laughed sharply. He turned to her. "You too, my darling."

"ICH HABE SIE FÜR DICH GETÖTET. VERSTEHST DU? WAS HAT SIE FÜR DICH GETAN?"

"I killed her," Margaret whispered, cupping Jim's ear. "Probably means Pat. I don't know why she thinks that."

"A priest in front of a hospital room would be easy to misinterpret," Jim whispered, or hoped he whispered, talking about Tad.

Dieter crouched between both women, sat a metre apart. With his arms outstretched, he touched both their knees.

"The authorities, that stupid busybody journalist. The net was closing in, Lise. And you seemed so happy at Cahoots. I didn't want to destroy your life."

"Are you really Tick-Tick?" she asked.

He looked down and away. "It was all for the cause."

"What cause?" she argued. "The GDR is long dead."

"No," he said, his voice growing louder. "It lives on if you want it to. You will understand, in time. We mustn't waste another minute of it."

"UND WAS IST MIT MIR? MIT UNS?" Nele barked.

"What about me?" Margaret whispered.

"*Schatzilein*, you're the other piece of my puzzle."

"NEIN, DU WILLST SIE, NICHT MICH." She pointed at Lise, her lip trembling, then more coughs. She looked like she'd just swept the world's dirtiest chimney. He's losing the dressing room, Jim thought. He's not getting out of this with one woman, never mind two.

"You want her, not me," Margaret translated.

"Nele, please," Lise said.

"We had each other, Dieter. After your death," Nele said the word death with great sarcasm. "Did you know that, Lise? Yes, we've lived together here in Leipzig ever since. My husband didn't know, but he didn't need to, either. He doesn't pay attention. Finally, we were together. And it was wonderful. It was what it should always have been. Before you. Before the cause. And then your wedding invite came. We made a plan to deal with the mute. Then I woke up to a note on the kitchen table. He was gone, again. TO GALWAY. His fragile ego couldn't take it, couldn't accept you remarrying. I was so angry. Who cares if you married again? You can have your rich idiot."

"He's not an idiot."

"He really is," said Dieter. "Spectacularly so."

Nele pointed. "We had everything, and he ruined it. And for what? Jealousy?"

"I want you both," Dieter said, looking between them. Nele knocked his hand from her knee.

"I understand," Lise said. "I think."

"*Als ob!*" Nele snapped. "You understand that he wanted to kill your fiancé, right? Wanted to make it look like an accident and then swoop in again and win you back. Exploding chandeliers? Hunting accident? Distillery explosions? Ludicrous plans. Subtlety was never his strong point, but you know that."

"There is no need for name-calling here, my dear," Dieter cautioned. "It's not like you were so successful yourself. Poisoned drinks no-one drank. Poisoned toothpaste no-one used. You couldn't even change a hotel reservation."

"I succeeded in the end. Did you?"

"If you want to claim it as success," Dieter said, flashing his teeth, suddenly wolfish. "But it was my plan."

"Well, I drove the car, didn't I?" Nele said.

Lise turned away in disgust, seeming to finally understand something, which was more than Jim, who was very lost. Dieter began to pace, monologuing, gesturing with an open palm at one or more of the women. "I have always loved you both. Equally. That's why I had to stop the wedding. I thought I could live without you, Lise, but it was torture."

Nele cackled. She really did have a hell of a cackle. Cut right through Jim like an icy breeze. *"JA KLAR. SELBSTVERSTAN-DLICH.* And now what? The three of us, ride off into the sunset in your stolen ambulance?"

"Yes," said Dieter. "I have it all planned. I have tickets. A cruise. Fake names. A triple room. We'll escape to Argentina."

This time, both the women howled with synchronised laughter. "Argentina?" said Lise. "That remind you of anyone?"

"Ja," Nele said. "What is it, 1945?"

"Don't," he barked, turning around a third chair and placing it between them, which only added to the weird vibe that this was a rehearsal for a terrible play. "The first time I ever saw you, it was here," he said wistfully, craning his neck to look out into the empty hall. "Did I ever tell you the story?"

"No," Lise said, lowering her eyes.

"Not you, my love. This is our place too, Nele. You were just seventeen and here with friends. With Lise, actually. I was twenty. It was winter. Dimly lit. Full of students, mostly." He perked up. "The energy. The excitement. The regime was so pure back then, wasn't it? There was so much hope, so much," he paused and while Jim couldn't see it, he was sure he was licking his lips, "potential. The band, well, it's safe to say they weren't The Beatles. Still, they had a certain something." He jived with his elbows. "An enthusiasm. Blues, it was blues. Some western hits too. I noticed you standing off to the side, back to the wall, arms crossed while Lise danced with abandon. You were beautiful. Of course, you were beautiful, you're still beautiful, but that wasn't it. It was how, with everyone staring forwards, lost to the music, lost to each other, lost to the moment––you were not. You were above them. Apart from them. Studying them. Then you saw me watching you. And you began to study me. Your gaze was not one I could hold, is not one anyone can hold. Even then."

"That person is gone," Nele said. "Used up."

Dieter shook his head. "*Nein.* I've hidden this long, Nele." He turned to Lise. "Lise. I can hide us again. I can hide us all well."

"Yes," Lise said, looking around. "I believe you, my love." She was trying to sound sincere, but it was a hard ask, and Jim wasn't even slightly convinced. "Now let me go so we can be together again."

Dieter got up but moved to Nele, kneeling, taking her hand. "You love Lise just as much as I do. As she does you. You're two halves of one whole––Lise the impulsive, artistic, empathetic part while you, my buttercup, are loyal, idealistic, and utterly ruthless. I need you both to live. Say 'yes' and let's go."

"Yes," Lise said, but Dieter wasn't asking her; she didn't seem to have a choice. Nele coughed some more, then wiped some ash from her forehead. Her free hand dropped to the floor.

"Okay," she said, voice thin and tired. "Now hold me."

Dieter leaned forwards to embrace her and as he did so, she pulled a small knife strapped to her ankle, and plunged it deep into his neck. "No," he screamed, pushing her hard and she, he, and the chair tumbled backwards onto the stage with a loud thud. He pulled the knife out of his neck and threw it onto the floor.

"Quick," Lise said to Nele. "Untie me and I'll get help."

"No chance," she said, wiggling out from beneath him. She got up, looming over him, nostrils flaring, as he wriggled and gurgled, his hand to his throat, blood spraying everywhere. Jim felt his heart stop. Margaret had her hand over her mouth, stifling a scream. Was this the moment to attack? But they were too shocked to move.

"We had our chance, you fool," Nele yelled. "We were happy. We had nearly two good years here, and yet you threw them away, and for what?" She pointed at Lise. "This old hag? To kill some idiot alcoholic paddy?" She kicked him in the face with the sharp point of her shoes. He was too far gone even to moan.

"She's lost it," Margaret said. "She's going to kill Lise."

"We need the gun. It's in his jacket pocket."

"I'll draw her away," Margaret said. "You get as close to the stage as you can, and as soon as there's an opening, charge for it."

Before he could argue, she'd run behind a nearby column and was moving quickly, bent low, using the furniture for cover, crossing the giant space. He watched with pride and envy at her decisiveness, how there was no hesitation or worry for her own safety. She was so restrained with her emotions, yet so fearless and impulsive with her actions when protecting others. Were all head teachers like this? He wished he'd paid more attention to his own and stayed in school a little longer. Adrenaline surged through his veins as he moved left round the back of the stage, keeping close to the wall and his eyes firmly on Nele's back. He felt like he was floating.

"You always got whatever you wanted, didn't you?" Nele turned and growled at Lise, baring her teeth.

"I didn't want to be tied to this chair. I didn't want my husband to fake his own death."

"Not even two years," she said. "Not even two. You had how many?"

"Too many. But in most of them, he was gone. Or I was on tour. When he was around, he was distant and angry and lying to me. It's all lies," she said. "At least you knew the real him. I'm glad you killed him."

Jim wasn't so sure he was dead yet. "My life's work," she said, not listening, looking around the room, as if the decay and debris in the concert hall were representative of the collapse of the GDR, the regime she seemed to have loved so much, yet Jim had only heard bad stories about. Except for the football teams, of course.

"Reduced to rubble," she continued. "You got to be the famous violinist. To tour the world. While I was here, second fiddle to the famous Tick-Tick, wasting my time infiltrating Native American enthusiast societies and choirs. Working for a second fiddle regime, in the second fiddle half of a formerly great nation." She picked up the knife from the ground and wiped it clean on her trousers. Her movements were fast, robotic almost.

"You don't need to do that," Lise said, looking around frantically, eyes pleading.

"I know."

"Let me go. We can pin all this on him. You can walk away. We can walk away together. You're a good person, deep down. He led you astray. Tilda will say whatever I want. She owes me. Come to Cahoots and live with me. There will be so many more good years left. So many great people to meet. New things to believe in. A community to build."

"I know that I don't need to do it," Nele hissed. "I want to do it." She twirled the knife in her hand, fast. Jim could see from her face that she was lost to the madness. Lise wasn't going to be able to reason with her. She took a few steps away. She was going to throw the knife. He was at the side of the stage, very close, at the bottom of the two steps that led up to it, desperately trying not to rush in, but losing faith in Margaret and sure this was it, this was Lise's end. What would he tell Connor? He climbed the first step as… birdsong rang out? Shy, but melodic. A series of notes rising and falling. "Chick-a-dee-dee-dee."

Nele's head turned, slowly and robotically. She walked across towards the edge of the stage, peering out into the cluttered auditorium. Lise tipped back her head and returned the call. The pitch was different, Lise's ending with a kind of warbling, like she was rapidly flicking her tongue against the roof of her mouth. Very convincing, it was; Jim was almost back in the woods of Galway.

Nele's head snapped back towards Lise. "Shut it, you."

"Chick-a-dee-dee-dee." Margaret's call rang out again, nowhere near as good, but recognisable. Nele turned back towards the auditorium. That was enough. Jim rushed onto the stage, grabbed the chair from the floor, tipped it upright and, using it as a primitive shield, in case Nele threw the knife, fell to his knees behind it and next to Dieter, who was either dead or unconscious, laying on his front. Jim rifled through his pockets, searching for the gun.

"*Nein*," Nele shouted. Jim risked a quick look up and saw her coming for him, knife in the air, as he searched Dieter's last inside pocket—did doctors really need this many pockets?—"Die," she said, as she ran and his hands felt something cool, gripped metal. He yanked the gun out and pointed it at the on-rushing figure of Nele, her face wild, more animal than human.

"Stop," he shouted.

She stopped, raised her hands, and then let out another high-pitched cackle. "You don't get to win."

It was Jim's turn to laugh. "We've already won. I brought a gun to your knife fight."

"But do you know how to use it?"

"Come any closer, and I'll be forced to take an educated guess. Drop the knife."

She held it out in front of her, staring forlornly at it. Lise stayed quiet, which Jim thought was probably wise. Where was Margaret? Nele could always throw the knife, probably before he could stop her even. He'd shoot her if he had to, wouldn't he? He hoped he would. Or rather, he hoped he wouldn't have to find out if he would. He would. Nele pointed the knife at Dieter who was motionless. "I suppose one out of two isn't bad."

"Drop the knife," Jim repeated. "It's over."

"Is it?" she asked as Jim climbed to his feet, gun gripped tightly in two hands, pointed at her chest.

"I think I'll decide when it ends," she said. "Me." Her hand suddenly flexed, the knife spinning, and then she gripped its handle and raised it up to her...

"No," Margaret yelled, running across the stage; but she was too late. A blur from Jim's left rushed straight into Nele, knocking her off her feet. It was Lise, still attached to her chair. She hit Nele hard in the side and they both toppled over, crying out in pain. Nele's head hit the corner of the stage. The knife fell from her hand. Margaret kicked it away and climbed onto Nele, pinning her down, arms by her side.

"Stay down," she said as Nele moaned and writhed.

"Black-capped Chickadee," Lise said, grinning. "Tilda's favourite."

Chapter 37

Epilogue: The Nikolaikirche (Margaret)

It was eerily quiet in the Nikolaikirche. Margaret was standing near the altar, her fingers knocking against her leg. The pastor had been so grateful that they had brought two former spies to justice, and saved the church from burning down, not to mention Tilda, that he'd agreed enthusiastically to let Lise and Connor hold their wedding here. The pastor had spent a decade as a political prisoner in a Stasi jail and told Tad he'd do anything for "defenders of freedom."

They could only use the front half, the nave, which hadn't been damaged. The church had hung large curtains blocking the ruined altar, sanctuary and apse. Even with the doors and windows open, there was still a heavy smell of both smoke and damp, from all the water needed to put out the fire, but you got used to it. It wouldn't have been Margaret's choice of venue, too many very bad, very recent memories, but Lise and Connor had always had a rather macabre sense of humour.

The room held its collective breath as they stood for the first notes of Bach's––Lise had insisted on it––*Air in G* played on the organ. Lise and Tilda stepped into the church, arm in arm, Tilda sporting a new, shorter haircut––a more fashionable tight bob. The relationship between the sisters had survived Tilda's confession, of course it had, so overshadowed by the greater treacheries of Lise's now definitely dead husband, and still alive former-best friend, in prison, awaiting trial.

Another foreign trip for Cahoots, another media sensation. Margaret was ducking all interviews again and, to her surprise, so was Jim. Had he found modesty, and so late in life?

Lise was slow and leaning heavily to her right––her injuries from last week's accident still plaguing her. Tilda wasn't any faster. Pat was bandaged up too, wearing nearly as much white as Lise, who was a vision in her cream wool dress. Margaret had never seen a knitted wedding dress, but Seamus had rallied to deliver something truly remarkable. While Jim had been off chasing Dieter, Connor had rushed to his aid. The way Seamus told it, Connor had kept him alive through the sheer force of his will. Maybe that was true, maybe it's that of all the places to be shot, a hospital is a pretty good one. His stomach had needed two different surgeries, and he'd lost a kidney, but his long-term prognosis was good. And stuck in bed, he'd knitted fast for an injured, heartbroken man. Jim had told her he was exceptional, and rarely for him, he hadn't been exaggerating. The dress he'd been able to create, even in his injured state, intricately embroidered with hearts and a daring v-neck that many brides of Lise's age wouldn't have risked, suited her bold personality perfectly. Wool being thicker than silk or chiffon, it was somehow more complimentary too.

A wolf whistle from on her left. "Connor," Margaret said, but laughing as she did so, still impressed by how freely he and Lise expressed their love. Seamus was in a wheelchair next to him. A spot that would have been Gary's. Jim had told her, on the sly, that Connor had actually asked Jim to be the best man, but that he'd been drunk at the time, and Jim didn't want to mention it again. Margaret wasn't sure she believed him. Jim and his stories. Jim and his ego. She'd agreed with him that it should be Seamus, though. Both he and Connor were wearing black woollen armbands just above the elbow, a traditional sign of mourning, something they would have done for Willie, but were now also wearing in Gary's memory.

Tilda and Lise reached the altar, that same impossibly wide smile, just one employed much less often by Tilda. The fluttering in Margaret's stomach intensified as Lise reached them. Connor broke from his position and wrapped Lise in a hug, lifting her from her feet and spinning her round. The church, and it was a surprise how many people had made it on just ten-days' notice, clapped and hollered.

"Decorum please," said Tad. Of course, the pastor had also given Tad permission to officiate. He had known of his charity work, even. Tad really did seem to be the real deal. Reluctantly, Connor put Lise down, and Jim and Margaret moved and took their places in the first row.

"Dearly beloved," Tad began, his booming voice echoing from the rafters. "We are gathered here today…" The service continued somewhat normally until, "Should anyone present know of any reason that this couple should not be joined in holy matrimony, speak now or forever hold your peace?"

"How long have we got?" Pat shouted in the raspy voice of hers that they had got used to in the past week. They'd had a lot of time to talk. Margaret had had so many questions. Had needed to resolve all this, to make sense of it, to decide how much blame she would have to live with for not figuring out it was Nele and Dieter earlier.

Thorsten had been right. Dieter had threatened Pat to drop her investigation. She hadn't listened. Dieter placed a bomb under her car. What he couldn't have known, or maybe didn't care to check, was that on that fateful Tuesday morning, her daughter's car was being repaired and so she'd borrowed Pat's to get to work. After her daughter's murder, Pat, ravaged with guilt, vowed not to speak again until Tick-Tick was brought to justice. It was all she worked on, day and night, just like the man she was sitting next to in the second row, the man with the cane: Thorsten.

Margaret respected their dedication. Since then, her and Pat hadn't stopped jabbering. She'd won Pat's respect now, she felt, too. The church howled with laughter at Pat's joke.

"Connor and Lise have decided to do their own vows," Tad said when it finally died down. Margaret flinched. She hoped Connor would keep the cursing and lewdness to a minimum; there were children present.

"Lise," Connor said, removing a sheet of paper from his back pocket. "As an Irishman, I know a thing or two about a good laugh, a good pint, and a good woman. And you, my bride, are the best of the best. I can't count how many portraits I've painted in my life, but it was your face in every one of the buggers. A whole country and several people doing its dirty work had to be toppled for us to find each other, yet toppled they were. I could vow that I will be your protector, but you don't need one. You're a force to be reckoned with--and not just at the board game table. This last week, death tried to do us very much part, and in its face, we turned and we laughed. We will keep laughing. We will keep loving. And it will be glorious." Connor choked on his emotion as he folded up his sheet of paper, wiping his eyes on the sleeve of his suit. A single tear tumbled down Margaret's face too, as she watched, transfixed. She didn't wipe it away.

Lise cleared her throat then began to speak, without notes or aids, a hand to her heart. "Connor," she began. Her eye shadow was white today, not its trademark blue. "For a long time, my life, or rather, my love was a lie. And worse than that, deep down, I knew it. I put on a brave, bold front, but it was fake. I was playing a role. Career musician. Dutiful wife. I don't ever want to act again. I want to be myself and to know that self is lovable, and I do, because you have only ever loved it, unabashedly. You don't care if I dance on tables with strippers. You don't want to control me. You set me free to live honestly. Which is how you live. Which is who you are. I see you, completely, and I am proud of you. And in how you see me, how you accept me, how you love me, I have learned to do the same to myself. I love you with an intensity I had never known possible. You said it best in the hospital, when you rushed to be by my side. We'll live well. Far beyond both our means and station. We'll make them gossip and scorn. And I, for one, cannot wait."

Connor let out a squeak, and Lise reached over to take his hand. "She's had a head injury," he shouted to the audience. "She doesn't know what she's saying."

"I've never meant anything more."

Another tear tumbled down Margaret's face. That was strange. She hadn't cried in the last ten years. Must be the air. Or the damp.

Next to her, Jim blew his nose on a tissue. The man was mush. "The vows always get me," he said, and squeezed her hand. After brief consideration, she decided to let him, since he was so emotional. A gesture of kindness.

Tad took back over. "The rings," he boomed. Seamus handed his to Connor. Tilda stepped forward, holding a small box that Margaret knew must hold her mother's ring. She smiled warmly at her sister and her brother-in-law. A few more formalities and then… "You may now kiss your bride."

Connor launched himself at Lise and their mouths opened widely as their tongues slipped across in what was a brazenly inappropriate display of affection that Margaret only pretended to find scandalous. More clapping, cheering, everyone up out of their pews and moving to the front to hug, slap backs, shake hands, and jig with the bride and groom as confetti filled the air and the organ player switched to *You Can Never Beat the Irish* by The Wolfe Tones.

Slowly, they filed out, Jim walking with Margaret, their arms interlocked. "Not bad, eh?" he said.

She smiled. "I've seen worse."

Outside, Daniella was waiting in the driver's seat of a white Trabi stretch limo, ready to whisk the happy couple through Leipzig and on to their honeymoon suite in Dresden's poshest hotel. Still East Germany, but less old memories and more space to create new ones. It had to beat the *Hofhandel*. Lise had one foot in the limo when she stopped and turned. "Almost forgot." With one quick movement, she lifted her bouquet over her head and threw it behind her, right into Jim's embarrassed arms. He went bright red.

"Well, I know a good priest and a wedding dress designer," Margaret said.

"The tricky part might be the bride. And I'm not going abroad for the honeymoon. It's Skeggie, or nothing."

She laughed. "Haven't you heard? Seamus has invited us to his place in Mykonos on the McGinley plane."

"Did he now, Mags?"

"Margaret," she corrected. "Did you see the huge bouquet Cahoots sent? I'm going to have to talk to Moneybags when we get back. They've gone wild over there without me. We have strict budgets."

"Apparently, the new girl knew a florist," Jim said.

"New girl?" she asked. She couldn't remember a new member's vote. And they wouldn't have held one without her.

"Yeah," he put on a fake posh accent. "Dr Charlotte Stone."

All the colour drained from the world. Margaret's knees buckled and Jim caught her as she was falling, and in the process, dropped his flowers.

"You okay?" he asked. "Too much emotion?"

It couldn't be, could it?

Thank you for reading!

This book was an experiment, a first collaboration between an award-winning memoirist and a University Lecturer of Children's Literature. We've grown very fond of Jim and Margaret and if you have too, please let us know by leaving a review. That'll way we'll know you want us to send them off on more adventures.

Until next time…

Printed in Great Britain
by Amazon